IN SEARCH OF FOREVER

MENDED HEARTS SERIES

An Anchor on Her Heart
Love Calls Her Home
A Kite on the Wind
Love's Autumn Harvest
In Search of Forever

IN SEARCH OF FOREVER

MENDED HEARTS SERIES

By

Patricia Lee

In Search of Forever
Published by Mountain Brook Ink
White Salmon, WA U.S.A.

The website addresses shown in this book are not intended in any way to be or imply an endorsement on the part of Mountain Brook Ink, nor do we vouch for their content.

This story is a work of fiction. All characters and events are the product of the author's imagination. Any resemblance to any person, living or dead, is coincidental.

Scripture quotations are taken from the New King James Version of the Bible. Public domain.
ISBN 978-1-953957-30-6© 2023 Patricia Lee

The Team: Miralee Ferrell, Tim Pietz, Kristen Johnson, Cindy Jackson
Cover Design: Indie Cover Design, Lynnette Bonner Designer

Mountain Brook Ink is an inspirational publisher offering fiction you can believe in.
Printed in the United States of America

The ache for home lives in all of us. The safe place where we can go as we are and not be questioned.

Maya Angelou

CHAPTER ONE

"Stay low, Private." Jayden Clarke rolled the injured man into a rocky outcropping along the side of the Jalalabad-Kabul road and patted his shoulder. "I'm going back up."

"No, Clarke!" The man rasped. "You'll be a target."

Jayden ignored his plea and turned away, crawling toward the burning Humvee in which he and four others had been riding only moments before. One wheel caught only a minor shock of an IED blast, but the vehicle had overturned, throwing them out. Enemy fire pelted the air above causing debris to churn like a sand storm. His courage waned the closer he got. An image of his hero dad flashed before his eyes. Had Dad braved a hailstorm of bullets like this when he was pinned down by enemy fire? Did he feel death coming at him? Did he persist in spite of it all? Jayden swallowed.

I will make you proud.

He dismissed the images and focused on his target. Were any more men stranded beneath the vehicle's overturned frame? Dust choked the air, making him wheeze. He slithered on his belly toward the wreckage, squinting through the cloud of smoke. Steadying himself on one knee, he scanned the area for other survivors. Seeing no one he turned to go back the way he came. Before he could clear the pavement, another deafening blast rocked the ground. The Humvee rolled to its back in the force of this new explosion, catching Jayden's right leg beneath its front tire. He screamed, the weight of the vehicle against his thigh pinning him to the ground. Pain raced up his calf, knee throbbing.

He tried to see through the haze, his safety glasses askew on his nose, but countless fragments flew from the cloud of smoke and blinded him. Shapes danced like images in a fun house mirror, grotesque figures that laughed from the reflection. In a last effort to make sense of what he saw he squinted, collapsing as everything around him dissolved to shades of gray.

"Man down!" The voice of his commanding officer, Parker Macgregor, sounded close to his ear. "Medic now!"

"I can't see!" Jayden breathed slow, erratic pants as he struggled for air in the surrounding chaos.

"Hang on, Clarke." Parker gripped his shoulder. "Help is coming."

More bullet rounds whizzed overhead, with his unit engaged in a counter attack.

"My eyes."

"Stay calm, Clarke." Parker's steady words spread peace against Jayden's panic. "We'll get you out of here."

"Sir. I haven't done my duty." Jayden pleaded. "I can't go home yet. I have to. . ."

"Soldier, stay calm." Parker's voice brooked no argument. "That's an order."

"But my dad. . ."

Hands gripped him under his shoulders as men lifted the wheel off his leg and pulled him onto a stretcher. He fought for consciousness. "Dad! I'm sorry."

CHAPTER TWO

Eighteen months later

THE HARLEY SPUTTERED TO A STOP on the asphalt, the country road empty. Jayden Clarke drew a deep breath. The turn signal still blinked, rhythmic evidence of his initial intent to maneuver the driveway ahead. His courage failed. He wasn't ready for a homecoming. For all the questions. Too many memories here held him back. That last stretch ahead loomed like an impossible wall, yet the need to remember this place drove him. One look. That's all he needed today. He stood, removed the key, and rolled the Harley to a spot behind a juniper, camouflaging it in the brush.

He knew the routine well. How many times had he done this with his mountain bike when he'd been a lonely kid in search of a friend? When he'd needed a refuge from his abusive step-father? When he sought peace away from the daily trauma of a horrific family life? Too many to count. Now if his knee could manage the climb.

As exertion accelerated his breathing, Jayden crested the top of the hill, positioned himself among the scrub pines and stared down at the familiar ranch scene below him. Horses grazed in the outer pastures and a collection of children played Frisbee within the perimeter of the yard. For a handful of years, he'd called this place home.

Not much had changed. The ranch house still stood at the end of the long twisting driveway, a curl of smoke climbing from the chimney. The new duplex which had been in construction when he'd deployed stood finished. If he remembered the blueprints, four summer staff studios and an office occupied one side. An apartment for the cook filled the other end. An addition of dorm rooms poked above what was once an unfinished garage. Jayden had watched that structure go up and had helped build the walls. Judging from the numbers of youngsters going in and out the door, the dorm rooms were getting a lot of use. While he'd been away, the ranch had become a working operation.

The barn to the right had lost its faded exterior, sporting a coat of fresh paint and a roof covered in new shingles. New fences replaced the sagging posts of the ranch's earlier days. A sturdier round pen had been built, and from up here he could see four riders training inside, their horses circling an instructor in the center.

The ever-present water trough still graced the outer wall of the barn, the wet and cold lessons he'd learned there vivid in his mind. The laughter reverberated in his heart. How often he'd been here in the past, a lonely boy come to visit Bennie Mueller, an understanding rancher who recognized a hurting child and welcomed him to his home. Now the years had matured him. The kindly old man was gone. Others had taken his place. Those days were etched in his memories.

A dog barked, chasing the flight of the spinning disc, its tail wagging in delight as it leaped toward the airborne toy. Another dog, black marked with white, lay nearby, its attention no less fixed on the activity around him. Unlike the exuberant pup, though, this dog didn't rise to the occasion. Its interest was not as keen as its companion, as if years had stolen its energy and arthritis pained every joint.

Duke.

Jayden's eyes blurred. He'd know that dog anywhere. Time and distance would never dim the adventures he'd shared with the faithful animal. His own existence once had been protected and loved by the devotion of that black and white border collie. Jayden figured the years in his head. Duke must be nearly fifteen.

A slender young woman Jayden didn't recognize, her hair gold in the sunshine, emerged from the barn. She patted her knee and called to the old dog. Something about her seemed familiar, though Jayden couldn't pinpoint why. She reminded him of his high school friend, Baylie, a young woman with whom he'd lost contact while overseas. He intended to find her again.

As Jayden watched, Duke rose on shaky legs and wobbled toward the barn, gait unsteady, head hanging low. The young woman bent down to pet the animal, whose tail wagged in appreciation, as she scratched behind his ears and hugged his neck. She held the door open, encouraging the border collie to go inside. She shut the door and strode toward the bunkhouse, stopping at the water spigot. She rinsed her hands, letting the water fill the trough below her before she continued on. The screen door banged. Like it always had.

Jayden was tempted to skirt the hill and wander into the yard, just to see Duke, but he held back. His mother now worked here as the cook and knew he was coming, but she'd promised not to tell the others. Nor had he told her when to expect him. Opportunity to again connect with this family would come, but not today. He wasn't ready. He adjusted his eye patch and put his weight on his cane, turning back the way he'd come.

At the bottom of the hill he found his Harley still parked in the juniper. Out here on a lonely stretch of road in Harney County, in the high desert of Eastern Oregon, not many would stop and try to haul it away. He folded his cane and stashed it in his saddlebag, donned his helmet, and turned the key. The motor sputtered and he gave the bike a little gas. He was rewarded with a roar and a puff of smoke. He accelerated slowly out of the bushy surroundings as tires connected with pavement. He wanted to see his former commanding officer Parker McGregor before he swooped into the lives of the family now living on the ranch. Parker would have wisdom he needed to hear.

A pickup, its lights on, came rumbling down the highway

toward him. A signal to turn flashed and Jayden hesitated. The truck looked familiar. The last thing he wanted today was an encounter. Jayden gassed the motorcycle and sped down the road. Time enough later to find his courage and share his tale. He didn't want their pity.

Baylie Summers walked around the ranch office, turning off lights and closing drawers. Her monthly newsletter still waited on the computer screen, the cursor blinking where she'd left it minutes ago. Satisfied she'd done all she could for today, she saved the file and shut the computer down. Tomorrow she'd hit send and ranch patrons would receive their monthly update.

Kurt and Lissa McKintrick owned the ranch and relied on her to keep the communications lines open and the donations pouring in. Keeping the ranch prosperous met a need in her life as well. After a long and grueling college experience, Baylie welcomed the sanctuary the ranch offered.

"That's your main objective, Baylie." Lissa McKintrick had outlined the job for her when she was hired. "Otherwise, the Bennie Mueller home for rescued horses and neglected kids will be no more."

Being responsible for the welfare of so many lives, animal and child alike, weighed on Baylie. She worked diligently each month to find heartwarming stories that helped the public connect with the needs of the ranch.

She'd grown up like a foster child herself, reared by her late mother's distant cousin, Mary Marshall, and her husband Troy. Her grandparents were named her guardians when she lost her parents at age four, but through kinship placement they chose Mary to provide the home environment they believed Baylie needed as she grew. When she left for college, Mary's home was no longer a resource for her, though the Marshalls assured her she would always be welcomed.

Baylie's circumstances had been without many challenges because of the family connection, but she knew other kids were not as fortunate. For them, she threw herself into her work. Every child deserved a forever home.

She glanced at the clock. She'd finished early today so she decided to wander over to the main house and see if Melanie Barnes, the ranch cook, needed any help with dinner. Feeding a crew like this took work. Baylie liked to pitch in whenever she could. Melanie was fun to talk to, someone with whom she could connect, just as she had with her foster mom. She left the office, locked the door to prevent any hide and seek games coming in here, and stepped into the yard.

A few minutes later, she entered the kitchen, greeted by the aroma of spaghetti sauce simmering on the stove. "That smells so good."

Melanie stood at the stove. She turned, apron spattered with spots of tomato sauce, and grinned. "Want to taste?"

"You know me well." Baylie reached in a drawer and grabbed a spoon. She dipped into the fragrant red sauce and blew on the steaming spoonful. Careful not to burn her tongue, she sampled. "Mmm. Wonderful as always."

"Thank you." Melanie turned back to her work, humming a tune that sounded vaguely like the "White Cliffs of Dover", a WWII melody.

Knowing Melanie had lost a husband in Afghanistan, her choice of song surprised Baylie. Melanie's son, Jayden, now served in the Marines. Choosing a WWII melody seemed out of sync with her circumstances, but maybe Melanie found the old tunes filled with more hope or better harmony.

"I finished my work load early today." Baylie set the spoon in the sink. "Need me to do anything?"

"Give me a minute." Melanie walked to the pantry and rummaged through the supplies. She returned with two loaves of French bread. "You want to slice these down the middle and butter them?" She held up a jar. "This is garlic butter. Use it and then wrap the bread in foil so we can heat it."

"Sure." Baylie washed her hands. "Heard anything from Jayden?" Mentioning the young man to Melanie always brought smiles to both the woman and to her. Melanie's son Jayden had been one of Baylie's closest friends in high school. They'd corresponded until Baylie stopped writing her senior year in college for reasons she'd never disclosed. Jayden's letters stopped coming as well. There'd been no letters since.

Melanie stiffened and sucked in a quick breath. "Not much to tell."

Surprised by her reaction, Baylie didn't press the conversation. She hurried on, trying to find footing in the awkward silence. "Do you want this sliced into individual portions as well as down the middle?"

"That's a great idea." Melanie handed her a serrated knife. "That will save time at dinner with twelve hungry kids."

She sliced the bread lengthwise and applied the garlic butter. Taking care to slice only to the back side of the loaf, she prepared ten slices and set them near the oven for warming, then reached for the second loaf. She turned to Melanie. "Anything else I can do?"

"Grab the big cooking pot and fill it with water." Melanie pulled out a large bowl. "When it boils, add the spaghetti. I'll toss the salad."

Baylie lifted the filled pot onto the range and turned on the burner. She glanced at the clock. Five o'clock. Dinner was served at six. "Shall I put plates down?"

"The twins have table setting duty this week." Melanie headed for the cooler, grabbed a head of lettuce from the shelf, and returned to the kitchen. She stopped to run a finger across the wall calendar where individual chores were assigned. "Krystal and Kendra are usually reliable."

"That's the job my foster sister and I had to do." Baylie remembered the countless times they had set the table. "Can't get the need to place plates out of my system, I guess."

Melanie laughed. "Jayden performed that same chore when he lived at the Herrick Valley Rescue Ranch with Peggy Blake and Kurt. I continued the chore routine here." She sobered. "Can you keep a secret?"

Baylie glanced up, startled by the request. "I can."

"Jayden's stateside."

"He is? Does anyone else know?"

Melanie shook her head. "He's injured and receiving therapy. He said he'll drop by when that ends."

"What happened?" Baylie couldn't imagine sending a son off to war and then learning he'd been hurt. She remembered her own fears for him when he had enlisted as soon as they graduated from high school. Now those fears had come true. Her heart ached for Jayden. He didn't deserve this. Was this why his letters had stopped?

Melanie shrugged. "He's not told me much. Very hush, hush. I only know he is alive and not badly wounded." Melanie looked at her, eyelids rimmed with moisture. "He's in God's hands and under His protection."

"And that's all you know?"

The twins came into the room, their chatter loud in the quiet kitchen. Baylie shrugged at the intrusion and raised an eyebrow toward Melanie, who smiled and made a face. She broke open the head of lettuce. "Yes, that's all I know."

Baylie nodded, then snapped the spaghetti into the boiling pot, counting the handfuls as she went. Feeding this brood meant plenty of noodles to fill the plates. She measured the salt into the water then set the timer.

Her boss, Kurt McKintrick, stepped into the doorway, knocking on the casing as he entered.

"Hello, Kurt." Melanie wiped her hands on her apron. "Dinner will be ready in about twenty minutes."

Baylie held her surprise. Kurt rarely visited the kitchen, especially this close to a meal. What would bring him here? She put the garlic bread in the oven and waited.

"I passed a Harley-Davidson on the highway when I was coming home a few minutes ago." Kurt tilted his head. "You wouldn't know anyone who might be riding one around here, would you?"

"No. Though I wouldn't be surprised if someone were." She folded her arms. "Who wants to know?"

"So he could be in the vicinity?"

"I'm sworn to secrecy." Melanie lifted her chin, a tease in her eyes. "Even a horse trough seminar couldn't make me spill. So you'll have to guess."

Kurt laughed. "Okay. I won't make you break your promise to Jayden. It is kind of suspicious when no one around here rides a Harley, except him."

Melanie laughed. "Yes, it is."

CHAPTER THREE

JAYDEN HAD FORGOTTEN HOW LONG THE trip was from the ranch in Burns, Oregon to the Willamette Valley on the other side of the Cascades. Two and a half hours after leaving the ranch he rolled into Pine River, the sun setting on the horizon. He checked his GPS to find the directions he needed. Tonight he planned to reunite with an old friend.

His commanding officer, Parker Macgregor, had completed his tour of duty in Afghanistan earlier this spring and invited Jayden to come see him when his rehab finished. Jayden jumped at the opportunity. What were the chances that this man who had led him on patrol halfway across the world lived close enough stateside for the two men to reconnect?

He gunned the Harley, his excitement at seeing his former leader fueling his ride. He couldn't stop the smile spreading across his face.

Parker had been a tough leader with a gentle heart. He'd stayed with Jayden when a roadside bomb exploded and the Humvee in which he was riding overturned.

"Man down!"

Jayden still remembered the shout and Parker at his side when the medics airlifted him to the nearest hospital in Germany. Parker had texted and connected by screen time, keeping updated on Jayden's surgeries. He followed his timeline for recovery, tracking his active duty status as Jayden's need for discharge became apparent.

When Jayden had been sent stateside to receive ongoing care, Parker had texted him to keep his spirits up. "How ya doing?" The three words became Parker's standard phrase when he wanted to check up on him.

Texting grew more difficult with Parker's duties still in the field and Jayden confined to a hospital bed. Parker didn't forget him. He made Jayden feel as if a part of Parker had been lost when Jayden no longer served under him. Parker never let his men down, wherever they were, Jayden included.

Man, I miss that guy.

Jayden maneuvered the Harley down a dozen streets, watching for road signs that would direct him to Parker's home. The man lived alone and had never married. His first fiancée had called it quits when she realized how often Parker's military obligations would call him away. That had been fifteen years ago, and Parker had never tried to fill the empty spaces of his heart. Jayden thought that was sad. The man would be a wonderful catch for some lucky woman.

Parker's street sign popped up at the next intersection and Jayden wheeled the Harley around the corner, noticing the affluent neighborhood and the tidy yards upon which the townhouses sat. He followed the numbers, stopping in front of a home that fit Parker's description in his letter—two story in brick red and charcoal gray trim. Though a light shone from an upstairs window the house appeared dark, as if no one was home.

He parked in the driveway and pulled the key from the Harley, grabbed his cane, and walked to the front door. The bell sounded inside, a Sousa march tune tinkling on a chime. Leave it to Parker to have his doorbell play something military.

Footsteps bounding down stairs inside made him smile. His former commanding officer never did anything without fervor, even answering the door. "Welcome home, soldier!" Parker spread his arms wide, grasping him about the shoulders. "Was that you on the Hog?"

"Yes, sir." Jayden returned the hug. How odd to embrace a man he would have saluted a year ago. "Don't leave home without your wheels."

"Let's have a look at your machine." Parker strode to the driveway and circled the bike. "Nice ride." He patted the seat. "You rode all the way from Portland to Burns and then here? Today?"

"Yes sir."

"You must do straight stretches at lightning speed."

"No, I played it safe." Jayden straightened and tapped his knee. "Not good in an emergency."

"Got it." Parker gestured to the house. "Let's go in." He led the way. "I hope you're hungry. I've got dinner on."

"You can cook?" He grabbed his duffel and followed Parker, breathing in a wonderful smell that floated on the air. The entry greeted him with an oval rug, an American flag in the corner, and a silk plant arrangement sitting in an alcove. Parker had a domestic side.

"I dabble a little. Tonight it's only hamburger stroganoff in the Crockpot, but I promise you the breadsticks are to die for."

Jayden laughed. "That sounds like an American soldier cookbook you're following."

"Follow me. We can eat."

The cheery kitchen was white with red checkered curtains and a blue tile floor. Jayden smiled at the ongoing military touches. A retro chrome table sat in the center. The four, red handle-back chairs sat pushed in, neatly rounding the prim dinette set.

Parker pulled out a chair. "Here, make yourself at home. I'll dish up some grub."

Jayden looked at his hands. "I should wash first. I've been gripping the Harley handles for a while and my fingers are grimy."

Parker pointed to a door off the kitchen. "Small bathroom in there. Help yourself."

A few minutes later he emerged to find Parker setting plates on the table, a steaming bowl of hamburger gravy taking up space beside a heaping container of mashed potatoes. Parker reached in the refrigerator and removed a bowl of salad.

"How did you know I'd be here for dinner?" He slipped into the chair Parker had left waiting for him.

"I didn't, but it stood to reason you'd show up at the end of the day knowing where you were coming from." Parker grabbed a chair for himself and sat. "Did you go see your mother?"

"No, I decided to wait." He laid his cane on the floor beside him. "I climbed the knoll above the ranch and took in the scene, but I knew if I went to the ranch house, I'd get embroiled in a reunion I wasn't prepared to handle."

Parker passed the potatoes his way. "They don't know about your eye?"

He shook his head. "All Mom knows is I was injured." He passed the potatoes back to Parker. "Their reaction might have deflated me."

"Is that the only reason?"

Jayden looked at his commanding officer. Two years before, on the battlefield, he would have given a ready answer to this man. Now Parker's question made him search for words. "I didn't expect to come back from the deployment like this."

"Like what?" Parker shoved the bowl of hamburger stroganoff his way. "Alive? Wounded? Discharged?"

He fisted the table. "I went to honor the legacy of my father and to emulate my foster dad, Kurt. They were great soldiers." He inhaled. "Instead, I'm a washout."

Parker put his fork down and gazed at him. "Your father was killed, Jayden. You were spared. From what you've told me, Kurt suffered survivor's guilt because he lost his best friend over there. You came home with injuries that won't keep you from a normal life. You did your job. You didn't wash out."

"I'm not the leader I wanted to be. Like my dad."

"Wasn't he part of a unit that was ambushed?" Parker stirred his potatoes with his fork. "He wasn't the commanding officer, was he?"

"No." Jayden glanced up. "He and Kurt were part of the same patrol. Dad was shot. Kurt went MIA."

"How is that better than your service?" Parker passed the salad and slid the basket of breadsticks toward him. "You were part of a patrol that was ambushed. You pulled a man from your unit out of the wreckage while wounded, remember? Thanks to you, he survived."

"I'd forgotten. I left the scene by stretcher pretty quickly." Jayden sighed. "I just wanted to do more, okay? Maybe I'll come to grips with this later."

"Got it." Parker offered him salad dressing. "I'm glad you're here."

They ate in companionable silence for a few minutes. Jayden savored the warm food and the company. "So are you planning to deploy again? Do another tour?"

Parker shook his head. "No. I've done four. That's my limit."

"Are you working?"

"Not yet." Parker offered him more potatoes which he waved off. "My military pension has kicked in and I'm able to get by on that for now."

"Nice house, by the way."

"Thanks. I bought it for a song a few years back. My mother lived here while I deployed. It stood empty after she passed two years ago."

"She can't have been very old." Jayden did the math in his head. "You're what, forty-ish?"

"I was the youngest of five siblings. Mom always said I was the one bringing up the rear."

"Still."

"Cancer got her."

"Sorry."

Baylie couldn't stop thinking about what Melanie had said about Jayden. He was stateside. After Kurt came to see if Melanie knew anything after spotting a Harley on the main road, Baylie's hopes rose. Jayden had preferred motorcycles to cars in high school. That he might be back here brought shivers of excitement running up and down her spine. But if he was here, why didn't he visit the ranch?

They'd been so close in high school—Jayden, Jamielyn, and Baylie—three foster kids braving the social barriers of a high school that majored in cliques. Often the mainstream students made life difficult for students without families, but the three of them had supported each other and finished their studies with notable grades.

"We did it!" Baylie had been the first to toss her graduation cap.

But not many weeks later, they went their separate ways. She chose college and pursued her dream of writing. High school had taught her the rigors of putting out a newspaper. The university taught her the need for concise copy. In the wake of studies, she lost contact with her friends. Now she had returned to the ranch, a place that held old memories.

A pan hit the floor and she jumped. Kevin, one of her kitchen helpers, stood frozen, eyes wide, as if expecting a reprimand. The fear of the consequences of his carelessness were written in worry lines across his forehead and the tight-lipped pucker of his lips.

"It's okay, Kevin." She smiled. "That pan must be full of jumping beans."

The child laughed, relief spreading across his face. "It sure jumped out of my fingers."

"Give it to me and you can go outside before we lose all the sunshine."

"Thanks, Baylie."

She watched the boy join his friends, glad that she'd eased his fright, sad that he expected punishment for so small an infraction as dropping a pan. Perhaps she should feature his story in the next newsletter. Names were never used, but when people learned of the histories of these children, they were often shocked into action because of the level of neglect and abuse the kids had endured before coming to the ranch.

Kevin would make a good feature. Mistreated by his mother's boyfriend, Kevin's history with that man echoed Jayden's experience with his step-father, George. She wiped down the counters and cleaned out the sink, her thoughts on what Jayden had told her. He'd not had it easy with his step-father. The man's drunken state and his temper had sent Jayden running. The original owner of this ranch, Bennie Mueller, had offered him sanctuary. Jayden's best memories were of his time with Mr. Mueller and his kindness to a hurting eleven-year-old boy who needed a friend.

"This would be a great place to work." Jayden had often talked about how the ranch had helped him. He always told her what the ranch could do for kids. A job here would be like living a dream, he'd said, but he built rooms, wrangled horses, and stacked hay bales. Not work she was suited for.

. When she'd accepted the position here, she didn't know if it was the job that called to her or the possibility she might see Jayden again. She'd never voiced that hope, though she knew the underlying root of her devotion to the ranch rested with him. If he came home, her joy would be magnified tenfold.

She dropped the kitchen towels in the hamper to await the next wash and exited the room. Bedtime routines weren't far off. Tonight, she had housemother duties at the dormitory.

Jayden carried his dishes to the sink. "Thanks for inviting me to stay here."

"Hey, glad to have the company." Parker put the last of the plates in the dishwasher. "Let me show you the guest room."

He grabbed the small duffel he'd stashed on the back of the bike and followed Parker up the stairs.

Parker opened the door to the room. "The space is a little on the feminine side. My mother had a thing for decorating, and she loved touches of pinks."

Jayden laughed. "This isn't bad." He glanced around, taking in the flowered wallpaper and the dark cranberry drapes. "It could be a lot worse."

Parker shrugged. "I'll give it an update one of these days, but the colors remind me of Mom."

"My mother would love this." He set his duffel down. "It feels more elegant than girlie."

"Bring her here." Parker leaned against the door casing. "If anyone would understand your injuries, she would."

"She lost so much when Dad was killed. The experience nearly broke her." Jayden pulled up a chair and sat. "I don't want my injuries to add another round of stress."

"Would it help if you went with someone?" Parker shifted his weight to his other leg. "Why don't we go together?"

"To the ranch?"

"Yeah. I'd love to see it. You could introduce me to all those people you are always talking about and you and I could spend some time reminiscing about Afghanistan."

"You going to ride the Harley?"

Parker smiled. "Set your duffel down. I've got something to show you."

Jayden frowned. The smirk on Parker's face told him he was in for a surprise. He followed Parker down the stairs and through a side door that led to the garage. When the lights switched on, he stared at a bright green Harley with a yellow and black helmet sitting on the seat.

"Parker, you got a bike?"

"After listening to you wax eloquent about the advantages of a motorcycle all those nights in Afghanistan, I decided to give one a try."

Jayden walked to the bike and ran his fingers over the shiny chrome. "And what do you think?"

"I'm a fan." Parker handed him a box. "I also got a spare headset for your helmet. All you need is a cell phone."

Jayden stared at the gift. "I haven't used one of these before. We can talk as we ride?"

"As long as you stay within a mile of me." Parker picked up his helmet and pointed to the unit on the side. "I bought the deluxe model so I can talk with more than one biker at a time."

"Bluetooth?"

"No, this is a dynamic MESH connection. Supposed to be better than Bluetooth."

Jayden laughed. "Imagine the adventure we'll have with two of us on Harleys?"

"Just remember." Parker snorted. "I want to come home in one piece."

Baylie left the kitchen and headed to her temporary room in the dormitory above the attached garage. The upper floor had six bedrooms, each with its own dormer window. The room she now occupied was used on a rotating schedule, she and three other ranch employees trading off the duties of residence house manager every three days.

This bedroom was in the middle of the dorm with two bathrooms across the hall. Children who got up in the night to use the facilities were almost always noticed. As the residence house mother on duty, she had to make sure all children were tucked in at night—and that they stayed there. She was grateful these kids remained where they belonged. Being treated well, fed regularly, and loved unconditionally went a long way toward maintaining order and keeping discipline.

Her mother's cousin, Mary, had operated much the same way. When Baylie and her foster sister, Jamielyn, became teens Mary relied on them to help the younger ones feel loved and stay happy. Baylie gave thanks every day she'd been part of a loving foster care situation.

She entered her temporary quarters and sat on the bed, leaving the door open. The ranch bell rang outside, signaling the children playing in the yard to put away whatever equipment occupied them at the moment—balls, horseshoes, jump ropes—and come in for bed.

The rumble on the stairs grew louder as the kids hurried in and retreated to their quarters. Three of the rooms were double occupancy for smaller children and the remaining two bedrooms each had a single bed. The boy and the girl who occupied those rooms were entering puberty and needed their privacy. Baylie stood and waited as every child took their turn using the bathroom, brushing teeth, and washing grimy hands and faces after a day outside.

"Charlie, be sure to scrub behind your ears." Baylie smiled at the six-year-old.. "Want some help?"

He nodded, grabbed the soap, and handed it to her, together with the washcloth.

She created a lather on the cloth and gently helped him wash his face and hands. She handed him a towel. "There." She smiled.

"All clean?" His bright smile could have competed with the moon.

Charlie had only been here a few days, but he showed great progress learning the routine. She shuddered to think of what the little boy had endured, found wandering on the street alone, his mother and her boyfriend passed out on drugs at home. Charlie had been dirty, hungry, and scared, tears making trails in the dirt on his cheeks.

Her boss, Lissa McKintrick, learned of Charlie's plight and her heart broke for him. Though he was younger than the children they normally received here at the ranch Baylie watched as Lissa hurdled mountains to claim him. With that kind of dogged determination, Baylie held hope for Charlie's future.

She guided him to his bedroom. The other boy in the room had climbed in his bed, the covers up to his chin. Was he cold? Or hiding something beneath the covers? "Kevin, do you need another blanket?"

Kevin's wide-eyed stare confirmed her suspicion.

"Whatcha got under there with you?"

"Nuttin." Kevin scooted lower in the blankets. A muted mewl met Baylie's ears.

"Why does nothing sound like one of the new barn kittens?"

Kevin sat up and the wobbly feline climbed out of the covers and blinked. "He sounded so lonely I brought him here."

"That was kind of you, Kevin. The kitten, though, will need his mother during the night." She picked up the little cat. "You don't want him hungry, do you?"

Kevin shook his head.

"Good. Charlie will be here with you, so you can sleep well knowing you are safe and the kitten is happy in the barn."

"Okay."

Baylie withdrew from the room, the kitten tucked in her arm. "Good night, boys."

She continued along the hall, checking each room for occupants and wishing the children a good night. Once all were accounted for, she tiptoed down the stairs and outside, turning in the direction of the barn.

Kurt stood outside the round pen. "Are you out after curfew?" He chuckled, the insinuation in his tone making her grin.

"I'm a little old for curfew." She held up the kitten. "One of the boys had this fella hidden in his covers." She held the cat out to Kurt. "Can you return it to its mother?"

"Sure." Kurt scooped up the kitten, dwarfed by his hands. "Let me guess, Kevin?"

"The one and the same."

"I'll have to give him feeding duties. He really loves those cats."

Baylie smiled. "Kevin still feels a little lost and is in need of a friend."

"He'll get there."

"He will." Baylie lifted a hand. "Good night."

CHAPTER FOUR

THE NEXT DAY JAYDEN AND PARKER rode side by side, the Harleys drowning out other noises along the highway. The MESH unit headset in Parker's helmet had been programmed to sync with his before they left Pine River. Now the headphones allowed them to chat comfortably as they burned miles beneath their tires, the reunion touching on experiences they'd shared in the sand as well as discussion about their individual lives stateside. Jayden appreciated Parker's candor, the duty-bound sergeant persona absent in this new environment. As they headed up highway 126, Parker pointed out places he'd frequented as a kid.

"Let's stop here," Parker said into the headphones. He signaled for a left turn. "Take a break."

Jayden glimpsed the sign marker which read Koosah Falls. "You into waterfalls?"

"After Afghanistan, who wouldn't be? The green here is like an oasis."

They parked their bikes on the shady side of the parking lot and followed the sound of rushing water to the falls. A breeze blew through, bringing with it cooler air. Parker tucked his helmet under his arm. "When I was eleven, my family's overnight camping trip near Cascadia involved a stint in a tent around a campfire."

Jayden removed his helmet and held it at his side. "Yeah. Kurt took me camping when I was that age."

"Nice." Parker pointed right. "This way."

Jayden trailed Parker, who rounded a bend and the falls came into view. They leaned on the railing to watch the water cascade over the edge, the mist rising from the edge of the falls as the river splashed into the pool below.

"My family took a day trip away from the campground and

came here out of curiosity." Parker chuckled. "I decided to follow the two-mile trail from Koosah Falls to Sahalie Falls, not knowing how long the jaunt would take. My mistake was I didn't tell anybody where I was going."

"Your parents must have been frantic."

"You don't know the half of it." Parker kicked the bottom rail of the protective barrier. "I was fascinated by the churning water that connected the two waterfalls. I'd never seen a stream like this, the force of the channel thunderous as the water crashed against rocks and challenged its banks. I lost track of time. I didn't realize how far I'd come until I looked at an almost night sky." He sighed, shaking his head as if lost in memory. "I knew my family needed to get back to our tent site and it was growing darker by the minute. I thought about heading back along the trail, but the blackness meant I might miss them if they came behind me."

"What happened?"

"I didn't know what to do. The only smart thing I did was stay put."

"Was anyone around to find you?"

"A state trooper found me. I was in big trouble with my dad." Parker rubbed the dirt on the trail with his boot. "Let's say I didn't do that again. The need for adventure, though, had been born. The experience cemented my future as a soldier who wanted to see the world."

"Did your dad ground you?"

Parker nodded. "My dad threatened me with a GPS attached to my back side." He pointed down the path. "Come on. The trail is only two miles. We can walk to the other falls and back before we head on over the mountain."

"Sounds like we're on patrol." Jayden cast Parker a crooked smile.

"Once a platoon leader, always a platoon leader." He gestured toward the trail and took off at a brisk clip.

Jayden fell into step behind him, steadying himself with his cane. "Hey, remember I'm just out of rehab."

"Sorry." Parker slowed his pace. "Don't want to do more damage to your leg."

The trail fascinated Jayden. The path paralleled the raging waters all the way to the next waterfall. Both were breathtaking. He remembered the trail he and Kurt had followed at the Paige Spring campgrounds along the Donner und Blitzen River. The memory sparked a sense of homesickness as thoughts of other adventures with Kurt resurrected themselves. He had treated Jayden like a son, not a lonely, hurting child. Jayden's need for a reunion was growing.

An hour later they returned to the motorcycles. Jayden donned his helmet and tested his headset connection. "Do you read me?"

"Loud and clear." Parker threw a leg across the seat and started his engine.

"Thanks, Parker. Following that trail brought back vivid images of many old escapades."

"Your tour will cost you lunch." Parker revved his motor. He pointed down highway 126. "Sisters is next up."

"Good food there?"

"There's a Mexican eatery that I like." Parker gripped his handlebars. "Or there was before I deployed."

"Sounds good."

Baylie opened the ranch office the next morning, booting her computer, and checked the daily schedule. The dormitory had been quiet last night. All her charges stayed in their beds and she'd not heard any night terrors. Bad dreams had a habit of stalking these children, their past lives often popping up in their sleep and waking them in fitful episodes of tears.

Charlie, the newest child, had whimpered, but he'd not awakened. When Baylie called him this morning, he'd studied her wide-eyed. "I'm so glad I'm here. I dreamt I was sleeping on the floor again, hiding from my mother and her boyfriend while they smoked that stuff that smelled so bad."

"Never again, Charlie." Baylie gave him a hug. "You're safe here."

"You even serve breakfast."

She ruffled his mop of curls. "Then you better dress, wash your hands, and head for the kitchen. What do you say?" She didn't have to ask twice.

Now she sat at her desk, re-reading the newsletter she had prepared for delivery this week. This edition focused on the horses the children shared. Each animal had its history, too. Why did neglect run so rampant among those who were most vulnerable?

Today she'd written about Whiskers, the grey gelding the ranch had rescued from a forgotten pasture. The horse had been abandoned after its owners decided not to keep trying to make their property profitable. They'd pulled out and headed over the mountains to the northern part of the state, leaving the horse to feed on pasture.

Baylie grimaced. In some areas leaving a horse on pasture would be a safe enough plan. Not here. The dry desert-like heat last summer had parched the pasture and dried up the creek. The horse had nothing on which to graze and no water for its thirst. She lifted her hands from the computer, remembering her first introduction to Whiskers.

"I found a horse that's in trouble." Baylie's boss, Lissa McKintrick, had texted, having spotted the forlorn animal while she was driving to Idaho to make arrangements for another child. "He's sagging against a fence in a distant pasture. His knees are buckled, head down."

Baylie noted Lissa's location and called the veterinarian to alert him and to inquire about the horse's owners. When none were located, Baylie reported the news to Lissa who went into action.

Whiskers, stumbling on his overgrown hooves and weak from hunger, was loaded into a trailer and suspended from a sling as he was transported to the veterinary clinic for observation. The vet called for community volunteers to help watch the horse around the clock, not certain if dehydration or starvation were the greater danger. Both threatened to steal his life.

"We won't know anything for a while." Lissa's words made Baylie fearful for the horse's future.

Lissa had hovered near the animal, keeping vigil over its progress for more than two weeks. Finally, after intravenous therapy and close attention to diet, Whiskers showed signs of improvement. The vet called and cleared the process for the ranch to adopt the horse.

"Whiskers is coming home!" Baylie and Lissa shared a high five.

The animal thrived here. Fresh grass, daily grain feedings, and lots of sunshine had combined with the children's competition for turns at brushing him, transforming what could have been a tragic end into a new beginning for Whiskers.

Baylie swallowed the lump in her throat. How like Whiskers she had been when she arrived at the ranch. Her university experience had left her struggling to find her footing, a broken shell of the young, starry-eyed freshman she had been. Devoid of hope, her quest destroyed, Baylie only retained shattered fragments of that energetic girl in her mind. She retreated to the ranch, hoping to reclaim her former self—soul barren, empty, and in need of transfusion. Some wounds, though, don't heal. Others leave scars. She and Whiskers shared a similar history.

She forced herself to study the screen once more. Time for remorse later.

The door opened, interrupting Baylie's proofread. She looked up as Melanie walked in. "Can you help me with dinner today?"

"Sure. My newsletter is about to fly. I'll be free then."

"Great." Melanie turned to go, her hesitant smile lingering. She looked back. "And no, there's no more word on Jayden."

Baylie blushed. How much of her friendship with Jayden did Melanie remember? Jayden only knew her former self. Could he be friends with this new version?

Jayden paid for their meal and followed Parker to the parking lot. "That was an amazing veggie burrito."

"Yeah. They prepare a good lunch." Parker checked the Harley. "Are we close to the ranch?"

"No. We've another two hours of driving. Why?'

Parker looked at him. "I think I should stop somewhere before we get there. You can ride into the ranch on your wheels alone."

"What about you?"

"I'll follow you in." Parker gripped his handlebars. "A little later."

"Any particular reason?" Jayden scratched his head. "Or do you have a hot date waiting somewhere between here and there and I'm the third wheel?"

"You are the returning soldier to these people." Parker jingled his keys. "You need to experience their joy at seeing you again."

"And you?" Jayden pursed his lips. "The escort service?"

"No." Parker grinned. "I'll show up a half hour or so later looking for you. That way you can introduce me, and I won't share your spotlight." Parker studied him, as if waiting to see if his instructions were clear. "You need this, Jayden."

Jayden sighed. "I hope I can manage."

"You can."

Parker turned the ignition and waited as Jayden put his bike in gear. "Tell me when you think we are close enough and I'll pull off the pavement."

"I know just the spot."

Ninety minutes later Jayden pointed to a pull-off on the highway and spoke into the headset. "This would be a good place to hang out."

"How far from here?" Parker wheeled his bike onto the graveled space.

"About thirty minutes, give or take a few." Jayden let his bike idle. "Long enough to get the Harley cooled." He grinned. "Might look kind of strange riding in on a cold bike, though."

"Point taken." Parker gunned the motor for effect. "That ought to heat things up."

Jayden adjusted his face shield. He turned the ignition and revved the engine. "Think you can find the turn-off?"

"Sounds easy enough."

Jayden took off down the highway, the wind at his back and the roar of the engine singing a tune he never tired of hearing. Time seemed to vanish as he rode and within what seemed like minutes he faced the turn-off to the ranch. As he had yesterday, he slowed for the turn, put on his signal, and braced himself for the reunion waiting for him at the end of the long driveway.

The pickup that had made him burn rubber only a day before approached from the other direction. This couldn't be, could it? What were the chances he'd run into Kurt McKintrick, his former foster dad, here *again*? This time, though, Jayden braked, waiting for the truck to make its turn. As he coasted toward the vehicle, the truck slowed and rolled to a standstill. The window lowered and a familiar voice called. "Jayden? Is that you?"

He stopped next to the driver's door, letting the engine idle. He raised his face shield and sighed. "How did you know it was me?"

Kurt laughed and leaned out his window. "You're the only man I know that rides a Harley around here. Most everybody else has a truck or sits a horse. You kind of stand out, you know?"

"Busted." Jayden pulled off the road, removed his helmet, and pulled his collapsed cane from his saddlebag and extended it.

The pickup parked off the asphalt, the door opened, and Kurt stepped out and crossed the road. "I thought I saw you in this same spot yesterday, but you rode on like you were chased by a band of terrorists intent on your capture."

"Maybe I was." Jayden held out his hand, waiting for the inevitable reaction from those who had known him. He lifted his face to Kurt, his leg trembling under his weight. "How are you?"

Kurt studied Jayden's eye patch and his gaze dropped to his lower leg. "From where I stand, I'm guessing I'm a whole lot better than you, son. What a man you've become." He opened his arms and waited. "Come here."

Jayden's mouth wobbled and he breathed deep. This man had been his anchor when he'd had none, his rudder in the storm of his life, and his constant guide while he matured. Kurt had also endured the rigors of war. Jayden had joined the Marines to honor his father's sacrifice and to emulate Kurt as well. He'd wanted to make them proud. Now here he was, broken and disillusioned. Parker said he needed this man. If anyone could help him reclaim his path Kurt could. He looked again at Kurt and stepped his way.

Kurt wrapped his arms about him. "It's so good to have you back."

Jayden fought the need to cry. After all, he was a medaled soldier. But as the big man held him against his shoulder, Jayden couldn't stop the tears. He was home.

CHAPTER FIVE

BAYLIE HIT SEND ON THE RANCH newsletter document file, then checked the e-mail queue before shutting down the computer for the day. She locked her office and stepped into the ranch commons area. A slight breeze blew in off the pasture bringing with it scents of sagebrush and juniper.

Charlie played with Kevin near the barn, both boys consumed with giggles. Between them they held a stick with a ball on a string and as they dragged it across the graveled path, a kitten played gotcha, only to have the ball suddenly snatched from its paws. Baylie wasn't sure who was having more fun—the boys or the kitten. Its tail straight in the air, the tiny cat reared up on its hind legs and pounced on the ball, wrapping the toy with its body like a layer of fluff. Kevin snatched the string away as quickly as he could, which left the kitten whipping its head from side to side trying to find where the ball had gone.

An engine, loud and menacing, sounded at the top of the drive. Baylie looked to the source of the noise and saw Kurt's truck returning to the ranch. "Boys. Kurt's coming. Take the kitten inside so it will be safe."

Kevin and Charlie scrambled to their feet as Baylie pulled the barn door open to let them enter. The kitten had fixed its claws around Kevin's hand and was kicking the boy's wrist furiously with his feet. The truck engine outside sounded louder than usual as the vehicle passed the barn. Duke, the old border collie, let out a howl and barked like a wild animal. What had gotten into him? The dog had trouble navigating the yard, let alone sounding off like an official greeter.

"Oww!" Kevin shook the kitten away from his hand. "He's mean."

Baylie caught the kitten and tucked it close to her side. "He's playing tiger and he thinks he's ferocious. He doesn't mean to hurt you. His grip is the way he plays."

"I like him better when he purrs." Charlie watched the kitten with the tender look of a child fascinated with a stuffed toy.

Baylie nodded. "So do I." She held the kitten aloft, letting his hind feet dangle. "All right, you." She brought the kitten to her face. "Enough rough stuff." The kitten mewed.

"Can we go play with the Frisbee now?"

"Yes." As Baylie held the door for the boys she looked around for signs of activity. Kurt's truck had pulled into its parking spot, but the driver had already disappeared. Duke was circling the pickup, tail wagging, frequent barks declaring his excitement. A motorcycle stood beside the pickup, its kickstand down, a red helmet on the seat. She hadn't realized the bike had come in with the pickup. No wonder there was so much noise. Baylie's pulse raced. Had Jayden come in with Kurt? Judging from Duke's reaction, he had.

She turned to the boys. "The coast is clear. Be sure to share the Frisbee with the other kids."

"We will." Charlie and Kevin slipped out the barn door and raced to the lawn area.

Baylie carried the kitten back to the loft where its mother meowed her protest. "I know. They kept your baby too long. He had fun." She returned to the barn floor and exited the building. Melanie was counting on her help. What were they fixing tonight? She needed to hurry, especially if Kurt had brought Jayden.

As she pulled the back screen door of the kitchen she heard Kurt teasing Melanie. "Can you set an extra plate for dinner?" He stood next to the cook, his hand on her shoulder. "I think you'll enjoy this new kid."

Melanie stood in the center of the kitchen staring up at Kurt, arms hugging her middle in a guarded stance. Seeing Melanie's tears and hearing her sniff, Baylie stopped near the back door, sensing something was afoot.

Kurt chuckled, then seeing Baylie, he winked. "You'll keep him in line, too."

Melanie shook her head, tears pooling in her eyes. "Are you saying what I think you're saying?"

Kurt looked over his shoulder at the main door. "I think she guessed our secret."

Leaning on a cane and wearing an eye patch, a muscular soldier in camouflage gear stepped through the door. His uniform provided the final piece of the puzzle—the name Clarke printed above the pocket. Jayden Clarke. "Hi, Mom."

Melanie squealed and hurried to the soldier. "You're home!" She put her hands on his shoulders and kissed his cheek, then laid her head against his chest. The pair stood inseparable for a few minutes, Melanie's cries audible in the steamy kitchen.

Baylie stayed back, containing her joy at seeing Jayden while she allowed mother and son an overdue reunion.

Kurt came and stood beside her, his grin wide enough to stretch to his ears.

Finally, Melanie straightened and wiped her eyes, smiling at the others in the room. She sniffed. "Jayden, do you remember Baylie?"

Jayden turned his head. "Baylie Summers?" His jaw dropped and he stared at her. "I don't believe this? How is it you are here?"

"You always said this was a great place, so I applied for a position." Baylie swallowed her nerves. Seeing Jayden was better than she'd thought it could be. If only they could be friends again.

"Was I right?" Jayden angled his head to the left, that cocky smile he'd sported in high school popping across his cheeks.

"Really happy I listened to you." Baylie smiled back at him. "This is a dream job." She gulped at the one deep-set brown eye, so much like Melanie's and the muscular form of the boy-now-turned man she'd once known. She wondered at the patch over the other eye. His face next to Melanie's reflected the image of his mother's. "Glad you're home."

"You two know each other?" At their nods, Kurt smiled, folding his arms across his chest. He nodded Jayden's way. "This kid kept me busy all through high school. I gave more horse trough seminars than I thought possible."

Jayden smirked. "You always said I was a slow learner."

"Ah, I thought you just liked being dumped in the water trough." Kurt laughed. "No?"

"It was a quick way to catch a bath." Jayden winked at her with his one good eye, sending shivers down Baylie's spine. Jayden hadn't lost his rascal side. "He treated me like a pesky little brother."

Baylie shook her head at the banter between the two. "Doesn't sound as if Kurt has changed much."

"Nor Jayden." Kurt raised a hand. "I've got to tell Lissa you're here. I'll see you at dinner."

Baylie stepped forward and spoke to Melanie. "Why don't you tell me what I need to do so you and Jayden can catch up?"

"Thanks, Baylie." She pointed to the refrigerator. "There are two heads of cabbage in there, one green, one purple. Shave them fine for coleslaw."

"Got it." Baylie retrieved the cabbage and moved to the cutting board. She pulled out the long knife reserved for vegetables, her attention on the mother and son.

Melanie turned back to Jayden. "You sit down and tell me why you said your injuries were nothing." She huffed. "You lost an eye?"

"Yes. The explosion blasted my face with debris. I'm fortunate to have only lost sight in one eye." He straightened. "I can still legally drive. I have to watch my visual perception. One eye throws off my ability to judge distance and space between objects."

Mom pointed to his trousers. "What's with the cane? Is your leg gone, too?" Tears pooled in her eyes. "Didn't you think you could tell me what happened?"

Baylie whacked away at the cabbage trying to remain as quiet as she could. Eavesdropping on a private conversation bothered her, but the situation left no alternative.

"Mom, there wasn't anything to say that wouldn't have worried you more." Jayden slid onto a stool at the work counter. "I thought I was going to lose my leg at the knee." He looked Baylie's way as if seeking her support. "I still have my limb and the only reminder is my limp." He stuck out his leg at Baylie. "See?"

"I didn't even notice, to be honest." Baylie meant it. The rest of Jayden was so muscled out that he did not resemble the scrawny kid she remembered from high school, the guy with the penchant for rolling pencils across his desk, a habit he used just to annoy her. She decided she couldn't comment on his physique. "Melanie, do you want a couple of carrots grated into this?"

"Yes. That will add color." She looked at Jayden. "And I will eat with my hero son, so tell the twins to add a plate." She put her hands on her hips. "Even if he hid his wounds. Just like his father."

"Should I mix the dressing?" Baylie reached for the mayonnaise. Anything to impress Jayden.

"Yes. Use the whole milk."

"Got it." Baylie looked up to see the twins entering the kitchen. "Here to set the table?"

"Yes." The simultaneous response, complete with an eye roll as if to say 'duh', merited a laugh.

"Well, tonight we have a special guest, so add two plates to the table. Melanie is going to join us."

"Actually, there will be another guest." Jayden's quiet statement reverberated off the kitchen walls.

Baylie jerked her attention back to the mother and son. Had Jayden brought a significant other with him? Her spirit took a nosedive.

"If it's all right with you." Jayden cast his mother a sheepish grin. "I am traveling with a friend who's not far behind me."

Melanie's cheeks pinked. She wiped her hands on her apron. "Any friend of yours is welcome, Jayden."

Baylie thought Melanie's initial reaction strange. Melanie, though, was all smiles as she prepared to welcome another diner at the table.

Jayden's grin widened. "Thanks, Mom."

Baylie's heart sank. Jayden had brought a friend. The way he said it could only mean one thing. So much for a reunion. She attacked the carrots.

Jayden heard the rumble of Parker's bike in the drive. "My friend is here. I'll make introductions in a minute." He exited the kitchen, eager to introduce his commanding officer.

Parker had pulled off to the side of the drive, his motorcyle the center of attention as several young boys circled him.

Jayden grinned at the company of hero worshippers studying Parker, awe on their faces.

"Are you here to work on the ranch?" One small voice asked.

"Do you want to share my bunk?" The boy raised an eager hand.

Parker laughed, eyes twinkling when he spotted Jayden

coming toward him. "I'm here with this guy. He used to live here, I'm told."

All four pairs of eyes turned on Jayden, the scrutiny joined by puzzled faces and wrinkled foreheads. He recognized two of the boys as Kurt and Lissa's sons. Four years had not changed them much.

"I don't remember him being here. " One of the McKintrick duo gave Jayden the once over. "Are you sure?"

"Yes, he's sure." Jayden stepped into the circle. "I'm Jayden Clarke. My mother cooks for the ranch. And I used to live here."

"Boys," Kurt came up the drive, "Jayden was the first foster boy I had the privilege of mentoring. Gunner, Gage, you were real small when he left. He's a soldier just back from Afghanistan."

"Oooooh." The chorus of voices took the news with respectful awe. With the exception of Gunner and Gage, neither of the other two were old enough to have been at the ranch when Jayden deployed.

"This man," Jayden pointed at Parker, "was my commanding officer in Afghanistan. His name is Parker Macgregor."

"Hello, Mr. Macgregor." The hero worshippers chirped in unison.

Parker saluted the kids. "You can call me Parker. Mr. Macgregor sounds like the owner of a dairy farm."

The boys giggled. "Want to play Frisbee with us?"

"Maybe a little later?"

"Welcome, Parker." Kurt extended his hand. "Thanks for taking care of our boy."

"The pleasure was all mine."

Jayden thumbed toward the kitchen. "Come meet my mother. One of my best friends from high school is also here." He turned toward the entrance, then stopped and looked at Kurt. "I can't believe Baylie's on staff."

"She's just as surprised by you." Kurt cast him a playful grin. "I take it that's a good thing?"

Jayden snorted, giving Kurt a thumbs up. He walked back into the kitchen, Parker at his side. "Mom, Baylie, I'd like you to meet my commanding officer, Parker Macgregor. He recently finished his tour of duty and lives in Pine River on the other side of the Cascades. Parker, my mother, Melanie Barnes, and my friend, Baylie Summers."

Face flushed, his mother wiped her hands on her apron and extended a hand toward Parker. "It's so nice to meet you. Jayden's letters mentioned you many times." She seemed to be squeezing his hand like he was a lifeline to her warrior son. Jayden choked back his embarrassment.

Parker didn't say anything for a second, a strange blush coloring his cheeks, a similar reaction of his mother a minute before. Jayden waited, surprised that Parker seemed flustered. Was his mother's praise of him causing his discomfort? Or, strange as it seemed, was something else the underlying cause?

"Ma'am. The pleasure is all mine. Your son is a soldier to be proud of." Parker swallowed, his Adam's apple moving along his throat. "He's matured into a fine young man."

His mother blushed again, her gaze reflecting a shyness Jayden hadn't seen before. Jayden loosened his collar. He hadn't counted on this. He turned the conversation to Baylie. "And this is my high school partner-in-crime, Baylie."

Parker stood at attention and focused on Baylie. "Nice to meet you. So was Jayden as ornery in high school as he was in our unit?"

Jayden gasped. "Hey!"

Baylie laughed. "Probably more so, but he made up his mind to be a soldier like his dad and there was no turning him from his appointed task."

Parker turned back to Mom. "I'm sorry you had to lose your husband to war. I can't think of any other pain more difficult to bear than losing a loved one."

"Thank you. I'm thankful I didn't lose a son, too." Mom inhaled a deep breath. "You understand."

Jayden grasped for something to say. "So, Mom, can Parker stay for dinner?"

"Of course he can." Melanie gestured to the dining room. "Any friend of yours is a friend of ours. We've already set a place for him at the table."

Parker smiled. "I hope you saved a spot for yourself as well, Mrs. Barnes."

"Yes."

Jayden hid his surprise. Mom wouldn't risk a relationship again after George, would she? Parker, though, was not George. This would be an interesting reunion.

CHAPTER SIX

JAYDEN SAT AT THE END OF the table, the place on his right reserved for his mother, who would be a while. On his left Parker sat quiet. He seemed focused on the activity around him. If Jayden guessed correctly, Mom would finish serving the food and set platters of seconds on the table. Jayden listened as the chatter of children's voices rose outside the dining room, memories of past meals at this table running through his mind. Each child wandered in and found a seat.

"Charlie, did you wash?" Melanie stood in the doorway, serving spatula in her hand. "Hold up your fingers."

Jayden pursed his lips.

Parker chuckled beside him.

The small blond boy looked down, smile sagging. He sighed and turned back toward the bathroom. Jayden guessed he was either new or forgetful, he didn't know which. He whispered to Parker. "He's apparently learning the drill."

"Where is he?" Lissa, Kurt's wife, swept into the room with a toddler on her hip, face damp. She squealed. "Jayden Clarke, as I live and breathe!"

Parker and Jayden stood as she swooshed around the table and set the little one on the chair, then turned to Jayden and opened her arms wide.

"Come here. I've been waiting for your return too long." As Lissa hugged him, he braced himself against the chair to steady himself. "Oh, it is so good to see you, Jayden."

"And you. It's been a long four years." Jayden nodded toward Parker. "I'd like you to meet my commanding officer, Parker Macgregor. This is Lissa McKintrick, Kurt's wife. When the state took me from Mom, Lissa and Kurt made sure I found a home with them."

Parker shook Lissa's hand. "You two made this guy into a fine young man. Nice to finally meet both of you." He smiled, looking at the child wobbling on the chair. "Who's this?" Carefully, he leaned forward, and the toddler raised his hands, so he lifted him. "He has to be yours. He has your eyes."

"Yes. This is Grayson Foster McKintrick." Lissa's face beamed. "He is our latest addition to the ranch. He was born shortly after Jayden deployed."

"Hello, Grayson Foster McKintrick." Jayden smiled at the bashful cherub. "That's quite a name for one so small. He's three?"

"Um-hmm. We named him Grayson because it was Kurt's dad's middle name and for Kurt's friend, Foster Blake, who died in an ambush." The child reached for Lissa, and she held him against her shoulder. "He was our miracle baby." Lissa kissed the little boy. "Because of my age, we thought we couldn't have any more children after Gage and Gunner were born. God had other ideas and here he is."

"You aren't that old." Jayden disagreed. "You don't look a day over thirty."

"Ha, you lie like a rug." Lissa's eyes sparkled. "I was over thirty when I met you." She laughed. "But I'll love you forever for saying that."

Kurt stepped up behind Lissa and whispered in her ear. "It's time for dinner, Lissa." He tickled his son under the chin. "The kids are hungry."

Jayden looked around the table. "You kids ready to eat?" Twelve children, who all looked to be under the age of fifteen, sat waiting. A mix of boys and girls, including one set of twins, watched him and Parker. He spotted Gunner and Gage as they filed in and sat on the opposite side of the table. Gunner had been five when he left, Gage three.

Kurt turned to the group. "Let's pray and then you can take your plate and file through the line in the kitchen. Baylie is serving coleslaw and Melanie will add lasagna." Kurt took Lissa's free hand and bowed his head. "Lord, for this food and for the safe return of Jayden to our table, and for the gift of our guest, Parker, we thank you. Amen."

"Amen." Jayden looked up, all the faces focused on him.

"Kids, for those of you who didn't meet him earlier, this is Jayden Clarke, just returned from Afghanistan. He was our very first boy to live at this ranch. He helped build some of your bedrooms." He nodded at Parker. "And this is Jayden's commanding officer, Parker."

Kurt looked his way. "Want to walk through the lasagna line first?"

"I can wait." Jayden's face grew warm.

Kurt shook his head. "You're both celebrated Marines. We honor you."

Jayden shrugged, picked up his plate, and gestured for Parker to go first. They headed toward the kitchen door. Jayden leaned on his cane so he wouldn't trip.

Baylie smiled as she lifted a spoon of coleslaw after putting a generous serving on his plate. "Need more?"

He shook his head. "That will be plenty." He moved to the baking dish where his mother held a serving utensil.

She lifted a square of lasagna to Parker's plate. "The garlic bread is on the table." She turned to him. As she lifted the lasagna, Jayden stumbled, and the portion hit the floor.

"Oh, man." Jayden could feel the heat racing across his cheeks. "Let me clean it up."

His mother stopped him. "Have another square and join your friend." She deposited the portion on his plate then squeezed his shoulder. "Messes in the kitchen are part of our routine."

"Not from a man my age." Jayden drew a ragged breath.

"You'd be surprised." His mother winked. "Now go eat."

"Yes, ma'am." Jayden passed on through the other door and reclaimed his spot next to Parker. By the time each child filed back to their chair and all were seated, his heart had stopped pounding and the uncomfortable warmth left from the embarrassment of his stumble had passed.

Kurt picked up the basket of garlic bread and passed it to him. "Pass it to your left. Otherwise we wind up with traffic jams."

Jayden chuckled. "Some things never change."

"Nope." Kurt raised an eyebrow. "You should see what spaghetti does to our table."

"Free for all?"

"Close."

Glad for Kurt's lighthearted dismissal of his problem, Jayden grinned at the children around the table. Baylie and his mother joined them, each with their plate in hand. Baylie helped the younger children on either side of her cut their lasagna into manageable bites. Once she had them settled and eating, she picked up her own fork. His mother focused on Parker, drawing him into conversation about his service. Jayden searched for words.

"So Baylie, how do you like being one of the crew? I expected you to be long gone to some far away city by now." Her cheeks flushed crimson for a minute as she chewed, surprising Jayden. Had he said something wrong?

She laid her fork down. "As you know, I went off to college to garner a Pulitzer, but when that didn't happen right away, I joined the ranch crew as their newsletter writer." She took a drink of water. "I also love the horses, so this is a good fit for me."

Kurt glanced at Jayden. "Baylie helps the kids learn to ride."

"Lady is my favorite horse." Baylie's eyes sparkled as she spoke. "Isn't she the filly you were always bragging about?"

A rush of melancholy surged through Jayden—not to mention a twinge of jealousy. "Yes, Lady, Duke, and I were once inseparable."

Baylie nodded. "Duke is the sweetest dog I've ever met."

"He is one of a kind." Jayden breathed deep as the memories came flooding in. "He saved me from many a lonely night when I needed rescuing."

Parker looked up. "Is that the border collie you told me about?"

Jayden nodded.

Kurt laughed. "He even forgave Jayden for feeding him cat food."

"I only fed him that once." Jayden held up his fork as if he intended to stab something.

Parker gave him a look. "I take it he survived?"

"Yes." Jayden tasted the lasagna. "When there's nothing else to eat, it was better than going hungry." He popped another bite into his mouth. "All I had were a few apples."

"I'd like to hear that story sometime." Baylie forked a bite of coleslaw.

His mother stepped away to bring the baking dish of lasagna to the table for refills, then scooted into her place next to him. "He had me so worried. After Mr. Mueller died and this ranch was unoccupied, Jayden disappeared and stayed here alone."

"Not alone, Mom. Duke was here. Mr. Mueller trusted him with me." Jayden wrapped an arm around her. "I would have come home if George hadn't threatened me."

His mother kissed his cheek. "I know, Son. I still feel guilty about what happened."

"It's old history, Mom." Jayden sprinkled parmesan over his remaining lasagna. Life had never been the same after his friend Bennie Mueller died. The unhappy existence he'd had with his stepfather George Barnes transformed into healthy relationships with Lissa and Kurt in foster care. He'd considered himself the luckiest kid in the world back then, and he owed it all to running away with Bennie's dog, Duke. "The Marines have given me new history to replace it."

Kurt passed him the garlic bread. "That's history I'd like to hear."

Jayden sat up straighter. "In due time, Kurt."

"I'll be waiting."

Baylie cleared the plates from the table, scraped the uneaten food into the pig's slop jar, and stacked the dinnerware for a scrub. Gunner McKintrick donned an apron and rinsed each plate, handing them to his brother Gage to load in the dishwasher. As Baylie wove her way back and forth from the kitchen to the dining room she caught snippets of the conversation between Kurt, Parker, Jayden, and Melanie. Not only had Jayden grown and muscled out since high school, he'd also gotten handsomer, even with the eye patch. She breathed deep to slow her heart.

After high school he'd skipped out on attending college alongside her and enlisted, following in his father's footsteps. She'd so needed him at school, the loneliness of a big university threatening to destroy her. If Jayden had been there, she wouldn't have gone so far astray. But he'd left, letters scarce and brief. All she'd known of him before tonight were the few mentions his mother offered. Like bread crumbs.

"Our platoon encountered an IED near Mosul." Jayden sipped his coffee. Beside him Parker nodded, as if placing a truth stamp on Jayden's words. "I took shrapnel in my eye when the jeep I was riding in overturned from the blast ahead of us. I was pinned beneath the rear tire."

"You were lucky it didn't take your leg." Kurt passed the plate of cookies to Jayden and Parker.

"It almost did." Jayden took another cookie and lifted his cup, tilting it until it was empty. He set it back on the table.

Seizing the opportunity, Baylie grabbed the coffee pot, stepped from her spot near the door and returned to the table. "Refills?"

"Sure." Jayden slid his cup toward her.

"I'll have one, too, Baylie." Kurt held his cup.

"Doesn't this remind you of that time we worked the businessmen's luncheon refilling coffee cups?" Jayden clearly was enjoying the memory. His laugh made his hand shake as he slid the cup back along the table.

"And Jamielyn drowned the math teacher?" Baylie hadn't thought of that moment in years.

"Did she fail math again after that?" Jayden laughed. "I don't think I ever heard the end of that tale."

"I don't know, but she did work hard at the diner that summer."

"Ah, the diner." Jayden closed his eyes. "Ice cream sundaes."

"Not as tasty as the ice cream treats we used to down in high school."

"Those were the days."

After she poured, Jayden smiled and lifted his cup. "Thanks."

Baylie returned to the kitchen, positioning herself near the door again. She couldn't hear much standing too close to Gunner and Gage rinsing plates and gathering silverware.

Jayden continued his story. "They whisked me away to the field hospital, then decided I needed an airlift out."

"I suspect they threatened to amputate?" Kurt sounded more serious than Baylie had ever heard him.

Parker chimed in. "It looked a lot more serious than it turned out to be, but amputation was on everyone's minds."

"That was a consideration." Jayden nibbled on his cookie. "But once the surgeon inspected my leg, he found most of the wounds superficial, no broken bones, only a muscle that had sustained injury along my right femur where the wheel had pinned me down. They stitched me back together and sent me on my way to rehab. The leg healed except for the limp."

"Will the limp disappear?" Kurt's expression reflected hurt for Jayden.

"Time will tell." Jayden looked at Melanie. Even from here Baylie could see tears wetting her cheeks. Jayden handed his mother a handkerchief. "We can hope."

Parker nodded. "I believe he'll be fine."

Baylie remembered the stiffened shoulders she'd seen on Melanie earlier that week. She had been worried about her Marine son, probably sensing the depth of the injuries he had refused to divulge. Mothers always knew, didn't they?

"Baylie?" The noise at the sink had stopped.

She jumped at the sound of her name and turned to face the young McKintrick brothers who had been washing dishes.

"Are these all the plates?" Gunner laid down his dishrag. Gage added the rinsed dinnerware to the dishwasher. "All that's left are the lasagna pans."

"Good job, boys." Baylie laid a hand on each of their shoulders. "I'll take it from here."

Gunner grinned at her. "Thanks." He turned to the outside door of the kitchen, his brother Gage on his heels. "Let's go toss a football around."

The screen door slammed as the two boys hurried to the yard. Baylie lifted the lasagna pans to the sink and filled them with soapy water, remembering the time she, Jamielyn, and Jayden had helped at a banquet for the town businessmen. That was the day Jamielyn first met her grandfather. Jayden announced he was joining the Marines, and she went off to college. Things had taken a sharp twist in their lives after that. Not all of them good.

As the bubbles rose Baylie scrubbed the sides of the cookware, grabbing a palm brush to loosen the cooked-on cheese, her intense attack easing the pain of memory. That luncheon had cemented their three-way friendship. She'd thought they'd stay friends forever. That hadn't happened. She'd faced college alone.

Once the pan shone clean enough for a rinse, she soaped the pasta dish. Grabbing the sprayer, she rinsed the pans, washing away her thoughts along with the last of the lasagna. She set the pans upside down on the counter to dry. If only her head could be cleared so easily. She wiped her hands on her apron and set the dishwasher to run.

"Do you have any more coffee?"

Again, Baylie jumped and pivoted, this time to Jayden's voice behind her. *I need to quit daydreaming.* "Sure." She pointed to the coffee maker. "You can empty the carafe so I can wash it. Deal?"

"Unless you have some Dairy Queen ice cream somewhere."

"I wish I did, but coffee will have to do."

"Sounds like a good trade-off." Jayden filled his cup, turned off the warming tray, and handed her the empty container. "So, you teach riding lessons?"

Baylie nodded, wishing the warmth spreading across her face would stop. "The horses are good therapy for the kids."

"I speak from experience when I say I agree." Jayden found the sugar on the counter and spooned it into his coffee. "The original owner of this ranch, Bennie Mueller, recognized me as a hurting child and taught me how to work around horses and let me play with Duke."

"How old do you think he is?" Baylie stuck a dishrag in the coffee carafe.

"I was eleven when Mr. Mueller first introduced Duke to me. I'm twenty-four now. So Duke's got to be nearly fifteen."

"That's old for a dog, isn't it?"

Jayden sipped his coffee. "He's lived a good life, though." He looked up at her, eyes bright with a sheen. "He will be missed when he goes."

"I hope that doesn't happen anytime soon."

"Me either." Jayden set his cup down. "But time has a way of catching up with all of us." He turned back toward the dining area. "Thanks for the coffee."

Baylie didn't know what to say. Time did indeed snatch moments away. If only she could erase those incidents of the past that still haunted her. Clearly, the dog and the man before her shared a lot of love between them. She'd love to hear Jayden's memories of Duke, if he would indulge her. Past experiences might mend the void in her own timeline. She still needed Jayden to be there for her. How long would he stay?

She rinsed out the clean carafe and dried it before putting it back on the coffee maker. Reaching into the cupboard she retrieved a coffee filter, spooning the ground beans into the waiting receptacle. She could hear the voices of the friends around the dining table. She didn't want to snoop on their conversation. Obviously they had fond histories between them. She only hoped one day she might claim a spot at the table, and she and Jayden could share their own.

CHAPTER SEVEN

As the stories about his time as a foster child tumbled out around the table, Jayden swallowed the lump in his throat. Faded memories of when he'd stayed away from home to avoid his stepfather George threatened his composure. Images of empty booze bottles flying across the room at him, the weekend drunk sputtering from his easy chair, the joy of school days which got him away from George, all danced in panoramic color across the screen in his mind.

"I still remember the bruise on your arm." Kurt's face clouded as he recalled their first meeting. A runaway, angry and confused, Jayden could have wound up in very different circumstances. But Kurt found him hiding in the barn.

"I remember the sheriff sending me out when you turned up at Peggy Blake's ranch." Lissa's eyes misted. "None of us could believe you'd stowed away in the horse trailer."

"No room on the front seat." Jayden winked.

Lissa laughed.

He shook the painful images away, clinging to the feelings of love and protection showered upon him by these people. He'd have never survived otherwise. They'd each played a role—encouraging and guiding him to maturity. Though Parker came later in the story, he'd played his part. A truer friend, Jayden could not have found. These people all made sure he kept growing in spite of himself.

"Hey, Jayden." Kurt stood and gestured toward the door. "Want to see the changes we've made while you were gone?"

"I'd like that." Jayden looked at his watch. "Parker and I probably need to be on the road soon, though."

His mother's head whipped around, her mouth open as if surprised. "Where do you have to be?"

"I haven't made arrangements for the night yet." Jayden

shrugged. "Parker's house is in Pine River. So he's going to need a spot, too."

"Arrangements?" Kurt frowned. "Why don't you stay here?" He glanced at Melanie. "Isn't there a spare bed in your apartment?"

"Actually, the extra bedroom has two twin beds." His mother gave him a no-nonsense stare. "I've been saving the room for you."

"We don't want to impose." Jayden stammered, feeling foolish in the scrutiny. He glanced at Parker, seeking his input. "You all have a lot of little guys to care for."

"And you can help." Kurt gestured toward the door again. "These boys can be rascals. Especially Gunner and Gage."

"They probably take after their father." Parker grinned.

"Has Jayden told you of my horse trough seminars?" Kurt's right eye squinted.

Parker folded his arms. "Briefly." He shot Kurt a knowing look. "Think you're up to it?"

"I'd like to see you try." Jayden laughed. "Parker is every muscle your equal."

Kurt grinned. "I won't go for Parker. It's you I'm considering."

"I may be on the mend, but I've a few more muscles than I had when I left here."

Kurt laughed. "Of that I'm certain. Come on, I'll show you around."

Baylie heard the screen door slam as the three men exited the dining room. Melanie appeared in the doorway, eyes misty. Baylie studied her. "Good to see Jayden again, wasn't it?"

Melanie nodded. "So good." She stood, head down, shoulders slumped, as if she carried the weight of the world there. "I remember the Marines who came to my door when my husband was killed." She sniffed. "I wanted to be dead beside Jordan." She rubbed a knuckle under an eye, catching a tear. "I'm glad Jayden's alive."

"I can't imagine how terribly painful that must have been." Baylie laid a hand on Melanie's shoulder. "When my parents were killed in a car crash, I was too young to understand what had happened."

"Baylie, I never knew." Melanie's eyebrows lifted, her mouth agape.

"That's how I wound up in foster care." Baylie focused on the activity outside the kitchen, watching the three men inspect the ranch together, caught in her own memory. "My grandparents were appointed guardians, but they thought Mary, my mother's cousin, would be a better candidate to raise me than they would be at their ages. Mary was already a licensed foster mom so she was the natural choice." Baylie glanced back at Melanie. "I always had my grandparents nearby, so I never felt as if I had no family. They embraced my foster sister, who didn't have any family that we knew of, as one of theirs as well."

"They sound like wonderful people."

"They are." Baylie inhaled a deep breath. "Grandfather had to go to assisted living last year, so that's been hard." She hung up the towel to dry. "But I still get to see them."

"Kurt and Lissa will adopt you if you let them." Melanie's eyes twinkled. "I can't tell you how grateful I am that they took Jayden under their wing when his stepfather was convicted of abusing him."

"Jayden only mentioned brief memories of his early family life when we were in high school together." Baylie frowned. "Of course, most of our interaction involved putting out the newspaper. But I thought I knew more about him than that."

"That's probably because by high school he was living with Kurt and Lissa here on the ranch." Melanie's smile reflected her joy, then dissolved into sadness. "After his attempt to kidnap

Jayden, my ex went to jail. I almost did. But because I was implicated in the attempted kidnapping, I lost Jayden to the state, and that's when he moved to the ranch. Life with Lissa and Kurt became a happier time for him. "

"And look where Jayden is now." Baylie glanced outside again. Through the kitchen door, Kurt, Parker, and Jayden shared a laugh, holding the football high above Gunner and Gage where the two boys couldn't reach it. "I think he's come home."

Jayden caught the football and tucked it into the crook of his arm. Gunner tried to wrestle the ball away, but Jayden bent low and twisted right, tossing the ball to Parker who zipped it back to Kurt. Gunner laughed and headed off to attack his dad.

Kurt slammed the ball into the dirt. "Touchdown!"

"You guys are good!" Gunner's admiration carried through his voice. "I want to play ball like that one day."

"You will." Jayden panted as he limped to catch up with the father and son. He'd have to stop the tour soon or his leg would be overtired. "Kurt taught me. Now he will teach you."

"Were you on the football team?" Gunner's eyes shone as he twirled the football on his finger.

"No, I wrote stories for the high school newspaper." Jayden stood straighter, letting his leg rest. "I was a skinny little kid, so playing football was not my strong suit. But my pen could make giants of the players who did play the game."

"I want to play." Gunner tossed the ball to his little brother.

"If you grow to be big like your dad, you needn't worry about the coach seeking you out." Parker winked at Kurt. "You'll be pursued."

"Eat your spinach." Kurt tousled Gunner's hair. "Muscles need healthy food and good workouts."

Lissa's voice called from the house.

"And obey your mother."

Gunner laughed and ran toward the house.

"He's going to be a handful." Parker watched the boy leave. "But in a good way."

"They're all good kids." Kurt gestured toward the barn. "Come see what we've done to make Lady and her kin more comfortable."

"Kin?" Jayden stared at Kurt. "Did she foal while I was away?"

"See for yourself." Kurt opened the barn door and Jayden and Parker stepped inside.

The building interior grew dim as daylight withdrew from the sky. The outline of the stalls remained as he remembered them and Jayden followed the familiar row of gates with his eye. "Lady?"

At the end of the aisle he heard a snort, then a whinny. The mare lifted her head over the end gate, her greeting loud and long.

Jayden hurried to the stall, reaching up to finger the velvety ears and stroke the soft muzzle. How he had missed this horse. Movement beside her drew his attention. He peered through the rails to see a fuzzy flicker of a black tail as the foal nuzzled his mother's udder. "He's got the Kiger markings!"

"Yep. Pasture for the wild horses on the Steens Mountain dried up and became scarce one summer. A local rancher brought one of the stallions from the Kiger Ridge herd to his ranch. The horse was suffering from malnutrition." Kurt leaned on the stall. "The rancher offered the horse to us, but the animal would have had too much energy for the kids we have here." Lady pushed her muzzle against Kurt's shoulder. "Before he could have him castrated I put in a bid for a foal. The stallion was a grullo color, that mouse grey shade you and I saw on the mountain that first time we went. I thought a foal might be striking."

"But Lady is cinnamon."

"Both animals had the distinct dorsal stripe down the back and the striped legs." Kurt scratched Lady's neck. "The rancher hadn't considered the possibility, so he agreed to the experiment. Two Kiger horses, an endangered breed. Two with the original markings. The first foal was a filly who looked just like her mother. This one looks like his daddy."

"Two?" Jayden couldn't believe his ears. "She's managed to birth two foals while I was deployed?"

"She's been busy." Parker touched the mare's muzzle and she snorted.

"Lady's been a good brood mare." Kurt palmed a piece of carrot and Lady scooped it off his hand, slobbering as she chewed. "The rancher claimed the first foal, and we're keeping this one. But this will be her last. She's twelve this spring. Time to go back to teaching kids to ride."

Jayden reached over the gate and rubbed Lady's neck. Caring for this horse had matured him into a better person. Lady taught him to believe in himself. "I'm proud of you, girl."

Baylie left the kitchen and headed to her current room at the end of the house. The three men were leaving the barn on the reverse end of the drive. Tempted to join them, she resisted and kept walking.

Jayden called after her. "Really good to see you, Baylie."

She waved. "Maybe we can do some catching up tomorrow."

Jayden grinned. "It's a date."

She looked over her shoulder and caught Jayden's gaze on her. She gave thanks the sky was darkening and he couldn't see the blush warming her cheeks. Having Jayden here might prove interesting, especially since the duplex-like structure of the bunkhouse she and Melanie occupied shared a common wall in the middle. Though her end of the structure had separate studios for the summer help, knowing Jayden lived with his mother in the full-sized apartment on the other side of the wall gave her pause. Did he snore? Worse yet, did she?

Jayden followed Kurt's directions to find his mother's private quarters in the duplex structure of the bunkhouse, Parker at his side. Kurt said to use the main entrance at the far end of the building. He found the door to the apartment and knocked, not yet comfortable walking in unannounced.

"Come in, Jayden. You too, Parker."

He opened the door and entered a small living space with two chairs, a braided rug on the floor, and bookshelves on one wall. His mother sat in one of the chairs, a table and lamp beside her, a Bible in her lap. "This is nice."

Parker set his duffel down beside him. "You sure we won't crowd you?"

"Not at all." His mother set the book on the table beside her. "You'll find the bedroom is quite spacious, even with two beds." She pointed to a door to her right. "The bathroom is between the two rooms."

Parker retrieved his duffel. "I'll go check it out so you two can have some mother and son time." He walked toward the bedroom door and disappeared inside.

"He's nice." Melanie reached for Jayden's hands. He moved to where she sat and extended his arms for the hug he knew was coming. She stood and wrapped her arms around him, the slight shaking of her shoulders giving away her tears. "I'm so glad you're here." The words sounded breathless, and ragged, a sound he'd come to know too well from the past. Mom had suffered through many trials.

"I'm glad to be here."

She released him and gestured for him to sit. "Is your rehabilitation finished?"

He took the other chair, laid the cane against the wall behind him, and settled back. "I have followup visits, but most of the critical physical therapy is finished."

"Do the doctors think you'll regain complete use of your leg?"

"I already have, Mom. The limp is only a leftover nerve that hurts once in a while. With time the sensitivity will stop."

Mom looked away, a sniff giving away her sorrow. Jayden ached for her, she had endured so much. Her heart had been shattered when his father Jordan was killed in Afghanistan.

"I'm sorry to bring more pain into your life because of the military."

"Don't ever apologize for following your path." Mom breathed deep. "I couldn't be more proud of you."

"Thanks, Mom." He looked at this woman who had remained steadfast in spite of mistakes she'd made. Most of those were for his welfare. She'd rushed into a second marriage to keep Jayden's life stable after Dad was killed. Too late she discovered George, her new husband, resented the heroic tales of Jayden's father Melanie told her son to keep Jordan's memory alive. "I'm proud of you for staying the course through it all."

"Some things I wish I could redo." She glanced at him and he nodded. He knew what she meant. George's jealousy created a powder keg of trouble and led to abuse. She'd lost Jayden to the state because of him. Years had passed as she leaped through the hoops of government bureaucracy to regain custody of her son. When she'd finally been reunited, Jayden had enlisted, and she'd lost him again, almost forever, to the same enemy that had claimed his father.

"I knew your injuries were more than you were telling me." Mom gave him a no-nonsense stare. "Men who are injured in battle and air-lifted to a field hospital aren't recovering from a hang nail."

"You knew about that?"

"I grilled the Marines at my door."

He chuckled. "I didn't know how much to tell you." He

ducked his chin, a question on his lips. "How did you keep news of the attack from Kurt and Lissa?"

"Everyone was running errands the day the Marines showed up." She folded her arms across her middle. "When you called that afternoon, I did as you asked and kept it to myself." She grinned. "It's okay. I held you up in prayer to God's ear every hour. I couldn't be there for you, but I knew He could."

"I'm grateful." Jayden leaned forward, elbows on his knees. "If you ever tell anyone this, I'll deny it, but I was pretty terrified when that bomb blew up." He studied her face, watching his words threaten her composure again. "Knowing you were here praying for me kept me from freaking out."

"Is your tour of duty complete?" His mother studied her lap as she asked the question. "If not, I can injure your other leg."

Jayden snorted. "That sounds ominous." He leaned back and crossed his arms behind his head. "Technically, no, I'm not through yet. But I expect an honorable discharge to follow. There's no reason to send me back."

"No time left on your enlistment?"

"Most of my remaining time was spent in rehabilitation." Jayden sighed. "Not exactly the way I wanted to follow in Dad's footsteps."

"Following in your father's footsteps would have gotten you killed."

"I know. But what I meant was how I wanted to honor his memory, emulate the soldier he was."

"Jayden, there was more to your father than a uniform and a rifle." She lifted a small box from beneath the table and removed what appeared to be a pack of letters. "You need to read these. Then you'll understand."

"Understand what?"

"Who your father truly was."

CHAPTER EIGHT

BAYLIE CLIMBED THE STAIRS TO THE dormitory for the second time that evening, the encounter with Jayden, Parker and Kurt still on her mind. Jayden had changed, which was to be expected, but his old quick wit and subtle sense of humor hovered beneath that solid soldier exterior he emanated. And boy, did he look good.

They'd been such good friends. He'd even been a little sweet on her, taking her to the prom their senior year and managing a date for her foster sister Jamielyn. Baylie had been devastated when he enlisted.

"Jayden, not the Marines!" She'd fought tears when she learned of his plans.

"Gotta follow my dad, Bayles. Been my dream since I was nine."

She thought their friendship would end, but he'd remained steadfast, writing her sporadic letters through college, encouraging her to continue chasing her dreams. When she'd come to a dark place her senior year in college, she'd stopped writing back. Jayden's letters stopped coming as well. She didn't know if it was because of her silence or if that was when he'd been wounded and couldn't respond. Guilt poked at her. She'd let her friend down in his time of need while she nursed her own private disappointments.

I'll make it up to him. She searched for the key to her room. *This is my chance.*

Jayden was here now, at least temporarily, and she intended to make things right between them. They might not ever be more than friends, but she'd learned friends were important in life, often what made living worthwhile, and she couldn't have too many. If she were honest, though, her heart hoped for more. Much much more.

She opened the door of her temporary quarters and reached for the flashlight. Time for a bedcheck. She inspected Charlie and Kevin's room, and found both boys asleep. Charlie's mouth hung open, and the soft boyish snores surprised her. Not much noise, but a lot for a little guy.

She moved on to the girls, hearing muted giggles as she approached. She opened the door and flashed the light, catching a swift tug of a blanket as two bare feet disappeared beneath it. "Krystal? Time to sleep."

Two blue eyes peeked out at her from the covers. "We were just telling stories."

"About what?"

"Our mom and us before we came here." Krystal's voice grew quiet. "I miss her."

Baylie's heart broke for the girls. "I know how that is. Both my parents were in a car crash when I was four." She switched on the light.

"They were?" Kendra sat up. "Do you remember them?"

"Not much. I have pictures, but I was so young their memory has faded." Baylie sat on Kendra's mattress. "You two have a lot more memories to think of and share because you are twins."

"But what if we are adopted or separated?" Krystal sat up on her bed, eyes welling with tears. "I don't want to lose Kendra, too."

Baylie went to Krystal and wrapped an arm about her. "I know Lissa McKintrick believes families should stay together. She's checking all the policies in the state of Oregon." She squeezed the girl's trembling shoulders. "If she finds you a placement in a loving home, you two will go together. Otherwise you'll stay here at the ranch."

"Promise?"

"Promise." Baylie stood and covered Krystal with her blankets. "Now both of you need to get some sleep."

"'Night, Baylie."

"Goodnight girls. Sweet dreams."

She tucked Kendra in, giving both girls a final peck on the cheek. "May God's angels watch over you through the night, and love's promises wake you in the morning."

"Amen." The mumbles came from beneath the covers.

Baylie walked on down the hall and found the pre-teens both asleep. She turned and headed back to her room. Below she heard Kurt locking the dormitory doors and setting the motion detector. Krystal and Kendra didn't need to worry. This ranch and its staff would keep them all safe. And together.

Angry voices outside the bunkhouse the next morning made Jayden peek through the bedroom window. A young man, probably not much older than fourteen, stood shaking his fist at Kurt.

"You're not my dad!" The kid shouted. "I don't want to be here."

"Calm down." Kurt held a pitchfork in his hand. A wheelbarrow lay on its side, the contents strewn across the pavement. "Wheelbarrows tip over all the time. You need to get a shovel and a broom and put the shavings back in."

"And what if I don't?" The kid folded his arms, spread his feet, and squared his jaw. "Who's going to make me?"

Kurt stood firm, waiting for the kid to cooperate.

Jayden wrestled with the need to help.

He had awakened a half hour ago to sun poking through his window, surprised that his mother had allowed him to sleep. Parker had already risen and left the apartment, so Jayden hadn't rushed. He'd wanted to explore the pack of letters she'd given him. Alone. But he hadn't gotten far when the noise outside disturbed him. The letters would have to wait.

Last night Kurt had explained their summer intern program. Teens needing work experience applied to help on the ranch in exchange for a meal and a reference. This kid must be part of that program. The ranch offered many learning opportunities, most of them dealing with the care and feeding of livestock. Learning to follow orders was something this kid obviously didn't know how to do.

With his military discipline kicking in, Jayden thought he could help. He hurried into his jeans and pulled on a t-shirt, in order to appear more civilian than soldier. On cue his stomach rumbled. He needed to eat, but right now Kurt needed him more. He hurried outside.

"Anything I can do to help?" Jayden stepped up beside Kurt and surveyed the situation. "Looks like we have a wheelbarrow down."

"Yeah." The kid sneered. "And it's going to stay that way."

Jayden looked to Kurt for permission to enter the scenario. With a nod Kurt stepped back and gave Jayden the go-ahead. "This is right up your alley."

"I'm Jayden Clarke." He extended his hand. "And you are?"

"None of your business." The kid snarled at him, then frowned at Kurt.

"Okay, none of your business."

The kid glared at Jayden.

"Seems to me you've got a lot of anger riding shotgun on your shoulder."

"What would you know?" The boy's spine straightened and his chin rose, a smirk on his face.

Jayden glanced around the yard and into the pastures beyond, memories flooding his head. He spotted Duke sleeping by the bunkhouse, his right ear twitching. Jayden returned his gaze. "I used to be a lot like you."

"Yeah, right." The kid snorted. "You don't even know me."

"My step-dad was a weekend alcoholic. I was his punching

bag." Jayden clenched his jaw. "I'm guessing from your anger, you've been there."

"You're stabbing in the dark. Some sort of self-appointed psychologist?"

"No. But I'm willing to bet behind that hateful exterior you wear, there's a decent boy who has a lot to give." Jayden took the pitchfork from Kurt. He bent over and picked up the broom that had flown off the wheelbarrow when it tipped. "I've been there." He offered the broom to the kid. "Why don't I pitch the shavings back in the wheelbarrow and you sweep the pavement."

The kid studied Jayden, a slight quiver on his mouth. Jayden didn't know if the kid would surrender or walk away in a huff. "Deal?" Jayden waited.

The kid took the broom. "Deal."

Kurt backed away, a grin on his face. "I'll leave you two at it then."

Jayden spoke over his shoulder. "Tell Mom to save me some breakfast, would you?"

Kurt nodded. "I don't think Cody ate before he arrived this morning, either. You can both eat when you're done."

"I'm only an intern part-time. I don't get breakfast." The kid sounded surprised. "Only lunch."

"Today you do." Kurt nodded at Jayden. "I'll see you soon."

"So it's Cody?" At the kid's nod, Jayden smiled. "Let's get this cleaned up so we can eat."

When Jayden pitched the last fork full of manure into the wheelbarrow and Cody swept up the scraps, Jayden took the tools and set them inside the barn.

Duke had joined them while they worked. Jayden bent down to pet the dog who wagged his tail. "Hey, fella, it's so good to see you this morning." Duke yipped.

Cody watched the exchange. "He seems to know you."

"Duke and I go way back." Jayden pointed to a pile at the side of the barn. "You want to dump the wheelbarrow?"

"Anything for breakfast." Cody lifted the handles and pushed the load toward the pile as if the promise of breakfast fueled his steps. Once he had dumped it he hurried back to where Jayden waited.

Jayden gestured toward the kitchen. "Let's go eat. I'm starved."

Cody looked at him. "Thanks."

"Think nothing of it." Jayden called Duke to his side. The dog followed them and lay down at the door.

They entered the kitchen, the smell of cinnamon lingering in the air. Parker leaned against the counter, sipping a cup of coffee. He held his cup aloft with a nod. "Hello, sleepyhead."

Mom looked up. "I wondered if you were going to join us for breakfast." She rinsed out a sponge and finished cleaning the counter. "Kurt said you'd be late."

"Cody and I had to clean up a spill before we came."

"I made you both a plate of ham and eggs. It's in the oven keeping warm." Mom pointed to a basket on the table. "The kids had cinnamon rolls. I saved you a couple."

"Wow. Thanks." He looked at Cody. "Let's get washed."

The kid made a face.

"You don't want horse dung mixed with your eggs, trust me."

They returned from the sink a few minutes later and Jayden peeked into the basket. "I haven't had these since. . ."

"Before deployment?" Parker nodded approval. "I know I haven't."

"Probably." He lifted a roll out of the basket and bit into the frosting. "Mmm. These are incredible, as always." He glanced at Cody. "Have one?"

Cody grabbed a roll, and took the plate Jayden offered him. He placed his pastry alongside the eggs, reverence in his gaze. He looked at Jayden. "Can we eat?"

Jayden lifted his plate, nodded, and spoke to Parker. "Did you have one?"

"Couldn't stop with one." Parker rubbed his stomach. "Your mother is quite the cook."

"I'm surprised there are any left for me." Jayden reached for another roll.

Mom snapped a towel at him. "Take your ham and eggs to the table. Diners in this kitchen are expected to sit." She smiled at Cody. "That goes for you, too, young man."

"Yes, ma'am." Cody jumped to follow directions. He carried his plate to a spot and grabbed a chair. "Thank you. I never get breakfast."

Cody's polite reply made Jayden smile. Perhaps this kid had another side, after all. He opened the other foil-covered plate, and set it next to the basket of rolls. He winked at his mother, "I'm only experiencing my new found freedom."

His mother grinned, a raised eyebrow aimed his way. "Heathen."

Parker snorted.

Even Cody grinned. "Is she your mother?"

"Yes." Jayden laughed, looking toward her. "You love me and you know it."

"Couldn't love you more." Mom pulled out an assortment of pots. "Now I've got to start lunch."

Jayden paused and offered thanks, looking up to see the surprise on Cody's face. "Habit of mine." He picked up his fork and dug into his eggs. Silence reigned as the two of them devoured the food, Cody appearing as ravenous as Jayden felt. He'd ask Kurt how Cody might qualify for breakfast on a regular basis. Hard to work and be civil on an empty stomach.

Soon Cody stood. "Thank you for breakfast. I've got more barn duties."

Jayden followed Cody's lead. "And I told Baylie we'd catch up today. Where would I find her?"

"Try the office." Mom jerked her head toward the door. "That's in the other end of the bunkhouse."

"Figured as much." He took his plate to the sink and rinsed it, indicating Cody do the same. "At least I remembered to clean up after myself."

"There's hope for you yet." His mother set a pot on the stove.

"Parker, you coming?"

"I'll be there soon." Parker stretched. "Melanie wants me to butter bread for sandwiches."

Jayden stared at the pair. He and Parker hadn't even been here twenty-four hours and the man had already volunteered to butter bread?

"You said you were headed to the barn, Cody?"

"I've got another stall to clean." The kid raised a hand in farewell and disappeared out the door.

"Speaking of clean, I better change after mucking out horse droppings this morning."

He left the kitchen and looked around for Duke, who had disappeared. He hurried back to his mother's apartment. After showering he slipped into clean jeans and pulled a tee over his head. He checked his face. Should he shave? Running a hand across his chin he decided there wasn't enough fuzz to merit a razor. At least not now. He shrugged his shoulders, flexing his biceps as they filled the shirt. He grinned. That would make Baylie notice.

Whistling, he stepped into his shoes and beelined for the other side of the bunkhouse. Kurt stood in the drive talking to Cody. The kid nodded and headed to the barn. Seeing Jayden, Kurt wiggled a finger. He walked over.

"Thanks for what you did this morning." Kurt sighed. "Cody's one of our volunteer teen helpers who get work experience for being here, but we've been having problems with him cooperating."

"I'd say there's unspoken issues going on with him outside of the ranch. I wonder how regularly he gets food. He ate breakfast like a man starved."

"You may have stumbled onto something." He gave Jayden a conspiratorial look. "I need to find someone to work beside him and keep him on task." Kurt studied him. "You think he could be persuaded to get here early enough for breakfast?"

"I'd say that's a definite possibility." Jayden grinned. "Let me know if I can help."

"Let's talk soon. I've got a meeting in twenty minutes so I've got to hustle."

Baylie sat at the computer typing profiles of the rodeo of horses the ranch maintained for the benefit of the children. *I may have to move on to cows,* she grumbled in her head. *I don't have that many more horses. Maybe Lissa will rescue another horse or two soon.*

Every month Baylie tried to pair a different animal with a child, along with the testimony of the child who chose that particular mount, and run a side story in the newsletter. The stories were often funny, and the newsletter audience routinely commented on the accounts.

Last month's feature was Lady and her new foal. The headline read: *Wild Horse Goes Domestic, Ranch Gains a New Addition.* She grinned at the picture. The foal peered at the camera from behind his mother's tail. Photogenic, you little cutie.

The human interest side of the profiles, though, made the ranch's patrons willing to open their wallets a little wider. She continually reminded herself the ranch couldn't stay afloat without those community sponsors.

No pressure.

Today she couldn't concentrate on the article. She knew why.

Jayden had arrived. Last night he'd promised to catch up with her. Maybe share his war story. Or other things. They needed to talk about Jamielyn and revisit their memories. Baylie longed to connect with Jayden again, the way they had found common ground when they were teens. But a man wounded by war was not the same person as the teenager with whom she'd shared ice cream in high school. Not only was he muscular, and worldly, he had to be the most handsome dude she'd seen in a long while. Oh, and that eye patch! Only added to his mystique.

Steady girl. Don't get carried away.

She wasn't the same girl, either. Her heart had run ahead of her brain in college, and the experience came close to ruining her future. Hopefully those lessons had engrained themselves in her collection of wisdom, and she wouldn't repeat the mistakes she'd made.

A knock on the door disturbed her reverie. She glanced up to see Jayden at the entry. She took a deep breath. "Come in, Jayden. Have a seat."

"Am I here at a bad time?" Jayden grabbed a chair from the wall and scooted it closer to her desk. "Wouldn't want to disturb the writing of your Pulitzer prize essay."

"Nothing so grand as that." Baylie swiveled in her chair. "I'm responsible for the publicity that promotes the ranch. Human interest stories, that sort of thing."

"Sounds as if it could be fun."

"It is." Baylie folded her hands in her lap to settle the jitters. "Not as much fun as the April Fool's paper we put out in journalism class, but less chance of censorship."

"Remember how the superintendent called our advisor on the red carpet?"

"I still feel guilty about getting her in trouble."

"You escaped without even a reprimand." Jayden leaned back

in his chair. "You should at least have had forty lashes with a wet noodle."

"Ha. Our advisor defended me, remember?"

"I do." Jayden glanced around the office. "Kurt and Lissa have certainly taken this rescue ranch seriously, haven't they?"

"Lots of kids out there who need love." Baylie studied her friend. "I remember when we lived in their shoes."

Jayden nodded. "Me, too."

"So what's next for you?"

"I don't know." Jayden's gaze landed on her. "I'm not completely finished with my military responsibilties. Waiting for the honorable discharge to come through."

"Will you go back to school?"

"I may." Jayden sat up straighter. "But I'd like to spend time with Mom first. We missed so many years because of my stepfather. We need to bond again."

"I'm sure Kurt can find work for you here. He hasn't hired the last wrangler for the summer." Baylie pulled out an employee hire list from her drawer. "That interest you?"

"This morning I volunteered myself to help a teen intern who has anger issues. Kurt told me he needs someone to work alongside the kid." Jayden leaned back and folded his arms. "Might be the job I need right now."

"Kurt will be back at noon. You should ask him." Baylie returned the list to the drawer. "Tell him Baylie sent you."

"In that case, I'm a surefire shoo-in, aren't I?"

"You'd be surprised how insider influence could help."

Jayden's eyebrows came together, a twinkle in his eye.

CHAPTER NINE

JAYDEN FOLLOWED PARKER TO HIS HARLEY the next morning. "Thanks for riding over with me." He extended his hand. "You were right. I needed this."

Parker scuffed his toe in the gravel. "After seeing you in action with that kid yesterday, I am confident coming home to this ranch will be the impetus you need to find your path." He studied Jayden. "You were a great soldier. Never doubt that. You acted bravely in a tough situation. That kind of courage will fuel your future."

"Will you come and visit agan?"

Parker grinned. "I think I just might do that."

The need to rib Parker about his interest in Mom was so tempting, but Jayden swallowed the tease he wanted to say. "Mom really enjoyed meeting my commanding officer." He stifled his grin. "She's always looking for help making food for the kids."

Parker didn't take the bait, but instead folded his arms and studied the skyline. "This is a good work environment. Your mother has made the most of the opportunity." He moved his gaze to Jayden. "So should you."

"I plan to find Kurt and talk more about working here this summer. Baylie said he hasn't hired the last wrangler yet."

"Probably waiting for you to ask." Parker lifted his helmet and put it on. "Keep the headset I gave you. When I return, we can go ride the high desert together."

"Don't forget the way."

"I won't." Parker lowered his face shield, adjusted his gloves, and turned the key in the ignition. He lifted a hand as he revved the engine. Putting the bike in gear he drove up the long driveway to the highway leading away from the ranch.

Jayden turned toward the barn where he'd seen Kurt working

earlier. Duke rose from a spot by the open door, tail wagging. Jayden stooped to pet the dog, then moved into the barn where he could hear a push broom sweeping hay along the aisle. "Kurt?"

"In here."

Jayden found the man in one of the stalls cleaning up the waste left by its previous occupant. A nearby wheelbarrow waited emptying. "Baylie told me you haven't hired the last wrangler for the summer crew."

Kurt leaned on his broom. "That's right." He looked at Jayden. "You applying for the job?"

"I have experience." He grabbed the handle of the wheelbarrow. "Want proof?"

Kurt smirked. "No need."

"I'll be right back." He wheeled the manure to the side of the barn and then returned. "Haven't lost my touch."

Kurt set the broom aside. "After watching you with Cody, I'd love to have you join us." Kurt closed the stall gate. "You'd work with the children, teaching them responsibility, safety, and help them learn confidence. But I really need someone to guide the summer interns. That's where I think you'd be the most help. Some of the teens we get in the summer only come in for riding lessons or for work experience references. Some of them are tough to handle."

"Like Cody."

Kurt nodded. "I believe there's a decent kid hovering beneath all that armor he wears."

"He's probably been hurt more times than we want to know. He shields himself from more pain." Jayden folded his arms. "The attitude is a defense mechanism."

"The anger is a problem." Kurt picked up a scoop shovel and cleared the aisle of lingering debris. "If we can find a way to help him let go of that, we'll prevent a future filled with trouble."

"I'm not sure I have the skills to steer him in the right

direction, but I can relate if he's living under a cloud of fear." Jayden studied Kurt. "My step-father George was no picnic, if you remember."

"Too well." Kurt finished shoveling the last of the debris into the wheelbarrow Jayden had left standing in the aisle. "Let me dump this and we'll go get something cold to drink while we discuss your employment."

After the waste was discarded, Kurt washed his hands and led Jayden to the office. Baylie sat at her desk, typing whatever it was that kept her busy. Jayden nodded at her and she smiled back, giving him a thumbs up as he passed.

Kurt opened a door at the back of the larger office space and entered a small glassed-in room with a mini-fridge and a microwave in the corner. He gestured to a chair for Jayden to sit. "This is Lissa's office, but I borrow it on occasion. She keeps snacks here that I like to raid." He grinned as he opened the refrigerator and withdrew a couple of sodas. From a box on top he grabbed two bags of chips. "I used to raid Peggy's stash when I first came home from Afghanistan to help her with the ranch."

"Did she mind?"

"No. I think it helped her cope with the loss of her son, Foster." Kurt's gaze wandered out the window as if caught in memory. "Foster and I were such good friends. For me to come home from Afghanisan in his place to work at the Rescue Ranch seemed brutally unfair."

"Did you know she was a foster mom before you came?"

"No, that didn't happen until you showed up as a stowaway in the barn."

"She took me in almost without question."

"Peggy is all about love." Kurt snorted. "And snacks for guys." He grabbed a chip for emphasis. "Peggy taught Lissa how important these things are to keep her boys happy. Glad Lissa agreed."

Jayden chuckled and tore the top off the chips. He popped the top on the soda can and took a swig. "How many times I wished I could do this in Afghanistan. Bet you remember the heat."

"I do." Kurt tipped his soda and lifted it to his lips. "Nothing like a cold one on a hot day."

Jayden waited as Kurt chugged his drink and tossed the can in the recyle bin beside him. With a satisfied smack of his lips he leaned back in his chair and finished his chips. Crumpling the bag in his fingers he shot the wad over Jayden's head where the bag landed in a trash can against the other wall. "Score three points for you." Jayden slid sideways to inspect the garbage. "You must have a lot of practice."

"Peggy instilled neatness in my brain. She wouldn't have her ranch cluttered up, not even by a friend of her son." Kurt's face sagged at the memory. "I had to measure up for the sake of Foster."

"Speaking of Peggy, how is she?" Jayden picked another chip from his bag. "Is she still running her rescue ranch?"

"Yes and no." Kurt leaned forward, elbows on knees. "When Lissa and I came back to this place, and you came here, then left for Afghanistan, Peggy decided to step away from the Herrick Valley Rescue Ranch.. Now a general manager runs her rescue operation under the supervision of the Herrick Board of Directors. Peggy still lives there and spends time with the rescues that come in, but it is mostly for her enjoyment, like keeping her hand in for memory's sake. But the actual care and feeding of the animals fall to the fellow the board appointed."

"Didn't she keep it for the sake of Foster?" Jayden remembered how much the woman missed her son.

"And Foster made me promise to come home in his place." Kurt's forehead sported wrinkles, his smile drooped. "We all needed healing and that's where it happened."

"I think I'll go see her." His chip bag crinkled in his hand and he shot it at the waste basket, missing the target, "But not before I perfect my jump shot."

"Good thinking."

Baylie had typed fewer than thirty words since Kurt and Jayden disappeared into Lissa's office. Through the glass, the two seemed to be doing nothing but drinking sodas and chomping down chips, but Baylie decided she should pray for their conversation. Selfish prayer on her part—keep Jayden here. Positive prayer for the ranch—keep Jayden on staff. Pleading prayer for Melanie—keep Jayden close for his mother's sake. She sighed. God didn't often listen since her downfall in college, but maybe this one time He would. It couldn't hurt to try.

Feeling justified, she continued her work on the computer, though she doubted she'd salvage many of her fragmented thoughts in the end. Jayden distracted her. Which was silly. She hadn't seen him in more than four years. Anything that had passed between them then would have to be rekindled now. From the looks of him, Jayden probably needed time to sort out his feelings and find his way after war, injuries, and trauma had invaded his life. She couldn't imagine how unsettled he must feel. He and Melanie needed to build a bridge back to a relationship as mother and son. From what Jayden had said earlier, Baylie surmised the split caused by the step-father had left a chasm of pain between him and his mother. Time. He needed time.

But, if he is working here, he can heal, and we can work our way back to friends. Or better.

Baylie smiled at the random thoughts. Tired of trying to focus, she gave herself a break. She exited the program, shut down her computer, and went to find a nice, whiskery muzzle to spoil in the barn. Lady's foal spent his days in the paddock at his dam's side, almost always willing to investigate anything a visitor might bring.

Today she retrieved a handful of carrot tops she'd saved from lunch fixings and carried them out the door. Several kids were engaged in a game of Frisbee on the other side of the driveway so they wouldn't notice her heading for the barn. She heard voices in the round pen as four kids and four horses practiced riding. With everyone engaged, the paddock would be hers alone. She liked that.

The foal lay on the ground when she arrived, muzzle resting on the soft dirt, eyes closed in a squint. Lady stood nearby, munching a flake of hay left for her. The mare's tail flicked occasionally as a fly buzzed her hindquarters. The foal's ears twitched, reflecting his need to send an insect away. But the peaceful scene warmed Baylie, mare and foal idling away a lazy afternoon.

Baylie shook out the carrot tops, climbing on the fence rails to tempt the mare. Lady didn't waste time. She nickered, the low rumble signaling her colt to raise his head and sniff the air. He rose to his feet as his mother ambled over to the waiting treat. Lady snatched a carrot top and chewed, her baby pushing in alongside to investigate.

"You want some too, don't you?" Baylie shook another handful of carrot tops at the foal. "You have to claim them yourself. Not steal from your mother's cache."

The animal inched closer, ears twitching as if he listened to what Baylie said. His short tail flipped like a flag on the president's limousine. He stretched his neck out so far he wobbled on his spindly legs, snatching a few carrot greens with his teeth. Baylie laughed. "You are a sneaky thief."

"Probably learned it from Lady."

Baylie jumped as Jayden approached the paddock, Duke at his side. He lifted one foot and rested it on the bottom rail, leaning his cane against the upright post. She found her voice. "I didn't hear you coming."

"Not much on this side of the barn to make noise." He folded his arms and rested against the top rail, his fingers reaching out to Lady. The mare snorted, her muzzle inspecting his hand. She curled her lips back as if she'd tasted something nasty. "Don't remember me?" A low rumble answered him, the mare stepping closer, head hanging over the top of the paddock railing. "Good girl."

"How did it go with Kurt?" Baylie groaned inwardly at her abrupt question. Nothing like being too eager. Jayden still needed to find his way. She hoped all went well, but chastised herself for being so pushy. "Feeling reconnected?"

"Not yet." Jayden scratched Lady's neck. "I'm at loose ends. But Kurt wants me to help here this summer."

"That's a start."

"Yes. Spending time with Mom as my mother, and not as the cook hired to work for the ranch where I was a foster kid, is important to me." Jayden raised sad eyes to her. "Though Mom was always there, I didn't feel like we were really mother and son while I was a ward of the state."

"Well, now you can."

"How are you doing?" Jayden probed her gaze. "Still see your grandparents?"

"Not as much as I'd like." Baylie inhaled. "Grandpa needed to go to assisted living last year, so it's hard watching him and Grandma make a new life."

"Are they together?"

"Yes. They share a compact apartment with enough room to allow them a small dresser each, a walker, television, their lounge chairs, a sofa, and a bed. Meals are communal and they share a bathroom with other residents."

"Are they happy?"

Baylie reached up to pet Lady's velvety ears. "They love each other, always have, and they love me. Their faith in God keeps them content."

"I sense a 'but' in there."

Baylie blinked back moisture threatening her composure. "They are all I have left of my family. Mary Marshall was a distant cousin and I lived as a ward in her foster home. She and her husband Troy were great. I still think of them often. Grandma and Grandpa, as guardians, were the real family watching over me from a distance." She turned her gaze on Jayden. "Their presence during my high school years made me feel less like a foster kid. I know you understand."

"I do." Jayden stayed sober a minute, then threw her a sideways grin. "I know Kurt and Lissa would adopt you in a heartbeat."

"I feel as if they already have." Baylie shifted her weight against the fence rail. "Your mother said the same."

"And you can claim me as your pesky big brother."

Baylie laughed, schooling her face to remain neutral. She didn't want a big brother. But time was on her side so she returned the tease. "That will never change."

CHAPTER TEN

JAYDEN SLUMPED INTO A CHAIR NEAR the table in his mother's apartment. Parker had gone home, Baylie had dormitory duty, and Mom had stepped out for a Bible study. Sleepy, after a long day of emotional highs and lows, he stretched, yawned, then lifted the letters his mother had given him to the table.

He opened the box, notes his father had written from Afghanistan, the missives his mother had saved for almost two decades. The paper had yellowed, but the familiar handwriting spoke from the envelopes as if his dad had sent these words a mere two weeks or so ago. He didn't know what to expect inside, probably a lot of sentiment between Dad and Mom as they waited to be reunited after Dad's tour of duty.

Except that never happened.

He opened the first one.

"My dearest Melanie……"

The line made him feel like an intruder, as if he were snooping in his parents' private business. They had been so in love. They had equally loved him. As a child he felt that love and rested secure in the family unit.

Dad had been his hero, his mentor, his buddy. Jayden had learned military maneuvers and wrestling techniques from him. His dad was a soldier, but also a loving husband. He'd watched how a man treated his wife as Jordan honored Jayden's mother. Those memories were embedded in his heart. If only that love hadn't ended so soon.

He read on.

"The heat is unbelievable. We have to wear our protective gear in daytime temps that often reach highs of 120 degrees. Nighttime temps can dip into the teens. The contrast makes this place a living hell. And the snipers are everywhere. . ."

He had only been nine when the Marines had arrived at their door with the report of Dad's death. He remembered how his mother had collapsed at the news. Her beloved Jordan had been killed in an ambush, never to return. Though she had tried to be strong, sorrow shut her down. With no family nearby to support her, Mom often spent hours in bed, forgetting she had a son who needed her. Jayden had tried to understand her grief, accepting the neglect with the hurt of a nine-year-old child. The loneliness had eaten at him. That's when he'd discovered the Mueller ranch and the loving rancher Bennie Mueller. The man had offered companionship and a work environment suitable for a young kid. Mom, sensing his eagerness, had given her permission for him to visit. He'd gained a friend. Not to mention Duke and that silly filly.

He read more:
"The only thing that keeps me going are thoughts of you and Jayden. I count the days until we can be together."

Jayden stopped reading, a lump in his throat that threatened to choke him. The truth still hurt. Dad never came home again. Reading his earnest desire to return brought back the pain of loss once more. Suffering had happened on both sides of the planet.
Jayden read the last paragraph:

"I lead a Bible study every evening here with the men and the unit joins me in prayer for you. Know how much I love you both. Jordan

Jayden put the letter down. Dad led a Bible study? How did he not know about that?

The door opened and his mother entered. She smiled. "Ready for some company?"

"Yeah. I have questions." He held up the letter. "Short, sweet, but full of things I didn't realize before."

"The Bible studies?"

"That was a surprise." Jayden put the letter down. "Was Dad a chaplain?"

"No, not a chaplain." Mom sat in the other chair and leaned back. "Jordan knew every man in his unit could face eternity at any moment. He was passionate about not losing any of them. He said Afghanistan was hell enough, he wanted his men to experience the joys of heaven."

"Wow." Jayden folded the letter and returned it to its envelope. "Certainly alters my image of the hero soldier."

"Your father was a hero among men and a soldier for God."

Jayden swallowed. "Makes it even more difficult to follow in his boots." He studied his mother. "That's not been my focus."

Mom picked up a book off the table. "Are you certain?"

"I've always looked up to him as my hero dad. The fearless soldier, the combat ready warrior. To think he spent his off-time leading Bible studies doesn't fit my perception of him." Jayden placed the envelope back in the box. "This other side of him will take some rethinking."

"He loved God more than the military. And he loved us." Mom ran her finger around the cover of the book she held. "Promise me you'll give it some thought."

Jayden nodded. "I will." He leaned back in his chair. "So how was the Bible Study?"

"Good." His mother laid her book in her lap. "We're studying Ruth."

"That's the one where the daughter-in-law follows her mother-in-law to a new land, right?"

"Yes." Mom studied the ceiling. "It amazes me how God put the forerunners of the Messiah in place years before Jesus made His entrance into the world."

"Maybe you are going to meet your Boaz." Jayden raised his eyebrow. "God might be putting pieces in place for you."

"I'm still in love with your dad. If I'd listened to my sensible side back then, George would never have happened." Mom gave him a no-nonsense stare. "How stupid I was."

"Everyone makes mistakes. Forgive yourself. Move on."

"I have, just not that direction." She rolled her eyes. "God would have to slap me upside the head to shake Jordan's memory from my mind. George certainly didn't."

"I don't know, Mom. Parker seemed to capture your attention." Jayden grinned as she quirked an eyebrow. "Prepare to be slapped."

Baylie packed her overnight case and changed the sheets in the room she'd occupied the last three nights. Another staff member would assume the role as housemother tonight and Baylie would return to her own apartment. The rotation worked well. Three nights on and then nine nights in her own place. With four staffers in the lineup, no one ever had to give up their own bed for long. The children always felt loved.

She carried the sheets to the ground floor. The sound of a washer running caught her attention. The woman who came in twice a week to manage the laundry stood sorting clothing. With twelve kids needing changes of clothes, the pile could grow high in a short time.

"Hi." Baylie held up the sheets. "Changing of the guard."

The woman smiled. "Just toss them over there."

Baylie aimed for the heap, succeeded, and then returned to the room upstairs. She grabbed the overnight case and garment bag, then headed to the apartment. Returning to her own space meant she'd be sharing the same roof with Jayden and his mother. She was glad her studio and the other three on her end of the bunkhouse duplex were separated by a main wall from Melanie's private quarters. She'd be tempted to pop up uninvited at Melanie's door if a hallway ran down the center of the building. Jayden would be worth the risk, but this way she had to behave.

She entered the bunkhouse, unlocked the office door, and checked for mail. Picking up the pile, she sorted out the correspondence meant for staffers. The business letters went to Lissa's desk. A return address caught her eye. Grandma had written. She stuck the envelope at the bottom of the pile, anxious to get to her studio and open it. She hurried on down the hall, slipping the posts she carried in each of the individual mail slots where they belonged.

Opening her door, she stepped into the room, positioning one of the two chairs she owned closer to the window, and sat to read. Her letter opener sliced through the fold of the envelope on the bottom. Bracing herself for bad news, Baylie scanned the page.

My dearest Baylie,

I trust this letter finds you well and happy. We hope you'll have a free weekend soon. We'd love a visit.

Your grandfather suffered a stroke last weekend and spent two nights in the hospital. He was moved to a rehabilitation facility where he remains. I'm told he is responding well to therapy. I've been to see him and am encouraged. I'm praying he soon will get strong enough to come back to share this apartment with me. I miss him.

Baylie stopped reading and wiped her eyes. *Grandma! Why didn't you call and tell me?*

She put the letter down. Grandma must have thought he wasn't seriously affected. She wouldn't interrupt Baylie's life for something trivial—but still. Baylie should have been informed. She sniffed. Poor Grandma. All alone in her assisted living apartment.

Though Grandma had more room than she did, the older woman's apartment was not spacious. Without her husband there to fill the space, Grandma was probably bouncing off the walls. How she must miss him.

She reread the letter. Grandma needed her to visit. She looked at her wall calendar. The newsletter had been sent. Her files were up to date. Nothing kept her from taking a couple of days to visit her grandparents.

Except Jayden being here.

A knock sounded on her door. She opened it to find Lissa standing there smiling. On her hip she juggled Grayson, whose grin was priceless. He raised his chubby hand and waved. "Hi."

"Lissa! What brings you to my humble abode?" She stepped back and gestured toward the table. "Please come in."

"I won't stay long. Grayson needs a nap soon."

Baylie laughed. "So do I."

"How was the dorm last night?"

"Fine." Baylie frowned. "Why?"

"We found evidence of an intruder by the downstairs garage."

"No kidding?" Chills ran up Baylie's neck. She hadn't heard or seen anything. "Did you catch him?"

"When the silent alarm was triggered, the floodlights flashed on." Lissa lowered Grayson to the floor. "Kurt went outside. He saw a departing figure on the driveway."

"What or who do you think they were after?"

"We have our suspicions, but fortunately they didn't succeed."

"How can I help?" Baylie didn't know if she could fire a gun, or even if she could wrestle a burglar to the ground—but she could scream.

"Nothing for you or the other staffers to do. Just make sure the doors are locked whenever you leave a room or building."

"Got it." Baylie held up her letter. "My grandfather had a stroke last week and my grandmother would like me to visit. Any chance of me taking the weekend off?"

"By all means, go. You're caught up, aren't you?"

Baylie nodded. "I don't want to leave the grounds if you need me here. If the children find out, won't they be scared?"

"We won't tell them. We can handle everything here. There's plenty of staff." Lissa grabbed Grayson by the hand. "Besides, Jayden is collaborating with Kurt on strategies to counter this intrusion. With two ex-Marines on alert I imagine we've more than enough security."

Baylie couldn't hide her chuckle. "Camouflage gear and a sniper scope?"

Lissa rolled her eyes. "You get the picture."

"I could stand on watch during the night if you have a lookout spot." As he launched into soldier mode, Jayden's adrenaline notched his heart rate a little higher. He glanced out the window of the office where he and Kurt were discussing the incident from the night before. "Do you think the intruder will be a regular?"

"I don't know. The person we suspect isn't allowed to visit." Kurt shrugged his shoulders. "I know how ugly George got when he came looking for you while we were off camping." He looked Jayden's way. "Peggy met him at the door with a Smith & Wesson."

"Did he threaten Peggy?" Jayden's mind went blank. He'd never known his first foster mother had challenged his stepfather. "How did I miss that?"

"We decided it would only frighten you more. You were eleven." Kurt breathed deep, the long-ago incident obviously stirring up unhappy memories. "Duke was on guard."

"Figures." Jayden tapped a pencil on the desk where he sat. "George was determined to get revenge, that's for sure."

"This guy may be of the same frame of mind."

"So, what's the plan?" Jayden could see low-lying hills and a distant mountain. The ranch sat at the bottom of a rise. He remembered the place where he'd scouted the scene when he first came. "I could stake out among the scrub pines at the top of the driveway."

"Squat behind a juniper bush?" Kurt snickered. "Somehow I sense experience speaking."

"You don't know how many times I snuck away from George. I would hide in the brush so he wouldn't find me, then slither down that hill just so I could spend time with Mr. Mueller."

"The top of the driveway isn't a bad idea." Kurt stood and crossed the room to the other window. "There's an old school bus shelter up there. We could turn it around to face the ranch."

"Too obvious." Jayden joined Kurt at the window. "I'll just park my backside against it. Maybe I can convince Duke to join me."

"You'll have to carry him up that hill."

"Think he'll ride the Harley?"

Kurt laughed. "Now that I have to see."

"Don't think I won't try." Jayden leaned on the window. "He climbed the bales of hay to join me in the loft when we were hiding. I didn't think he could do that, either."

"He was a lot younger then." Kurt's jaw flexed as if he fought a smile. "Maybe you can talk Baylie into joining you," Kurt's crooked grin gave away his tease. "She loves Duke, you know."

Jayden cleared his throat. "I don't think she should be out where a weapon might be used."

"Uh-huh." Kurt punched Jayden's shoulder. "I hope you plan to stay here for a while. Lissa and I will love watching you two."

"I don't think there's anything to watch." Jayden felt heat creeping along his jaw. "We went our separate ways after high school."

"Have you always been clueless?"

CHAPTER ELEVEN

Baylie's drive to the assisted living facility in Bend where her grandparents resided seemed extra long and tedious today. Her head ached. Waves of nausea tortured her stomach. Tight muscles convulsed across her shoulders. What would she find when she arrived? Was Grandma holding up? How weak would her grandfather be?

She tried to pray, a habit instilled in her at a young age—one she had relied on even after her parents were killed when she was little—but she couldn't seem to focus.

Baylie knew why.

She'd lost her belief in answered prayer during her senior year in college. Had brazenly disobeyed God, fallen into a sinful lifestyle, and someone else paid the consequences. Talking to the Lord now about anything deeper than a need for patience seemed like a waste of time. How could He forgive her fall from grace? Overlook what it had done to her faith? Not punish her for her behavior? Here she was two years later, and her shame followed her everywhere. And her faith?

All but gone.

The residence loomed in the distance, a hotel-like apartment building with two sides representing different types of care. The front entrance led to apartments for the ambulatory residents who came and went as they pleased, their retirements a time of relaxation and leisure. On the back side of the facility another entrance led to those residents who needed assistance with day–to–day living. That is where Baylie aimed the car. Grandpa had needed the extra help and Grandma went with him. Baylie liked that her grandparents were looked after, visited daily by professional staff. If they still lived at home, she would never escape the worry.

The corridor leading to her grandparents' apartment smelled clean and fresh, a refreshing change from other facilities she had visited in the past—those which smelled stale or soiled by waste items left by careless housekeepers. She found the door to her grandmother's apartment and knocked. A rustling inside assured Baylie Grandma was home. When the door opened, Grandma Laura began to cry.

"Oh, Baylie. My sweet girl. You've come." Grandma widened her arms and Baylie stepped into them, holding this dear woman tight.

"I would have been here sooner if you had called me."

"I didn't want to burden you." Grandma sniffed. "You've got your own life."

"Let's talk on the sofa." Baylie whispered. "You shouldn't stand for long."

"Thank you, dear." The woman wobbled to the nearest cushion. "I'm feeling especially weak today with your grandfather absent from our home."

"Any word on his recovery?"

Her grandmother sighed. "All they say is he keeps improving."

"Can we visit?"

Grandma's eyes lit up. "That would be so wonderful. Do you have the time?"

Baylie hugged her. "I'm here for the weekend." She kissed Grandma's cheek. "We can go as often as they will let us in."

Moisture trickled down Grandma's cheek. "You are such a blessing."

"So are you." Baylie opened her phone. "Who do I call?"

Jayden wandered into the kitchen the next morning to catch Baylie before she got involved with her weekend plans. Mom stood cleaning up breakfast dishes, two children he hadn't met helping to load the dishwasher. She raised an eyebrow. "Need a second breakfast?"

"No, I missed Baylie this morning and hoped to find her here helping you."

"She's gone to Bend to visit her grandparents." Mom gave the counter another swipe. "She's not due back until Sunday evening."

"I needed to talk with her, but it'll wait." He peeked into baskets of leftovers on the counter. "I'm glad she has an opportunity to visit them." Jayden found a biscuit and helped himself. "I know she mentioned they'd moved into assisted living recently."

"Her grandfather has had a health event of some kind."

"That's too bad." Jayden buttered the biscuit. "Not serious I hope?"

Mom shrugged. "Could be."

"I'll catch up with her when she gets back." Jayden headed for the door. "I'm helping Kurt plan surveillance of the property."

"No guns!"

"As if." Jayden laughed. "All we have here are trespassers." He winked with his good eye. "Catch you at dinner."

A respectful silence hovered over the hospital as Baylie and her grandmother entered. Masked personnel stirred with importance around them, an attendant waiting by the entrance to the recovery section of the ICU. "Are you here to see Mr. Levine?"

Baylie nodded. "We called."

"Please put on a mask and follow me." The attendant led them down a corridor, signs indicating they were going to an intermediate care section of the hospital. Soon the attendant stopped outside an open door. She knocked lightly on the casing. "Mr. Levine, you have visitors." She stepped back. "He's groggy. You have ten minutes."

Baylie's breath caught. Only ten minutes? How serious was Grandpa's condition? She followed Grandma into the room and her heart sank. Her grandfather was hooked up to an array of monitors, his pulse and oxygen levels displayed on a nearby screen. His pale skin had a bluish tint and his eyes were closed. Baylie resisted the urge to cry.

Grandma walked to the edge of the bed and took his hand. "Joseph. It's me, Laura." She kissed his wrist. "Are you awake?"

Baylie held her breath as they waited for Grandpa to respond. A lifetime seemed to pass before the man's eyelids fluttered and he looked at them.

"Lawwa?" At her nod, he lifted her hand to his lips. "So goo…" Grandpa stopped mid-sentence as his eyes closed again.

"Baylie is here, Joseph." Grandma looked at her, gesturing toward the bed. "Come where he can see you, dear."

Baylie approached the bed, legs stiff as if she were frozen in time. She forced a smile, fear sending her heart into a staccato rhythm. *Please don't die. Not here. Not yet.* She found her voice. "Grandpa Joseph? It's me, Baylie."

The man's eyes opened again, and his gaze found her. "Baywee, my dahlin' girr. I muss be dreamin' ift I . . ." He stopped, his slurred speech slipping into nonsensical gibberish. Wetness rimmed his eyelids. He lifted shaking fingers and she took them in her own.

"I'm so glad to be here." Baylie bit back the cry threatening to ruin her composure. "I wanted to see you this weekend, so here I am."

Grandma piped up. "She's here all weekend. I'll be glad for the company."

"Goot." Grandpa grunted.

"Yes, it will be good." Baylie squeezed the limp fingers she held. "I'll bring Grandma to see you again tomorrow."

Grandpa's eyes drifted closed again. One of the monitors began to beep. Within seconds a nurse appeared and hurried to the noisy machine. She adjusted the dials and soon the noise stopped. She glanced at her watch. "I'm sorry, but your ten minutes are up. We need to tend to some issues for Mr. Levine."

"Of course." Grandma turned away from the bed, gripping Baylie's hand like a lifeline. "Thank you for taking such good care of my Joseph."

The nurse smiled but didn't speak. She gave Baylie a nod of her head, gaze intent as if sending a silent message. Baylie didn't know what the nurse was trying to communicate, but she sensed the news wasn't good.

She led Grandma from the room, her ability to speak comfort to her grandmother momentarily suspended. They walked in silence toward the exit, stopping at the nurse's station to make an appointment to see Grandpa tomorrow. When they reached her car, Baylie opened the door and helped her grandmother slide into the front seat. Grandma wiped her eyes.

Baylie leaned in and hugged the dear woman. "Grandma?" She wrapped an arm around her, pulling her close. "Don't cry. He's in good hands. They are watching him around the clock."

"I know. But it is hard to see him so weak, unable to speak, and barely cognizant of who we are." The tears flowed down her cheeks. "I'm not sure he'll make it out of the hospital."

"You need to pray." Baylie kissed the woman's forehead. "You want to do it now?"

Grandma nodded. "Will you?"

"Let me get in." She hurried to the driver's side and keyed the ignition. "Okay?"

Grandma nodded. "Prayer is good."

Her conscience screamed. Hypocrite! Baylie grappled for words, seeking the confidence she lacked. Being so out of touch with God, would He listen to her? Would He know who she was? She hadn't bothered Him in quite a while, and considering her past failures, He might not want to hear what she had to say. Bitterness filled her as remorse for those awful days she'd not been the Christ-follower she should have been surfaced. She cleared her throat. *Here goes nothing.*

"Father, we lift up Grandpa Joseph to you, asking that you surround him with your angels and bring comfort and healing to his broken body." Baylie searched for the words she'd once known so well. She pushed on. "And if it be your will, we ask you will return him to Grandma's side so they can have many more years together." She needed to get herself out of this so Grandpa had a chance. "Forgive me for any unconfessed sin, Lord, and don't hold my trespasses in the way of my prayers reaching your ears. Thank you, in Jesus' name, Amen."

Satisfied she'd done the best she could, she opened her eyes and found Grandma Laura looking at her. "Thank you, Baylie. From your lips to God's ears."

Baylie hugged the woman. "Are you hungry?" She started the engine. "What would you like to eat?"

"I think I'd like a burger. I never get to have those anymore outside the facility."

"Then burger it is, with a shake on the side?"

"Ooh, strawberry would be lovely."

Baylie laughed. "Let's see what we can find."

Jayden rode his Harley to the top of the driveway later that day. The school bus shelter sat among the junipers, close to the road, covered in sagebrush, knapweed, and Russian thistle. Obviously, the structure hadn't been used in a while and the noxious vegetation hadn't been addressed, something the local authorities usually did. But its ramshackle exterior made it the perfect place for surveillance.

He stumbled through the brush, chopping at stubborn tangles with his cane. The effort created an open space at the back of the shelter where he could sit and spy on the ranch below. He considered finding a stool, a short one that would raise him just enough to look out over the sagebrush. This would be a perfect spot to keep an eye on the ranch during the night. If he could get Duke up here, the nighttime duty would be like old times. As a younger dog Duke used to bound up this hill like a battery-operated wind-up toy. The dog seemed to forget that Jayden didn't live here and Duke's owner was Mr. Mueller. But Duke only had eyes for him. His loyalty knew no bounds. Nor had his energy.

Those days were gone.

Jayden remembered when he had first entered foster care and lived at Peggy Blake's rescue ranch. Duke had joined him there after Mr. Mueller died. The dog became his constant companion. That was when his stepfather George used a side road to drive undetected along the upper boundary of the property. George forced Mom to be bait to lure Jayden to the waiting pickup. Duke jumped into the middle of the attempted kidnapping to stop George's misguided plan. If it hadn't been for Duke's barking George might have succeeded. Instead the man went to prison.

A noise caught his attention and he looked around. A blur of black fur, a lolling tongue, and a steady panting came through the sagebrush. "Duke?" The border collie wagged his tail and wobbled toward him. "How did you get up here, fella?"

Duke barked, happy little yips which Jayden interpreted as pride in his effort. To have climbed the hill today, the dog must be exhausted. Jayden would have to see if he could lift Duke on the Harley to go back down. He owed the dog that much. Jayden hugged his old friend, glad for his company once again.

Jayden's life had taken a turn the day the abduction failed.

He'd gone from a temporary placement at Peggy's ranch and wound up a permanent ward of the state. His mother couldn't reclaim him because of her suspected part in the scheme, even though she was an unwilling participant. But the courts wouldn't budge. Mom filed for divorce which satisfied the state that George would not return to their home once he finished his sentence. By the time all the legal hoops had been jumped, Jayden was eighteen. He and his mother lived like strangers throughout his high school years.

Recapturing their relationship as mother and son became his priority. Now that he was home from Afghanistan, his military duty almost complete, he and Mom could spend real time with each other. Fifteen years were lost to the past, but the future loomed bright and promising.

Grandma sucked on her straw with noisy abandon, surprising Baylie with her enthusiasm. The woman smacked her lips and emitted a loud burp. "Excuse me, but that was wonderful!" She gave the straw one more slurp then set the glass on the table. "I'd forgotten how good a strawberry shake is. Thank you, Baylie."

"You are most welcome." She picked up the lunch tab and reached into her billfold for her debit card. "I'm glad we could have this time together."

Grandma grasped her hands. "Let me pay for this. Please?"

"No, I am treating you." She flashed the plastic card at the waitress who took the bill to the cash register. "You've paid my expenses many times in the past, and they weren't for a four-dollar milk shake. It's my turn."

"Okay. If you insist." Grandma closed her wallet. "What time did they say we could come tomorrow?"

"I asked for a morning visit." Baylie opened her phone. "I thought Grandpa might be more alert earlier in the day."

Grandma's eyes pooled again. "I hope so." She sniffed. "It was so hard seeing him like that today." She looked at Baylie. "What if he never recovers?"

"Don't think like that." Baylie grabbed her grandmother's fingers and squeezed. "You asked God to restore him, so leave the outcome in His hands."

"You've always had so much faith, Baylie. Your parents instilled that in you from the time you could walk."

Guilt wrapped Baylie in shame. If Grandma knew how little she prayed these days she'd be shocked. Prayer didn't come easily for her anymore. Cloaked in feelings of unworthiness, she feared approaching the throne of God. Every time she tried praying in earnest, images of her college senior year flashed before her, blocking the communion she needed with her Savior. Baylie had yet to push through the barrier that held her back. Like her grandfather's struggle to speak and communicate, a condition from which he might never improve, Baylie's recovery of her faith might be no less of a battle.

"Shall we go back to the apartment now?" Baylie signed the payment slip, took her card, and stood. "Don't want this day to get too long for you."

"With you here, the day will never be long enough." Grandma rose on shaky legs and tucked her hand in Baylie's elbow. "You are a treasure."

If only that were true—a treasure. One with a broken lock on the chest, the contents damaged and neglected. She doubted anything could restore her to the person she once was. The deterioration was real. The regret irreconcilable. Baylie remained silent as they walked to the car.

"Come on, Duke." Jayden called the dog to him after spending an hour inspecting the terrain at the top of the drive. He'd considered all angles he might need to observe a trespasser in the act. "Let's go home."

Duke came wagging his tail, head low.

Jayden patted the seat, coaxing the dog to jump up. Duke yipped, but he remained on the ground. Jayden climbed aboard and encouraged the dog to crawl onto his lap. Duke lay down on the gravel, paws stretched out in front of him, head on his legs and eyes fixed on Jayden. A low whine followed the wag of his tail.

"Come here, boy." He reached for the dog's collar and pulled. Duke resisted, his body a dead weight at the end of the tug. "Duke, come."

The dog's sad eyes watched him.

"I'm trying to help you get home, Buddy." Jayden caressed the dog's back and scratched behind his ears. Duke didn't weigh as much as Jayden's pack in Afghanistan. He could easily lift him, though straddling the animal across his lap while keeping his own balance might prove disastrous. Jayden wasn't sure he could. "I wish I could just say 'herd, Duke' like I used to and you'd take off."

Duke sat up, ears alert. He barked, looking around the hill.

Jayden didn't know what brought the response. He said it again, only this time like a command. "Herd! Duke!"

With a bark and a whoosh of his tail, Duke trotted off down the driveway. He continued to bark as he hurried, covering half of the length of the roadway before Jayden could engage the Harley. *This will be embarrassing if an old dog beats me and my bike home.*

The motorcycle responded with a roar. Jayden rolled onto the graveled driveway with care lest he spin out on the loose rock. He gave the bike a little gas and fell into line behind Duke, finally catching him on the straight stretch. The dog alternated his trot with excited bounces as his tail kept time to his barks.

"Let's go home, Duke!"

The dog didn't need encouragement. He broke into a dead run as they neared the barn. Jayden pulled up beside him at the water trough. Duke stood on hind legs and lapped from the trough, abating his thirst like a weary traveler.

Jayden killed the engine and climbed off. He bent down on his good knee and held out his arms. "Duke, you've still got game. You great, sweet fella."

The dog hurried to him, his stiff legs reflecting the exertion he'd just exhibited. He rested his head on Jayden's shoulder. He gripped the dog about the neck, fighting the sudden interference of tears. "If you've still got moxie, buddy, then I'll have to find mine, too." He hugged him once more. "Thank you for the kick in the pants."

CHAPTER TWELVE

THE NEXT MORNING WHEN BAYLIE AND her grandmother arrived to see Grandpa Joseph, the nurse on duty greeted them. "He's not shown much improvement since yesterday. The stroke affected his left side and attacked his facial muscles which is affecting his speech. We're not seeing any change in that."

Baylie's stomach cramped. Poor Grandpa.

"He's aware of what's going on around him," the nurse said, "but right now he can't respond the way you wish he could."

"What should we do?" Baylie didn't know how to help him if she couldn't understand him when he spoke.

"Nod and smile when he attempts speech." The nurse noted their visit on the white board outside Grandpa's room. "That will encourage him to keep trying, even though it won't encourage you. Half of his journey back will be believing he can recover."

"I believe he can, with God's help." Grandma put on her mask. "Baylie, let's go help him."

Baylie glanced at the nurse, who nodded, then followed her grandmother into the room. Grandpa lay asleep, eyes closed and mouth askew, loud snores filling the room.

Grandma approached the bed. "Joseph, it's me, Laura."

Grandpa's eyelids blinked open and he stared, as if unseeing, around the room. Finally, his gaze fell on Grandma. "Lawra, my dahling." He held out his hand to her. "Yuu're heer."

"Yes, Joseph. we have come again." She squeezed his hand. "Baylie is here, too."

"Grandpa, so good to see you." She touched his shoulder. "I brought Grandma."

Her words sounded lame to her ears, but she couldn't think of anything meaningful to say. "Saving Grandma gas money." She laughed.

"She bought me a hamburger, Joseph, with a strawberry shake."

Grandpa opened and closed his mouth several times. "Yummm."

Baylie resisted a gasp. He had understood them. She tried again with something different. "My friend from high school is back from the military. He's going to work at the ranch this summer."

"Be goot." Grandpa said, then chuckled.

Grandma laughed. "Joseph, you rascal. Don't tease her so." Grandma looked her way. "Is this Jayden who is back?"

"You remember him?"

"Of course. He took you and Jamielyn to the prom in blue jeans. Watched the show from behind the ball cages in the gym, if I remember correctly."

Baylie blushed. "That was the best evening I ever spent. The three of us shared a milkshake."

"I would have bought each of you your own if you had asked."

"I know, but this memory is one I cherish." Baylie closed her eyes remembering. "Jayden spent all the money he had in his pocket to buy that shake."

"Does he have more money now?"

"He's riding a Harley-Davidson." Baylie grinned at Grandma's shocked face. "Those don't come cheap."

"How can he date you if he rides a motorcycle?" Grandma clutched her chest. "Is this a new era kind of thing?"

"He hasn't asked to date me, Grandma." She touched the woman's shoulder. "I'll be happy if we can only be friends again." Baylie crossed her fingers. Who was she fooling? Being friends with Jayden would be wonderful, but having him on the same premises made her want much more.

Lissa had told her of Kurt's journey back from war memories.

Jayden might need to tread the same lonely road. She'd pay close attention to see if his war experiences hovered. He might need healing, both from wounds she could see, and from those she couldn't. She had time. Her own journey still waited unfinished.

"He followed you up the hill?" Kurt's open-mouthed stare made Jayden smile. "I didn't think that dog had it in him."

"He came up the hill panting, but going down he seemed to float." Jayden set his helmet on a table. "All I said to him was 'Herd' and he was off like a shot."

"Amazing." Kurt sank into a nearby chair. "What did you think of your surveillance probe?"

"The school bus structure will serve my purpose." Jayden glanced about the room checking the furniture. "What I need is a low stool to raise me up above the sagebrush. Do you have anything like that around here?"

"What about a milking stool?" Kurt folded his arms across his chest. "We have two or three in the barn not in use."

"That might be the exact height I'm looking for." Jayden grabbed his helmet, tucking it under his arm. "Point me in the right direction and I'll go check them out."

"Probably in the tack room at the end of the stalls."

"Great. Thanks." Jayden headed for the door. "Baylie's still gone?"

"Yes. Due back tomorrow, I believe." Kurt's mouth twisted. "You going to get her in on the surveillance duty?"

"Maybe." Jayden made a face. "I don't know what nights to be out there."

"The last intrusion was on a Thursday, so I would think that's a good place to begin." Kurt rubbed the back of his neck. "Whoever it is may have a night off and try again."

"Or decide the possible trouble is not worth the risk." Jayden studied Kurt. "Who do you suspect?"

"Charlie's mother's boyfriend." Kurt sighed. "He was responsible for the neglect of the child, hooking the mother on drugs. He threatened to get even. Blamed Charlie for causing him to be sent to jail."

"Boy, that has a familiar ring to it."

"I thought you might find the story hits close to home."

"Makes Charlie seem like a kindred spirit." Jayden reached for the door. "All the more reason to try."

"I wish you could stay longer." Grandma hugged Baylie as she prepared to drive home. "But having you here this weekend meant a lot."

"I was glad to be here." Baylie kissed the cheek of the forlorn woman standing before her. The worry over Grandpa's stroke, coupled with the years they'd loved each other, had taken a toll on her grandmother's face. Puffy skin hovered around a sagging chin. Moisture clouded the already glazed look of her eyes. How Baylie loved this sweet little lady who had always put her first. "Promise me you'll keep me updated on Grandpa's condition. His progress."

"I will. I'm praying I only have good news to send you."

"You send me all the news, Grams." Baylie rested her hands on the woman's shoulders. "Don't hold back if his condition worsens. Okay?"

Grandma sighed. "Okay. If you insist." She slid a knuckle under her right eye and caught the beginning of a trickle. "But I might make you worry more."

"Grandma," Baylie found her most serious voice. "You'll need support if Grandpa continues as he is. I know you believe I can't handle this, but I can. After four years at the university I'm quite good at managing heartbreak. Having me be your shoulder to cry on in a time of need would be payback for all the times you let me cry on yours."

"You sure?"

"I'm quite sure." Baylie hugged the trembling woman. "Now before I make you cry any more, I need to get out of here. It's a ways back to the ranch."

"Shouldn't you call ahead?" Grandma spoke in her be sensible tone. "They should know you are leaving here late."

"Can I use your landline? My cell phone is low on power."

"Sure. Write the number by the phone, too, will you?" Grandma handed her a pad of paper. "If something happens, I may be too shaken to find the number."

"Is that what happened before?"

Grandma nodded. "Besides the tears I couldn't stop."

Baylie dialed the number and got the answering machine. Better than nothing. "Hi. Baylie here. Leaving Bend late. Didn't want you to worry. See you in a few." She hung up the phone. "That should do it." She wrote down the number on the pad, then added her cell phone. "Now you do the same if anything happens. Promise?"

"I'll keep you posted, my dear girl."

"Thank you. I'll see you soon."

Darkness had descended on the ranch and Baylie still had not arrived back. Jayden paced his mother's apartment, worry fueling his steps. The empty stretches of road were not places anyone, especially a woman like Baylie, should be out traveling after dark. After maneuvers in Afghanistan, he understood the dangers of patrolling a dark landscape. Baylie didn't have that experience. Had a tire gone flat? Did her car break down? The worst possible scenarios flooded Jayden's mind, his soldier brain kicking in without invitation.

A knock sounded on the apartment door and his mother went to answer it. "Kurt?" She stepped back. "Please come in."

"Have either of you communicated with Baylie today?" The question sounded like an innocent inquiry, but Jayden sensed a layer of worry beneath the words. "She called last night from her grandmother's apartment and told Lissa she planned to stay one more day and be home this evening."

"No." Mom glanced Jayden's way. "Did you?"

"No. I haven't heard anything."

"Lissa and I have been wondering where she is." Taut muscles strained Kurt's cheeks, his forehead furrowed with deep wrinkles. "She called the landline about seven and said she was leaving later than planned."

"If she left at that time, she should be close to home." Jayden looked to his mother, who nodded.

"So it would seem." Kurt shifted his weight to his other foot. "That's why I wondered if she'd called or texted either of you."

"Cell reception is not the best out here, you know." Jayden studied Kurt. "Has anyone called her grandmother?"

"I don't know who she is." Kurt appeared thoughtful. "Even if I did, calling her might worry her unnecessarily."

"Does your phone record incoming calls?" Mom crossed the room and sat down. "The number should be available as well as the time of the call."

"I think she called the house landline." Kurt's jaw clenched. "That won't help us."

"Did you check voice mail?" Mom looked from Kurt to him. "Maybe she had to stay another night."

"That's my guess." Jayden recounted all he knew. "I remember her grandmother from high school. Her name is Laura Levine. She's moved to assisted living in Bend."

"So she's somewhere between Bend and here." Kurt frowned.

"If she left at the time she intended, she could be close." Mom folded her arms. "There aren't too many places to go on that highway. If she's out of gas or changing a tire, she'd be easy to spot."

"After we check the answering machine"—Jayden grabbed his jacket—"why don't we go look for her?"

Returning five minutes later, Kurt's frown and the set of his jaw gave Jayden concern. "She called again." He pursed his lips. "This second message said she left about nine, so she could be anywhere."

"But she should be here, don't you think?" Jayden mentally calculated the miles against the time. "I still think we should go look."

"That's a hundred and thirty mile stretch of highway!" Kurt's frustration filled his eyes.

"We'll go to plan B." Jayden pointed to the door. "If we don't find her close by, then we'll call her grandmother."

"Meet you in the drive in five." Kurt waved as he walked out.

"Where do you suppose she is?" Mom appeared as flustered as Kurt had been nervous.

"Kurt and I are into surveillance." Jayden grinned. "Trust two ex-military to knock the rust off their training."

"Baylie is in good hands."

"Pray we find her soon." Jayden headed out the door. "That's a long section of road."

Baylie tried the ignition again. Her car had sputtered to a stop in the middle of nowhere. She opened her phone. 12:00 am. On this stretch of deserted highway few cars would be passing by so close to midnight. She turned on her four-way flashers and prayed. "I know we haven't talked much in a while, Lord, but it seems as if you are forcing me into situations where I have nowhere else to turn. I'm not worthy of your concern, but if you remember who I am, please send help."

Her common sense had failed her this time. She could only blame herself. *Why did I leave so late? I should have stayed the night.*

Baylie knew the answer. She had been about to leave her grandmother's apartment and head back to the ranch when the hospital called, and the day turned dire. Grandpa had lapsed into unconsciousness, his condition deteriorated.

Panicked with worry, she again drove her grandmother to the hospital. Staff explained Grandpa was comfortable and there was nothing they could do but wait for morning. Seeing her grandmother's exhaustion, Baylie convinced her to go back home and rest. Tomorrow would bring new answers.

"You need to get back to your job, Baylie." Grandma urged her to return home. "This facility will provide transportation to the hospital in the morning."

"But Grandma. . ."

"Go child. I'll feel better knowing you are home and safe. There isn't anything any of us can do for Joseph. He's in God's hands."

"Who is going to hold you up?"

"My Lord." Grandma patted her hand. "I will call you if there is any change."

"Do you promise?"

"I do. The doctor said he could be like this for days." Grandma squeezed her fingers. "I'll keep you posted." A kiss on the cheek followed. "Get on the road before it grows any darker."

Now Baylie wondered how many hours she might have to sit in this car and pray for someone to come along and help her. She guessed she was more than halfway home, which was good, but it also meant little traffic. Out here alone, she felt vulnerable. Stuck.

She didn't like the dark. In it, her imagination grew wings. Outside her window she thought she saw shadows moving. What sorts of critters lived in the sagebrush and juniper? Would they harass her in the car?

She wanted to call someone. She should have called the ranch one more time before she left Bend. At least then someone would have been alerted to her traveling even later than she originally believed she would. But now she couldn't. Cell phone reception out here was almost non-existent. Feeling defeated, she leaned back into the car seat—her only option wondering and waiting. She turned the key and the gas gauge indicated half a tank. Were there engine problems? Why wouldn't the car start? Worst of all, would it be expensive to fix?

Something jumped on the hood of her car. Baylie freaked. She stifled a scream. Four legs. A tail. She gulped for air, her heart pounding. As quick as the animal came, whatever it was, it left. Only the glow of its eyes as it glanced back in the four-way flashers haunted her.

That did it. She locked her car doors and slid down into the front seat to avoid prying eyes, if there were any, and to mask her scent from the acute noses of passing wildlife. Surely someone would come along.

She uttered another prayer, just in case God hadn't heard her the first time. "Please forgive my past failings and hear my plea. Send someone soon."

The darkness enveloped her—no lights, save for the flicker of her four-way flashers, no sign posts—almost total empty blackness. Above her stars littered the sky, but no moon hung there with them. What she wouldn't give for a full moon. Her eyes felt heavy, but she resisted sleep. As time ticked on, she struggled against the weariness, only to soon lose the battle.

Jayden and Kurt had been searching the highway for an hour, but with no sign of Baylie or her car. Jayden's worry grew by the mile—Baylie was no match for a villain with ulterior motives. Out here anyone could be lurking in the shadows, waiting for an unsuspecting quarry. The high desert provided a variety of hidden hideaways for those who had mischief on their minds. Enemies who stalked innocent prey. How well he had learned that lesson from George. He shuddered to think of all the possible scenarios.

"What's that over there?" Kurt's question broke the stillness of the truck cab. "See the dim flickers?"

Jayden peered through the windshield. "Looks like four-way flashers. Albeit dead ones."

"That's what I thought." Kurt slowed and pulled off the road. "But that is Baylie's car." He rolled down his window, the cold night air filling the cab. "No sign of anyone around."

"I hope she didn't try to hoof it back to Bend from here." Jayden's breath grew erratic, his mind in soldier mode. He jerked the door open and took a combat stance. "Aren't we about sixty miles away?"

"Baylie is smarter than that." Kurt climbed out his side of the cab. "Grab the flashlight."

Jayden crept on quiet feet to the car, flashing the light in through the windows. The interior appeared to be empty. He sidled up to the driver's window and peered in. Baylie lay on the seat, knees bent and feet tucked up against the door. He signaled Kurt with the flashlight over the top of the car. "She's asleep on the seat."

"Tap gently." Kurt put a finger to his lips. "She'll scream if we pound on the door."

Jayden nodded. He touched a knuckle to the glass and knocked. No movement. He struck the glass a little harder, the sound sharper in the silence. "Baylie?" He rapped again. "Baylie? Wake up. It's Jayden."

He raised his fist to beat the glass but stopped when movement on the front seat caught his attention. "I think she's coming around."

"About time." Kurt folded his arms. "I was beginning to think she'd succumbed to fumes from the engine."

Baylie struggled to open her eyes. How long had she been asleep? She squinted in the darkness, too groggy to remember where she was. As the dashboard came into focus she remembered—stranded on Highway 20 in the middle of nowhere—her only visitors a pair of eyes and a set of ears that looked in at her when she'd stirred a while ago.

Now someone tapped on her window. She lay still. Who could it be? Was she safe to sit up? She waited. Chills from fear wracked her body. The knocking came again. "Baylie Summers? Wake up!"

Only one voice would call her by her full name. Jayden! Had God heard her prayer? She pushed up from her seat and smiled. He peered into the car and signaled for her to roll down her window. She reached for the handle, only to be startled when a second person appeared outside on her passenger side. She groaned. Her boss. Kurt McKintrick. Nothing like calling out the troops.

Instead of opening the window she pushed the door handle. She swung her legs out and sat sideways on the front seat, steering wheel pressed against her side. "Hi."

"Have a nice nap?" Jayden's tease came through in his voice. "Kind of a bad place to stop and snooze, don't you think?"

"When you're tired, you're tired." Baylie's quick wit had abandoned her in the moment. "Besides, sleeping kept me from having to converse with the deer and the antelope dropping by for coffee." She yawned and tried to shake off the grogginess. "But when your car quits in the middle of nowhere, you don't exactly take off down the road in the dark."

"You would if you had Taliban behind you." Jayden chuckled.

"Some soldier you'd make."

"Not planning to enlist any time soon."

Kurt joined them. "Did you run out of gas?"

"No, I don't think so. The car just sighed and died."

"Why don't you crawl out of there and we'll take a look?" Kurt leaned against the top of the car. "Maybe it is something simple we can fix here."

"Thanks." She touched a foot to the pavement. She shivered. The night air had cooled while she slept.

"You can climb in the pickup if you're cold. Let me move the truck in front of your car so we can use the headlights to see. From the look of your four-way flashers, we may have to jump your battery." Kurt turned toward the pickup's driver's side, climbed in, and started the engine.

Once the pickup was aimed at her car, and the lights on, Baylie crawled into the warm cab. Kurt and Jayden leaned over the engine, their backs to her. She watched them move wires and check connections, their voices low as they discussed what they found.

Jayden moved to the truck's driver's door. "Your keys?"

"In the ignition, I think." Baylie didn't remember removing them.

Jayden pivoted and walked to her driver's seat. He reached inside, held the keys up in the headlights where she could see them, and climbed behind the wheel. Kurt attached cables to something under the hood. She didn't know the first thing about jumping a battery. Soon the ignition could be heard squealing as the mechanism tried to engage the engine, but nothing happened.

Kurt disconnected the cable. The whirring slowed as the battery's power waned in Jayden's efforts to start the car. He stopped and climbed out. Baylie slumped. She had so hoped the car might magically respond to his touch, but it hadn't. What would they do now?

Kurt went to the back of the pickup, removed a large chain and held it up. Jayden shook his head. For several minutes they talked out of Baylie's hearing. Finally, they closed the hood of her car, locked the doors, and walked her direction.

Jayden opened the passenger side door. "Slide over. We're going to drive into Burns and leave instructions for the car to be towed."

"Towed?" Baylie's mouth tasted dry as she slid across the seat. "Is there a mechanic there?"

"Kurt knows people who know people." Jayden grinned. "He will contact them in the daylight to see if they can figure out what is wrong."

"Okay."

Kurt climbed behind the steering wheel. "Something is not making connection, Baylie. We'll have to find a mechanic to test it out."

"Thank you. I'm sorry to make so much trouble."

"No trouble." Kurt started the truck. "We're Marines. No man, or woman, is ever left behind."

Jayden snorted. "Expect recruitment papers in the mail."

Baylie laughed. "Okay, okay. I can take a joke."

Kurt chuckled and reversed the truck onto the highway.

Baylie listened to their conversation as long as she could, but the rumble of the engine made her sleepy. Her eyes refused to stay open, her head nodded. Just as her chin hit her chest, she would jerk upright awake. Suddenly Jayden's arm came up around her shoulder and pulled her against his chest. "Get some rest, Baylie. We've got a fifty-mile trip ahead of us."

"But. . ."

"Shh. Just sleep."

CHAPTER THIRTEEN

THE SUNBEAMS DANCING ON THE FLOOR beside her bed startled Baylie. The window in the apartment faced west, so bright light didn't enter the room until at least noon. How late was it? She squinted at the clock trying to see the time. Twelve-thirty? She bolted upright, gasping at the lateness of the hour. She glanced around her, confused. She didn't remember returning to the ranch. Nor walking into her apartment. How did she get here? Was she carried?

She stared at her pajamas. When did she change into these? Her cheeks warmed. No, don't go there. They wouldn't. They just wouldn't.

She found fresh clothes and hurried to the shower, bits and pieces of the previous night replaying in her memory. Jayden had carried her when her sleepiness refused to let her walk. Melanie had guided her to bed. The ordeal rewound in her head.

Minutes later, she emerged from the bathroom, all the grubby remains of her long nightmare washed down the drain, damp hair dangling along her neckline. Using her fingers, she made curly tendrils along the sides of her face.

As she glanced in the mirror circles under her eyes told more of the story than she wanted to admit. The long night had taken its toll. She dabbed on moisturizer and a little light foundation and called it good. Her stomach growled.

"Food coming right up." She patted her stomach, then looked around for her apartment keys but couldn't see them. Rummaging in the pockets of her dirty clothes from yesterday produced nothing.

A knock sounded at her door. She stopped searching and zipped across the room. When she opened the door, Jayden leaned against the casing, hand uplifted, her keys dangling from his fingers.

His goofy grin and twinkling eyes spoke mischief. "Did I wake you? Thought I should return these."

"Thank you." Baylie felt her cheeks warm. "Did I sleep through the entire ride home?"

"You were zonked." Jayden's eyebrows narrowed. "Do you know you snore?"

"I do not." Baylie grabbed at the keys, but he snatched them out of her reach. "Do I?"

"Could hardly hear the engine over the noise." He hooted.

"Jayden!" Baylie resisted the urge to slap him. "You are taking unfair advantage of my breakdown."

"True." Jayden handed her the keys. "But you've a lot to live down."

"By the way, how did I get here?" Baylie grit her teeth, not sure she wanted to know. "And into my pajamas?"

"The pink ones?" Jayden's grin turned ornery.

"Jayden!"

He laughed, the noise making Baylie more and more uncomfortable. "You don't remember?"

"Not much."

"I carried you in." He breathed deep, let out a sigh, and with a chuckle said, "Mom came over and helped you get into bed."

"Oh, thank heavens." Baylie sagged against the door.

"Had you worried, did we?" Jayden straightened. "Kurt and I are men of honor. You'll never have to worry about us taking advantage of your reduced state of consciousness."

"Then how did you know the pajamas were pink?"

Jayden broke into another fit of laughter. "Just a lucky guess. It seemed like your color, you being blonde and all."

"You're mean." Baylie's stomach growled again, loud and long.

"And you're hungry." Jayden stepped back and gestured toward the entrance to the bunkhouse. "Mom saved you a plate of eggs and bacon. I'll even share the biscuits."

"You are too kind." Baylie stuck her keys in her hip pocket. "Any word on my car?"

"Yeah, the garage just called." Jayden nodded for her to follow. "I'll tell you over breakfast. I haven't eaten either."

"Really?" Baylie stared at him. "It's afternoon."

"You aren't the only one who was tired coming in this morning at three-thirty."

"I am so sorry." Baylie touched his shoulder. "I owe you and Kurt big time."

"I intend to collect." They had arrived at the kitchen entrance and Jayden opened the door. "Now that I know you're good at nighttime activity, I want to use you on surveillance for the ranch."

"More intruders?"

Jayden nodded. "We caught somebody in the driveway when we arrived last night. He ran into the brush and we couldn't follow. But at least we know how tall he is, and we know it's a man."

"Sounds scary."

Jayden sat on the opposite side of the table. He could look directly at Baylie as they tackled their breakfasts, even though it was afternoon. Most of the interns and the children had finished their lunches and left. Good thing Mom knew how to keep things warm. This late breakfasting was becoming an annoying habit, one he hoped to break soon.

"So tell me about the car." Baylie bit into her biscuit, a drip of strawberry jam hanging on her lips. Jayden reached across the table and swiped it off with his thumb. Baylie blushed. "Thanks."

"Welcome. Can't have our editor working with jam stains on her shirt." Jayden cleaned his hand with a napkin, then lifted his own biscuit to his mouth. "Mmm, these never get old."

"Your mother is a gifted baker."

"I know." Jayden took another bite and swallowed. "When I think of all the breakfasts we used to share when my stepfather left us to drive truck cross country, then all the years his stupidity caused us to be apart, I am glad to come full circle and enjoy her food again."

"I never knew about your stepfather until Melanie told me." Frown lines formed on Baylie's forehead. "You never mentioned him in high school."

"He wasn't someone I wanted to talk about." Jayden scooped up some eggs. "But I landed in a better place because of his drinking."

"Here?"

"Peggy's ranch first, then here. Mom suffered though." Jayden laid his fork down. "Now about your car. You want the good news or the bad news first?"

"There's both?"

"Uh, yeah." Jayden resisted a snort. "Your car will drive again. That's the good news."

"The bad?"

"Your timing chain broke. It can be fixed. Won't be cheap. And you may have a wait before the car is ready to hit the road again."

Baylie lowered her head, not looking at him. She closed her eyes and her mouth twisted, as if she fought tears.

"Baylie? What is it?" He reached across and lifted her chin. "Money? Fear? What?"

"My grandfather is in really bad shape." Baylie raised teary eyes to him. "That's why I left so late last night. The hospital called and said he'd had a setback. I took Grandma there one more time before I headed home."

"How was he when you left?"

"Basically, comatose." Baylie drew a ragged breath. "And

with my car in the garage I can't go back and see them."

"Ever ride a Harley?" Jayden watched her react to his question then chuckled under his breath.

"I wouldn't know where to begin."

Jayden sipped his coffee. "We'd start with a helmet, and then show you how to sit on the back."

"You mean ride behind you?"

"Since I know what I'm doing, I think that would be safer than you at the throttle."

Baylie laughed. "You've got that right." She frowned. "How long would a bike take to get to Bend?"

"Not much longer than a car, but my Harley is new and runs good. You won't have to sleep in the juniper, while you wait for a rescue."

"Ha, ha. Very funny." Baylie tasted her coffee. "Could we go next weekend?"

Jayden nodded. "But first we need to catch that intruder."

"How can I help?"

"We'll try surveillance on Thursday night." Jayden searched her face. "Think you'll be caught up on your sleep by then?"

"Yes. I'll make sure of it."

"It's a date."

Baylie entered the office a little while later and found Lissa standing at her desk reading a letter. She looked up. "How are you doing this morning?"

"Much better." Baylie walked to her boss's desk. "Thank you for letting me go see my grandparents."

"Not a problem. Family is important." Lissa's eyes grew soft, a tenderness in them that warmed Baylie's heart "How is your grandfather?"

Baylie swallowed. "Not good, but still here. He took a downward turn last night just before I was heading home. That's how I wound up on the road so late."

"If you need to go back, just say the word." Lissa touched her shoulder. "These people are important in your life. Take every opportunity you have to spend time with them."

"Thank you, Lissa." Baylie breathed deep to hold the tears that threatened to intrude. "Jayden's getting my car repaired. In the meantime, he volunteered to take me back."

"On his Harley?" Lissa's mouth gaped. "You up for that?"

Baylie shrugged. "We'll see."

Lissa's eyes twinkled. "Might be kind of fun."

Baylie studied her boss. She'd taken the words right out of Baylie's mouth. Adventure waited.

Lissa waved the letter. "This is from one of our regular patrons. They wrote to thank us for the wonderful stories we tell in our newsletter."

"Really?" Baylie drew a sharp breath. "Oh, I'm so glad."

Lissa handed the letter to her. "In fact, they want to donate three more horses and funds for their upkeep to the ranch. I'd say your features are doing our little community here a lot of good."

"I needed this today." Baylie felt her lip tremble as she read the kind words. She'd honed her writing skills in college. God could honor that, if nothing else. Maybe He hadn't abandoned her after all.

Thursday after dinner Jayden walked up the hill with Baylie. He carried binoculars, a spotlight, and a small stool. The weapon he might need remained concealed in his jacket. He wasn't supposed to carry one on the ranch, but up here away from the hub of the operation, he felt justified. He didn't believe he'd need it, but night surveillance could turn up meaner foes than a daytime encounter.

"Do you think anyone will show up?" Baylie's breathing accelerated as she climbed higher.

Jayden stopped to give them both a break. His knee throbbed and he didn't want to overdo it. "No way to know. But we'll be ready if someone does."

Intruders on the ranch were most likely curious onlookers or a disgruntled parent, but after his experience with George, Jayden wouldn't take any chances. He didn't want to put anyone in harm's way, especially not Baylie, who had volunteered to take the first shift. Her job was merely to keep watch, not interact or intercept anyone she saw, and call him if she did. What she didn't know was that he would be hiding off-road waiting to ambush whoever might show up. His military training would come in handy here.

A noise behind them made him turn. Tail wagging, tongue lolling as he panted, Duke had his nose to the ground as if he'd caught a scent.

"What do you smell, boy?" Jayden leaned down and stroked Duke's ears. The dog yipped and looked up. "You can keep Baylie company. What do you say?"

As though he understood, Duke leaned into Baylie's leg. She laughed. "I didn't know he had so much energy left in him." She reached a hand down to the dog's head. "He's not the same dog he was before you came home."

"He might have been in mourning for me, as I was for him. We share a bond that goes back to Mr. Mueller's time."

"I believe it." She glanced around. "How much further do we need to go?"

"See that school bus shelter?"

"The structure that looks as if it could collapse any second?" Baylie's voice squeaked.

"You're not going inside, so relax." Jayden walked toward the dilapidated building. He set the stool down at the back, handed her the binoculars, and held out the spotlight. "Your tools, ma'am."

Baylie giggled. "Is this what spies use?"

Jayden resisted an eye roll. "You are to keep watch. Use your phone to text me if you see someone or hear footsteps. In this dry underbrush sounds will carry a ways, and I'm betting whoever is trying to trespass isn't all that careful." Jayden made his voice stern. "Do not engage your suspect."

"Aye, aye, Sarge."

He reached in his pocket and handed her a small canister. "You know how to use pepper spray?"

She took the container from him. "Just aim and push?"

"Basically." He pointed to her slacks. "Clip it to your belt."

"I can handle it." She sat on the stool and Duke flopped at her feet. "Duke knows what to do."

"I just hope he doesn't bark." Jayden waved and turned. "Don't forget to text."

The night grew colder. Baylie untied the sleeves of the hoodie she'd draped across her shoulders and put the garment on, pulling the hood up over her head. She hadn't needed it when they'd hiked up the drive earlier, but she did now. Careful to be quiet, she zipped the front closed. She felt warmer, but a breeze blew in off the hill, making her shiver. She leaned closer to the building, seeking a wind break. She didn't know how she would hear someone sneaking through the brush when only a blast of air made everything around her rustle. Would she be able to tell the difference?

Beside her Duke lifted his head, ears on alert. Baylie grew still. She hadn't expected to feel fear, but Duke's attention to whatever it was he sensed made the little hairs on her arms stand up. She didn't see anything. Should she text Jayden?

Duke rose to his feet. A low growl came from his throat.

Baylie grew more alarmed. Her breathing erratic, she jerked

the phone from her pocket. **Duke senses something**.

A reply appeared. **Yeah. I see something too.**

What do I do?

Nothing. Stay hidden.

Baylie sank back against the wall, trying to breathe normally, but Jayden's words made her shake. Her heart pounded.

Be reasonable. You aren't some loopy teenager falling apart at every little thing. Be an adult.

Easier said than done.

She breathed deep, trying to calm her edginess, and peered into the darkness. The night seemed peaceful, but Duke's attention remained fixed. The waiting grew unbearable. Is this what Jayden did in Afghanistan? She'd never enlist, of that she was certain.

A shout and Jayden's voice sounded to the west of her. Voices rose in the darkness. She strained to see what was going on. Three figures stood in the drive. She recognized Jayden, then Kurt. The third figure didn't seem familiar.

"Baylie! Spotlight please."

She grabbed the spotlight, turned it on, and aimed at the figures she'd seen. Duke let out a howl and took off toward the group. Baylie followed, knees trembling. As she neared the trio, she heard Kurt speaking in firm tones. "You know the rules we keep here."

"My girlfriend is sick over losing Charlie." A man, from what little she could hear, sounded broken. "I only came to look and make sure he's all right." The man's voice wobbled. "But I never found the courage to walk the driveway."

"You tried to enter the garage last week."

"What? No. That wasn't me." The man sounded panicked. "This is my first night here."

"Are you sure?"

"I swear it. But my girlfriend will be disappointed I didn't do more."

"Your girlfriend will have to wait for the hearing. Charlie is no longer in her custody."

"Am I going to jail?"

"Trying to interfere with a child who is a ward of the state is serious business." Kurt pointed down the driveway. "You need to come with me."

As the pair walked away, Jayden came to where she stood. "Kurt suspected who it might be. He also knew when the guy had a night off. That's why we planned the stakeout for tonight."

"That seemed awfully easy." She handed him the spotlight.

"He claims this is his first visit." He turned off the bright light. "So we may have another snoop on our hands. This could get complicated. Some burglars aren't real good at what they do."

"Neither are spies."

CHAPTER FOURTEEN

Early Saturday morning Jayden stood in the parking lot comparing two helmets, trying to decide which would be a better fit for Baylie. One was a spare he'd had in his belongings, the other he found in the ranch's craft room—no idea whose helmet it might have been. Neither was wired for communication, and the long ride ahead of them would grow tiresome if they weren't able to talk between themselves. He'd hoped to use the kit Parker had left behind and create a temporary intercom, but he wasn't succeeding.

"Good morning." Baylie came out of the bunkhouse, dressed in jeans and a long-sleeved sweater. "Ready for our adventure!"

"I'm assuming you don't have a helmet."

"No. Not in my private collection." Baylie frowned. "Why?"

"We won't be able to talk back and forth because these helmets aren't wired."

"I can't just yell in your ear?"

"The wind would carry your voice away." He offered her the pink helmet. "You'll have to poke me when you want to stop."

"Okay." Baylie held up her fingers. "One for food, two for bathroom."

"Right." He glanced at her clothes. "You have a jacket? Or thermals under your jeans?"

Baylie blushed. "I can get a jacket, and add an extra layer under the sweater, but I don't have thermals."

"You might get cold riding that far."

"I'll just scoot closer to you. Your body heat will probably be enough."

Jayden fought the retort he wanted to say, the warmth generated by her comment making him uncomfortable. "No, you don't want to scoot closer to me." He pointed to the seat. "You sit back here on the flat section and keep your body straight. The backrest is for you." He made a sweeping motion with his hand. "When we do turns you want to tip toward my back. Don't tilt into the turn."

"What do I hold on to?"

"My waist, if you need it. The seat side, otherwise." Jayden pointed to the backrest. "This is for you to lean against. It's called a sissy bar, but it will make you more comfortable. Keep your feet on the pegs at all times. Never put them down." He touched the exhaust. "This gets hot and will melt your boots." He looked at her feet and groaned inwardly. Shoes with shoelaces. Not going to happen. He glanced up. "Do you have any boots? Shoelaces can come untied in the intensity of the wind and get tangled in the brakes."

"Yikes." Baylie glanced down at her shoes. "I didn't think to wear my boots. Important?"

"Much safer."

"Riding boots are all I have." Baylie worried her lip in her teeth. "As in horse riding lesson boots."

Jayden nodded. "They'll work just fine."

Baylie's relief whooshed out. "Whew."

"When I slant into a turn, look over my shoulder that's on the side of the turn. Don't lean into the tilt. Stay neutral."

"Like a sack of potatoes?"

He nodded. "Exactly. Any jerky movements or anticipation of the turn could send us tumbling."

Baylie's face reflected her panic. "I'm not sure about this."

"We don't have to go if you don't want to."

She shrugged.

"You'll need these." Jayden pulled a second pair of gloves from his pocket and handed them to her. "I promise to stop every twenty miles or so to see how you are doing."

"If I poke?"

"I will immediately pull over." Jayden swallowed. This was going to prove interesting. He'd have to stay focused to keep his mind on the road and not on the girl riding against his back.

"Let me go get my jacket and add another layer under the sweater." She started to turn away, then stopped. "Can I take time to call Grandma? Let her know we're coming?"

"Good idea."

She pivoted and headed toward the bunkhouse. "Be right back."

"Find your boots." Jayden watched her go. The girl he'd known still had spirit. He liked that. He needed to watch himself.

Kurt stepped out of the ranch house and strode toward him. "Good morning. You ready to ride?"

"Taking Baylie to Bend so she can visit her grandmother."

"That's quite a trip."

"Yes, it is. The highway is pretty straight and usually not heavily trafficked." Jayden fought the smile that threatened to warm his cheeks. "But her car is still out of commission and she's worried about her grandfather."

"She must be really worried to ride that far on a motorcycle." Kurt straightened, a lop-sided grin on his face. "Or excited to be riding with you."

"I doubt that's the reason." Jayden avoided Kurt's gaze. "She says she'll be okay."

"Probably more than okay." Kurt winked and pointed to the barn. "I've got a mare and foal anxious for their breakfast, so I better get to it."

"Lady will be hungry." Jayden lifted a hand. "Give her a neck scratch for me. See you later, Kurt."

Kurt turned back. "By the way, I meant to tell you. Charlie's mom said she never sent her boyfriend to rescue him."

"You believe her?"

"Yes. Apparently, the man is a lot like George." Kurt's face clouded. "He intended to use the child as collateral to get the mother to leave with him."

"Boy, does that sound familiar." Jayden gritted his teeth. "Why do women fall for such losers?"

"They're mothers." Kurt touched his shoulder. "They'll do just about anything to protect their young."

"The whole mama bear syndrome?"

"Now you're getting it." This time Kurt walked away and didn't look back.

Baylie appeared again wearing a fleece-lined jacket, a knit cap on her head, and a pair of gloves dangling from her fingers. She smiled like a cat who had found the missing super ball in the corner.

"Did you reach your grandmother?'

"No answer this morning, but I want to go anyway." She stopped at the bike and examined the seat, checking out the hand holds on both sides. "I hope I can do this and not fall off."

"I'll take the first stretch slow so you can find your balance." Jayden adjusted his mirror. "We should get going soon."

"Think I'll be warm enough?" She flashed the front of her jacket. "I'm really warm right now."

"You'll cool off when we hit fifty miles an hour and the wind is crawling down your spine."

Baylie paled. "Makes me shiver just thinking about it."

Jayden laughed. "You'll be fine." He pointed to the helmet. "Will that fit over your hat?"

"I didn't think about that." She adjusted the knit hat and lowered the helmet over it. "Tight squeeze but it works."

"Okay." Jayden held back his snicker. She looked like a cherub bundled up for a snow outing. "The knit will provide extra cushion for your head if you hit the pavement."

"You are not giving me confidence here."

"Hop on behind me." He raised his right leg carefully and

stepped over the seat, tucked his folded cane in his saddlebag, and waited. Baylie slid onto the back and positioned herself close to him. He pointed where she should put her feet and started the engine. The Harley puffed, followed by a roar, making Baylie squeal. "Hang on."

He rumbled out the driveway, taking the hill slowly. Baylie kept her balance as they climbed. When he reached the highway, he stopped. "Okay, so far?"

"Yes." Excitement tinged Baylie's voice. "This is kinda fun."

"Good." Jayden revved the engine and eased onto the highway. He found a straight stretch and gradually increased his speed. The faster he drove the tighter Baylie's hands gripped his waist, her chin resting on his left shoulder. He straightened and focused on the road, forcing himself to ignore the girl who could prove to be a distraction. For safety, he needed to remain alert.

Baylie found the hum of the motorcycle almost musical as Jayden put miles beneath their tires. Her legs were cold, but the man in front provided sufficient windbreak to keep her from freezing. The extra layers he had insisted upon proved wise. The leather gloves he'd loaned her were a lifesaver. Comfortable, she could enjoy the ride.

She took advantage of her position sitting at his back and studied the scenery. Landscapes she'd never noticed when driving rose up from the barren hills like sculptures finely carved by a gifted artist—the same hand who had designed her. Only these creations accepted their placement without protest. She had dared to challenge hers, and look what it cost her. She returned to the landscape, willing the memories to fade.

The high desert offered a savage beauty, its stark barrenness a canvas for lesser flora and fauna, plants and animals ignored by those who cultivated more delicate varieties. Sage brush covered sandy patches. Juniper, gnarled by hot summers and brutal winters, stood in fierce contempt of the setting in which it was forced to thrive. An occasional cluster of horses appeared among the patches of vegetation. Once in a while she glimpsed the tail of an antelope, or was it a white-tailed deer?

The motorcycle rushed by, leaving the creatures in a blur. She only wished her past would do the same. That her memories would fade, and God would resume his rightful place. She'd lost so much.

The engine slowed and Baylie sat up straighter, doing her part to remain neutral in the seat. Jayden had warned her not to anticipate turns, slowdowns, and stops because she could move in such a way as to throw off his maneuvers and dump both of them. She'd anticipated plenty of turns and slowdowns in college, and her reactions to those had left her in a heap of tangled troubles not even God could fix. At least here on the bike she could control her movements and help maintain balance. If only it had been this easy then.

Jayden pulled off the road and brought the bike to a stop. He put both his feet firmly on the ground. Removing his helmet, he spoke over his left shoulder. "Climb off and we'll stretch our legs."

She swung her leg over the back and stepped down from the floorboard. "I think I'm getting the rhythm of this."

"You've done well for a beginner." Jayden climbed off, set the kickstand, and moved to the back of the bike. He reached into a saddlebag that hung beneath her seat and offered a bottle of water.

"Thanks." She unscrewed the top and took a sip. "I didn't know I was riding shotgun over our supplies."

Jayden grinned. "Raiding the saddlebag could have tipped us over so I remained mute."

"Trust me. I'm not brave enough to do acrobatics back there."

"Granola bar?" Jayden held a wrapped protein snack in his hand. "These are chocolate, peanuts, and raisins."

"Don't have to ask twice." Baylie smiled and took the

proffered food. She unwrapped it and took a bite. "Yum. Tastes more like a dessert than a nourishing food bar."

Jayden nodded, unwrapping his own. "That's why I like these." He bit the end. "Healthy snack is promised on the package, sheer goodness on the inside."

"Did the military provide these when you were deployed?"

"Similar." Jayden's forehead wrinkled as if remembering something unpleasant. "But we didn't complain."

"Do you miss Afghanistan?"

"I miss the soldiers, the sense of doing something great to help an oppressed people. I don't miss the country, the homesickness, nor the hot days and brutal nights."

"Sounds like eastern Oregon."

Jayden laughed. "Not much different in many ways. No antelope though. Afghanistan makes this landscape look like an oasis."

"Or wild horses?"

Jayden shook his head. "None of those." He pointed off across the road. "If you need to powder your nose, there's a rest stop, of sorts."

"Reserved for me?" Baylie turned to the wayside, the square block house standing like a deserted bomb shelter. She wondered if she really needed to use it. "I hope it's clean."

"You are welcome to try sagebrush." He called over his shoulder, the wind catching his laugh and carrying it away. "I've got a juniper reserved in my name. Be right back."

Jayden figured they'd come about halfway when he pulled off at the wayside. The dilapidated structure didn't offer much in the way of luxury, but it would afford Baylie some privacy if she needed a pit stop. Most of the sites along this stretch were merely remnants of people's earlier attempts to survive, the inhabitants staying long enough to go broke and move on.

The last leg of their journey would be a fairly straight stretch, the kind that can lull an unsuspecting rider to sleep. He'd warn Baylie to stay alert. He didn't need her drifting off and sagging in the seat behind him. He planned to goose the engine every once in a while, to keep them both on their guard. At least here he didn't have to look for snipers, or watch for IED's, and wait for the bombs to explode. Made for an enjoyable trip, despite the bleak countryside.

Baylie emerged from the small building and crossed the highway with care, though no cars could be seen either direction for miles.

"Feel better?" Jayden squinted her direction. "The little stone building and its hidden inhabitants didn't try to snatch you?"

"Yes, I feel better. Thanks for the privacy." Baylie's eyes danced. "Though I had a hard time convincing the snake to leave."

"Did he rattle his thanks?"

"No, he spoke in a forked tongue."

Jayden groaned, then picked up his helmet. "Ready for the last leg of our trip?"

"How much further, do you know?"

"Fifty miles or so." Jayden put on his gloves and climbed aboard the bike. "We've made good time."

"Yes." Baylie glanced at her watch. "Another hour or so?"

He nodded. "Just don't get sleepy and drift off. You have to remain upright and neutral to the flow of the motorcycle."

"I'm wide awake." Baylie gestured around her. "Plenty of countryside to see."

"It will be more of what we just passed. Rather barren and deserted."

"That's okay. I want to drink it all in."

Once Baylie was situated, Jayden revved the motor to life. He lowered his visor and checked to see if his passenger had her feet where they belonged and her helmet secure. "Ready?"

She smiled through her visor and nodded. Her hands rested on his waist. She leaned forward as if she'd been riding behind him all her life. Jayden breathed deep. He could get used to this.

The facility loomed large and unfriendly as Baylie climbed off the bike and headed for the entrance, Jayden at her side. She dreaded what she might find here today. What she might learn of her grandfather's condition. Her grandmother had not called or left a message at the ranch all week. Baylie hoped that was a good sign.

She checked in at the lobby and got clearance to proceed to her grandmother's apartment, assured that Grandma Laura should be there. When she knocked, she prayed for good news, afraid of what the truth might bring.

Grandma Laura's eyes pooled when she opened the door. "Oh, Baylie. You sweet girl." The woman reached forward and hugged her, then stepped back. "Please come in. You are a sight for a tired old lady."

"You remember Jayden Clarke from high school?"

Grandma Laura studied Jayden for a moment. "I do! But I wouldn't have known you, son, you've become such a man." She winked at Baylie. "Wow!"

Jayden stepped in behind her and closed the door. "It's nice to see you again, Mrs. Levine."

"Come sit down, both of you." Grandma gestured to the sofa. "I'll make us some tea."

"How's Grandpa Joseph?" Baylie sat next to Jayden, her focus on the elderly woman whose steps today seemed feebler than they had last weekend. "Any improvement?"

Grandma stiffened at her question, then lifted the teapot and poured three cups at the counter. "Here, Jayden, can you carry this tray for me?" She set the teapot down. "I can't walk and carry something like this anymore."

Jayden sprang to her side. "Glad to help out." He carried the tray to the coffee table next to the sofa. Grandma followed, settling herself on an armchair nearby. "Help yourselves. I've got cookies."

"Grandma, how's Grandpa?" Baylie repeated, her voice tense. She studied the woman's movements. "Have you heard anything more?"

"Yes, I've been to see him every day this week." Grandma's eyes filled. "He doesn't know I'm there."

"No improvement?"

Grandma shook her head. "No, he's slipping away more each day."

Baylie clutched her middle as if she'd been punched. She tried to breathe, but air refused to fill her lungs. She'd prayed so hard. Every day.

But God hadn't listened.

Again.

No surprise there. He didn't seem to have time for Baylie anymore. She couldn't blame Him, not after what she'd done at the university. But her grandfather shouldn't have to pay for her mistakes. Anger rose from her throat, unspoken words aimed heavenward. *He's not the one You need to punish. I am. When will You forgive me?*

"Grandma, is there anything I can do?" Baylie's voice failed, her words wobbly and frail. "Anyone I need to contact?"

Grandma shook her head. "I've called those who need to know. I didn't call you because you were here last weekend." She looked at her hands. "I doubt he will last the week."

"No." Baylie sagged against the back of the sofa. Grandpa was dying and nothing she could say, no bargain with God she could make, would reach the ears of the most Almighty God. She would have to live with her shame the rest of her life.

"Baylie."

The voice startled her. She'd been so lost in thought.

Jayden took her hands and made her look at him. "Call Lissa and tell her what's happening. I think you should stay with your grandmother."

Baylie studied the sincerity she saw in Jayden's face, but she was more taken by the warmth of his hands wrapped around her fingers. His tenderness would be her undoing if she wasn't careful, and she didn't want to cry in front of her grandmother. Grandma's strength had reached its limit. Baylie refused to add to her burdens.

"Can you call her for me?" Baylie feared she'd lose it on the phone. Jayden would do a better job. "Please?"

CHAPTER FIFTEEN

After calling the ranch and making arrangements with Lissa and Kurt, Jayden left Baylie with her grandmother and started the long trip home. She'd call him when she felt she could leave her grandmother, or if the inevitable happened, when she could tell Grandma Laura goodbye and leave without worrying about her grandmother's loneliness with Joseph gone.

Jayden worried about Baylie's perception of her circumstances. When he'd asked if they could pray together, something they used to do in high school over every situation, Baylie just shook her head.

"God's not listening to me anymore. My prayers would fall on deaf ears."

Shocked by her response, Jayden had prayed alone. Not only for Mr. Levine and his wife, but for Baylie.

What had happened to this girl who had been the champion of everything spiritual? Who saw no obstacle too great for a miracle from God? Something in her recent past kept her from the enthusiastic go-getter he'd known earlier. What secret did she carry? What pain? He knew well the trauma that could scar one's mind and leave the victim overwhelmed by regret. He'd seen enough of that in Afghanistan.

Jayden gunned the bike's motor and zipped along the highway toward home. He and Baylie needed to have a conversation soon. He'd known his mother's prayers had covered him while deployed and had assumed Baylie's petitions had held his welfare before God as well. So far, he'd managed to avoid triggers of the post traumatic stress that threatened him in darker moods.

The ride home took less time than the trip over, with Jayden able to ride faster without his passenger riding behind. He knew the road better, too, so straight stretches and little traffic afforded him freedom to test the bike's strengths and hone his own skills as a rider. As the heat coming off the desert grew uncomfortable, Jayden's skin begged for relief. He sped up, allowing the bike to create its own wind, the breeze generated by the air flow bringing a welcome coolness.

He slowed as he pulled off the highway and rode down the winding driveway toward the ranch house. Horses grazed in the pastures, cows stood swishing their tails. Lady stood quietly in the paddock, the foal nudging her for an afternoon snack. Everything seemed as peaceful as when he and Baylie had left this morning.

Then he stopped.

A shiny green Harley sat parked next to the duplex. Parker? Why hadn't he said he was coming? Jayden maneuvered his bike next to the other one, removed his helmet, and beelined to the apartment. Finding no one, he pivoted toward the kitchen. Duke barked his greeting, tail wagging and legs bouncing as the dog came to Jayden. He reached down and fondled the soft velvety ears. "Good boy."

From the doorway he heard laughter, Parker's deep baritone carrying above the sounds of pots and pans clanging. Jayden breathed deep. Was he okay with this? He had hoped he and his mother could spend time as mother and son, finding the bond they'd once shared. Parker might prove an obstacle to that plan. Jayden wasn't sure he was ready. He squared his shoulders. How many sandwiches needed bread buttered this time?

Jayden entered the kitchen and found Parker at the double sink next to a young boy. Parker had his sleeves rolled up to the elbows, hands covered in soapy water. The kid had a towel. They were laughing as if cleaning dirty tableware was the most hilarious occupation anyone could have.

"What's so funny?" Jayden drew nearer to the sinks.

Parker whipped around, the silly grin on his face disappearing as he shouted. "Hey! You're back! How was the trip to Bend?"

"Uneventful for me. Heart wrenching for Baylie."

Mom came from the pantry. "Jayden?"

"Hi, Mom." Jayden leaned in for her hug.

He looked at Parker who still waited for an answer. "No issues, really. Baylie made it there safe and sound. I left her with her grandmother because her grandfather isn't doing well."

"I'm so sorry to hear that." Parker's sincere concern made Jayden feel less threatened by his friend's presence. Parker pointed to the sink. "Kevin here put in the wrong soap and we had mountains of suds climbing the walls."

"I thought I was going to lose them in a cloud of bubbles." Mom looked at him. "Have you eaten?"

"Granola bars and water."

"Let me heat some of the chili I fixed for lunch." Mom grabbed a pan. "Dinner's only an hour away."

"I can wait for dinner, Mom." Jayden propped himself against the counter. "So Parker, how long you here for?"

"I wanted to see if you had time to ride." Parker studied a spot on the floor.

Jayden grinned inwardly. A trip across the Cascades to see if he had time to ride? Right.

Parker caught his eye roll. "I tried to call you on your cell this morning, but it wouldn't go through."

"I was already on the road with Baylie. My phone was turned off." Jayden straightened. "You know anything about timing chains?"

"Some. You having trouble with one?"

"Baylie's car is in the shop with a broken timing chain. That's why I biked her to Bend." Jayden studied his friend. "How long should repairs take?"

"Depends." Parker dried his hands on a towel. "They pull the engine to get to it."

"I will have to go back to Bend to bring Baylie home, and I hoped to take her car for a test drive. She doesn't feel safe driving that highway after she broke down midway."

"Can't say I blame her."

Jayden glanced toward his mother who busied herself at the stove. She appeared disinterested, when in truth she obviously hung on every word. "I could ride tomorrow." He smirked. "Baylie won't be back for a week."

"Melanie, you want to try out a Harley?" Parker wore a twisted grin.

"Seriously?" Mom stared at both of them. "I'd love to."

"Then it's set. Tomorrow after Sunday dinner." Parker picked up his towel.

Jayden couldn't resist an ornery tease. "Which of us you going to ride behind?"

Mom stared at him, a twinkle in her eye. "Who says I'm the one riding behind?"

Baylie helped her grandmother into the facility van. After Jayden left yesterday, she had prepared a light meal for Grandma Laura, cleared the dishes, and sat with the woman on her sofa sharing stories of Grandpa Joseph. She would have liked to go see him, but Grandma said she'd already visited that morning and didn't feel strong enough to go back. "He doesn't know me, child, and it hurts to see him so confused."

"We'll go first thing in the morning, then." Baylie prepared them both a cup of chamomile tea. She had needed to calm herself after riding with Jayden. She hoped he made good time on the return trip. He'd left early enough to do so, but after her own car problems, Jayden's safety on the long empty road worried her. She should pray, but what good would it do?

This morning Grandma Laura seemed stronger, her impatience to get going making her brusque, a change from her usual complacent personality. The phone rang and she answered. Putting the receiver back, she grew more agitated. "Let's go now."

Baylie understood her pain. Grandma Laura must be beside herself, watching her husband continue to fail and nothing could be done. Baylie hurt, too, seeing her beloved grandfather on the brink of eternity. How would she cope with the loss? These two had been a constant source of strength throughout her childhood and teen years. Now, as an adult, she'd hoped to repay their dedication by being there for them.

The ride to the medical facility took fifteen minutes. Grandma Laura had grown quiet, fewer than two words escaping her lips. She glanced at Baylie often, little thoughtful side glimpses as if she wanted to say something, but didn't. As they climbed from the van, Grandma squeezed her hand. "Thank you for being here. It's so much easier than facing this alone."

"I'm here for you, Grandma."

Grandma's gaze searched hers. "Pray with me?"

Baylie swallowed the lump in her throat and nodded, feeling like the hypocrite she was. At least Grandma would think Baylie prayed from faith, and not from a heart steeped in past sins. She took her grandmother's hands and bowed her head. "Father, we. . ." Baylie glanced up to find Grandma's gaze upon her.

"Go on, child." Grandma urged her. "God is listening."

Baylie hesitated. She couldn't admit her sin here, not when Grandma was counting on her to bring Grandpa Joseph before the Lord. *Please God, don't hold my past sins and ongoing problems over that dear man's fate.*

"Baylie?" Her grandmother stood there expectantly, as though waiting for the words she longed to hear.

With a deep breath and a nod, Baylie spoke, phrases she'd used many times in the past tumbled off her tongue. "We humbly acknowledge our helplessness to change Grandpa Joseph's condition, but we believe you have that power. We ask if it be your will, that Grandpa will be restored to us, and if that is not to be, that you will hold him in your arms as he enters eternity. Give us strength, Lord, for whatever comes."

"Amen." Grandma's voice shook. She glanced up. "Thank you. Now we are in God's hands." The woman straightened. "Let's go in."

Baylie trembled as they navigated the corridors to the dreaded hospital room. *If he's already dead, I'll never be able to live with myself.* Outside the door, Grandma stopped. "Let me go in first. I'll call you when I think the time is right."

Baylie frowned as the older woman entered ahead of her. What was she doing? Baylie found a chair in the hallway and sat, waiting for her summons. The minutes ticked by with no sign of Grandma.

She studied her phone. Who could she call? Sketchy service on this side of the mountains continually plagued her. Not that she had many people to call, but it would be nice to be able to do so if the occasion arose.

"Baylie?"

She tucked her phone in her back pocket and stood. The look on her grandmother's face made Baylie shiver. Was Grandfather gone? She stepped toward the door. "How is he?"

Grandma Laura's mouth trembled. "That phone call before we left?"

"Grandma?"

The older woman nodded. "That was the doctor letting me know Joseph had joined Jesus about an hour ago."

Baylie slumped against the door casing, knees buckling as she staggered to take in the truth. Grandpa Joseph was gone. God hadn't heard her prayers. Again. Bitter tears filled her eyes as she stood in the spotlight of her sin. Now Grandpa Joseph had joined the list of those she'd failed. Her shame mocked her. "I'm sorry, Grandma. I'm so sorry."

Grandma Laura wrapped her arms about Baylie's shoulders. "There's nothing to be sorry for. We should rejoice. Joseph is now with the angels, receiving his reward. He has won the victory."

Baylie couldn't stop her tears. "But we'll miss him so much. Didn't God know we wanted him here?"

Grandma kissed her on the top of her head. "Of course He did. But that was not His plan, it was ours. And as much as I wanted to keep him here, Joseph deserves to stand before his Savior and hear the words, 'well done.'"

"Well done?"

"The words from the book of Matthew. Well done, thou good and faithful servant. Enter into the joy of your Lord." Grandma's face grew serene, a smile firmly in place. "Joseph deserved to hear those words." She sighed. "We will mourn his loss, but we will go on."

Baylie's shame overwhelmed her. God would never say 'well done' to her. Not now. Not ever. She wiped her eyes. "Can I see him?"

Grandma nodded. "Yes, he is ready."

They entered the room together, Baylie clutching Grandma Laura's arm. Her grandfather lay in his bed as if asleep, hands folded across his chest. Baylie thought she was going to be sick. "How long will they leave him here?"

"Not long. I asked them to leave him until we arrived. But they will be in to take him soon."

Baylie wrestled with confusion. "Grandma, why did we pray outside before we entered when you already knew he was dead?"

"For you, Baylie. I sensed you needed to prepare yourself for this visit. By talking to God, we allowed Him to sustain our spirits, too. God isn't in the business of abandoning His children in their hour of need. You asked God to give us strength, remember?"

"I do."

"And is He?" Though Grandma remained solemn, her eyes smiled. The warmth coming from her soothed Baylie like an insulated blanket.

"He is." Baylie shook at this new revelation. Perhaps God had not forgotten her. Hope swelled in her soul. She longed to be back in the fellowship of her Lord. To also be told well done. Was it possible?

A noise caught their attention and they turned to the door. A white-coated assistant stood waiting, a gurney at his side. "Sorry to interrupt you ladies, but we need to remove Mr. Levine from this room."

Grandma took Baylie's hand. "Yes, of course you do. Give us one more minute?"

The assistant nodded and stepped back into the hall.

"Come Baylie, and say your good-byes. I've already had my time with him." Grandma pulled her to the bed. "This is the last time we will see him this side of heaven."

Baylie came near the bed. She touched Grandpa's cold hand, then leaned forward to kiss him on the forehead. "Thank you for all the love you gave me. Because of you I made it." Tears welled, streaming down her cheeks, one landing on her grandfather's hand. "Save me a spot next to you in heaven." She turned to her grandmother. "Thank you for letting me say good-bye."

"Ready to go?"

Baylie nodded. Grandfather wasn't here. He'd gone on ahead of them. But one day she hoped to see him again.

Jayden grinned at his mother as she donned the extra helmet he'd handed her. Like Baylie, she looked nervous and apprehensive, but she climbed on his Harley and turned the ignition as if she'd started an engine a hundred times. "Have you done this before?"

"It's been a while." She laughed. "Many years ago, with your dad. Before you were born."

"Seriously?"

Mom nodded, a conspiratorial look in her eyes. "We both biked early in our marriage. When your father deployed the first time, I was pregnant, so we sold the bikes."

Parker walked over to his bike, casting Jayden a goofy grin. "So which of us are you riding behind?"

Jayden didn't know what to say. "Why don't I stay here and you two go out and enjoy the afternoon?"

"No, Jayden. I'll ride behind." Mom started to dismount.

"I insist." He handed her his helmet and reached for the one she wore. "My helmet is radio connected to Parker's. You can communicate through the headset."

"But what will you do while we're gone?"

Jayden squeezed her shoulder. "I need to read more of Dad's letters but haven't had time." He stepped away. "Go for it, Biker Babe."

She blushed, adjusted the face shield, and glanced at Parker who started his engine and pulled ahead of her. His mother maneuvered the driveway like she'd been doing it all her life. What else did he not know?

He turned toward the bunkhouse, Duke joining him. Kurt stood in the doorway of the office.

"Was that Melanie riding up the driveway?" Kurt's eyes were wide, eyebrows raised.

"The one and the same." Jayden laughed at Kurt's dazed expression. "Surprised me, too."

"Wow, our cook is a motorcycle mama."

Jayden punched Kurt's shoulder. "Never know."

"I guess." Kurt held out a message slip. "Baylie called to say her grandfather died, and the funeral is Tuesday." He sighed at the gravity of his words. "Poor kid."

"I was afraid of this." Jayden exhaled. "Did she sound okay?"

"She's anxious to get back to the ranch, but I told her to take some time with her grandmother." He looked at Jayden. "When is her car going to be ready?"

"I don't know." Jayden re-read the message. "But I can go back to Bend and get her."

"I think her grandmother is giving her some things, so she'll need more than a saddlebag to bring it here."

Jayden nodded. "Maybe I could borrow the ranch's Suburban?"

"I'll talk to Lissa." Kurt turned toward the ranch house. "See you later."

Jayden entered the empty apartment, his mother's motorcycle ride on his mind. Parker would keep them safe, but what was this thing they seemed to have between them? Obviously, Mom was okay with it. A bike ride could cement the deal. Jayden frowned. Slow it down, Mr. Macgregor. She's my mom.

He lifted out the packet of letters and found one dated the week before his dad was killed. He swallowed, not sure if he was ready to read his father's last written words. Had Dad known he was headed into enemy fire?

Dear Melanie,

The Taliban have been active recently. Scouting missions report sightings of small bands of armed gunmen skirting the hills.

I continue to meet with my men for prayer and Bible study. One of my fellow soldiers, Foster Blake, accepted the claims of Jesus last night. He is close friends with a soldier in my unit named

Kurt McKintrick. Foster's mother, Peggy, lives somewhere near where you are. Runs a rescue ranch for horses, I understand.

Keep my men in your prayers. The enemy is always on our minds.

Love to you and Jayden,
Jordan

Jayden re-read the letter. How sad to think of his dad alive and active, knowing at any minute his life or the life of one of his men could be snuffed out. What a responsibility to carry the eternal outcome of the souls of his men on his heart at all times.

Jayden felt ashamed of his own lack of attention to the eternal futures of his fellow soldiers. His last moments on the battlefield resurrected themselves in his mind. A sensation of cold breezed by his neck. As the terror he'd faced raised its ugly head, his breathing grew shallow. The bang of his heart against his breastbone choked off his ability to swallow. He inhaled slow, deep intakes of air, hoping to stem the rising panic. Hands on his knees, he bent forward, letting blood flow to his brain. Moments ticked by as he fought for control. The horror of all he'd endured slowly withdrew. Covered in sweat, he chilled as his body temperature returned to normal. He needed a shower.

Had he failed his fellow soldiers? All he had cared about was being the best soldier he knew how to be and to honor the memory of his father. Now he realized Dad had been on a completely different path. Jayden wished he'd understood that sooner.

An image of Baylie crossed his mind. Was whatever had destroyed her faith in prayer the reason she suddenly quit writing? He remembered how faithfully she'd sent letters from college, telling him about her studies, agonizing over how much she wished he'd gone to school with her and not joined the Marines, and lamenting how overwhelmed and alone she felt in a huge university.

She'd needed him.

He returned the letter to its envelope and added it back to the stack. He hadn't been the soldier his dad had been, but he could endeavor to be the man his father modeled. He was more convinced than ever that returning to the ranch had been pre-ordained, and the fact that Baylie had been hired here placed her directly in his path for a reason.

He understood the disappointment of not living up to one's expectations, of not fulfilling a lifelong dream. He'd not succeeded in following in his dad's footsteps on the battlefield, but the few letters he'd read told him Dad's objective had pointed a different direction. Jayden could step into that role, a counselor for the burdened. He'd experienced loss, knew how it felt to be left alone. Perhaps Baylie could be his first objective. Together they could conquer their failures. A fair exchange.

"Lord, I believe in your power. Reveal the source of Baylie's agony and help her heal. Amen."

CHAPTER SIXTEEN

THE FOLLOWING FRIDAY BAYLIE STOOD IN her grandmother's apartment waiting for Jayden to arrive. Fighting the unbidden moisture threatening her composure, she hugged her grandmother goodbye. "Are you sure you'll be all right?" She rested her hands on the older woman's shoulders, memorizing every line on her forehead, every wrinkle in her cheek. How she would miss this dear lady. "This facility will feel quite different with Grandpa Joseph gone."

"Joseph and I lived our lives with expectancy." Grandma kissed her cheek, then stroked it with a gentle caress. She spoke in a soft, controlled voice. "We knew one of us could be gone quickly, without warning. Joseph said men usually go first so he made me promise that I would go on and live life. Not mourn him."

"But without him, will you be able to cope?" Baylie couldn't imagine herself remaining as strong as her grandmother in the wake of death. "This room won't feel deserted?"

"I will learn how to cope, Sweetheart." Grandma's smile sagged a little. "The memories are here to keep me company."

A knock at the door interrupted them. Baylie went to open it and found Jayden standing there, a transport cart behind him. Baylie laughed. "I see you came prepared."

"Kurt said you had stuff to bring back, so I made sure we could transport it without killing ourselves." Jayden offered an arm to Grandma, wrapping her in a brief hug. "I'm so sorry for your loss, Mrs. Levine. Grandpa Joseph was a kind man."

"Thank you, Jayden." Grandma's face lit up with a smile. "We will see Joseph again." She touched his shoulder. "Thank you for making sure Baylie got here safely and is going home in your care."

"My pleasure to do so." He nodded toward the wheeled

flatbed behind him. "I went to the front desk and asked if I could borrow something with wheels."

Grandma stepped up beside Baylie, eyes twinkling. "I do believe you could empty the entire apartment with that."

"No, ma'am, that was never my intent, but I know Baylie." Jayden cast her a lop-sided grin. "The front desk made me pay a deposit on the cart, so don't get any ideas."

"Jayden!"

Grandma laughed. "She's only taking a few family heirlooms with her. The chiming clock from our mantle, the cross-stitched rocker that belonged to my mother, and a small curio cabinet. I trust you aren't riding the motorcycle?"

"No, not this trip. Baylie's boss loaned her the ranch Suburban." Jayden glanced at Baylie. "But only for the day." He stepped further into the room. "We should load your things. Daylight is waning."

Grandma turned and pointed at a stack in the corner. "That little pile over there is for Baylie."

"Not as much as I thought there would be." Jayden pulled the wagon closer to the items and loaded the assortment of mementoes. He faced them. "Is this everything?"

"Yes." Grandma looked over the room. "I don't see anything else."

Baylie hugged her grandmother. "I wish I could load you in the van."

"Not this trip, dear." Grandma took her hands in her own. "I have friends here with whom I will enjoy spending time. This is my home."

"I'll visit."

Grandma nodded at Jayden. "He's always welcome, too."

"Thank you, Mrs. Levine." Jayden pulled the wagon toward the door. "I'll look forward to seeing you again, soon." He glanced at Baylie. "Ready?"

Baylie nodded. "Let's be on our way."

Within a half hour they had arranged the pieces of furniture in the back of the SUV and secured the smaller items in and around the remaining space.

"I'll return the wagon to the front desk." Jayden walked away, the small flatbed following him like an obedient puppy. "Don't want to lose my deposit."

Baylie sighed, heart hurting for her grandmother. She promised herself she'd return soon and get Grandma out for an excursion. When Jayden reached the driver's door a few minutes later, Baylie hopped in the passenger side. She glanced his way. "Any word on my car?"

"Actually, yes. They returned the engine under the hood where it belongs and said it should be ready for pickup on Monday."

"Any idea what the bill will be?"

Jayden grinned. "Probably big enough to keep you working full time for at least another year."

"Great." Baylie sagged against the seat. "I'll have to budget carefully for a while."

Jayden started the ignition. "You'll be fine." He popped the SUV into gear. "You have friends in high places."

Baylie looked at him. What did that mean?

Jayden enjoyed the drive with Baylie back to the ranch. Unlike the ride on the motorcycle, he could talk to her in the comfort of a truck cab with a bench seat and air conditioning. He searched the digital readouts of the radio seeking some quiet background music. "Anything you'd like to listen to?"

"I don't listen to the radio much." Baylie reached for the search button. "Channels here are often static because they are broadcast from the other side of the mountains."

A voice popped up and then disappeared. Jayden glanced her way. "That sounded like a channel."

"Let me try to get back to it." Baylie punched the back button. Soon the voice came on and music with a rock beat played. "How's that? Too lively?"

"No, it will be fine." Jayden tapped the steering wheel, searching for a way to lead into the conversation he wanted to have with Baylie. Finally, he decided to mention their past. "How do you think the youth group is doing at our old church?"

"New Hope Community?" Baylie glanced at him, narrowed eyes skeptical. "I have no idea."

"That group was so much fun. So many activities to welcome newbies and make us a cohesive unit of teens serving Christ."

"It was." Baylie stared out her window as if reliving memories in her mind. "Great prayer walks in the town."

"You were always calling us to prayer, remember?" Jayden kept his eyes on the road, but he could sense the tension rising. "We had many answers to our petitions."

"We did." Baylie clasped her hands together. "God heard us in our innocence."

"When I volunteered to pray with you for your grandfather, you surprised me with your answer." Jayden cast her a quick side glance. "That's not the Baylie I remember."

"I'm not the Baylie you remember."

"What do you mean?" Jayden resisted glancing her way again, for fear of shutting her down. If only she would open up. "Baylie Summers no longer exists? Or Baylie Summers has given up on prayer?"

Baylie sat silent for a few minutes. Jayden thought she wasn't going to answer him. Finally, she huffed. "I didn't stay true to my faith in college." She breathed deep, the air ragged and halting. "I asked for forgiveness, but God has yet to do so."

Jayden frowned. "That doesn't sound like the God I know."

"I really messed up, Jayden." Baylie looked out the window. "Big time."

Jayden searched for the right words. "What makes you think God hasn't forgiven you?" He couldn't imagine what terrible sin Baylie might have committed to kick her out of favor with the God of the universe.

"He doesn't answer my prayers anymore."

Jayden looked across the cab. "How so?"

"Like this week. I had prayed Grandpa Levine would pull out of his stroke and return to live with Grandma." Baylie's breath caught, the suppressed swallow visible as she fought it. "But God took him anyway. My prayers were ignored."

"But Baylie, some things aren't within our power to change. Your grandfather had lived a long and fruitful life. God had ordained this as his time to move on to heaven."

"Then what's the use of praying? If God doesn't hear us or answer us? Why should we bother? Tell me that."

"He asks us to pray. He says not to be anxious over anything, but to make our requests known." Jayden swallowed hard. He was heading into unchartered territory. "I believe praying gives us peace as we walk through our circumstances."

"Peace." Baylie tapped on the window. "But the person you pray for still loses his life."

"Not always. God has a will, you know."

"No doubt about that."

"And if we pray seeking His will in a situation, we know that the end result was what He intended from the beginning."

"So no matter what we pray, God does it His way. Is that it?"

"No, we've had the privilege of communing with a high and holy God to achieve the end He put in place in the beginning. That's kind of awesome."

"It doesn't take away the guilt or the pain we feel when God says no, and we are left with the remnants of our actions." Baylie glanced his way. "That rejection is like a punch to the gut. Trust me."

"Would you like to talk about it?"

"No." Baylie leaned back against the seat, her gaze on him. "I'm going to nap while we travel. This week has left me drained. Do you mind?"

"We can talk later." Jayden turned the radio a little louder. "You'll see things differently when you've had some time to rest and recover."

"I doubt it, but thanks for understanding." She turned her face to the door.

Baylie slept fitfully as the Suburban ate up the miles between Bend and the ranch. She kept her eyes closed, though she wasn't asleep, occasionally peeking out the window to catch a glimpse of the sun growing lower in the sky. The orange globe shot rays of yellow and crimson across the high desert, illuminating the low-lying terrain, the scrub pines, and the occasional tumbleweed. Crooked juniper took on a surreal beauty when caught in the light of a probing beam intent on revealing its location. The further they traveled the sparser the terrain became.

"Baylie?" Jayden spoke quietly from the driver's side as though he feared waking her. "I'm going to make a pit stop at that wayside we visited on our last trip over." He waited. "Thought you might like to stretch your legs."

Baylie toyed with the idea of continuing to pretend she was asleep, but truth be known she could use a break. Her backside had tired of sitting, and her neck had started to kink. She raised an arm to stretch, and then slowly sat up, glancing over at Jayden. "Sorry to be such rotten company."

"No need to apologize." Jayden slowed the SUV and eased off the highway. "You've had a rough week. A little time to yourself is perfectly understandable."

"Have you always been this considerate?" Baylie studied the man beside her. "All I remember from high school is you rolling pencils and staring at the wall."

"I did write all the sports columns, you know."

"Oh, yeah. Now I remember." Baylie grinned. "Anyway, you've become a very nice adult."

"Glad you think so." Jayden thumbed toward the wayside. "Want to see if your snake is still in there? Or should I go and flush him out?"

"I'll go." Baylie opened her door. "But come running if I scream."

Jayden laughed. "Got it."

Baylie grabbed the emergency flashlight from the dash and headed for the wayside. She stomped through the door to alert any nefarious creatures of her presence. But the place was deserted, and she had her privacy. She emerged a few minutes later to find Jayden scrounging around the back seat. He stepped out, a jug in one hand and a sack in the other.

"What are those?" She gave his cargo a once over.

He held up the jug. "Running water for your hands." He shook the sack. "Sandwiches for your stomach, if it is empty."

"Wow!" Baylie's middle growled as if prompted by the sound of the sack. "You think of everything."

"Can't take credit for this." He sat on the running board of the Suburban and handed her a sandwich. "Mom sent these. She knows how I like to eat."

"Melanie is great." Baylie took the sandwich. "How she gets everything done, I'll never understand."

"Especially when she takes an afternoon to go motorcycle riding with Parker."

Baylie stopped chewing. "She did?"

"Yep." Jayden popped the last of his sandwich in his mouth. "Took my bike."

"Melanie and Parker took your bike?"

"No, Mom took my bike and rode it out to the highway." Jayden wiped his hands on his jeans. "Found out she and Dad used to own a pair of Harleys and rode together for a while."

"No kidding?" Baylie wasn't sure he was telling her the truth. "Did she enjoy her time with Parker?"

"Uh, yeah." Jayden grabbed a bottle of water and popped the top. "They were gone three hours." Jayden looked at her. "I think something's going on between them."

"No doubt about it."

"I'm going to need you to pry a little." Jayden smirked. "She'll tell you things she won't tell me."

"Spy?"

"Surveillance is a better word." Jayden placed his bottle back in the tote. "Got to check out the opposition."

"Back in soldier mode, I see." Baylie took another bite of sandwich. "But who are you protecting from whom?" She waited. "Surely Parker's not a threat."

"He's moving in pretty fast." Jayden offered her the cookie bag. "Not sure I'm ready for this."

They enjoyed their food for a few minutes when Jayden pointed across the desert terrain. "I think I see an antelope. See that flash of white?"

"Yeah." Baylie squinted. "Not a deer?"

"Too distant to tell for sure. But I saw my first antelope with Kurt when I was eleven. That looks like what I remember." Jayden took another bite. "So I vote antelope."

"Cool, though."

"Yes, it is."

Baylie smiled. "This country never disappoints."

Jayden stood and wadded up the sack. "Ready to travel?"

"We're not far now, are we?"

"No." Jayden held out his hand and pulled her up. "But I couldn't return home and still have uneaten sandwiches in the Suburban."

Baylie laughed. "You'd never hear the end of that."

"You think?"

The ranch below looked beautiful in the late afternoon sun. Baylie hugged herself. This place represented home to her. If she did her job well the ranch could become permanent. She'd been fortunate to live in only one home most of her younger years, making her feel secure and anchored. College living had been more disjointed, a series of questionable apartments with an equal assortment of interesting roommates that bounced her around like a ship without an anchor. She'd so needed Jayden there with her to keep her tethered. The separation had been a fatal link to her failure. Now, as Jayden descended the long driveway, she viewed the inviting home as her refuge, promising herself she would cling to this opportunity with all the resolve she could muster. Here she could find her way. Going astray would not happen again.

"Ready to be back on the job?" Jayden's question startled her.

"Yes. As soon as a newsletter goes out, a new one has to be designed and prepped."

"You have a list of themes you follow?" Jayden pulled the Suburban around to the back of the bunkhouse.

"I do. It's a holdover from when we produced the high school newspaper. I like to know what's coming."

"I imagine it makes it easier to stay on deadline."

"That's right." Baylie pointed. "Looks like Duke is missing you."

The eager dog came running across the back field where he'd been harassing cattle that often wandered in from the free grazing land. Duke barked and beelined for Jayden's door, his excited yips coming almost as fast as his front feet danced.

Jayden hopped out and bent down to hug the exuberant dog. "Hey, fella. Catch any rodents today?"

Baylie exited the vehicle and walked around the front to Jayden. Duke barked at her, his excitement at seeing them evident. "Rodents?"

"Prairie dogs, snakes, chipmunks." Jayden stood straight, his hand on Duke's head. "Never know what the high desert is going to provide for entertainment. Duke mostly likes to herd cows."

Baylie looked out over the expansive terrain beyond them. "He's lived quite a life here, hasn't he?"

"Yep." Jayden jangled his key ring. "Shall we unload your cargo?"

"I'll unlock my studio door." Baylie pulled out her keys. "We need a transport wagon like the one at Grandma's facility."

"I'll find a wheelbarrow." Jayden called Duke to follow. "I'll even dump out the manure for you."

Baylie wrinkled her nose. "How thoughtful you are."

"You can count on me." Jayden cackled, picking up a stick and throwing it. "Fetch, Duke."

Baylie watched the man and the dog for a minute, then hurried inside the bunkhouse straight to her door. She opened the apartment and stepped inside, happy to be back in her own space. She emptied the table so Jayden could set the smaller items there and moved the chairs to make room for the rocker Grandma had given her. Her dresser would hold the antique chiming clock. How nice to have family things of her own. With Grandpa gone and Grandma so far away, these treasures would give her the sense of belonging and connection to her real family. She'd always yearned for that tie growing up.

Her only real tie to her past was her friendship with Jayden. She cherished her memories with him, wishing there wasn't a barricade of circumstances standing between them now. She wanted to depend on Jayden for many things. But if he knew of her recent past, he might not want to know her at all.

"Knock, knock." Jayden stood at the door, Kurt behind him. "I found us a victim. . . I mean helper. . .to unload your stash."

"Hi, Kurt." Baylie held the door wider. "The rocker goes over there and the clock on the dresser."

"This is a nice clock." Kurt carried it to her dresser. "Is it loud?"

"Better not be." Jayden positioned the rocker. "I sleep on the other side of that wall. I don't want to wake up every hour to a gong or two."

Baylie laughed. "It has a gentle chime." She looked at Jayden. "And if it disturbs you, you can let me know and I'll move it to the other wall."

The clock made a sound, as if it was about to take a breath, like a break before a cymbal in a symphony, then chimed out a sweet and mellow bell. "Dong. Dong. Dong."

"I can live with that." Jayden studied the clock, listening to it announce the hour. The little wheels and gears inside clicked as they moved the hands on the clock face into the next sixty minutes. "Sounds like home."

CHAPTER SEVENTEEN

AFTER KURT AND JAYDEN LEFT, BAYLIE showered, dressed, and hurried to the kitchen. Melanie stood at the stove sautéing a pan of onions. She looked up and smiled at Baylie, reaching to turn down the burner. "You're back." She wiped her hands on her apron. "I was so sorry to learn of your grandfather's passing." Melanie hugged her. "How are you coping?"

Baylie blinked back moisture that threatened to smear her mascara. "Grandma keeps reminding me he's in a better place now, but I miss him. She made me promise to rejoice in his homegoing."

"Sounds like good advice. How is she?"

"She kept up a brave face while I was there, probably for my benefit because she's always protected me. First, when my parents were killed, and again now. I imagine she's suffering alone and probably shedding many much-needed tears with me gone. I wish I could be there to hug her." Baylie breathed deep. "They were married a long time and they'd known their share of sorrow."

"Be sure to keep in touch so she doesn't feel forgotten. When the reality of your grandfather's death hits home, your grandmother will need a shoulder to cry on. She'll look to you."

"Thanks, I will." Baylie glanced around the kitchen. "Can you use any help with dinner?"

"We're having stir fry and sausage tonight. The vegetables are cut, the rice is in the cooker, and all that's left is slicing the sausage into chunks and heating it."

"I can do that." Baylie reached in the knife drawer. "How did you get all those vegetables chopped so early?"

Melanie blushed. "I had outside help."

"Oh?"

"Parker was here. He chopped the carrots and celery. I fixed the onion, peppers, and squash."

Baylie remembered Jayden's request that she do surveillance for him. "Is he becoming a regular?"

"No. Nothing like that." Melanie returned to the stove. "He's Jayden's commanding officer. His friend."

"But he showed up here at the ranch even though Jayden was picking me up." Baylie pressed her lips together to keep from giving away her mission. "I doubt chopping carrots was at the top of his list."

Melanie picked up the spatula and turned the stove on. "He likes to be busy."

Baylie couldn't stop the laughter. "Melanie. Jayden told me about the bike ride. Level with me."

Melanie's face couldn't have been redder had she been sunburned. She focused on the vegetables, not answering Baylie.

"Melanie."

The spatula banged the side of the pan and Melanie raised her face as she studied the ceiling. She looked at Baylie. "Parker and I exchanged letters a little when Jayden was hospitalized." She straightened and faced Baylie. "He was friendly. I was worried about Jayden. We got to know each other because of our mutual concern for Jayden."

"But I thought you'd never met him before Jayden showed up here with Parker behind him."

"I hadn't met him." Melanie checked the rice cooker. "Only shared a few letters."

"From the looks of things, he's here to share a lot more than letters."

Melanie handed her a rope of sausage. "Let's get this sliced. The vegetables will soon be hot."

"You like him?"

Melanie ignored the question for a minute, her mouth changing from a reluctant smile to a perplexed pout, ending in a sigh that seemed to come from her toes. "Yes. But I jumped into a relationship after Jordan was killed. It ended in disaster. I'm gun shy. I don't trust my judgment." She glanced Baylie's way, a knowing look in her eye, a grin on her face. "And you can tell Jayden I said so."

Baylie bit her lip. Melanie had guessed. But more than that Baylie realized how alike Melanie's experience was to her own story—the one she didn't tell anyone, the one Jayden would never know, the one God couldn't forgive. A handsome smooth talker, a lonely college girl, and friends who didn't share her values. Recipe for trouble. "I can understand your hesitation." She sliced the sausage into small pieces. "Take it slow and be sure. Don't hurry things."

"You have a lot of wisdom for one so young."

"Been there, done that." Baylie scooped the sausage into the waiting frying pan. "And that's all I have to say." She stepped away from the stove. "Anything else?"

"Let's put out cookies for dessert." Melanie reached into a cupboard and removed a serving plate. "I took a tub of oatmeal chocolate chip cookies from the freezer this morning to thaw."

"Shall I arrange them on the plate?"

"Yes." Melanie sighed. "For all the good it will do. Two seconds and the plate will look like a scrambled mess."

"Why don't we put the cookies on a napkin at each place?" Baylie opened a cupboard. "We have some cute ones here left from a picnic or something. They have checkered squares on them."

"Enough for all of our crew?"

Baylie flipped through the stack with her thumb. "I count twenty."

"Perfect." Melanie handed her the tub of cookies. "That will keep our mess to a minimum."

"Well, at least napkins will remove one plate to wash." Baylie fought the smirk tugging at her mouth. "Parker washing dishes again tonight?"

"No, he's meeting with Kurt after dinner." Melanie raised an eyebrow. "Marines love to share their war stories."

"Jayden, too?"

"Probably."

"I'd love to be a mouse in the corner."

Jayden fist-bumped Parker as they gathered in the living room of the ranch house where Kurt, Lissa, and their boys resided. Jayden claimed a corner of the sofa. He looked around the room, appreciating the homey touches Lissa had given the space. "Lissa is quite the decorator."

Kurt sat in a rocker. "She wasn't when she first came home from deployment." He tilted his head back as if staring into space, a grin on his face. "She'd lived on a naval ship for fifteen years. Her idea of decorating was a plant stuck on a table that had a corner molding to keep the pot from sliding off in an ocean storm."

"Spartan, I'm guessing?" Parker slid into a recliner and shoved the back to an angle. "Kind of like living out of an army pack in the middle of the Afghan wilderness. No fuss, no extra weight."

"I remember those days." Kurt pointed to a picture on the wall. "My unit before we were ambushed."

Parker stood and moved closer to the print. "You don't look much different Kurt."

Jayden leaned in for a closer look. "That's my dad." He glanced at Kurt. "I don't remember you showing this to me before."

"That's because I didn't know I had it. Lissa found it in some of my Marine gear when she was cleaning out a closet. You were deployed."

"Can I get a copy?"

Kurt nodded and reached into an end table drawer next to him. "Lissa already had it made for you." He handed two pictures to Jayden. "One is our unit ready for patrol. The other is all of us gathered for Bible study and prayer."

"Mom said Dad felt the need to gather his men for evening devotions." Jayden studied the second picture.

Parker sat back in the recliner. "How many of these men made it home?"

"All but three." Kurt's forehead wrinkled, his mouth set in a straight line. "My best friend, Foster, was caught in a booby-trapped cache of weapons. Jayden's dad, Jordan, and another man, Carl Stevens, were ambushed on patrol."

"The same patrol when you were missing in action?" Jayden tipped his head toward Kurt.

"The same."

Parker sat up straighter. "Hard to believe we all served in the same area of the world— same enemy—but years apart."

"And all of us faced the same tactics—ambush, IED's, and weapons caches." Jayden winced. "I still remember the double explosion that threw our Humvee on its side. We missed the first bomb enough for all of us to roll from the truck. But the second explosion flipped it on its back. That's the explosion that caught my leg under the wheel."

"At least you weren't in the truck." Kurt closed the drawer on the end table.

"We wouldn't be sitting here talking if I had been." Jayden slid back on the sofa, the pictures resting on his lap. "I hate war."

"We all do." Parker reclined again. "But soldiers do what they are told."

"What are your plans, now that you're a civilian?" Kurt rocked the chair as he waited for Parker to respond. "You seeking employment?"

"Haven't really looked." Parker laced his hands behind his head. "I'm trying to take life a bit more slowly, spend some time alone, and savor each day without the military hanging over me."

"Is that why you bought the Harley?" Jayden studied his commanding officer. "To have some alone time?"

"Pretty much." Parker snickered. "And to keep up with you."

"What's the deal with Melanie?" Kurt's direct question startled Jayden. "We like our cook."

"She's one of a kind." Parker agreed. "I was amazed she knew how to ride a motorcycle."

"You and me both." Jayden slid forward on the couch again. "She had never mentioned riding motorcycles with Dad."

"Probably one of those bittersweet memories." Parker studied his shoes, before looking up. "Seeing you take an interest in bikes, and remembering Jordan when they rode together, might have been something she savored in private, since I understand your stepfather— George, was it?— was jealous of anything related to Jordan."

"He was." Jayden closed his fist, then relaxed it. "My dad was a hero, not only in my eyes, but in Mom's memories as well, and George couldn't compete."

"Jordan was a man worth remembering." Kurt studied the picture still in Jayden's lap. "His ability to lead men, not only on patrol, but through the Scriptures, guaranteed heaven to a number in our unit."

"I'm glad to know that about him." Jayden let out a sigh. "I only thought he was a brave soldier. Not a motorcycle-riding, Bible-toting, Renaissance man."

"And now we have our very own leather lady." Kurt laughed. "I'm guessing you plan to spend more time around here, Parker?"

"That has not been decided." Parker glanced Jayden's direction. "But I'm open to the idea."

Jayden kept silent. He liked Parker a lot, but he hadn't

expected to share his mother with the man. At least not so soon. He'd just gotten here himself. But it appeared Mom was eager to explore the relationship. Jayden didn't want to interfere, so he'd just let it happen.

After she and Melanie finished cleaning up dinner, Baylie left the kitchen and entered her apartment. She loved the ease of the chore tonight, one large skillet, a cutting board, and a couple dozen plates took all of ten minutes. She'd assisted with the washing while Melanie wiped down the counters and the table. Though it wasn't a night off, the simple meal felt like one.

She sat in the new rocking chair like a queen in her realm. Her great grandmother had needle-pointed the seat, the arm rests, and the back cushion. Colors of purple and blue dominated the floral pattern, mixed with gold threads that interspersed minute touches of green, pink, and lavender. Baylie shuddered to think of the hours of stitching woven into the intricate design. She lacked the patience to achieve such a feat, but she appreciated the efforts of anyone who did.

Her phone pinged. A text from Jayden. *Hope your week is happier. So sorry about Grandpa Joseph.*

Baylie swallowed hard. She typed in a quick message. *He will be missed. Thanks for helping me get back to the ranch.*

Another ping. *Your car will be ready for pickup in the morning.*

She smiled. Such thoughtfulness. *Great. What time?*

900 am. Harley okay?

Can't wait. See you then.

Learn anything new from my mother?

No.

The phone fell silent and she set it on the table beside her. The clock on the dresser chimed nine. The sound soothed her, like a group of monks doing evening prayers. She remembered when evening prayers filled her nighttime routine. The need to try again haunted her though she doubted God was listening.

Lord, thank you for helping me through this week. Guide me back to a right relationship with you. I've been gone too long. Jayden won't let this go. I need to talk with someone, but I can't tell him. I just can't. But he will insist. I know it. Please prepare his heart so I don't lose him forever. I wouldn't survive.

She stood and headed to the bathroom. After brushing her teeth and washing her face, she returned to her dresser and donned pajamas. Her shoulders slumped thinking of the inevitable conversation waiting in the future, as if she carried the weight of the world there. At least it seemed that way. She needed rest. Her last thought was of Jayden.

Jayden and Parker returned to Melanie's apartment after their evening with Kurt. Jayden gestured toward the sofa. "Have a seat. Want anything?"

"No. I'm good."

Jayden's head spun with the conversation they'd had in Kurt's home. "It's still hard for me to believe my dad and Kurt were together in the same unit. Talk about a coincidence!"

"I'd say that was more than a coincidence." Parker sat on the sofa. "Seems as if you might have had divine intervention on that one."

"Yeah, I have to agree." Jayden leaned back in the armchair. "When I was nine, it all seemed a mistake. But now in retrospect, I can clearly see where God was leading me and guiding my life."

"Kind of makes life ahead more inviting, doesn't it? You can rest in the fact that God has your back."

"Overwhelming, is more like it."

Parker grew silent, and Jayden sensed the man wanted to say something. "What's on your mind?"

Parker glanced up, fingers tapping the end of the sofa. "I really like your mother."

Jayden's jaw tensed, but he relaxed and forced a grin. "I kind of like her, too." Parker's Adam's apple moved, the swallow evident in the tenseness of his skin. Seeing his discomfort, Jayden felt sorry for the man. "So you going to be a regular visitor around here?"

Parker glanced his way, eyes wary. "How would you feel about that?"

"If Mom says it is okay, I'm good." Jayden waited for the man to say more. "You're certainly a better choice than George was."

Parker chuckled. "Thanks. I think." He leaned forward. "Melanie hasn't told me much about the man, but I can tell she's reluctant to try again because of the experience she had with him."

"Can't say I blame her." Jayden's fist closed, thinking of his past encounters. "She's still in love with my dad."

"I know." Parker sighed. "I can't compete with a love like that."

"Yes, you can." Jayden looked at his friend. "She's lonely— and you have my approval."

The door opened and Mom walked in. "Sorry to be an absentee hostess." She joined them on the sofa. "You fellas have a good discussion with Kurt?"

Jayden held up the photos. "Kurt took pictures of his unit when Dad was with him. Want to see?"

Melanie took the images, studied them for a moment, and burst into tears. "Oh, Jordan!"

Jayden shot a glance at Parker, then stood and wrapped his arms around his mother.

Parker nodded and excused himself. "I think I'll head for bed and leave you two alone.”

“Goodnight.” Jayden held his mother tighter, watching his friend leave them and disappear into the spare bedroom. From Mom’s reaction it was obvious Parker had a long road ahead of him. Sadness for his friend, as well as for his mother, overwhelmed Jayden. He prayed the road ahead would have fewer pot holes.

The next morning Baylie paced as the hands on the clock neared the appointed time to meet with Jayden. Today she would get her car back. Not to mention the bill. *I hope it is affordable.*

She gave her hair a swipe with her fingers and checked her teeth in the mirror. She’d chosen her skinny jeans which slid inside her boots. She grabbed the vest she’d worn before even though this ride would be shorter. Jayden said the mechanic worked out of Burns.

The sound of boots in the hall met her ears, the uneven step from Jayden’s limp a reminder he was still healing. Her heart fluttered. Jayden had been so kind, helping her through this crisis. She put a lock on her emotions in an effort to keep her feelings at bay. She couldn’t assume anything. Jayden had not asked her to go anywhere. Had not offered to watch a movie together. She kept reminding herself she had known he was coming home. He hadn’t known she’d be here. A relationship might be the furthest thing from his mind—especially after surviving injuries and rehabilitation.

She jumped when the knock sounded, chiding herself for being so jittery. She opened the door, taking a deep breath as she did so. “Good morning.”

“Ready to sign your life away?”

“What do you mean?”

“Auto repair bills.”

“Don’t say that.” Baylie stepped out of the apartment, keys

jingling in her hand. "I'm hoping the bill isn't that big."

"This guy is reasonable, I'm told." Jayden turned and they walked toward the front door of the bunkhouse. "If Kurt and Lissa use him, you know he can't be super expensive."

"I hope that's true." Baylie followed Jayden to the motorcycle. "But he may do favors for them because of the ranch."

"Aren't you part of the ranch?" Jayden handed her the spare helmet.

"Technically, yes." Baylie dropped the face shield over her eyes. "But I'm not one of the owners. I'm a simple hired hand."

Jayden tapped her helmet. "Nothing simple about you."

"Thanks." She ducked her chin, feeling the blush creep across her jaw. If Jayden only knew.

"Let's ride." Jayden slipped his leg over the seat, and Baylie followed him into her spot. "Remember how?"

"My memory serves me well."

The bike roared to life, and Jayden shifted into gear. Baylie sat up straight, making sure her feet were in the right place. Riding behind Jayden, she hesitated to put her hands on his waist, but the never-ending fear she might lean too far one way or the other still plagued her. She needed him for balance. *Stop being silly. You are only touching his belt.*

She bit her lip, forcing herself to show restraint. If she had her way, she'd wrap her arms around Jayden's waist and never let go.

CHAPTER EIGHTEEN

"WE'VE COME FOR THE MUSTANG GRANDE that was towed here last week." Jayden stood at the counter, his muscular presence filling the small lobby. "I understand the repairs are complete?"

"Yes sir. The timing chain broke in two." The mechanic handed Jayden the keys. "Glad there weren't any other cars directly behind when it happened." He looked at Baylie. "The engine completely stopped, didn't it?"

Baylie nodded. "I let the momentum carry me to the side of the road." She winced at the memory. "All it would do when I tried the ignition was sit there and whir."

"Yep. That's all it could do." The mechanic went to his computer and typed in data. "Be glad you have a guardian angel."

"How much is the bill?" Baylie held her breath

"No bill." He handed her a receipt. "Like I said, be glad you have a guardian angel."

"I don't understand." Baylie's confusion made Jayden smile. She looked his way. "Did you pay for this?"

"Not me." He held his hands up, palms outward, as if in a sign of surrender. "I'm low-paid military personnel." But he suspected who might have. "I'd say you have been blessed."

"Who then?" Baylie's eyes searched his.

"My lips are sealed."

"You know who, don't you?"

He ignored her question and held his hand out to the mechanic. "Thanks for taking care of this."

"No problem." The mechanic returned the handshake. "Glad to be of service."

Jayden turned to Baylie. "Ready to go?"

"You have to tell me." She grabbed his arm. "I'll get it out of you, one way or another."

"I'm resistant to torture, you know." Jayden snorted. "I was trained by the U.S. Marine Corps."

"Jayden."

Baylie started her engine and the little car that had been the source of bad dreams the week before purred now like a kitten returning home. She followed Jayden out of the parking lot, her mind checking off all the names of people who might have been her benefactor. Working at the ranch had its perks, but for someone to pay a bill that must have cost hundreds of dollars went beyond her ability to comprehend. Who would do such a kindness?

Jayden's motorcycle roared ahead of her, the man giving the bike a boost of speed as he zipped away in a flash of light. She laughed, knowing he was showing off just because he could, and she was helpless to do anything about it. Soon he appeared in front of her again, having allowed the bike to slow down so she could catch up. She was tempted to honk, but decided he'd probably consider that a signal that she was in trouble and resisted the urge. He stuck his hand up and wiggled his fingers, more evidence he was playing a game. She'd get him later.

A sheriff's patrol car sat in the drive as she and Jayden returned to the ranch. What was he doing here? Baylie's stomach did a flip flop as she considered the options. Had one of the kids run away? Was one of their group being transferred? That was always a possibility among foster kids. She parked next to the bunkhouse and stepped out. Jayden maneuvered the bike around to Melanie's apartment entrance. Kurt and Lissa stood talking with the deputy.

"Baylie? Jayden?" Lissa motioned them over. "This is Sergeant Sloan."

"What's happened?" Baylie hoped no child had been affected.

Kurt straightened. "We had another intruder last night. You and Jayden left before we discovered the break-in." He pointed at the back door of the kitchen. "Whoever it was managed to enter there."

"Did he steal?" Jayden's jaw clenched.

"Nothing appears to be missing." Lissa folded her arms. "We didn't notice anything until Melanie found an empty bottle in the trash."

Baylie worried her lower lip. "What kind of bottle?"

"Jim Beam."

"Not much call for that kind of thing around here." She looked at Kurt. "But a lot of these kids came from home environments where liquor fueled tempers, didn't they?"

Kurt nodded. "We called the sheriff to have a look around."

"I'm glad no children were involved." Jayden glanced around. "Where's Mom?"

"Fixing lunch." Lissa nodded at the kitchen. "The kids still have to eat."

"Is the intruder after her?" Jayden tucked his helmet under his arm. "Seems strange that whoever it is would prowl the kitchen."

"Not if he's hungry and looking for food." Deputy Sloan wrote on his tablet. "The kitchen would be a good place to start." The deputy glanced up. "But since this is the second incident and the first one involved the garage, I'm thinking there's more to the story."

Kurt nodded. "I agree."

"The question is what." Baylie glanced at Jayden who was leaving the scene, headed for the kitchen. "Hey, Jayden, wait up."

Jayden hurried into the kitchen through the side door, Baylie right behind him. "Mom?" He glanced around the cupboards before poking into the pantry. "Mom?"

"In the store room." Mom's voice sounded as if she stood in an echo chamber. "Be out in a minute."

A few seconds later she popped out of the back of the pantry. "Sorry about that, but I wanted to check the staples." Mom's smile sizzled a little too bright, face pale. "A quick inventory of our supplies."

"Did the intruder take anything?" Jayden sensed not all was right with the evidence she'd found. "Did he leave the chocolate bars?"

"Chocolate bars?" Baylie laughed. "You've been holding out on me, Melanie."

Mom pointed a finger at Jayden, raising her thumb as if firing a pistol. "You tease." She looked at Baylie. "Sorry, no private stash back there."

"Bummer." Baylie stuck out her lower lip. "Got my hopes up."

"What did he take?" Jayden probed his mother's face, looking for clues to her stiff manner and clipped words. "Surely you don't have a stash of liquor."

Mom's face flushed. "Of course not, silly."

"Then what is it?" Jayden leaned against the counter, arms folded across his middle, a dread seeping up from his toes. "That bottle you found suggests a thousand answers."

"Why don't we let it go for now since I'm behind making lunch?" Mom glanced at Baylie. "Any chance of soliciting your help?"

"Sure." Baylie reached up in the cupboard and grabbed an apron. "I need to work extra hard to repay a mysterious benefactor who covered the repair bill. Even though I don't know their identity, I plan to find them and repay the costs." She tied the apron at the back. "And thank them that I've got wheels again, so I can drive." She continued in a falsetto, assuming a stance like a character giving a soliloquy on stage. "I'm at your service. I'll do any other odd jobs needed as well. Just put donations in my apron." She curtsied.

Jayden grinned. "Good luck with that.'

Mom didn't crack a smile. "Good. Start on carrot and celery sticks." Her manner abrupt, Mom walked to the stove, surprising Jayden.

Baylie frowned at the brush-off and looked at him, a question on her face. At his shrug, she walked to the cooler and retrieved a bag of carrots and a stalk of celery and carried the vegetables to the cutting board at the front of the kitchen.

"What can I do?" Jayden grabbed a second apron, moving in beside his mother. He spun in a circle. "Look, I can pirouette in my tu-tu. Top that, Baylie." He lifted his foot and pointed the toe at the floor. "What do you think?

"I think you'd be more help getting the condiments out for the hotdogs, clown boy." Mom snapped a towel at him.

"What? Mustard? Ketchup? Pickle relish?" Jayden opened the refrigerator door. "You need these wieners?"

"Yes."

"How about some Jim Beam?"

Mom paled again. "That's not funny." She put her hands on the counter and hung her head, chin resting on her chest.

"What are you hiding?" Jayden studied his mother, voice a whisper. "Baylie's out of ear range."

"Let it go." Mom's jaw clenched. "Please."

"George?"

Mom snatched the wieners from him and picked up a cooking pan, lifting it to the stove and reaching for the control knob. He grabbed her wrist. "Mom."

She set the pan on the hot element and dropped her chin again with a sigh. "He sent me a letter about a month ago. Said he'd be in touch." She looked at Jayden, eyes wary. "I told him not to bother." She made fists, tapping them on the counter. "I don't want to deal with that man again."

"Nor do I want you to have to, but he's not letting it go?"

"He sent copies of the divorce papers, unsigned." Mom closed her eyes. "I wondered why I never received anything more, but apparently I failed to follow up." She put a hand on Jayden's shoulder. "When he disappeared after he was released from jail, I assumed everything was finished, for good." She focused weary eyes at him. "And in the middle of losing you to the State, I didn't follow through."

"You are still married?"

"It appears as if we may be. I don't know how this works." Mom knuckled a tear sliding down her cheek. "Apparently the proceedings moved us into a contested divorce that has yet to be resolved. I'll need to contact my attorney."

"Seriously?"

Baylie walked toward the stove, the carrots and celery washed and cut, ready for lunch. "What else do you need help with?" She set the platter of vegetables on the counter.

"There are a couple of bags of chips in the pantry." Mom glanced at Jayden as Baylie disappeared into the storage room. "Can you put the condiments at the end of the counter where the kids can stop and fix their hot dog buns before they move to the stove for their wiener?"

"Sure." Jayden retrieved the items from the refrigerator and slid the bottles to the end. "Would it help to put each one in a dish with a spoon?"

"That's a great idea. Less mess." Mom smiled at him, then turned to Baylie. "Would you put the chips in a couple of bowls?"

Jayden caught Baylie's questioning look as she walked away. Like him, she appeared to have sensed a change in his mother. When she returned, he nodded at her and shrugged his shoulders again, trying to send a signal that he knew she was worried. They'd catch up on this later. He would tell her if he could, but Mom didn't seem ready to divulge the news. Baylie turned, mid-step, eyes bright. "What about a piece of fruit to go with this?"

"There's a bag of apples in the cooler. Wash several." Mom sighed. "I didn't think the morning left me so rattled, but I am so glad you both are here to help." She glanced Baylie's way. "Why don't you slice three or four of those apples and make smaller portions for the younger children?"

"Will do."

"Mom, we can finish the lunch." Jayden laid a hand on her shoulder. "Take five and breathe." He pulled her away from the stove. "This must all be unsettling."

Mom shuddered, eyes rimmed with tears. "I thought I was through with him thirteen years ago." She raised her arms and tilted her head back, then let them drop to her sides. "To think he's back here, ready to cause trouble, is more than I can handle."

"Big difference though." Jayden brought a stack of small bowls from the cupboard and set them near the condiments for filling. "I'm no longer eleven."

Baylie sensed something about the morning's activities at the ranch had shaken Melanie to her core. She didn't know what might have caused the woman's stress, but she kept her speculations to herself and let Jayden deal with his mother. Had Parker left without saying goodbye? They had seemed so solid before she went to Bend.

No, it had to be something else. Jayden's low voice as he conversed with his mother suggested Baylie shouldn't eavesdrop or pry. More than ever she wished she still believed her prayers could effect change. She would pray for Melanie, if she did—but her grandfather had died in spite of her prayers. If anything, she may have made things worse, a person with her history daring to approach the throne of the most holy God.

She grabbed a knife and sliced three apples, placing the slices in a bowl. Glancing at the clock, she turned to the cupboard and lifted down a stack of plates. She counted out twelve glasses and set them at the end. "What are the kids drinking with this?"

"Milk today." Melanie's voice sounded flat, robotic.

"Shall I pour?"

"Please. I'll get the buns and wieners set up at the other end." Melanie carried the buns to the far end.

Jayden waved a spoon in the air. "I'll spread the mustard."

Baylie snorted. "You keep slinging that spoon and we'll have mustard colored walls."

For the first time since they'd come in the kitchen, Melanie smiled. "You two are the best."

"We're only doing our jobs." Baylie twisted the cap off the milk jug. "You are the captain of this ship."

Melanie's smile appeared forced. "I don't feel much like a captain today. I'm more like the rescued survivor from a life raft."

Jayden hugged her. "We'll get through this together."

Baylie tensed. Get through what together? When would Jayden clue her in?

CHAPTER NINETEEN

After lunch was served and cleanup finished, Baylie went to find Kurt. She heard him whistling in the barn and made tracks that direction. The sound of a broom sweeping the aisle accompanied his off-key rendition of *The Sounds of Silence*. When she entered the open doors, he worked busily cleaning a stall. The summer intern Cody pushed a scoop shovel.

Cody looked up and nodded, then spoke to his boss. "Kurt? Company."

Kurt stopped, and seeing her, grinned. "Baylie, how's that car running for you today?"

"Seems to be like new." Baylie walked down the aisle to where the two men waited. "That's why I'm here."

"Oh?"

"Somebody paid the bill." She studied him. "Do you know who might have done that?"

"Maybe." Kurt's eyes twinkled. "We have sponsors who volunteer to pay for unexpected events here at the ranch. One of them learned of your loss, followed by your car troubles, and footed the bill."

"Really?" A stranger had stepped in and helped someone they didn't even know. "How do I thank them?"

"The same way you thank all the sponsors." Kurt leaned on his broom. "Keep telling those wonderful stories our community loves to read. People do care about foster kids, but they don't always know how to help."

"Would it be appropriate to tell my story as a way of thanking them?"

"I think that's a great idea." Kurt swept a pile to the side. "Awareness helps pair children with parents. Every child needs a forever home."

"Thanks, Kurt." Baylie turned to go. "That means a lot."

She headed to her office and sat at the desk. Her head spun with what she'd just learned, but her heart felt ready to burst. She'd prayed for rescue. Kurt and Jayden had come. She'd prayed for Grandpa, but he'd died. She'd agonized over the cost of repairs for her car and an unknown benefactor gave her a paid-in-full receipt. All of these were concerns for which only God could have decided the outcomes. His will prevailed. Grandpa had joined eternity, but her needs were met. She was left eternally grateful. She wanted to cry. The God she thought no longer cared for her obviously did and had for some time. She'd have to revisit her thinking.

Ashamed of her doubts, but bolstered by her joy, she booted the computer. She prayed, a habit left dormant too long, but one she intended to return to active status immediately. Receiving the newfound freedom in knowing she was forgiven came like a breath of fresh air, a warm breeze on a cloudy day. Perhaps her future could be bright.

She dabbed at her eyes. How silly—sitting here crying over good news. But she couldn't stop the happiness running rampant in her soul. She'd been held prisoner by guilt too long. She typed her first sentence. "My grandfather recently died."

The door to the office opened and Jayden entered. At the sight of him, she gulped air and groped for composure. "Hi," she squeaked. "How's your mom?"

Jayden pulled up a chair and sat across from her. "Doesn't appear she's much better than you right now." He handed her the box of tissues on the corner. "What's going on with you?"

Baylie sniffed, giggled, and glanced up at him, feeling even sillier, caught in her reverie. "I'm just overwhelmed by the goodness of God." She looked at Jayden's concerned face, the skepticism in his eyes. "I've not believed He's cared about me for a long time."

"I know you told me you messed up big time." Jayden leaned back in his chair. "But I've not wanted to pry. Are you ready to talk about it?"

"Maybe." Baylie hedged. "Soon." *But you must never know.* She brightened her smile. "First tell me what is going on with your mother?"

Jayden sighed, staring at the ceiling, then fixed his gaze on her. "This is between you and me, okay?"

"Of course." Baylie grew concerned. "Is it Parker?"

"I wish it were." Jayden drummed his fingers on the desk. "My infamous stepfather has made threats of returning to our lives."

"That guy. . . George?" Baylie fell mute. At Jayden's nod, she pressed on. "I thought he went to prison."

"He did—thirteen years ago. But he's out now, having served his time, and went back to long-haul trucking." Jayden clenched his jaw. "He wants to see Mom again."

"To what purpose?" Baylie's ire rose. "Surely he doesn't expect to pick up where he left off? Aren't they divorced?"

"Supposedly, but he didn't sign his divorce papers. Mom was in a state of despair over losing me because George implicated her in the kidnapping. She narrowly escaped jail time herself." Jayden shook his head, as if the memory fueled his anger. "She filed for divorce, but either she or her attorney didn't follow through. The proceedings were left in limbo and the courts ruled the divorce contested."

"How weird."

"Yeah, totally." Jayden blew out air, shoulders rigid. "But there's good news."

"What's that?"

"This time he can't use me to manipulate my mother."

"That is good news."

"I'm going to contact Parker. He should know what's going

on." Jayden's tease played in his eyes. "He has a vested interest in these matters."

"You think he's serious about your mom?"

"I don't know. But having him in the picture could make George back off—for good."

Jayden skipped all the pleasantries when he called Parker the next day. "This guy George is bad news. Mom is shaken now that he's back in the picture."

"Has she contacted her attorney?" Parker sounded calm and in control. "I'd think that would be the first thing she should do."

"She will. This all hit yesterday." Jayden ached for his mother. "She's in shock. And dealing with my stepfather was never easy."

"She told me about him." Parker paused, a door bell chiming in the background. "I've got company arriving today. Like right now. They'll be here a day or two. Can I get back to you?"

"Sure. Nice to talk with you, sir."

"Leave the sir in Afghanistan. I'm Parker here in the states."

Jayden laughed. "Old habits die hard."

"And I'll text your mother. I promise." The door bell chimed again. "See you."

Jayden clicked off his phone. Maybe George wouldn't show. He could only hope.

He exited the apartment and went to find Kurt. Today he was scheduled to work alongside Cody checking fences in the lower pasture. He hadn't seen the kid yet and wondered where he might be.

He popped into the barn, then walked around back to the paddock where Lady and her foal were munching on hay. He heard noise in the tool shed and headed that direction. Cody stood with his back to him, a cell phone to his ear. "Yeah. I'm on it. They found the bottle."

Jayden stopped, waiting for Cody to realize he was there. The kid turned. His expression froze when he saw Jayden. "You looking for me?"

"We're supposed to work on fences. You ready?"

Cody shrugged. "As ready as I'll ever be." He thumbed toward the wall. "What tools do we need?"

"Hammer, the post-hole digger, shovel." Cody's willingness to comply surprised Jayden. Was the kid trying to cover the phone conversation he'd heard? What bottle was he referring to? Jayden's military training kicked in. Something was off. But he needed more evidence.

"Are we walking?" Cody interrupted Jayden's thoughts.

"It's not far." Jayden picked up a shovel and balanced the handle on his shoulder. "Give me the post-hole digger. You grab the hammer and the can of nails."

The lower pasture corralled the ranch's small herd of cattle. Jayden couldn't count the number of times he had to deal with these ladies. Bossy, the lead cow, liked to lean on the fences, seeking the greener grass on the other side. Often, she pushed the posts out of their holes, and when she succeeded, she'd step into the freedom of the open range and take the rest of the herd with her, trotting down the highway interrupting traffic. More than once, he and Kurt had gone looking for Bossy and her girls, trying to convince the bovine to return home. Regular maintenance of the upright posts proved the only way to curb Bossy's appetite for forbidden territory.

Jayden pointed to a post leaning at a forty-five-degree angle near the corner of the pasture. "Bossy has been at it again."

Cody snickered and followed him to the spot. "She's big enough to push over every fence post here."

"That's why we have to be diligent." Jayden set the shovel down. "Some future spring, she won't calve and she'll meet her fate at the processing plant."

"Won't she be tough as shoe leather, being that old?"

"We'll have her made into hamburger." Jayden laughed. "She will feed these kids for months."

"Poor cow." Cody shoved the post to an upright position. "Being an animal stinks."

"God gave us the animals to sustain us." Jayden positioned the post-hole digger. "In Afghanistan where I deployed, the people had little to eat." He tested the hole. "A lamb or a chicken were delicacies. The general population lived on grain dishes."

"Grain dishes?"

"Rice, wheat. . .that sort of thing."

"Bossy would be a welcome addition to their diet, then, wouldn't she?"

"They probably wouldn't know what to do with her."

"Worship her?"

"No, not there. Cow worship is further south in Hindu country." Jayden laughed. "But I'm not bowing to an ornery, trouble-making cow." He pointed to the post. "Lift that out of the hole, if you can, and I'll deepen the opening."

Cody tugged the post up, and Jayden scooped out the soil. "Now drop it in and I'll tamp the dirt solid."

The post dropped into position. After tamping around the base, Jayden gave the upright a shove. The wood stayed firm. "Don't know if that will deter our derelict cow, but it ought to slow her down."

Cody's phone pinged. He checked the screen. "Mind if I take this?"

"No, go ahead." Jayden ground his lower lip. At this rate they'd be here all day.

The kid turned and walked to the next fence post, some distance away, but not out of Jayden's hearing. "I did what you asked." The whisper turned to a hiss. "You shouldn't call me when

I'm working here."

Jayden picked up the shovel heading toward the next post but as he went Cody said, "She's a nice lady. You should forget your past grudge."

The hair on the back of Jayden's neck prickled. Who was a nice lady? Was it somebody Cody knew off the ranch? Or someone here? He didn't want to jump to conclusions, but the morning had left him edgy. How much did Kurt know about this kid's background?

The coincidence was not lost on Jayden. Cody had access to the kitchen and he behaved with utmost respect around Mom. Was that a front for a grander scheme? And why?

The bigger question—was Cody speaking of Jayden's mother? Someone from her past? Jayden could only think of one person who might be carrying a grudge, the man whose name kept coming up in conversation, the one person nobody ever wished to see again— George Barnes. But what did Cody have to do with him?

Baylie scrolled down her screen, studying the story she'd written about losing Grandpa Joseph. She'd kept it light, focusing on the wonderful source of strength he'd been in her life. She touched on her years as a foster child, a girl without parents, but with real grandparents not far away. She'd never felt alone. Grandpa Joseph's guidance had hovered over her, giving her direction when she had been confused.

She closed the document and leaned back in her chair. The article wasn't finished, but she always liked to give any written copy time to rest. When she read it later the story would seem fresh and a new perspective could help her spot the flaws. Kurt's words kept resonating in her mind. "Every child needs a forever home."

Strange how true that was, even though she remained the exception. She'd never had a forever home. Not in the truest sense.

Mary and Troy had taken good care of her, but she'd been one of several they took in under their wing. Their home never seemed permanent. She hoped to count the ranch, but it wasn't forever yet. Maybe it would be some day.

She pulled up her photos. She needed a horse to spotlight this month. Or a cow. Maybe she should even consider one of the pigs. The door to the office opened, and she glanced up to see Jayden in the doorway. Her heart did a double beat. His face held no smile, and the set of his jaw told her something had happened.

"Hey!" She tried to sound casual. "Did you reach Parker?"

Jayden slid a chair over to the front of her desk. "Yes, I did." He leaned forward, eyes intent on something distant, not her. "Can you look up the records for the interns?"

"I don't have access to their personal histories. Lissa keeps all those." Baylie gave him a puzzled look. "Why? What do you need?"

"I suspect someone has planted an intern here to make trouble."

"Really? Who?"

"Cody."

Baylie frowned. "I know he's had some problems following orders and getting his work done." She opened her file of story leads and glanced at the roster of summer help. "But he's managed to stay one step ahead of the pink slip." She sensed something was on Jayden's mind. "Why?"

"He and I were out working the lower pasture today."

"Cows?"

"Cow—as in an ornery old cow named Bossy." Jayden blew out a puff of air.

"Hey, I'm looking for an animal to feature this month." Baylie flashed a smile. "Would Bossy be a good candidate?"

"Bossy is not why I'm here." He sounded almost angry. "Cody got this text while we were out there and walked away to read it.

Then his phone pinged, and I heard him say to whoever it was to leave someone alone."

"What someone?"

"I don't know. But I heard him say she's a nice lady and that whoever was on the phone shouldn't carry a grudge." Jayden shared the barn incident. "I also heard him say they found the bottle."

Baylie gasped. "Wow. "

"That's what I thought."

"You don't suppose he's targeted Lissa?"

"Or Mom." Jayden's eyes narrowed, smile grim. "I know George always held a grudge."

"But how is he connected to Cody?"

"That's why I wanted to check Cody's files."

"I have an idea. We'll have to tell Lissa and she'll probably tell Kurt." Baylie tapped her lip with an index finger. "I could feature Cody in a newsletter. Lissa would let me see his file for that. But I'd have to be careful not to reveal anything personal."

"Could you look, then decide he wasn't right for the story?"

"Hmm." Baylie glanced at her computer screen. "That might work. I still think we need to tell Lissa."

Jayden slumped. "I hope I'm wrong. But if it is George I need to know."

"Why would you even suspect him?"

"Mom said she'd heard from him. That he wanted to connect." Jayden's eyes flashed. "The booze bottle in the trash yesterday shouted George like a calling card."

Baylie stood. "Let me go talk to Lissa." She pushed her chair in. "Wait here. We might be able to snoop within a few minutes."

"Thanks, Baylie."

Jayden leaned back in his chair, his thumb poised over his cell phone, tempted to call Parker again. But he didn't want to appear as if he were pushing them together. If Cody was somehow involved with George, though, he trusted Parker to be in the mix. Mom needed an ally.

His head reeled with all the possible scenarios, knowing that to suspect Cody was grasping for facts without evidence. He'd had enough stealth training to keep a level head. But thinking like a soldier again conjured up images of his time in Afghanistan and quickened his pulse. He'd managed to escape the nightmares since being at the ranch, but he knew triggers were never far from his mind. He walked a narrow tightrope. A relapse could happen at any time.

The door to the office opened and Lissa walked in with Baylie. She looked at Jayden, a smile gracing her lips. "Sounds like we need to vet you for security purposes."

"What does that mean?"

"We clear you to see sensitive material with the understood promise that all information will be kept confidential."

"Really?"

"When you work with kids in the state's jurisdiction, their privacy is of utmost importance."

"Do I need to sign in blood?"

Lissa laughed. "No, but you do need to sign a statement that says you understand the terms of your involvement here." She handed him a document. "You'd have to sign eventually, anyway, but Baylie's made the case for adding you to the team now."

Jayden glanced at Baylie. "You told her of my suspicions?"

"I think this is worth pursuing."

"So do I." Lissa handed him a pen. "On the dotted line, please."

After reading its contents Jayden signed the document. He held it out to Lissa. "I'm not a snitch."

"I know." She turned to Baylie. "Folder please?"

Baylie took a seat at her desk and opened the file in her hand. Lissa grabbed a chair and joined her. Jayden leaned over the desktop. "Anything jump out?"

Baylie gasped and pointed. Lissa lifted the file to see. Jayden wanted to swear. "What?"

"Cody's mother has a restraining order against a live-in male companion." Lissa looked at him. "George Barnes."

"So he *is* back." Jayden hit the desk with his fist.

Outside an engine backfired, loud and annoying.

"We have company?" Baylie glanced at him, surprise in her eyes. "Talk about timing. You don't suppose he'd come in broad daylight?"

"The man is wacko enough to do that, but I'm here to see that George Barnes will not interfere with our lives again." He rose and strode towards the door, stopping to look over his shoulder. "Thanks, Lissa. You, too, Baylie." The door closed with a decidedly loud click.

CHAPTER TWENTY

BAYLIE HURRIED TO THE KITCHEN TO help Melanie with dinner preparations. At least she told herself that was the reason for going. If she were truthful, she wanted to see how Melanie took the news of George Barnes poking around the ranch.

Jayden certainly hadn't reacted well when he'd heard. He stormed out of her office, fists tight, jaw set. One would think the man in question worked for the Taliban. The door slammed in the wake of his temper.

Could this kind of conflict stir up war memories? Would Jayden exhibit symptoms of PTSD, behaviors that had not yet manifested themselves? At least in her presence, they hadn't. Baylie didn't know much about the condition, but she had to consider Jayden's war history. He'd encountered an improvised explosive device that overturned the vehicle in which he and his fellow Marines had been riding. A foot to the right and Jayden's unit would have suffered the full force of the IED. He would have been killed.

Baylie shuddered. A brush with death like that would give anyone nightmares. No guessing what it may have done to Jayden. He'd survived, but how had the incident left his mind? And if he'd died, what would have been her response? Losing Jayden to senseless war maneuvers in a peace keeping mission? Any hope of Baylie's desire to renew her relationship with her Savior would have been severed. If God couldn't deliver on His promises, neither could she. But Jayden had come home, and he'd given the credit to God. So must she.

She opened the back-kitchen door and entered, ashamed that she so easily put blame on a creator who had treated her well. God had given her a fulfilling career here, a lead role in an enterprise she was glad to represent. She and Jayden had once again become friends. The promise of so much more waited on the horizon. For that she gave thanks.

Laughter sounded in the kitchen, the male voice familiar, though she didn't recognize the speaker. She glanced around for Melanie, who was standing at the stove, chuckling as Parker stirred the pot. He'd donned a chef's hat, white and poufy, and was singing "This is the night. . ." loud and off key, a song she recognized from the spaghetti scene of an old animated version of a children's film.

Baylie crept into the room, not wanting to interrupt the levity. She leaned against the counter and waited. Parker glanced over, silly hat bouncing as he belted the cadenza, "and the heavens are bright. . .".

He stopped and laughed. "Hi, Baylie."

She applauded. "Don't quit singing on my account." She stepped toward the pair. "You have a nice voice."

Melanie turned her way, cheeks rosy. "He does, doesn't he?"

"Does this mean we're having spaghetti and meatballs?" Baylie grinned at Parker's flushed face next to Melanie's. "Or did you just feel inspired to sing?"

Melanie nodded. "I had lots of sauce left over from my last foray into spaghetti land so I thought it would be a good time to use the abundance. Parker is making meatballs to go with it."

"What can I do to help?" Baylie spied the large bowl on the counter. "Make a salad?"

"That would be great." Melanie glanced at her watch. "But it's early, so maybe we could assemble the ingredients and toss the salad nearer to dinner time."

"Got it."

Baylie retreated to the counter feeling like a snoop. Though Jayden had played down his call to Parker, clearly the man's presence meant he'd responded to the urgency of the matter and come to see Melanie. Baylie made for a third wheel. How could she gracefully withdraw? Murmured voices between the man and the woman confirmed what she believed. They were growing closer. Where had Jayden disappeared to?

The door to the kitchen opened and Jayden entered. "Hey, Parker. Saw your ride outside."

"Your call set off warning bells in my head. My company left early so I thought I'd come join the surveillance team." Parker's wink toward Melanie suggested another reason for the visit.

At Parker's words Jayden's demeanor changed, eyes again stormy, jaw rigid. He managed a smile for his former commander. "We could use an extra set of eyes. I don't want George coming around here."

Parker again looked at Melanie, an unspoken agreement seeming to hover between them.

"We both think you should calm down, Jayden." Melanie put her hands on her hips. "You don't know it's George."

"You know as well as I do, this is his calling card." Jayden's words were clipped and short.

Melanie shook her head. "It could be the behavior of a lot of drinkers."

"Mom." Jayden huffed. "Seriously?"

Melanie studied him. "I don't want you to vanish into soldier mode."

"I'll be careful." Jayden waved a hand as if dismissing the warning. "I had help with coping skills during rehab."

Parker stepped beside Melanie. "She's right, Jayden. This could trigger thoughts you don't want to give free rein." He clapped Jayden on the shoulder. "Nip it in the bud now."

Baylie frowned. What did she not know?

Jayden drew in several deep breaths, techniques he'd been taught to handle unwelcome memories and stave off violent reactions. His body relaxed. Surprised by the level of resentment he still carried against his former stepfather, he promised himself to deal with the fury and not give power to a man who no longer had any influence in his life. He'd been free of George's control for more than a decade. He wouldn't let the man affect him now. Nor would he allow George to put his mother in harm's way.

He glanced at Parker. "Thanks. You're right."

Parker nodded. "Glad I could help." He pulled off the chef's hat. "What kind of strategy do we need to catch this guy?"

Mom stirred the spaghetti sauce, then turned toward them again. "If it is George, I am the target. He wouldn't be here for any other reason."

Baylie cleared her throat. "Actually, there could be a reason." She aimed her question toward Jayden. "Have you told them what we discovered?"

He took another breath to control the venom that kept choking his thinking. He studied his mother, who held his gaze. "We found a connection between George and one of the interns."

Parker folded his arms. "No kidding."

Mom paled. "Why does that not surprise me?"

Parker touched Mom's shoulder. "Didn't you say the divorce is contested?"

"All he has to do is sign the documents and we're finished. . .for good." Mom walked to her workstation. "I told him that when he called me last month, but he never did listen to reason."

Parker shifted his feet and leaned against the counter. "Maybe he doesn't want the divorce to be final."

Jayden agreed. "Exactly what I was thinking."

Mom shook her head. "I have no intention of renewing my relationship with that man. We are done!"

Baylie looked at Jayden. "What do you think Melanie needs to do?"

Jayden spread his hands outward, then let them drop to his

side. "I don't know. But her attorney could tell us."

Parker agreed. "The sooner, the better, Melanie."

Mom squared her shoulders. "I shouldn't have let this go this long." Her saddened eyes gazed his way. "I will put an end to this one way or the other."

Jayden walked to his mother and wrapped his arm about her shoulders. "We're all rooting for you. Together we'll figure this out."

Mom kissed him on the cheek. "Won't he be surprised when he discovers the man you've become?"

"Yeah. I'd like to see him throw a Jim Beam bottle at me now." Jayden smirked. "I've developed a pretty good aim and could probably level him with a return throw."

"I'm sure you could." Parker agreed. "But that would only escalate what may only need to be a simple meet and greet."

Jayden blew air between his teeth. "I'll try to contain myself."

Mom turned toward her work desk and shuffled through some papers. "My attorney gave me his personal number. I'll go contact him on the office phone and see what he thinks I should do. I'll also try to reach George." She left her apron on the counter and walked out the back door, Parker at her side.

After the kitchen discussion, Jayden hurried to find Kurt and tell him of his mother's fears. He entered the barn and heard sweeping at the far end. "Kurt?"

Cody stuck his head out of the last stall. "He went up to the ranch house."

"Thanks, Cody." He pivoted and headed for the door.

"Jayden? Can I talk to you a minute?"

Jayden glanced back at Cody and stopped. "What's on your mind?"

Cody walked up the aisle, gaze darting from one side of the barn to the other. "I need to tell you something."

"Okay." The boy's nervous demeanor made Jayden suspicious. "Shoot."

"You are George Barnes' stepson, aren't you?"

Jayden felt the hair on the back of his neck prickle. "I was once, many years ago."

"He thinks you still are." Cody stopped and studied the barn floor. "He knows your mom is the cook here, too. When he found out I was an intern for the ranch, he started asking me a lot of questions about her."

Jayden ground his teeth. "Such as?"

"When she is in the kitchen. Where she stays. How many helpers she has. That sort of thing."

"Could you provide answers to those questions?"

Cody shook his head. "No. Not really. I had to be evasive because I'm not here all day or every day."

"Is that all he wanted?"

"He asked me to plant the Jim Beam bottle in the trash yesterday."

"Are you the one who raided the kitchen last night?"

Cody shook his head. "No, he came hunting for her."

Jayden again took deep breaths and focused on the hill behind the ranch. He could feel his heart banging against his sternum, each beat a little quicker than the last. His breath grew short and fast. He had to stop the panic attack before it got away from him.

Cody stood there, waiting for him to say something, but he couldn't. He held up a hand and bent over, hoping the blood would rush to his head. He thought he was going to lose the battle when a strong hand touched his back.

"Steady, Jayden." Kurt's voice was calm, tone deep. "You've got this."

He took another set of deep breaths and the rush of adrenaline withdrew. He straightened and breathed a sigh of relief. "I almost lost that one."

Kurt glanced at Cody. "I heard part of what you told Jayden. Is George close by?"

"He could be." Cody cast a sheepish smile at Kurt. "I told him I wouldn't help him anymore and he blew up. Threatened me the same way he threatened my mother. Only she has a restraining order against him. I don't." Cody glanced around him again, eyes wary. "That's why I wanted to warn Jayden. His mom has been super nice to me. I don't want George to hurt her."

Kurt held out his hand. "That took courage, Cody. Thank you for coming forward." He looked at Jayden. "Why don't you go check on your mother?"

"She's with Parker at her apartment."

"Still, she should know what Cody said."

"Got it." Jayden hurried toward the bunkhouse, his bad leg hurting again, the limp magnified by the tension he felt.

Baylie could only imagine the turmoil inside Jayden's head as they waited for Melanie to contact George. Jayden left to do barn chores with Kurt while Parker walked Melanie back to her apartment. Baylie chose to fill the time by tossing the salad for tonight's meal. With the spaghetti sauce finished, all that needed doing was cooking the pasta nearer to dinnertime.

She spied the French bread on the counter, a meal addition Melanie likely intended to slice and butter to accompany the dinner. Baylie had had plenty of practice making this meal, one that was often repeated, so she set to work. Cooking for a group this size meant lots of repetition. Baylie figured that was the only way Melanie could stay ahead of the endless menus.

She had to be diligent. Often a child in his first days on the ranch would hoard food or overeat. Once their trust was established those behaviors disappeared. The children here seldom complained, many grateful they had three square meals a day without fear of hunger. Baylie sighed. Perhaps she should feature Melanie in a newsletter. She certainly had earned the spotlight.

Bossy, though, would be her next headliner. An ornery old cow with an agenda would entertain her readers and probably conjure up some belly laughs if she wrote the story right. Sounded like fun. Plus, it would serve as a great distraction from the troubling thoughts that kept plaguing her.

Outside Duke barked, something he only did if he didn't know an approaching stranger. A noise behind her made her turn. A man she didn't recognize stood in the doorway, scowl emphasizing a furrowed brow and drawn cheeks. Baylie took a breath, steeling herself for a confrontation. "May I help you?"

"Where's Melanie?" The voice, low and venomous, sounded gravelly and out of breath. "This is her kitchen, isn't it?"

"She left to make a phone call." Baylie forced a smile she didn't feel, unwilling to elaborate. "Would you care for a cup of coffee?"

"No." The man glanced around the room, taking in the surroundings as though he were memorizing the layout of the kitchen. He focused back on her. "Who are you? Assistant cook?"

"No. I help out when my work is done."

"What kind of work is that?" The man sneered. "Mucking horse manure?"

"No, I write the ranch newsletter." Baylie inhaled to keep her voice from wavering.

"A newsletter?" The man's eyebrows rose. "The ranch can afford a writer?"

"I earn my keep. The ranch won't run itself."

The man leaned against the counter. "Last time I was here only an old man lived on the ranch, as did my stepson when he wanted to avoid his chores."

Baylie swallowed. So this was George, Melanie's ex-husband. Jayden's nemesis.

Her pulse quickened, breathing ragged, as she studied the one person she'd heard a lot about, but hoped never to meet. The silence in the room magnified her fear. She grappled with something to say. "We've got lemonade, if you are thirsty."

"Call Melanie." George stepped toward her. "I'm sure she has a phone?"

Baylie glanced toward Melanie's work area, the phone she used silent against the counter. "No, she didn't take her personal phone with her." Baylie pointed to the device waiting on Melanie's desk. "I could call the ranch's landline."

"As long as you get Melanie and not a host of other do-gooders who want to come to her rescue."

"I can't promise who will answer the main phone."

George slammed the counter. "Look, Missy." He pointed a gnarled finger at her. "You get Melanie or there will be a price to pay." He jerked his chin up. "Got that?"

Baylie stood helpless. What was taking Melanie so long? Parker? Jayden? Anybody? As if time stood still, she faced the man. She glanced at the clock on Melanie's work station. Had it only been ten minutes? She heard the squeak of the screen door.

George heard it, too. "You move over here. I'll use you as my bargaining chip."

"Isn't your argument with me, George?" Melanie stepped into the kitchen through the back door. She looked at Baylie, sorrow in her eyes. "Why don't you take a break?"

George straightened. "She's not going anywhere. You think I'm stupid? First thing she'll do is alert the powers that be." George's lower lip curled, finger aimed at Baylie. "She stays."

Baylie's knees shook, her entire torso trembling. How could

she get help? She'd stuck her phone in her jeans pocket. George would notice if she reached for it. If only Jayden were close, but with him helping Kurt he'd be gone until dinner. Where had Parker disappeared to? *God, hear me. Melanie and I need help.*

"If she stays, I'll stay with her." Jayden entered the room, shoulders rigid, fists pressed against his belt. His eyebrows met in the middle, his frown that of a man ready to explode. "Hello, George. Long time no see."

Baylie slumped against the counter. God had answered! She grabbed the edge to steady herself.

George paled. "Jayden?"

"Yeah. Jayden. Surprised?" Jayden stepped toward the man, tone laced with ice. He breathed deep, exhaling like an enraged bull. "No longer eleven, and no longer intimidated by your threats." Jayden stopped a few feet short of where George stood. "Want to throw a Jim Beam bottle at me now?"

"You join the military?" George's voice wobbled, his gaze traveling over Jayden's frame.

Parker stepped into the room from the other door, Kurt beside him. "We're all military." Parker walked to Melanie's side. "And you are trespassing."

With three Marines surrounding him the air appeared to fizzle out of George, as if he were a balloon poked by a pin. "I don't want any trouble." He raised both hands in a sign of surrender. "I wanted to discuss our marriage. . .uh, er. . .my marriage to Melanie."

"The only discussion that I intend to have is about you signing the divorce papers." Melanie sounded in control and authoritative. "Something you should have done twelve years ago."

George straightened, jaw set. "I thought by not signing and with Jayden now grown and gone, you might have a change of heart. Maybe give me a second chance." He gazed at Melanie. "Guess not."

"No guessing about it." Melanie walked to her desk. "I have

the copies you sent me here. Sign them. I'm sure all my friends here will witness the act." She handed him a pen. "Look for the yellow highlights." She stepped back and waited. "Don't leave town until I have a chance to show these to my attorney. After all this time I may need to file new documents."

Eyes narrowed, mouth pressed in a straight line, George sat at the desk, found the marked places, and affixed his signature. He handed Melanie the pen. "Want to check and see if I got them all?" Sarcasm dripped from every word.

Parker walked to the desk. "I'll do that."

"Who are you?" George frowned.

"I plan to be your replacement in Melanie's life." Parker picked up the documents. "She deserves someone who will cherish her."

George's smile froze, lips curled in a nasty snarl. "I did cherish her, but that kid of hers always took priority over me." He glanced at Jayden, fire in his gaze. "I never stood a chance in his father's shadow." He focused on Parker. "You Marine types are all she sees."

Parker's voice grew soft. "Perhaps she sees us as men."

Baylie glanced at Jayden. He still huffed, his chest heaved, and his face had turned the color of crimson. Baylie's knees wobbled. Would Jayden suffer a setback?

As Kurt and Parker escorted George out of the kitchen, Jayden glanced at Baylie who had taken a chair. Her pale skin accented tight lines in her face, but her breathing had returned to normal. "Baylie, you okay?"

She cast him a weak smile. "I will be." She drew a deep breath. "He scared me."

"I'm sorry, Baylie." Mom put an arm around the girl's

shoulders. "I never meant for you to get caught up in this."

"It's okay." Baylie sat up straighter. "You didn't know he'd walk into the kitchen unannounced."

"When Cody told me what he knew, we all hurried here because I suspected George might be hanging around." Jayden folded his arms across his midsection. "Actually, that's the way George used to show up after a cross-country truck haul. Unannounced and usually after dropping by a bar." He lowered his arms to his side. "Some things never change."

Baylie tried to smile. "I didn't smell any booze on him. I don't think he was drunk today. Just agitated." She looked at Mom. "I've seen angry drunks. They are a lot more aggressive."

Her reply surprised Jayden. How did she know that? He needed to have that long overdue private discussion with her. She'd eluded him, but from this response Baylie had a few secrets of her own. He wanted to know what they were.

He turned to his mother. "Parker plans to replace George in your life?" He leaned against the counter. "When did all of this happen?"

Mom blushed, a deep hue of pink coloring her cheeks. "We really connected the last few weeks. He's brought the subject up several times, but I told him this was way too fast."

Jayden's pulse throbbed beneath his breastbone. "You think?" He pulled up a chair and sat near Baylie, gesturing for his mother to do the same. "Mom, you only met him, what, two weeks ago? Three?"

Mom didn't look at him, gaze on the floor. Finally, she gave him her full attention. "Actually, we got to know each other while you were in rehab."

"What?" Jayden leaned forward. "How?"

"He often called to update me on your progress. Especially when you wouldn't tell me anything. We talked a lot about your past." Mom's smile said she loved the memory. "We didn't meet face to face until you brought him into the kitchen the night you showed up on your bike." Mom grinned. "But I knew he was coming."

"Amazing." Jayden didn't know whether to laugh or wring his mother's neck. "He never said anything to me."

"I asked him not to." Mom's gaze searched his face. "Are you angry?"

"No. Only surprised." He took her hands. "I can't think of anyone I'd rather see you with. Parker's the best. And that's what you deserve."

Mom agreed with a nod. "That's what I think, too." She touched his chin. "Are you going to be all right?"

Jayden shrugged. "This George thing set off some ugly memories for me. I may have a few recurring nightmares. Wear ear plugs."

CHAPTER TWENTY-ONE

Baylie's head swam as she recalled the events of this afternoon. Her encounter with Jayden's stepfather George had left her shaken. His behavior reminded her of another's actions, a past acquaintance she hoped to forget.

Until today.

The past had caught up with her, threatening to resurrect the remorse she'd buried and to expose her shame.

Parker's declaration that he and Melanie were more than friends surprised her. How had this happened so fast? The news made her yearn for the same. How she longed to have a commitment with Jayden like the one Parker and Melanie shared with each other. Surrounding the entire confrontation, though, remained Jayden's violent reaction to it all—indicators war trauma continued to plague him.

"Take a few minutes for yourself." Melanie touched her shoulder. "You seem jittery."

"I think I'll go to my apartment."

Melanie's nod said she approved. "I'll have tonight's kitchen help assemble the salad."

"No need. I finished most of it before George appeared." Baylie paused at the door. "I'll be back. Truly."

"Take your time. We'll be fine."

Baylie walked to the bunkhouse and pulled out her key. Melanie's calm amazed her. When had the woman learned to be so strong in the face of aggression? George reminded her of the man she too had thought she loved, but whose behavior betrayed her. Her experience with him at school, similar to what Melanie had endured with George, left her fearful, not strong.

She shuddered as her mind replayed the fateful, unhappy

evening. The memories begged to be revisited. Baylie had buried them for as long as she could. She marveled that she'd escaped the horrible confrontation as well as she did. Only her guilt remained.

Hunter's visit had been expected, her anticipation of where they were headed that evening making her breathless. She shoved aside the values she held dear, forbidden desires taking her down a path she knew she shouldn't follow. Hunter was such a wonderful boyfriend. She never saw him drink, carouse, not even smoke. How he became the monster who stood before her that night, she didn't know. But he had. Drinking gave him boldness. He burst through her door, unsteady on his feet. Her knight in shining armor vaporized before her eyes, the rusted shell of a counterfeit in his wake.

Instead of being wooed by a romantic suitor she found this lewd and lustful drunk revolting. As if God was shaking her by the shoulders, she woke up in time to stop a decision she now knew she would have regretted forever.

"Baylie?"

She startled and turned to the voice. Jayden waited in the open doorway. She gulped in a breath of air. "Is your mother okay?"

Jayden nodded. "She's encountered George before."

"Obviously."

"But you haven't." Jayden shifted his weight. "May I come in?"

"Um . . . sure." Baylie pointed to a chair, nerves poking at her conscience. Jayden's face said he wanted a serious conversation. She didn't feel ready for it. She had to sidestep his questions. "I just came to catch a break. Then I need to help Melanie."

Jayden took the proffered seat. "She's got everything under control. . .as usual."

"She's amazing."

"So are you." Jayden's gaze was intense. "You kept a cool

head while you dealt with George. I was surprised when you said you'd encountered angry drunks before."

"In college you see a lot of things." Baylie shifted the focus to him. "You seemed agitated by his presence. Are you okay?"

"I will be. Aggression triggers a negative response in my brain. I launch into soldier mode."

"How do you get out of it?"

"They taught me in rehab to aim my focus elsewhere, so if I can, I pray. Today, though, all I could do was take deep breaths. Sometimes I bend over to send the blood to my head." He tipped his chin up." But every morning I usually take a long walk and pray as I go." Jayden shrugged. "The combination keeps me from going nuclear. A good workout helps me sleep, which is often when the terrors get a grip." He looked at her. "And I force myself to talk about it, though I don't want to. Most guys bury the memories." Jayden drummed the table. "I still have the occasional night terror. Mom has witnessed one or two."

"What happens?"

"That's just it. Night terrors usually don't wake their victims, nor do they have a memory of them. But others around them witness the effects. Nightmares, however, wake me up and I recall the dream."

"Does the time in Afghanistan plague your dreams?"

Jayden nodded. "Images of things I witnessed pop up."

"And?"

"I wake. I go for a walk. I can't run yet, but I will." Jayden grinned. "I cope." He leaned toward her. "Now how does Baylie cope with her memories?"

"By helping Melanie finish dinner for a dozen or so hungry kids." She stood and nodded the direction of the door. "You coming?"

"You are avoiding the issue of drunks in your past." Jayden squinted at her, closing his one good eye. "Don't think I didn't notice when you sidestepped the issue."

"All I said was I'd seen things while away at school."

"You made it sound personal." Jayden reached for her hand. "Why don't you sit and tell me about it?"

Baylie feared looking at him, across a table, straight into his eye. What if she told him what happened and he was disgusted? What if this part of her past ruined all promise of their future? She swallowed, not sure she could bear the humiliation. He held on to her fingers, gently pulling her to the chair next to his. She had nowhere to run.

Jayden patted the seat, waiting. "What was his name?"

She bit her lip. Could she do this? She exhaled. "Hunter." She settled into the chair, heart pounding, breathing ragged. "We were a couple my senior year."

"Serious relationship?"

"I thought so." Baylie laced her fingers together, resting them in her lap. "He said all the right things. Planned all the right moves. Made me feel like a princess. I was sure we were headed to a future of happiness."

"What went wrong?"

Baylie gazed at Jayden's solemn face, taking in the rugged cut of his jaw, the intensity of his good eye, the whisper of a smile on his lips. How could she ever have thought Hunter outshone her longtime friend? She raised her shoulders, as if letting them drop could bolster her courage. She moistened her lips, praying Jayden would understand and not despise her.

"I was so alone at the university. Every year I thought it would get better, but it didn't." Even now the memory of that loneliness threatened to elicit tears. The days of walking invisible to class. Of passing groups of friends laughing together who didn't notice anyone around them. Of being only a name on a professor's roll sheet. Hours and hours of feeling detached. The hurt still lingered.

She faced Jayden. "Some students come with so much money and are able to do so many things I couldn't afford, I felt left out. A foster kid on scholarships with no extra cash, no real home to go to on the holidays, no mom or dad waiting to bail me out if I failed. I didn't fit in."

"I can understand your loneliness. Your letters were full of your feelings."

"I needed somewhere to vent my frustrations." She squeezed his fingers. "You were an easy target."

"I'm your friend. I was honored that you chose to confide in me."

"But what could you do? All I did was heap guilt on you."

"I didn't feel that way. It gave me a way to connect and pray for you. Until you stopped writing." Jayden lifted his gaze to hers. "I thought something was wrong."

"That was when I met Hunter."

The door to the bunkhouse opened and Baylie heard the twins, Kendra and Krystal, calling her.

"Down here, girls." Baylie waited as the pair wandered to her apartment. Internally she sighed in relief—saved by the girls.

When they reached her open door, they stopped. Kendra gave Jayden a shy smile, then looked Baylie's way. "Melanie asked us to help with the French bread, but we don't know what to do."

"Can you come help us?" Krystal clasped hands under her chin. "Please?"

Baylie looked at Jayden who gave her a nod. "Sure, let's go get dinner finished." She stood and walked to where the girls waited, appreciating their presence.

"We'll talk about this again, Baylie." Jayden spoke behind her. "I won't let you run away forever."

Baylie closed her eyes, the truth of what she needed to tell him a piercing spear in her side. She couldn't do it. She doubted she ever could.

She turned and studied him, the burden of the knowledge she carried burying her smile. "Yes. You deserve to know."

But you never will.

She rejoined the twins and headed for the exit, feeling like she'd escaped execution from the guillotine, the reprieve welcome. She'd live another day to summon her courage. All was well. For now.

Jayden headed to his mother's apartment, the afternoon's drama weighing on his mind. Baylie hid something, and from the strain reflected on her face, telling him would not be easy. She still behaved like the natural leader she'd been in high school, still performed her duties with a smile. But talking about this guy—Hunter, was it—whatever he'd done in her life weighed on her like a ball and chain. Jayden promised himself he would do whatever it took to help her get beyond this demon that plagued her.

If she would tell him.

Parker entered the apartment, carrying his helmet. "I'm bunking in the barn tonight."

Jayden frowned. "Why?"

"Melanie and I are spending a lot of our days together when I'm here. It's probably best if we don't spend our nights in the same apartment, don't you think?"

Jayden folded his arms across his chest. "What's this about you taking George's place?

"I hope Melanie will give me a chance." Parker scuffed his boot on the floor. "You were the biggest obstacle until you gave me the go ahead."

Jayden held his hands up, palms out. "Mom knows her own mind. I'm fine with the two of you hitting it off. I had only hoped to have more time building a new relationship with her. We lost a lot of years to George's shenanigans."

Parker straightened. "I will not interfere with that." He spun the helmet in his hands. "I can't be here that often, so a lot of our getting to know each other will be through e-mail and texts." He clipped his heels together and saluted. "You, sir, will be free to spend all the time you want with your mother."

Jayden held out his hand. "Take good care of her. She deserves a man like you."

"I will. Now, can you show me where to bunk in the barn?"

"As a kid, I spent my nights in the loft. Hay makes a great bed to sleep on." Parker didn't look impressed. Jayden laughed. "But there is a bed in the tack room where we sleep if we have an ailing cow or horse in need of nighttime attention. We're close to the animal, yet comfortable."

"That sounds great." Parker gestured to the door. "Lead on."

"Trust me. This will be an experience."

Jayden led the way into the familiar maze of stalls and walls of buckets, the smell of hay and grain mingling with the always present odor of manure. No matter how clean the barn, that pungent stink always lingered. For him these reminders of his years growing up as first Peggy's foster teen, then Kurt and Lissa's, brought back great memories. How Parker viewed this earthy experience remained to be seen. The man might not be enamored with a whiff of horse muffins.

"Really brings us to the heart of the ranch, doesn't it?" Parker chuckled behind him. "Is the spare bed in a stall?"

Jayden pointed to the tack room. "No, the bed is in the room with the saddles and blankets. Less manure smell, but still lots of horse."

"I'll be fine." Parker stepped through the door. "Remember, I had to sleep in a tent with sweaty, grime-covered Marines." He pushed on the bed. "This even has a decent mattress. Definitely a step up from a cot."

"We cater to an elite clientele." Jayden leaned against the door casing. "The horses will serenade you to sleep with their snorts and hay crunching."

"Sounds like a high-priced show at the local theater."

"Right." Jayden glanced at his watch. "We better head for the kitchen. Mom may think we're late for dinner so we can weasel our way out of dish duties."

Baylie put the finishing touches—chopped cucumbers, shredded carrots, and tiny bits of tomato—on the pile of lettuce she'd assembled earlier. She set the salad on the counter by the plates and went to the cooler for bottled dressing. When she returned Jayden and Parker had come and were teasing Melanie. She stiffened. She needed to distance herself from Jayden for a while—cool his scrutiny of her past. Telling her secret would sever the friendly rapport she'd enjoyed with him since his arrival home.

She focused on the twins filling a container with the French bread. "Girls, cover the bread with a clean towel so it stays warm."

When she looked again, Melanie's cheeks burned pink. Her laughter in the company of the two men made Baylie relax. Parker's attentions drew Jayden's focus away from her and fixed it on his mother. Baylie appreciated the anonymity.

Melanie glanced her way, a knowing smile on her lips. "Why don't you lightly coat the salad with the Italian dressing, so we don't have kids turning the bottle upside down over their plates?"

"Got it." Baylie grinned at the memory Melanie's comment evoked, appreciating the way the woman re-directed Baylie's thoughts. She remembered the incident well.

Kevin had been the culprit. The child really liked ranch dressing. His lettuce had landed on a lake of white in the middle of his plate. The bottle had little left to dribble over the remaining salad. Though she and Melanie had laughed, they made a mental note not to leave Kevin unsupervised near the condiments again. Or, for that matter, any child. Around here history had a way of repeating itself.

She opened the spicy vinaigrette, sprinkling it on the lettuce. She tossed the ingredients with the wooden spoon to distribute the flavor more evenly. She tipped the finished salad toward Melanie, again offering thanks for the skillful way the woman had pulled Baylie away from thoughts of the afternoon's events with a chore.

"I think we're ready to serve the kids." Melanie motioned to Jayden and Parker. "Want to let the troops know they can wash their hands?"

Baylie stepped in beside Melanie at the counter and picked up the tongs. "Shall I serve the noodles?"

"No, I promised Parker he could help." Melanie cast her a sideways grin. "You've earned an evening off."

Baylie's panic sent her heart racing. She needed some task to cover for her. "I think I'll lie down, then, if you don't mind."

"Are you ill?" Melanie's concern etched worry lines between her eyes.

"No. Just a bit worn out from all the excitement." Baylie pasted on a smile. "Do you mind if I skip out?"

"Of course not. You weren't hired as kitchen staff, yet you willingly do it anyway."

"I'm always glad to help. However, I think you have an eager helper waiting to get a little closer." She winked.

Melanie blushed. "I don't mind that a bit."

Baylie untied her apron and slipped toward the back door. Duke raised his head, giving her a quiet woof. She held the screen so it wouldn't bang and walked in the shadows of the buildings to her apartment.

Her stomach growled. Lissa's office door stood open as she passed. She stopped in and grabbed a bag of chips from Kurt's stash and a bottle of iced tea from the refrigerator. She'd repay them tomorrow. For now, this would provide dinner and a safe getaway from Jayden's questions.

When Jayden returned to the kitchen, he searched for Baylie, but not seeing her, asked his mother.

"She said she needed to take a break."

He frowned, then turned his attention to helping the kids get dinner. Parker played sous-chef, dishing out noodles at Mom's side. Jayden stepped up to the salad bowl and helped the smallest children with the lettuce.

"There's garlic bread in the stainless-steel bowl." Mom pointed to the container. "Add that to their salad."

Jayden picked up the tongs and served the bread chunks. The smell of garlic and warm butter rose from the bowl. These kids ate well with his mother at the helm.

When all of the children had been served, he and Parker each grabbed a plate and filled it. Jayden picked up a third plate and stepped up to the noodles.

"You especially hungry tonight?" Parker's eyes teased as he placed another tong of noodles in front of Jayden.

Jayden shook his head. "I thought I'd take a plate of hot food to Baylie since she left without dinner." He glanced at his mother. "Don't you think that's a good idea?"

"It's a nice gesture, but she was quite shaken with the events of the day. She may not have an appetite."

"She can put it in her mini-fridge if she can't eat it."

Mom studied him. "Go for it."

Baylie sat on the edge of her bed, popping chips into her mouth.

The earlier conversation with Jayden had dredged up unwanted memories of that fateful night with Hunter. She'd so willingly gone along with his plans that the reality of what they planned to do hit her like a bucket of cold water.

She sipped her iced tea and stared out the window at the sun going down over the hill. Her stupidity still baffled her, but Hunter's charm had blinded her ability to reason. Dashing, and unbelievably handsome, he'd come from money. He drove a luxury sports car, had a beguiling smile, and charmed her with his words. He'd called her his special angel. She'd basked in the attention.

She stopped, shaking her head. How foolish she had been. Enamored by her fairy tale prince, she couldn't see anything else. She inhaled a sharp breath as more memories surfaced. She and Hunter had grown more and more involved. Dates. Trips. Fraternity parties. Study nights. She'd loved it all.

They'd also grown more affectionate. Kissing. Holding hands. Hours of cuddling in his car. She'd craved the physical attention as much as the verbal praise. Hunter kept pushing for sex, but she'd resisted. The continued pressure had worn down her resolve.

That's when Hunter asked her to spend the weekend with him. His parents had a cabin. A great getaway. They could be alone. Dinner, a fire, huge windows to watch the stars. Each other.

"You know how much I care about you." Hunter had whispered in her ear. "Think how great our next step will be."

Baylie shuddered now at her willingness. He'd manipulated her heart to a place of surrender. They'd chosen the following weekend for their tryst. Almost as soon as her heart warmed to the idea, her feet grew cold. Her upbringing in a Christian foster home, years spent in a youth group, and personal study of Scripture all seemed to chime in, screaming at her to resist. But their voices were silenced by the appetite of her rebellious heart. She wanted this. To belong, to be loved, to be Hunter's desired companion.

A knock on her door interrupted her reverie. She waited. Only one person could be there. She didn't want to see him. She sat on her bed gazing out the window. He would want the truth. Giving it to him would forever sever any hope of a future relationship.

The knock came again. "Baylie? It's Jayden."

She didn't move. *Go away, please. I need to be alone.*

He knocked again. "Baylie, are you all right?"

He wasn't going away. Fine. *Let's get this over with.* Baylie stood and walked to the door. She opened it a crack, looking at this perfect figure of a man she'd once called friend, a person who'd soon discover she wasn't someone he wanted to know. "I'm fine. Just rattled from the afternoon."

Jayden held up two plates, the aroma making her mouth water. "I didn't think you'd eaten so I brought you a plate."

"Who's the other one for?"

"I thought I could keep you company."

"I'm pretty sure you'll regret it."

Jayden cast her a lopsided smile. "Let me be the judge of that."

She stepped back. Once again, her resolve had failed.

CHAPTER TWENTY-TWO

J AYDEN ENTERED THE APARTMENT AND HANDED Baylie the loaded plate. "I brought silverware." He fished in his pocket, pulling out a bundle he'd rolled together in a towel. "And napkins."

"Aren't you efficient?" She took the food and gestured toward the small table. "I think we can both sit there."

Jayden moved to the other side, careful to slide the chair out so there was enough room for him in the corner where it sat. "These apartments are nice, but not generous with space."

"No." Baylie sat across from him. "But they were designed for temporary summer help."

"You aren't temporary, are you?"

"Thankfully, no. At least not yet."

Jayden studied his friend. "What does that mean?"

"If the ranch falls behind in support, layoffs follow. My job and your mother's position are considered essential to the operations of the facility, but there's always the possibility of a funding shortage."

"Has there been a problem?" Jayden didn't remember his mother expressing any worry.

"No." Baylie unwrapped the silverware and handed him a fork. "But I haven't been here long. This wasn't my first gig out of college."

"Where were you before?"

"I did a brief stint as a reporter while I was still in Eugene." Baylie wrinkled her nose. "It wasn't my cup of tea." She swirled spaghetti on her fork. "I was tired of the campus scene and didn't like the demands of the job. I needed a change of scenery after four years at the university."

"So you opted for the wide open spaces of Eastern Oregon."

"This felt normal, like I'd come home."

Jayden smiled. "I approve of your choice, for all the right reasons. Let's pray." He didn't miss the pale fright that passed over her face as he bowed his head. When he finished, he stuck his fork in his noodles. "Parker accused me of being super hungry when I took a second plate. So eat up. I can't go back with leftovers."

"How do you like Parker and your mother being together? Are you feeling better about them?" Baylie's question tabled his next comment on her job choices, so he forked a mouthful and chewed. She studied him. "Sure happened fast."

Jayden nodded. "Mom told me she knew him while I was in rehab. The exchange of letters or e-mails or texts. . . I'm not sure what device they used. . .must have been intense."

"Your mother had to have been super worried about you. She said you wouldn't give her any information."

"I didn't know how much to tell her." Jayden set his plate down and wiped his chin. "I couldn't just say, hey, Mom, I'm losing my leg today. Send flowers." He looked at her. "The eye would have totally freaked her out."

"She would have come running." Baylie laid the fork on her plate. "She'd have supported you no matter what happened."

Jayden glanced at her, the opening he'd been waiting for inviting him in. "Just like I will support you no matter what your story is." Baylie's face paled in the dwindling light outside her window. He'd touched a nerve. He waited in the quiet, hoping she'd let him into her private hell. "Tell me more about Hunter."

She fidgeted for a minute, as if her willingness to tell him the story fought her reluctance to do so. She sighed and looked at him. "We met our senior year. I'd been so alone for three years, working to get my degree, having no time or money for much social activity. Hunter came along like the proverbial knight on a white horse."

"He swept you off your feet?" Jayden studied her, the

emotions playing across her face reflecting pain, regret, and fear. She didn't respond. "Baylie?"

"Yes." The whispered response sounded faint even in the silent room.

"Did you fall in love with him?" Jayden held his breath, hoping she'd say no.

Baylie slumped. "I don't know." She looked at the floor for several minutes. When she raised her gaze to his, unshed tears brimmed the rims of her eyes. "Jayden, you don't really want to know this." She sniffed. "You'll never want to be around me again."

He reached across the table. "Anything you have done can be forgiven, Bayles. I believe in the forgiving God of the universe. So do you. If His Son could die for me, why would He not hold out His arms to you?"

Baylie inhaled, her chest heaving. "I did think I loved Hunter. He said all the right things, took me to all the nicest places. I thought we were headed to a great future."

"What happened?"

Baylie held up her hand. "Let me finish. We were growing more and more affectionate. He pushed for sex. I resisted."

Jayden didn't flinch.

"You aren't shocked?"

"I've been to war. I've known Marines. A lot of guys have only one thing on their mind." Jayden leaned closer. "Did you give him what he wanted?"

Baylie sagged in her chair. How could she acknowledge her willingness, yet explain her innocence? "I intended to." She glanced about the room, not making eye contact with him. "He said he wanted to take our relationship to the next level. I didn't know what that meant, but I was willing to find out." Her voice cracked and she cleared her throat. "We planned a dinner date at a fancy restaurant, then a rendezvous at his parent's weekend cabin. I bought lingerie."

"Really?"

She looked at him. "Yes, really. See. I told you this would send you running."

"I'm not going anywhere." Jayden patted her hand. "I shouldn't have said that. I was just trying to lighten your mood. I can tell this is difficult for you."

Baylie glanced at the clock her grandmother had given her. "I shouldn't have left Melanie in the lurch."

"Parker's got it covered."

Baylie stood. "But still, I . . ."

"Don't run away." Jayden kept his voice soft, almost a whisper. "Clearing the air will help you escape the hold this has on you."

"But will my story trigger a negative reaction in you?" She stared at him, one eyebrow raised. "I thought you were going to lose it today when we encountered George."

"No, you are helping me focus on something other than my past encounters." Jayden leaned back in the chair and crossed his left leg over his right. "As your friend, I want to hear your tale."

Baylie closed her eyes, her face a mirror of the pain she must have suffered. Jayden prayed she could find the strength to unburden her soul. When she opened her eyes, she raised her gaze to stare at the wall, again avoiding direct eye contact. "I'd purchased a strapless blue dress I couldn't afford. Dangling earrings." She looked at him as if searching for evidence that he was repulsed by what she said. Jayden kept his face composed, determined not to react. "I wore my hair in a messy bun." She held up her fingers as if making air quotes. "Wispy tendrils trailing down the sides of my face." She blushed. "Hunter's gaze told me I'd succeeded in meeting his expectations." She studied Jayden again as if anticipating the damning reprimand she deserved for her behavior. His heart broke for her.

Jayden could well imagine the scene. Hunter's reaction. He

remembered how Baylie had looked when he took her to their high school prom. Her grandmother had purchased the dress for her birthday, a green satin that accented her eyes and highlighted her golden hair. A shy teen with a gorgeous girl on his arm, he'd been intimidated by her beauty, He understood the hunger aroused in Hunter. "Where did you go for dinner?"

"We didn't get that far. Hunter swaggered into the room, arms outstretched, leering like a lion who'd found his prey. He slurred his words. Dessert first, he said. Meaning me." Baylie's jaw tensed. "He didn't want to wait for the cabin. I told him I wouldn't go. Not now."

"Was there really a cabin?"

"I think so." Baylie shrugged. "I don't know. He crossed the room toward me. As he drew nearer, I could smell the liquor on his breath. I called him on it." She grabbed her midsection, as if in pain as she recounted Hunter's betrayal. "He said he had a lot to celebrate. Then he'd smiled and his smirk turned my stomach. He became aggressive, pinning me in his arms, and kissing me like he'd succeeded in trapping his kill."

"Did you get away?"

"I yelled at him to stop! I shoved him back and slapped him. The sound cut the silence in the room." A smirk escaped her lips and she shook her head. "All I could think to do was ask if we didn't have dinner reservations?"

"I'm guessing he wasn't interested in dinner?"

"I told him this wasn't romantic. I was disgusted." She grabbed her shoulders and dipped her head. "He called me a prude. Grew sarcastic. Asked me how I thought the evening was going to go."

"Obviously you had no clue." Jayden leaned forward again, forcing himself to remain calm. How he wanted to wrap Baylie in his arms and tell her everything was going to be alright. He drummed the table to relieve the stress he felt, fighting the urge to release his anger at Hunter with the force of a fist on the unsuspecting surface.

"He lunged for me and I sidestepped his grab. He stumbled off balance and swore. I picked up a volume of journalism law, the biggest book I owned. Holding it with both hands above my head I brought it down on his shoulders, and he moaned. I told him to get out." Baylie put her head down on the table. "I said I hadn't agreed to this."

"Did he leave?"

"He was furious. His rage scared me. I didn't expect to escape the situation." When Baylie looked up her tear-stained face reflected the horror she'd endured. She continued. "'You are nothing but a tease,' he said. He roared and shook his fist." Baylie mewled, a small desperate cry escaping her throat, hands covering her face.

"Baylie?"

"He kept yelling at me. 'I can have any woman I want. And I have.' Then he laughed. 'Look at your shocked face,' he said. 'What? Did you think you were an exclusive? Dream on, little miss innocence. You are just one in a collection of many.'"

"I'm not surprised, Bayles." Jayden sat up straight. "Can I get you a glass of water?"

"I'm almost finished." Baylie's distraught smile formed a faint curve on her lips. "Are you sure you want to hear more?"

"You can't get rid of me that easily." Jayden cast what he hoped looked like a crooked grin, trying to lighten the tension in the room. "I'm your friend."

"Thank you, Jayden." Baylie swallowed, licking her lips. "I pointed to the door and told Hunter to get out now. He stormed out, stopped on my step, and aimed an angry finger at me. He said he wouldn't be back."

"And you slammed the door, right?"

"Oh, Jayden. I failed him." She looked at him, tears running down her face. "I shouldn't have sent him away angry and drunk. I should have made him coffee. Tried to calm him down. Maybe even offered to pray with him." She scoffed. "I was so stupid."

"I doubt he would have listened."

"But I failed God, don't you see? Instead of me influencing Hunter, he influenced me."

"Did he ever come back?"

"No." Baylie tensed, eyes wild with fright. She sobbed into her hands, the cry that of a wounded animal. "God can never forgive me." She stood and ran out the door.

"Baylie, wait!"

Why did she tell Jayden her story? She'd sworn she never would. But she had. Every painful detail. Except for the last one. She couldn't tell him that.

He hadn't appeared to be shocked. Yet he had to be. Disappointed. Disgusted. Disinterested. She'd so needed him as a friend. Now he'd be justified avoiding her. Another stupid error in her judgment. A promising relationship ruined.

She entered the barn, slipping through the half-open side door. In here the dwindling outside light became dusk, shadows mounting the walls as the sun finished its descent beyond the hill. She walked with care, listening to the sounds of the horses stabled here. One nickered, as if greeting the trespasser it heard in the barn, a welcoming comfort to Baylie's fragile heart.

She sucked in a ragged breath. The crying from minutes before wracked her body. Every breath became irregular. She didn't know the barn well, at least not beyond the row of stalls she passed now. A noise to her right made her jump. Duke whined at her from an empty stall. "Go back to sleep, fella." She hurried on.

The tack room door stood open and she stepped inside, pulling the latch behind her. A small low-watt lamp had been left on, a spindly string dangling from the socket. She tiptoed to the waiting cot, sinking into the mattress and burying her face in her hands. The silence soothed, as if she'd entered a sanctuary where she could sit and meditate without interruption.

The quiet of the space reminded her of the prayer room she'd kept in her closet when she'd needed comfort during her college years. The place where God joined her—but not anymore. How she longed to have that fellowship with Him again. Would she never sense the presence of her Creator whispering healing balm to her mind?

"Father, I need your forgiveness. I need your presence back in my life. I failed you. I failed Hunter. I know you brought him into my life for a reason and I let him down. I let you down."

She stopped, listening to the hush around her. Only the occasional stomp of a hoof on the barn floor or a snort from an itchy muzzle interrupted the peace. She leaned back against the wall, the distress of the last few minutes leaving her drained. The cot felt inviting. She lay on her side and closed her eyes. No one would find her here.

Jayden hurried out of the bunkhouse as fast as his bum leg would let him. "Baylie! Wait!"

But Baylie had been running, had slammed the front door to the building before he could grab his cane and leave her apartment. His frustration triggered bitter memories—breathing labored, heart pounding in his throat. The war had stolen the ability to move quickly, diminishing his manhood. He couldn't help his friend with her pain. For that he wanted to yell.

Once outside, the fading light further decreased the visibility. "Baylie!" He saw no sign of her, but only so many places existed here on the ranch that could hide her. He'd search each one. Should he start with the main kitchen? She might think Mom still needed help with dish duties and seek out her counsel. A good choice. Should he interrupt them?

The barn waited to the right. Baylie didn't do much in the barn beyond teaching an occasional riding lesson, but she did like the horses. Would she go there? He knew from experience how safe a barn could make a person feel. He hesitated, indecision fouling his thinking. "Baylie?"

"You lose somebody?" Parker came up beside him out of the shadows, startling Jayden. "Or are you playing hide and seek?"

"A little old for that." Jayden faced the man. "Baylie and I were having a deep discussion about something from her past. Retelling it made her emotional and she ran out of the bunkhouse and disappeared."

"Want me to help you look for her?" Parker's warm voice reached out through the growing twilight. "We're both good at surveillance."

"She's really fragile right now." Jayden fought the wobble in his voice. "I better do this alone. I don't want her to think I'm sharing her secrets."

"Good thinking." Parker clapped him on the shoulder. "I'm heading to my bunk for the night after I grab my pack from your mother's apartment. If I see Baylie in the barn, I'll send her your way."

"Better still. Come get me." Jayden sighed. "She probably doesn't want to talk to me any more tonight."

"Sounds deep."

"It was." Jayden turned to the kitchen. "I'm going to talk to Mom. Baylie might have sought her out for a listening ear."

"Melanie is still there, but not for long. Didn't see Baylie." Parker raised a hand in farewell. "Good luck finding your girl."

"Thanks."

Jayden wandered toward the kitchen first. Mom stood wiping down the stove. She smiled. "Need something?"

"Did Baylie come in here?"

"No." Mom tossed her sponge in the sink. "Did you two finish your plates? I'd like to get them back."

"I'll bring them next trip. Okay?" Jayden turned to the door.

"Is everything all right?" Mom put her hands on her hips. "You seem agitated."

"Just looking for Baylie." Jayden didn't want to give Mom any details. "I'll catch you later."

He ducked through the back kitchen door before she could question him further. He checked the laundry room, then doubled back to the end of the barn where the recreational equipment was stored. No sign of her. The only remaining option was the barn interior. Stepping back outside, he headed to the double doors, remembering the paddock behind the barn where Lady and her foal spent their days. He'd stop there first. She wouldn't have gone to the pastures, would she?

CHAPTER TWENTY-THREE

At the sound of footsteps in the barn aisle, Baylie sat up, blinking in the dim light. Duke, awakened from his spot in the first stall, let out a small yip. A male voice answered him.

Baylie's heart punched against her breastbone, a staccato rhythm. She didn't want to face Jayden right now. If she told him the rest of the story, he'd never speak to her again. She stayed still in the quiet of the tack room. Would he find her in here? She waited, chest heaving. The steps came closer and the door opened. She sucked in a breath.

Parker stepped through the opening, set his pack on the floor, and seeing her, stopped. "Oops. Sorry. I didn't think anyone was in here." He glanced around the room. "Jayden told me I could bunk here for the night."

"I'm so sorry." Baylie stood. "I needed some time alone." She choked back a sob. "I'll leave right away."

"Wait." Parker held up a hand. "Jayden told me you were upset." He sat on the chair across from her. "From the sound of your voice, I'm betting you could use a friend." He crossed an ankle over his knee. "Am I right?"

Baylie nodded.

"I'm good at listening."

"I don't want to burden you with my problems." Baylie took a step toward the door, embarrassed to be caught with a tear-stained face, non-stop sobs, and frequent sniffs. She rubbed her cheeks.

"Anything you say will be kept confidential. Sometimes telling your story to an outsider gives you perspective." Parker gestured to the cot. "Want to try?"

Baylie hesitated, but Parker's warm, patient smile and his easy-going demeanor was inviting. "I don't know." She wrapped her arms about her middle. "Jayden doesn't know the whole story. I ran before I finished it."

"Perhaps you'll get further this time?"

"I guess."

"Have a seat." Parker pointed to the bed again. "Unless you'd prefer a saddle."

"Thanks." She chuckled, returning to the cot. She searched Parker's face seeking a place to focus. Finally, she found her voice. "I'm guilty of pushing away someone who needed help. Jayden doesn't know that. I can never be forgiven for what I did."

"That sounds pretty complex." Parker leaned forward, elbows on his knees. "Why don't you start from the beginning?"

She retold the story, the details vivid as she relived the nightmare of that evening. Parker listened, leaning back in the chair. When she finished, she heaved a big sigh. "I really let God down."

"This guy had no responsibility in what happened?"

"He wanted a good time. So did I. Then I realized what I was doing and lost my nerve."

"He became angry?"

"I tempted him and turned him down. If I had been the person I knew I should be, he wouldn't have shown up drunk at my apartment in the first place. He accused me of being a tease." Baylie's voice broke. "He wouldn't have stormed off."

"Did he return?"

"No, he lost control of his car." Baylie grabbed her middle, the truth assaulting her again. "He didn't take the safe way home. I heard his tires squeal as he turned onto Skyline Boulevard, a winding street with lots of curves and sharp turns. We'd taken it many times when we wanted a private place to pull off and kiss. The noise of the crash exploded over the neighborhood a few minutes after he left." She put her hands over her ears as if hearing the collision again. "He made a wrong turn and took a curve too fast. His car slammed into a tree." She cried out in pain. "He died!"

"That wasn't your fault." Parker looked at her for a minute.

"But I might have saved his life."

"That's a lot of would have, should have, and could have." Parker squinted at her in the dim light, a straw stuck between his front teeth. "Did you know what he was suggesting when he invited you?" He rested a hand on his ankle. "I've met girls who had no clue what signals they were sending a guy."

"That is definitely me." Baylie shook her head. "I was expecting a romantic evening. Even fantasized about what our time would be like in my dreams. I was totally unprepared for the reaction I got."

"This fella should have realized that and not taken advantage of your innocence." Parker folded his arms. "Doesn't sound like a nice guy to me."

"But he was killed! That rejection cost him his life." Baylie wanted to scream. "Don't you see? I don't know if he knew Jesus. I may have sent him to hell." Her voice grew louder, tension choking her words. "How can God forgive that?"

"Hmm." Parker remained quiet and reserved, as if Baylie's outburst didn't phase him. "Well, first of all, I have good news."

Baylie stared at Parker. "You do?"

Parker nodded. "Last time I checked God doesn't give mere mortals the power to send someone to hell." He gave her a long appraisal. "You look like a pretty, and not-so-ordinary young woman, but I don't see any wings on your back or a halo over your head."

"No wings here, and certainly *no* halo." She bit off the words like she was spitting them.

"Ah, so this guy made his choices on his own." Parker touched his chin, as if thinking. "You're off the hook there."

"But he came expecting a good time. I anticipated our evening together. I didn't know what all would happen, but I was willing.

Then he showed up drunk. I was shocked. He was way too eager to celebrate his good fortune. I was disgusted and said no." Baylie blinked back tears she hadn't thought she still had. "He left in a rage. I didn't do anything to stop him." Baylie slapped the mattress. "I failed. I can't ever face God again."

Parker reached into his pack. "Do you mind if I share a little scripture with you?

"Go ahead." Baylie dropped her chin. "I'll warn you, though. Reading it only makes me feel more guilty." She knuckled her cheek, wiping away another gush of tears. Folding her arms, she sniffed again. Would her crying ever be spent?

Parker reached in his pocket and handed her a handkerchief. "Here, I keep this tucked away for emergencies."

"Thanks." Baylie dabbed at her wet cheeks and wiped her eyes.

Parker lifted his Bible and aimed the neck of the lamp at the open book. "Let me find the verse I love." He flipped the pages. "Here it is. I John 1:9: 'If we confess our sins, he is faithful and righteous to forgive us the sins and. . .'"

Baylie blurted out. "But I have confessed, over and over."

Parker put a finger to his lips. "Hear the rest of the verse." He read on. "'He is faithful and righteous to forgive us the sins and to cleanse us from all unrighteousness.'"

"But why don't I feel forgiven?"

"You haven't forgiven yourself." Parker closed the Bible. "You blame yourself for this man's death even though he is the one who showed up with sinful intentions, flew into a rage, and stormed out."

"But I could have calmed him down, made him coffee, de-escalated the situation. I knew what to do, but didn't." Baylie shuddered. "All I wanted was for him to leave."

"You were right to make him do so." Parker leaned back in the chair. "He sounds as if he clearly was setting you up for conquest that night. You were no match for a drunken, lust-filled oaf. You probably would have been raped. I'm pretty sure you would have lost him anyway, once he had his fill."

"He didn't love me, did he?"

"I don't know. Maybe, in his own twisted understanding of the word. But you would have lost so much more if you hadn't resisted his plans. Even worse, he could have insisted you go with him. Both of you could have been killed."

Baylie closed her eyes. Parker was right.

"And Jayden wouldn't have come home to find his best friend working in his mother's kitchen."

"I doubt Jayden and I will be friends after this." Baylie bit her lip. "I'm sure he is disgusted. May never speak to me again." A noise at the door made her look up.

Jayden stepped into the doorway, that half-cocked crooked smile on his face. "Probably not. But I don't know the entire story." He moved toward her. "I assure you though, I can't imagine never speaking to you again."

Baylie gasped. "When did you arrive?"

"A minute ago. About the time you said I would never speak to you again." Jayden tipped his head, the gaze of his warm brown eye fixed on her, that wonderful smile still on his lips. "But how can I deny you the forgiveness you seek when Christ has forgiven me? That's kind of selfish, don't you think?"

"Did you hear our conversation?" Baylie held her breath.

"Only the last part when you said I'd never speak to you again." Jayden clapped Parker on the shoulder. "This guy has a lot of wisdom to share." He looked at her. "You should heed his advice."

"I'm so ashamed, Jayden."

"I'm proud of you for standing up to a man who only had sex on his mind." Jayden reached for her hand, pulling her to her feet.

"Want to come walk with me? Parker's driving home in the morning and needs to catch his z's. And we need to finish this discussion."

"I'm sorry for keeping you from your rest." Baylie put a fist to her mouth.

"Not a problem at all." Parker held out his hand. "I'm joining Melanie at breakfast before driving home. I'll let Jayden take it from here."

"Thank you for the listening ear." Baylie grasped his fingers.

Parker smiled. "I listened, God spoke." He winked at her. "I think you're headed to a better place." He held up his Bible. "Remember, you are forgiven *and* cleansed from all unrighteousness. You've been washed clean. Cling to that."

Jayden led her out the door, stopping in the aisle. Duke rose from his bed and wiggled toward Jayden, wagging his tail. He leaned down and gave the dog a pat on the head, then sent him back to his empty stall, and stood. "I am so glad you finally told me. I felt like I'd lost the Baylie I knew. I blamed myself."

"Why?"

"Because I joined the Marines to prove myself worthy of my father's trust in me and left you needing your best friend." Jayden led her out of the barn. "I'm sorry you felt so alone, Bayles. But I'm here now. Can you forgive me?"

"Jayden, you had to follow the path you believed God put before you. I know that now." Baylie faced him, the sliver of a moon letting her see the outline of his features. "I needed to grow up."

"And so you did." Jayden caressed her cheek with his hand and kissed her. "Quite beautifully."

Baylie gulped. "Jayden?"

He grinned. "I've wanted to do that for a while. Just waiting for the right moment."

She stared at him, voice mute in the shock of what had just

happened. Jayden had kissed her?

"Baylie? You okay?"

"I think I'm moving in a dream and any minute I'll wake up and face reality." She dipped her head, feeling foolish, then peeked up at him. "Did you just kiss me?"

"It was either you or a passing wood sprite." Jayden glanced around, acting frantic, waving his arms in the air like a confused traffic controller. "It was you, wasn't it?"

She wanted to kiss him back but resisted. "You nut." She gulped in the fresh night air. "This is the Jayden I remember."

"Oh good. I thought I lost more than an eye in Afghanistan."

She swatted his upper arm. "You will, if you don't stop."

Jayden reached for Baylie's hand, and they walked across the driveway toward the bunkhouse. "Are you tired?"

"Exhausted, actually." Baylie shivered. "That breeze coming off the hill has a bite to it, doesn't it?"

"This will warm you up while I walk you to your apartment." He wrapped an arm about Baylie's shoulders. "Mom is worried about her plates and I promised to return them to the kitchen."

"The ones in my apartment?" Baylie turned her face his way.

The nearness of her took Jayden's breath. "That would be them."

They reached the bunkhouse and entered, traipsing down the hall to her studio. Baylie fumbled in her pocket for a minute. "I didn't grab my keys when I left!" She looked at him, stricken. "Lissa will kill me if I disturb her now."

"Relax." Jayden pulled a ring of keys from his pocket. "I saw them on the table and took them with me when you rushed out."

"Oh thank goodness." Baylie reached for the key ring, but Jayden held them aloft. "What are you doing?"

"Opening your apartment." Jayden inserted the key in the lock.

He swung the door wide and gestured for her to enter. "After you."

"Should I return the plates to the kitchen now?"

"Yes, let's take them back, then we can walk along the back of the barn and talk." Jayden followed her into the apartment, picked up the forgotten plates, and rolled the silverware back into the towel in which they'd come. "You can carry the utensils." He glanced sideways, a grin on his face. "Just don't stumble in the dark and stab me in the back."

"I'll walk beside you. If I trip, I'll only hurt myself."

Jayden stepped back into the hallway. "Who's on duty with the dormitory tonight?"

Baylie locked her door and turned to the exit. "I think it's Bryn the recreational director." She pushed open the bunkhouse door for him. He maneuvered through with the plates. "Because of my grandfather's death and funeral, I've missed my rotation. I'll be catching up on my turn soon."

"I'm glad the staff can share those responsibilities." Jayden headed to the back door of the kitchen, stopping so Baylie could grab the door. They entered and turned on the lights, then rinsed the plates and left them in the sink for tomorrow's dishwasher load. "Mom will be pleased. Her plates have made it home."

Baylie laughed. "She's not as protective as all that."

"She is when the culprit is her son. I was notorious about keeping dishes in my room."

"So you're living down your reputation?"

He looked at her, cocking an eyebrow in affirmation. "Let's head outside. It's still early."

Exiting to the back of the building they skirted the parking lot, passing behind the dormitory. Lights were still on in one of the rooms and through an open window they heard crying. Jayden glanced at Baylie. "Someone's having a hard time."

"I know." She looked up at the window. "That's Krystal and

Kendra's room. They are usually happy campers. I wonder what's wrong?"

"Can you go in and investigate?"

"The entry doors are locked by now." Baylie pursed her lips. "I'll have to find out in the morning. But it does worry me."

The slam of a door on the front of the building caught their attention. A silhouetted figure ran across the yard toward the main house. The crying upstairs grew louder.

"Let's go see what's happening." Baylie grabbed his hand and together they hurried to the main entrance. As they approached the double doors, Lissa came up beside them. Baylie spoke to her boss. "What's wrong with the twins?

"Oh, Baylie. Thank goodness you're still up." Lissa looked from Baylie to him. "Both of you." She gestured for them to follow her. "I think Kendra has appendicitis. She's in a lot of pain."

Jayden followed the women up the stairs. "I can carry her down if you need to transport her."

"Better yet." Lissa spoke as if winded. "If you could go with me to the hospital, then Kurt can stay here with the boys."

"Happy to help." Jayden glanced at Baylie. "We'll have to have that talk later."

Baylie nodded, then glanced at Lissa. "Do you want me to stay with Krystal?"

"That would be wonderful." Lissa's intake of air made a whoosh in the deepening night. "The staffer on duty has to calm down the rest of the children and Krystal is hysterical. Afraid she'll never see Kendra again."

"Let me go grab my overnight bag. I'll be right back." Baylie took off running toward her apartment.

Jayden faced Lissa. "So what are we driving?"

Lissa fished in her pocket and produced a key. "We'll take my four-door." She pointed to the end of the driveway. "Warm it up and pull it over here. Kurt's already upstairs getting Kendra ready to transport. I'll call him."

"I'll tell Mom where I'm going. Be right back." After relaying his message, Jayden hurried to the car and slipped inside. The engine rumbled its protest but cooperated with his persistence, and soon the heater was producing warm air. He drove to the dormitory and parked, stepping out to open the doors for Kurt who had Kendra in his arms. In Kurt's capable embrace she looked younger than her nine years. She whimpered as Kurt nestled her into the seat, but Lissa slipped in from the opposite door and cradled Kendra's head in her lap. Jayden gulped at the child's pale face. "Ready to go?"

Lissa whispered comfort to Kendra before looking up. "Take the main highway into Burns. Harney District Hospital is easy to find. I'll guide you."

Jayden put the sedan in gear and as he headed up the driveway, he caught a glimpse of Baylie, bag in hand, joining Kurt at the stairs. *I'll be back, Baylie. We will talk.*

CHAPTER TWENTY-FOUR

Listening as Krystal's sobs echoed in the hallway, Baylie hurried up the stairs. She opened the door and found Bryn, the night staffer on duty, sitting on the bed rubbing the child's back. Bryn glanced up. "I think she needs you."

"Krystal, I'm here." Baylie sat on the mattress and held out her arms. Krystal fell into them. Her cries tore at Baylie's heart. "Shh. It's going to be all right."

Bryn stood and tiptoed away. "I have to check the other kids."

Baylie nodded. "We'll be fine. Try to get some sleep."

After she left, Baylie sat Krystal up and brushed tangled locks away from her tear-stained face. She doubted her own face looked much better, after an evening of confessing her past and crying about her failures to Jayden. Using the handkerchief Parker had given her, she dabbed at Krystal's eyes and rubbed the child's cheek dry with her thumb. Pulling her closer, Baylie listened as the sobs lessened in their intensity and the little girl relaxed in her arms. "Think you can sleep?"

Krystal shook her head. "I miss Kendra."

"She's in good hands. Lissa and my soldier friend Jayden took her to the emergency clinic in Burns. The doctors will check her out and find what is wrong."

"But what if I never see her again? Like my mom and dad?" Krystal's tears started again. "I can't lose her. I can't."

"Why don't we talk to God about Kendra?" Baylie couldn't believe she was even saying these words. "Ask Him to be with her and to give the doctors wisdom?"

"What's wisdom?"

"The right answers to a problem the doctors need to solve." Baylie lifted Krystal's chin. "God knows exactly what is wrong and how to fix it. After all, He created Kendra before she was born."

"He did?" Krystal's eyes grew wide. "Kendra and I were together in my mother when she had us."

"You were, but not before God gave Kendra her special self. Just like He gave you your special self. Even though you are twins, you are different people. God designed each of you to be unique."

"Will God hear us?"

"Yes. He most definitely will hear us." Baylie smiled, the answer making her heart soar. How different she felt about prayer after confessing her past to Jayden and then receiving Parker's counsel. The weight off her mind made her feel as if she'd discarded the past four years and was once again the prayer warrior she'd been before. *Thank you, Lord, for taking me back.*

"Baylie, can you help me talk to God? I don't know how."

"Talk to Him like you would a good friend."

Krystal bowed her head. "God, this is Krystal. Kendra has gone to the hospital. Please help the doctors know what to do. I need her back here. Please don't take her away." The last few words dissolved into sobs, but Krystal finished with a wobbly amen.

"Lord, hear Krystal's prayer and be with Kendra and the doctors. We ask that the tummy ache is nothing major and that Kendra can come home soon. Be with Lissa and Jayden as they stay with her and wait."

"And help me to sleep. I'm really tired. Amen."

Baylie chuckled at Krystal's honesty. "Want me to tuck you into your bed?"

"Can you stay with me?"

"Sure. I brought my overnight bag. Shall I sleep in Kendra's bed?"

"Will you fit?" Krystal's eyes grew round. "You are a lot bigger than my sister."

Baylie laughed. "I think I can squeeze into it."

"Tuck me in first." Krystal crawled under the covers. "And say those words you always say over us."

Baylie straightened the comforter and brushed the hair away from the little girl's face. "May God's angels watch over you through the night, and love's promises wake you in the morning."

"Amen." The muffled response disappeared into the covers and little girl snores followed almost immediately. Baylie stood and crossed over to the other twin bed. She hoped she'd hear Krystal if she awakened in the night, but Baylie sagged under her fatigue. Sleep could not come soon enough.

Jayden waited in the lobby as Lissa joined the doctors in the examining room. Kendra moaned all the way to the hospital, fueling Jayden's need to drive carefully. He'd heard soldiers moan when they were wounded, had seen injuries that threatened a man's life, but hearing that small child in pain ripped open his soul. Why should one so small have to suffer?

An unbidden image from Afghanistan sprang across his memory. His unit had been on patrol. Small village. Deathly quiet. No children playing anywhere. Suddenly a small girl wandered into their path, holding out her hand. One of his men reached for her offering, only to discover a grenade waiting, the pin in her teeth.

"Grenade!" The soldier shouted, grabbing the device and tossing it into a nearby outcrop. The grenade bounced off the stone surface, then rolled into the crater formed by several boulders together. His men scattered to whatever cover they could find. The explosion shook the ground, the debris from the shattered rock flying in every direction. All of his unit survived, but when the dust settled the child lay motionless in the sand, fragments of granite embedded in her forehead. She'd been the bait and paid with her life.

Jayden's breathing ramped up and his heart banged beneath

his breast bone. He put his head between his knees and forced himself to breathe deep. He couldn't risk a panic attack here in the hospital lobby. He shouldn't have allowed his mind to wander to the children in Afghanistan. Shouldn't have let that little girl's face enter his memory. He focused on his breathing.

"Jayden?"

He looked up and found Lissa staring, concern written across her forehead.

"You okay?"

Jayden shook his head. "I will be. Kendra's suffering reminded me of the children during the war." He sat up straighter. "How's she doing?"

"They are prepping her for surgery." Lissa sat next to him. "It's appendicitis, as I suspected. She'll be in and out before morning."

"That's fast."

Lissa nodded. "Apparently a preliminary test revealed an elevated white blood cell count and that indicates infection. All the other symptoms—the nausea, the pain, the lack of appetite—match."

"You want me to wait here for you?"

"I think you can go home. I'll be back in a minute."

As Lissa left, Jayden decided to focus on something else. No more panic attacks tonight. Baylie haunted his thoughts. She'd experienced her share of hurts, and though much of those troubles had been of her own making, he couldn't stop the feelings of guilt for his part in her agony.

He'd known she wanted him to go to college alongside her. They talked of nothing else that last year of high school. But when his scholarships didn't supply enough funds to cover his expenses, he had to take another look at his plans. He so wanted to become the soldier his dad had been. A lifelong ambition. The lack of money pointed him in that direction rather than college. He remembered how disappointed Baylie had been, but he'd been confident she could handle whatever came her way. She was the outstanding student. The upright faith-driven example of a soldier for Christ. The girl who would tear up the campus with her level-headed approach to life. Souls were waiting to be saved and Baylie was the girl for the job.

But the story he heard tonight shocked him. He never would have guessed she'd feel lost or left out. How she must have suffered from the loneliness, the feelings of conquering the university alone without a friend at her side.

Her best friend.

Him.

Guilt tormented him now. That guy Hunter would never have tempted her if she could have talked it out with Jayden. She would never have considered the charm and advances of the man if Jayden had been around. He would have helped her see through the façade. But he'd been off fulfilling his duty as a soldier, serving his country, never mindful of Baylie's angst. He couldn't blame her for giving in to the man's seduction, but he gave thanks that God protected her and intervened before she made a decision she could never undo. She didn't believe God had been there, but it was clear to Jayden a host of angels stood guard.

Tomorrow they would talk. She needed to know he still believed in her, still thought a lot of her, and most of all, accepted responsibility for not being there for her when she was tempted. Even King David had been caught by the temptation of sexual sin.

He leaned back into the padded lounge chair and closed his eyes. These long days and short nights were taking their toll. Just a quick little snooze, that's all he needed.

"Jayden?"

He felt someone shaking his shoulder. He peeked at the voice.

Lissa stood beside him, worry lines again creasing her

forehead.

He sat up, glancing at his watch. "Wow! I've been asleep for an hour?" He focused on Lissa. "Sorry."

"No problem."

"How is Kendra?"

"She's in surgery now." Lissa sighed. "They want to keep her overnight, which I figured they'd do from the beginning."

"You're going to stay?"

"Yes. I sent Kurt a text and told him. You can go back to the ranch. Kurt will pick us up in the morning if Kendra is able to come."

"The boys?"

"They're good. I don't tax the staff with my kids when there are foster children who need their care. Kurt will load them up and bring them here tomorrow."

"Okay. Tell Kendra I'm praying for her."

Lissa touched his shoulder. "Thanks."

Baylie opened her eyes, confused when a hand shook her shoulder and she didn't recognize her surroundings. Bent over the bed, Bryn smiled down at her. Recognition dawned. Baylie had spent the night with Krystal. She sat up and rotated her shoulders. The small bed had left her stiff. "Any news this morning?"

"No. Someone came back late last night, but I haven't heard anything." The girl pointed to the door. "Jayden Clarke is downstairs waiting for you."

"Outside the dormitory?"

She nodded. "I heard him throwing rocks at the window. It's a wonder he didn't wake Krystal."

"I'll go right down. Let me run a brush through my hair." Baylie stood and stepped across the hall to the bathroom, overnight bag in hand. Retrieving a brush, she peered into the small mirror, her puffy eyes and drawn cheeks telltale reminders of her distress the night before. She pinched her cheeks, hoping to bring up a little color and rubbed her eyebrows in an effort to lift the sag from her eyes. The action didn't help. She pressed her lips together, forced a smile, and headed downstairs. Outside in the crisp morning air, she grabbed her shoulders for warmth and squinted at the bright sun.

"Good morning, Bayles." Jayden sounded chipper even though she was certain he'd had less sleep than she had. "Sleep well?"

"Not as well as I'd hoped." She put a hand to her forehead, shielding her eyes from the sun. "You'd think the sun would be warmer, as bright as it is."

"Looks like a nice day. The sun needs to crank up its Bunsen burner."

"Hope it hurries." She shivered. "Let's go get coffee. I'm sure Melanie has a pot on by now." She pivoted toward the kitchen gesturing for him to follow. "How is Kendra?"

"She had emergency surgery, so the hospital kept her overnight. Lissa stayed behind. We should know more this morning."

"There's Kurt with the boys." Baylie nodded ahead to where Kurt stood at the kitchen door. "He must know something."

"Hi, guys. The boys and I are heading into Burns to get Lissa and Kendra."

"She's coming home?" Baylie sucked in air, relief overwhelming her. "What was wrong?"

"Appendicitis. Apparently, it is an in and out procedure. Lissa said they are releasing her in a couple of hours. We'll be monitoring her for awhile."

Jayden reached for Grayson. "Come here, big guy."

The three-year-old grinned and climbed into Jayden's arms. "Go see mama."

Jayden laughed. "I know when I'm not wanted." He handed the child back to Kurt. "Anything in particular you want me to do today?"

"The stable can use some help." Kurt grinned. "Parker would appreciate a job, I'm sure."

"Besides working in the kitchen?" Jayden winked at Baylie. "I doubt we can pry him away. But he did say he planned to drive home later today."

Baylie smiled at the two men. "Maybe spending the night in the tack room convinced him the barn needs daily care."

Kurt's eyes widened. "He slept out there?"

"Yeah." Jayden shifted his weight on his cane. "He said he's spending a lot of time with my mother and thought it would look better if he wasn't sleeping in the same apartment. I agreed with him."

Kurt quirked an eyebrow. "They must be growing closer than I thought." He transferred Grayson to his other arm. "I'm glad he chose to sleep elsewhere without my having to ask him."

Baylie nodded. "Parker's wisdom and sense of propriety define him."

Kurt agreed, then called the two other boys back from the yard. "Gunner. Gage."

As he herded his kids in the direction of the SUV, Baylie called after him. "Have a safe trip, Kurt."

With Jayden at her side, she pointed to the kitchen. "I need coffee."

"Me, too." Jayden glanced at the departing Suburban.

"He's such a good man." Baylie kicked a piece of gravel, sending it flying into the grass. "All of you Marine types are."

Jayden opened the kitchen door. "Do you flatter us to avoid any future counseling sessions in the middle of the night?"

"Maybe. Is it working?"

Jayden wrinkled his nose. "Not a chance." He gestured for her to enter. "We need to talk."

Jayden smiled at his mother who stood laughing with Parker by the stove. "Good morning, you two." He couldn't resist a tease. "Mom, don't get too close to Parker. He probably smells like horse sweat."

"I'll have you know Melanie saw me emerging from the barn at dawn and while you slept in, she let me in to your bathroom so I could grab a shower."

"He smells just fine, thank you very much." His mother made a face at him. "Is Kendra okay?"

"Appendectomy. Lissa stayed at the hospital. She sent me back. We just saw Kurt on his way to bring them both home."

"Without his breakfast?" Mom frowned. "He must be a man on a mission." She shrugged. "By the way, thanks for returning the plates."

"Thank you for a wonderful plate of food." Baylie walked to the coffee pot. "I need a cup of this. Jayden?"

"Thanks, yes." Jayden glanced at his mother. "Breakfast over?"

"No. The kids will be here in another half hour. You want yours now?" Mom pointed to the stove. "The pancakes are on the griddle. The scrambled eggs are in the warming pan."

"I'm starving." Jayden grabbed two plates. "Baylie, want to have breakfast with me? I promise not to give you indigestion."

Her face reddened as if she dreaded the coming discussion. Jayden gave her an encouraging smile. "I'll go easy on you."

"Hope you keep your promise." She took the proffered plate and they helped themselves to eggs.

Mom set a plate of pancakes on the serving counter. "Have some. I'm working on a second griddle."

"Thanks." Jayden served Baylie two pancakes and gave

himself three. "Let's sit at the small table so we can have a little privacy."

Baylie followed him to the corner. Her skin pale, the set of her mouth appeared frozen as if she was about to face a firing squad.

He handed her a fork, then offered his palm. "Let's pray."

She took his fingers in hers and bowed her head.

"Lord, bless this food and the hands that prepared it. Guide our conversation in a way that honors you. Amen."

When he finished, Baylie glanced up at him. "Jayden. . ."

He pressed a finger against her lips. "Shh. Eat your eggs before they're cold."

He waited a few minutes, letting the silence surround them. He passed her the butter and a bottle of syrup. As she buttered her pancakes, Baylie appeared to relax, stopping once to comment on the taste of the sweet breakfast.

The children arrived, noisy and full of energy. Bryn managed to get them to form a line at the stack of plates. Parker whistled and the cacophony of sound hushed. "Let's pray. Kurt had to go get Lissa this morning."

The children bowed their heads. A couple of boys peeked out to inspect the breakfast. At the amen Melanie directed traffic. "Take a plate. I'll give you a scoop of eggs, and you can have two pancakes to start. Butter and syrup are on the table. Seconds on pancakes after you eat your eggs."

Jayden grinned at Baylie, glad for the distraction of clatter. He and Baylie could talk without worry of any eavesdroppers. "About last night. First, I have to apologize for leaving you alone to attend the university. I was so caught up in my quest to emulate my dad I didn't see how scared you were. Please forgive me."

Baylie shook her head. "There's nothing to forgive. As I said last night, you had your own journey to follow."

"Nevertheless, I could have supported you better through

letters and e-mail. I'm sorry."

"Jayden, I stopped writing to you because I didn't want you to know about Hunter. I knew I was flirting with temptation. You would have told me to be careful. I didn't want to hear that."

Jayden nodded. "I get it. Hunter probably chose you to charm because he saw you as an easy target. You were innocent, easily flattered, and eager for his attentions."

Baylie's eyes pooled. "I thought he really cared about me."

"He probably did, at some level." Jayden cut his pancakes with his fork. "I'm guessing he hid his drinking from you."

"I thought he was completely sober. Never imagined him drunk."

"Didn't drink at parties?"

"He always had a soda, as far as I knew." Baylie sampled her eggs. "He could have spiked it, I guess."

"Took you home at a respectable hour?"

"I had to study. I told him I couldn't stay out late."

"Which worked in his favor." Jayden sipped his coffee. "Leave you off at your apartment, meet his friends at a bar."

"Really?"

Jayden wanted to take her hand. She looked so vulnerable. "Baylie, he played you. Groomed you for a showdown. Dazzled you with dinners, movies, walks along the river. A spider weaving his web."

"I shouldn't have been so stupid, but I liked our relationship."

"Of course you did. You were hungry for friendship. You are only human, but he saw an opportunity and deceived you into thinking the two of you were headed for a happily ever after. The cabin, the long weekend, all part of the plan."

"Your advice would have fallen on deaf ears. I was so clueless." She put her fork down. "Knowing you would have supported me makes the pain go away. I didn't want to lose you as a friend."

"That will never happen, Bayles."

"Promise?"

He reached across the table and took her hand. "I want to be more than friends." He kissed her fingers. "And that's a promise."

CHAPTER TWENTY-FIVE

After breakfast Baylie floated back to her apartment, or at least that's how she believed she arrived at her door. Jayden wanted to be more than friends. Had he really said those words? In her deepest anguish, he had spoken to her greatest desire. She had to be dreaming. Real people didn't live in fairy tales. Had a mistake been made?

But the touch of his lips on the tops of her fingers lingered. The warmth of his hand around hers filled her senses. Jayden wanted to be more than friends. She kept repeating that to herself as if trying to convince her heart it was true.

Outside the bunkhouse a motorcycle roared to life. She left her studio and went to the office to look through the front windows. Parker shared a laugh with Melanie, shiny helmet tucked under an arm, free hand gunning the engine. She stood with her hand on his shoulder. Parker leaned over and kissed her on the cheek.

Baylie grinned at the picture. Those two were falling head over heels in love. What a cliché. But it fit the scene outside. She just knew it. Jayden probably wouldn't be pleased it was happening so soon, but Baylie sensed he welcomed happiness in his mother's life.

Helmet in place, Parker climbed on the Harley, dropped his face shield, and put the bike in gear. He waved and with a burst of gas started up the driveway, bits of gravel flying beneath his tires. Melanie watched him go, never leaving her spot until he disappeared over the hill. Yep. Parker and Melanie were definitely headed to a happy future together.

Almost as soon as Parker rode out of sight, the ranch Suburban appeared at the top of the drive. Kurt and company were back. Baylie walked out of the bunkhouse to greet the returning family. Kurt parked outside the ranch house, near the dormitory. Lissa popped out of the passenger side and hurried to open the rear doors. She helped the boys out the back, grabbing Grayson before he jumped. Kurt swung wide the passenger side door and lifted Kendra from the middle seat. Baylie stepped closer to the girl, surprised to see her wide awake and smiling.

"Baylie!" Kendra's broad grin brightened her face. "Is Krystal all right?"

"She's missing you. Are you feeling better?"

"I had to have an operation."

"Now you can get well."

"Baylie, can you get the dormitory door for me?" Kurt's brisk step made her hustle toward the building. She opened the door and held it for him.

"Thanks."

"Want me to come up and help get Kendra settled?"

"That would be wonderful. Lissa needs to feed the boys." He caught his lower lip in his teeth. "Something I totally failed to do before we left."

"You need a doghouse to retreat to?" She followed Kurt up the stairs.

"Don't give Lissa any ideas." Kurt reached the upper floor and carried Kendra to her room where she was met by excited squeals. Krystal sat on the edge of Kendra's mattress and hugged her sister as if they'd been apart for years and not a few hours in the middle of the night. Baylie sank onto Krystal's mattress, enjoying the reunion.

"Remember, Kendra," Kurt's tone said he meant business, "you are to remain in bed the rest of the day."

"I will, I promise." Kendra nodded. "My incision aches."

Kendra's contrite smile looked genuine, but her glance at Krystal reflected mischief. Baylie didn't miss the hidden message in Krystal's glance at her sister.

Apparently, Kurt didn't miss it either. "Do I need to put Krystal in another room for the day?"

"No! I'll be good. I promise. Krystal and I can play with our jewelry kits on the bed. That won't be breaking the rules, will it?"

"No. That should be fine." Kurt touched the child on the head, looked at Krystal, and winked at Baylie. "I'm counting on both of you to keep your promises. Baylie will check in on you."

"Can she play, too?" Kendra's hopeful smile melted Baylie's heart.

She chuckled. "I'll see if I can't squeeze in an hour a little later. Okay?" She stood to leave.

The twins nodded, smiles across their faces as wide as the distance that separated them on the bed. Baylie blew them a kiss.

"I need to go to my superior and repent of my dereliction of duty." Kurt's contrite smile and a rise of his eyebrow reflected his intent to appease Lissa about the forgotten breakfasts.

Baylie chuckled. "Hope it works. We'll be fine here."

Kurt waved and stepped out of the room, boots thundering as he descended the dormitory stairs and went outside. Baylie would have liked to eavesdrop on their conversation. She'd never known Lissa to be upset, especially when it came to her hero Kurt. She doubted they'd be at odds for long. Probably kissing and making up before Grayson could spill his breakfast cereal.

Would she and Jayden grow into a relationship like that? At least today the promise seemed more hopeful than it had since he'd returned from active duty. She grabbed her elbows in a self-hug.

Leaving the barn where he'd set out some tools for the day, Jayden glimpsed his mother as she returned to the apartment. The unmistakable sound of humming met his ears when he walked up behind her. "You sound happy."

She jumped and turned, a hand on her throat. "You startled

me."

"Sorry." Jayden tipped his head, grinning. "Did you give Parker a send-off? From where I stood, you looked pretty cozy."

Mom blushed. "Yes. He's gone." She studied him. "How are you faring? You didn't return to the apartment until late, then rushed off to the hospital with Lissa. What kind of fuel are you running on?" They resumed walking to the apartment.

"I'm okay. I slept at the hospital while Lissa waited with Kendra." They stopped while Mom inserted her key in the lock. He leaned on the door casing. "I'll clean the two stalls that were neglected while I was fetching Baylie this week, then grab a few winks."

"Is everything all right with Baylie?" Mom opened the door. "When you two came in early for breakfast this morning, she looked exhausted."

"She'll be fine. She's been struggling with a personal issue that she needed to get off her chest so she can move on." Jayden grinned. "And I kissed her and made it all better."

"You rascal." Mom chuckled. "I know what good friends you were in high school. I'm sure you'll be a comfort to her."

"I plan to be more than a comfort to her. We are going to compete with you and Parker on becoming a couple."

Mom gasped. "What makes you think he and I are a couple?"

"Aw, come on, Mom." Jayden twisted his mouth into a pucker. "I heard the motorcycle and saw Parker kiss you as he left. Quit denying the obvious."

She glanced down at the floor. "Are you okay with this?"

"You deserve to be happy. Now that George is out of the picture for good." He stopped. "He is, isn't he?"

"George?" She grimaced. "Yes. Finally." She hung her key on the hook by the door. "My attorney filed all the necessary documents that he should have filed thirteen years ago, and we are officially, completely divorced. George said he'd never be back. I guess Cody's mother, who was seeing him, sent him packing, too."

"Do you think he'll get help for his weekend drinking sprees?"

Mom shrugged. "He probably doesn't realize that's what's destroying his chances with everyone he meets. Sad. He can be a decent man when he isn't living in a bottle."

Jayden wrapped his arms about his mother's shoulders. "That's why I love you so much. You always see the good in everyone, no matter what they've done. Don't ever change, Mom."

"Thanks, sweetie. But I've stumbled like everyone else. I know what it is to need forgiveness."

He sighed. "I have to clean those stalls soon before I drop. The lack of sleep is starting to get to me. If you find me snoozing on my shovel, just drop a pile of hay nearby so I hit something soft when I land, okay?"

Mom laughed. "Go get it done and come back. I'll have your bed ready for you to collapse into when you get here."

"Thanks." Jayden reversed direction and walked back outside, heading for the barn. He was surprised to hear the swish of the broom as he approached the door. Kurt stood over the wheelbarrow shoveling horse muffins onto the pile. Gunner had the broom and was pushing it with all the gusto of a nine-year-old. "You guys doing my chores today?"

Kurt stopped, resting on the shovel. "You should get some sleep. You were the one who drove to the hospital in the middle of the night."

"That'd be great." Jayden breathed a sigh of relief. "I told Mom to let me fall into a pile of hay if I fell asleep at the broom. I could sleep that way all day."

"No, go get some rest. Monday will come soon enough." Kurt scooped up another pile. "This is your day off you know."

"Officially, it is. But I missed a day of work to go get Baylie.

Don't I need to make it up?"

"No, your chores will be handled by subs. You were doing a good deed."

"Thanks." Jayden raised a hand in farewell. "I'll remember you in my dreams."

He walked on unsteady feet toward the apartment. His right leg ached from lack of rest, reminding him how tired he truly was. Slipping in through the front door, he called. "I'm back. Heading for bed."

"Sleep well." His mother jingled her keys. "I've got kitchen duty."

Jayden crawled under the covers and rolled onto his side. The blinds were pulled so the room's light barely outlined the objects around its perimeter. The extra bed where Parker used to sleep was made, the tight corners evidence that the man had done the job before he moved to the barn. Military training never left a seasoned soldier.

The dresser surface appeared empty, except for an envelope leaning against the lamp. He blinked. An envelope? Where did that come from? He rose up on one shoulder, squinting at the square object sitting alone. What was this? Jayden's eyes burned so much he didn't want to get out of bed again, but seeing the envelope he doubted he'd fall asleep until he examined the contents.

He groaned, sat up, and rose to grab the letter. This better be good, Macgregor. He slit the seal with his thumb nail, then stopped. Suppose Parker intended this letter to be found by his mother? He didn't want to pry into something private between them. But no, his name was on the front.

He continued, removing the paper and unfolding the missive. Parker's distinctive cursive, done in a bold, uniform blue gel pen, covered the page. Jayden let his gaze skim the meticulous handwriting, catching the essence of the letter.

Jayden,

I can understand your initial hesitation about Melanie and me growing closer, especially since you didn't know we corresponded while you were in rehab. She's your mother and you didn't get a lot of time with her when you were younger because of George. Please know I did not intend to rush into this relationship. But when you gave us your blessing Melanie and I decided to see where life takes us. I've not had a permanent woman in my life since my fiancée bailed on me early in my military career. Melanie knows the military life so she's a real prize in my eyes. It's no wonder you are such a fine, young man. You had the best influences you could have had. If my presence gnaws at you at any time, please tell me.

Your friend,
    Parker

Jayden returned the note to its envelope. In the beginning Parker had sensed his resistance to a budding friendship with his mother. Jayden slipped back into his bed, ashamed he'd been plagued by jealousy early on. Mom couldn't go wrong with a man like Parker in her life. Jayden would interact with his mother in the days between Parker visits. That would suffice. Besides, he now had a girl to chase himself. He closed his eyes and savored the memory of the kiss on Baylie's cheek. That only promised many more to come. Sleep overtook him as his thoughts drifted to Baylie.

Baylie tiptoed up the stairs to Kendra's room, keeping her promise to check on the girl and make sure she took it easy today. From the silence in the dormitory Baylie guessed that Kendra was catching up on some much-needed rest.

She peeked in the doorway. Krystal lay curled up beside her sister in one bed, both girls sound asleep. Baylie's heart warmed at the sight, knowing how traumatic the night had been for them, separated by an unbidden illness. She backed out of the room, pulling the door closed, and went to find her boss.

Lissa sat at the desk in the office, the door open. Baylie knocked.

"Come on in." Lissa's night at the hospital had taken its toll. The woman's face was lined with fatigue, color pale, and mouth sagging.

"Shouldn't you be sleeping?" Baylie studied her. "I know Jayden is catching up on his z's. He got more rest than you."

"I'll catch an early bedtime. The boys go to bed about seven, so I'll join them."

"Sounds like a plan." She took a chair and sat. "Any word on Kendra's recovery time?"

"Nothing concrete. Time will tell." Lissa gave a shake of her head. "The antibiotics and rest should have her better quickly."

"That's a relief." Baylie puffed out the breath she'd been holding. "We'll have to be diligent to make sure she takes it easy, so her recovery time is shortened."

"Even more so, now that the girls are being considered for a permanent home." Lissa's smile appeared forced. "Three couples have applied for girls their ages."

"They won't be separated?" Baylie leaned forward, grabbing the edge of the desk. "That is their greatest fear."

"I know. Each of the couples have been sent a complete bio—the family history, other potential relative placements, abuse reports, caseworker reports, medical issues—that sort of thing. The committee is currently reviewing the applicants." Lissa sank against the back of her chair. "The girls belong together, but not many families want a set of twins. So this may be a tough road ahead."

"What can I do?" Baylie's chest heaved, a lump the size of a boulder weighing heavily against her lungs. Krystal and Kendra separated? It could not happen. *Lord, I need you to hear this prayer more than any other I've ever prayed. Keep the twins together. Life without Mom and Dad is tough enough without losing your twin sister.* She glanced at Lissa. "After seeing Krystal's tears last night when Kendra went to the hospital, any kind of separation will be traumatic."

"Pray that one of these families will want them both." Lissa's jaw was set in a firm line. "When the state moves on a child in their custody, permanent placement is their goal, but it is Oregon policy that siblings stay together. Being older twins may make finding that placement more difficult."

"I can write letters." Baylie grit her teeth. "Tell me who and where to send them."

"Better yet, pray for the hearts of the couples as they consider adopting twins. That would be the perfect solution."

"You always have such wisdom, Lissa." Baylie's insides grew warm as she considered the better solution. Krystal and Kendra might have a family of their own again. "I will pray to that end."

CHAPTER TWENTY-SIX

After waking early the next morning, showering and dressing, Jayden headed for the kitchen. His stomach reminded him how long it had been since he'd eaten. Yesterday morning at breakfast? He passed Duke's food dish as he entered. Even that looked appetizing to his growling belly.

"Hey, Mom." He walked to the counter where she was mixing dough that shouted a batch of cookies. He spied a quart measuring cup of chocolate chips and a small bowl of chopped nuts sitting next to the mixer, confirming his suspicions. He reached in the silverware drawer and removed a long-handled spoon. He waved it at his mother, grinning as she stopped the mixer. "Taste?"

"Boys will be boys." She lifted the beaters, took his spoon, and swiped it through the dough. After touching the glob to the chips and then the nuts, she handed it to him. "Enjoy."

"You are too much! Thanks. Any breakfast leftovers?"

"Pancakes and sausage in the warming oven." She lowered the beaters into the dough. "Did you catch up on your sleep?"

"I didn't know I could be that tired." Jayden finished licking the spoon and carried it to the sink. "After breakfast, I'm asking Baylie to go to church with me."

"That sounds wonderful." Mom's eyes twinkled. "She hasn't regularly attended since she arrived at the ranch. "

"Aren't you going?"

"I'll attend the evening service." Mom winked at him. "Wouldn't do to have your mother spying on you."

"I have nothing to hide. It's church."

"With Baylie." Mom's no-nonsense stare studied him. "Hurry home for lunch."

"You're no fun." Jayden cackled. "Baylie's not that type of

girl, anyway."

"I see the looks passing between you two." Mom grabbed two cookie sheets from a nearby cupboard. "I know there's more going on than you divulge."

Leave it to Mom.

"I can only hope."

He poured a cup of coffee and sat at the table, savoring the eggs and leftover pancakes. A bottle of syrup remained after the kids left. He poured some over his pancakes. Stomach satisfied, he carried his dishes to the sink and rinsed them, nodded thanks to his mother, and hurried to find Baylie.

She stood near the ranch house, talking with Lissa, back to him. He approached, getting a wave from Lissa which made Baylie turn. She smiled and waved as well. Feeling like the eighteen-year-old he had been when he asked her to the prom, he stopped beside her. His panic attacks didn't make his heart bang harder than what it was doing right now.

"What's up?" Baylie's smile lit her face, eyes full of warmth and welcome.

"I thought I'd drive to church this morning at New Life Community, our old stomping ground." He swallowed as his voice threatened to wobble. "Would you like to join me?"

Baylie's face paled, then flushed. "Are we in time for that?"

"I think so." Jayden looked at his watch. "It's only 9:30. If we leave right away, we can make it." He looked at her jeans and frilly blouse. "Grab a jacket and we'll take the Harley."

"To church?" Baylie's mouth popped open, then curved into a grin. "Talk about an entrance."

"If people don't remember us from before, they will now."

"You think?"

"Come on, go get your jacket. I'll grab the helmets."

Baylie laughed. "Be right back."

Baylie sprinted to her apartment, ran a brush through her hair, applied some lipstick, a little mascara, and grabbed her fleece jacket. She kicked off her shoes and pulled on her boots. Her heart skipped a beat or two, the rhythm interrupted by her happiness in anticipation of a church date with Jayden. What a wonderful way to move forward from where she had been.

The motorcycle pulled up outside the bunkhouse, and as usual, Jayden revved the engine, letting her know he was ready to go. She locked her door and hurried to the main entrance.

Holding her helmet out, Jayden waited as she adjusted it before he snapped his face shield into place. She climbed on back, making sure her boots were where they needed to be, and reached for his belt. His nearness thrilled her, the attraction between them now a reality. She didn't need to wish for his presence, he had come to her of his own accord. So much had changed in a mere forty-eight hours. She closed her eyes, then blinked them open, in case this wasn't real and she was only dreaming. But the Harley kicked into gear and she was riding behind this man, this guy she had waited to claim for so many years. *Please Lord, help us to find our way to happiness.*

As far as Baylie was concerned, the ride to the church building took way too little time. Jayden parked in a bike spot at the edge of the parking lot and together they carried their helmets to the main entrance. Parishioners greeted one another as she and Jayden headed up the steps to the sanctuary. Baylie's memories whizzed through her mind—like the day so long ago she received a scholarship to the university. The entire church knew.

"Baylie Summers?" A voice to her right sounded familiar. She glanced that direction and caught the broad smile of the pastor, those around him staring at her as he walked with brisk steps to where she was.

"Hello, Pastor." She reached for his outstretched hand. "It's been a while."

"I heard you had returned to the area after college, but when you never showed up here I thought maybe you had decided to worship closer to wherever you are."

"No, I fell out of the habit at college and didn't try to resume attending when I returned to Harney County." She gulped at her honesty, but truth was truth. "Recent events in my life have made me realize what I've been missing and convinced me to recapture what I lost."

The pastor's smile filled his face, understanding in his gaze. "All we like sheep have gone astray. I'm glad you've found your way back to us." He turned to Jayden. "You seem familiar as well."

Jayden snapped to attention, his hand stopping mid-air as he almost saluted. "Jayden Clarke. Recently discharged from the Marines."

"Jayden?" The pastor's surprise reflected in his face. "You've become quite the man, haven't you?" He glanced at Baylie. "Didn't he write sports stories for that high school newspaper you edited?"

Baylie laughed. "The very same. Good memory."

The pastor held out his hand. "You were one of ours, too, if I recall."

"Yes, sir." Jayden returned the handshake. "I plan to be again."

"That's wonderful." The bell in the tower sounded above them. "Why don't we go in? Can I welcome you from the pulpit?"

"Uh, no." Baylie swallowed. "We prefer not to be singled out. As you said, we've been gone a while."

The pastor nodded. "I understand."

Baylie followed Jayden to a vacant space on a rear pew. If the pastor knew the truth of her reluctance to return to church before today, he might not understand. Nor would the people here who used to know her. She felt especially guilty about her neglect of Mary and Troy Marshall, her foster family growing up. She glanced around but didn't see them. Another time, perhaps.

This was a day of new beginnings and with Jayden at her side, she intended to keep moving forward. She hadn't thought she could feel like this again. God *was* in the business of miracles.

Returning home from church, Jayden delivered Baylie to the kitchen back door, took her helmet, and idled the bike in low to the front of the bunkhouse. He parked, removed his helmet, and slipped into Mom's apartment.

Church had been a wonderful breath of fresh air. He saw Baylie smile several times as the pastor delivered a message from Matthew chapter 6. "Seek ye first the kingdom of God." The message seemed targeted to Baylie's current situation, and Jayden couldn't have been more pleased. With consistent reinforcement, she would find her way back to where she'd once been.

Jayden pledged to find his own solutions as well. He'd seen so much in Afghanistan, the images would be a long time fading from his memory, but Baylie's presence kept him focused on the good things around him. The events that triggered flashbacks and night terrors were fewer. Unwanted memories which influenced his behavior faded with each passing day.

He stashed the bike gear in his room and exited, intent on grabbing lunch with the rest of the ranch. Sundays meant a smaller crowd—the interns had gone home for the weekend—so Baylie and Mom's responsibilities catered to the nine foster children and Kurt's brood.

He entered the kitchen, the lunch line in progress. Kurt and Lissa were directing traffic, sending the smallest children through the line first. Baylie stood at the end, spooning mashed potatoes on the plates and adding a ladle of gravy. Mom laid slices of turkey and a spoon of green beans on their plates. He worked his way to the cooking pots. "Anything you need me to do?"

Mom glanced up. "Sure, bring the other pan of turkey slices, would you?" She checked the basket at the end. "Oh, and the other basket of rolls."

"Got it."

He opened the oven and removed the stainless-steel pan of turkey, reaching for the second basket of rolls. He turned the warming oven off and carried the food back to where Mom served. "Anything else?"

"No. This will do it. Grab a plate."

"Don't have to ask me twice." Jayden joined the end of the line and glanced up when he reached Baylie and the mashed potatoes. He winked with his good eye. "I'll save you a place at the table."

Baylie beamed, her smile radiating a happiness no one could miss. "Thanks. Two scoops or more?"

"Three and a double portion of gravy, please." He lifted his chin.

"You are hungry."

"I'm always hungry." Jayden chuckled as she filled his plate with a generous helping of potatoes and gravy. "I'll have to do penance for overindulging."

"You'd better." Baylie furrowed her brows, trying to look perturbed, but all it did was make her more beautiful. "Ten laps around the parking lot."

"You couldn't look mean if you tried."

She scrunched her nose and walked to where the plates were stacked. Everyone had gone through ahead of her, so Jayden waited while she and Mom made plates for themselves. She joined him, and together they found the small table in the corner where they'd shared biscuits and eggs not long ago.

"I like this corner." Jayden set his plate down. "More privacy."

"Less chance of being smeared with errant potatoes, too."

He held out his hand. "Let's give thanks."

Baylie's eyes grew wide. "Kurt already did."

"I wasn't here and praying for both of us would be a privilege."

Baylie's face flushed and she closed her eyes, bowing her head.

Jayden grinned to himself. "Lord, for this food, this day, and our many recent blessings, we thank you. You are most gracious to us. Amen."

He looked up to find Baylie's gaze on him. "What?"

"You're something else."

"That's good I hope."

"Better than good." She grinned. "Amazing."

With Sunday lunch over and the McKintricks doing dishes so Melanie could have an afternoon off, which meant Baylie could, too, she walked with Jayden to the paddock behind the barn.

Lady stood munching hay, the foal catching an early afternoon snack, its flagship tail flipping in happiness. Lady nickered as Jayden approached, stepping away from her nursing baby to see if Jayden brought treats. She nuzzled his hands and leaned over the top rail to examine the pockets she could reach. Jayden laughed at the mare's intense search, finally producing a quartered apple for her. He offered a slice to the foal who slobbered it in his teeth.

"She certainly knows how to find anything hidden, doesn't she?" Baylie envied Jayden's easy-going style with the mare. He'd often told her the horse, the dog, and the ranch were among his favorite childhood memories.

"Yes. She's always been a persistent pocket thief. When I first met her, she was a pesky foal, and half of the fun was hiding carrots in my jeans for her to search." Jayden's face beamed. "She filled a lot of lonely hours for me."

"I'm sure the kids here at the ranch are glad for the opportunity to nurture and love a horse."

Jayden nodded. "This place should be great therapy for those kids who have come broken."

"Lissa told me Kendra and Krystal have caught the eye of three couples seeking to adopt girls their ages."

"Really?" Jayden gave Lady a pat on the neck. "That's great."

"I know."

"Baylie? Jayden?" Lissa came toward the paddock, step brisk, voice anxious. "I can't find either Kendra or Krystal. Kendra is supposed to be in bed, but she's gone."

"They like to hang out in the Frisbee field." Baylie studied her boss. "Not there?" Baylie tried to think of somewhere else they might be. "Find one. You'll find the other."

"That's just it. The caseworker is coming here in an hour to meet with them about their possible adoption."

"Here?"

"Yes." Lissa nodded. "I wanted them to both be here so the caseworker can meet with them privately."

"Did the girls know that?" Jayden sounded annoyed.

"I hadn't had a chance to discuss it with them before they disappeared." Lissa glanced around the barnyard, worry lines furrowing her forehead.

"The girls took it upon themselves to be unavailable." Baylie glanced at Jayden.

"We'll see if we can find them." Jayden reached for Baylie's hand. "I remember what it was like to be eleven and the need to stay out of sight. We'll keep you posted."

Lissa looked relieved. "Thank you."

Baylie watched as Lissa headed back toward the dormitory,

checking the recreation equipment room and peeking into the kitchen entrance. She turned to Jayden. "Where do you suppose they could be?"

"Follow me." Jayden turned toward the barn, grabbing her hand. "When I was hiding out here after Mr. Mueller died, I spent a lot of time in the loft. Hay bales make surprisingly good cover and surveillance spots, not to mention easy climbs which a girl in Kendra's condition needs."

"Sounds like early training for your military career."

Surprise spread across Jayden's face. "I never thought of it that way, but you're right." He pointed to a ladder leading straight up the wall. "Think you can climb that?"

Baylie sized up the rungs. One after another with no rails on the side for hand holds. "I'll give it a try. But I've never been good at rock climbing or that sort of thing."

"Just don't look down. Follow me."

Baylie laughed. "The view isn't spectacular."

"Don't like the soles of my boots?"

"I was thinking something else."

Jayden glanced over his shoulder. "I'm shocked. We need to take you to church more often."

"Sounds like a plan." Baylie groaned as she pulled herself up the rungs. "But if I can ride a motorcycle and not fall off, I can climb this ladder." She saw Jayden's boots disappear over the ledge above and she worked her way to the top and followed him. Crawling into the loft, she glanced around the open floor plan, amazed at how spacious the barn seemed up here. "Wow. This is kind of nice."

"Be careful to watch where you step. The floor contains open holes to drop feed to the animals below. You probably would wind up on a mountain of hay, but a hungry horse might have his head in the way, too."

"And would object to my dropping in uninvited?"

"That's the least of your worries. A spooked animal can be dangerous." Jayden rose from the loft floor and offered his hand again. "Let's explore the loft, shall we?" He put a finger to his lips and nodded toward the far corner. He walked to an opening in the floor that looked down on an empty stall. He pointed.

Baylie followed his line of sight and saw two blonde heads duck behind a stack of hay in the stall. She grinned at him.

Jayden nodded back to the place where they'd climbed up. Together they circled the outer perimeter of the area, grabbing the ladder and descending, walking steadily in the direction of the hiding twins.

"I don't think they're in the barn." Jayden spoke in a loud voice. "Too bad they're going to miss out on the ice cream sundaes Mom has planned for the Sunday afternoon snack."

"Lissa will be disappointed, too. She so wanted their caseworker to meet with them. A permanent home sounds wonderful."

"Would they share a room?"

"That's what I did growing up. Though Jamielyn, my foster sister, and I were unrelated, we had matching bedspreads, fluffy rugs, and frilly curtains. I always felt like I had a twin."

"Sounds like a great way to spend your high school years."

Baylie sighed. "It was. Especially with you as our third team member."

"Maybe Kendra and Krystal will find a third friend to share their adventures, too."

"Not if we don't find them before three o'clock." Baylie watched for movement in the stall. The rustling sound of hay suggested the girls were moving.

Soon Kendra and Krystal emerged from behind a mound of piled hay, bits of straw and seed clinging to their clothes.

Kendra spoke first. "Will we really get to be together with matching bedspreads and rugs?"

"And ice cream sundaes today?" Krystal chimed in.

"That's a good possibility." Baylie held out her arms. "Lissa didn't get a chance to tell you all of the news. She hopes one of these couples will have hearts big enough to take you into their family."

"We thought we were going to be separated." Kendra rubbed her side.

"I know you did." Baylie hugged both girls close to her. "But remember I told you Lissa believes families should be together. She's learned recently that the state of Oregon believes that, too. She didn't know that for sure before." She studied Kendra. "Did you hurt yourself?"

"I'm a little sore, but we stayed on the main floor, so it wasn't bad."

"Okay." Jayden glanced at his watch and extended a hand. "We ought to get you girls cleaned up. The caseworker may not appreciate all the hay and seed on your clothes."

Krystal brushed off her blouse. "I never knew hay could smell so good."

"Or itch like crazy." Kendra shivered. "I need a barn brush."

"That can be arranged." Baylie laughed. "Let's go, shall we?"

CHAPTER TWENTY-SEVEN

While Baylie hurried the twins to their room to change into clean clothes, Jayden went to find Lissa. She stood talking to Kurt outside the ranch house, hands moving as fast as she spoke.

"Lissa?" Jayden stepped up behind the couple. "We found the girls."

Lissa turned, a look of relief across her face. "Oh, good. The caseworker is due any minute." She studied the driveway where a SUV now wound its way to the ranch and pointed. "That's probably her now."

"Baylie is helping them clean up." Jayden squinted into the afternoon sun. "She'll bring them here soon."

Lissa curved her hand above her eyes, shading the sun from her face. "Would you please tell Melanie we'll be ready for the sundaes in about twenty minutes?"

"Sure. I'll help serve."

"Great." Lissa smiled, nodded, and stepped forward to greet the woman climbing from the car as Jayden turned to leave. "Hello. I'm Lissa McKintrick. I don't think we've met."

"No, I'm new to this case load." She glanced around. "What a nice facility."

"Thanks. We aim to make the children feel as welcome as possible in their stays here." Lissa turned to Kurt. "This is my husband, Kurt."

The woman extended her hand. "Nancy Simms." She gave Kurt her full attention. "Must be lots of work."

Kurt returned the handshake. "We get a lot of help from our staff." Kurt gestured toward Jayden. "Jayden was our first foster child when we opened ten years ago. He's been to Afghanistan and is now here working as a volunteer until he decides the next step in his life."

Jayden extended his hand. "Nice to meet you." He thumbed toward the kitchen. "I'll let the cook know you've arrived. Be right back." He stepped inside the door and returned before Kurt, Lissa, and the caseworker finished a circular inspection of the ranch.

Nancy shifted her briefcase to her other hand. "This would be a difficult place to leave." She focused her attention on Lissa. "I hope the twins will be happy when we place them."

"You're offering a permanent home. That should mean a lot." She looked over her shoulder. "Here they come now."

Jayden heard noise coming from the dormitory and looked where Lissa had pointed. Baylie approached with the twins in tow. The threesome laughed at some joke, Kendra and Krystal giggling as they held on to Baylie's hands.

Baylie arched a brow as she caught Jayden's attention, the question on her face asking what he thought. He shrugged, giving her an up and down nod of his head, hoping to convey approval. The twins fell silent at the sight of the caseworker, the exuberance of minutes before gone as they became self-conscious in her scrutiny.

"Why hello!" Nancy stepped toward the girls. "You really are twins!"

"Identical." Krystal laughed. "Not much chance of missing that one."

Jayden chuckled under his breath as Baylie squeezed Krystal's shoulder. "Say hello, girls."

Kendra and Krystal both smiled, mumbled their hellos, and cast side glances at each other as they sized up this stranger.

Nancy spoke to Kendra. "How are you doing after your surgery? Okay?"

"Yes. I'm glad it's over. Krystal and I didn't like being separated that night." Kendra jutted her chin. "We are a two-for-one package deal."

Krystal agreed with her sister. "We're sure the family you've chosen is very nice, but unless you have a place for us both, you can't have just one."

"That's not part of the plan, I assure you." Nancy glanced at Lissa. "How much do they know?"

"Not as much as they need." Lissa stepped into the conversation. "We have afternoon snacks planned for this meeting. Why don't you and the twins follow us to the dining room where you can sit and get acquainted?"

Nancy held out her hands to the twins. "I'm delighted to meet you both."

Kendra took the woman's hand. "The kitchen is this way."

Jayden stepped beside Baylie. "What are you thinking?"

"That Kendra and Krystal may be on the verge of having their dearest wish fulfilled." Baylie grasped his fingers. "A dream come true."

"Was that ever your dream?"

"Not really. I was content with Mom's cousin, especially since Grandpa and Grandma were a regular part of my life, but I was never adopted. I didn't feel like the Marshall home was permanent even though they insisted I was always welcome." Baylie took a deep breath. "I've come to realize how important a forever home might be."

"I know Peggy, then Kurt and Lissa, gave me that at home feeling. And with Mom working as a cook with the state's blessing I didn't feel separated from her. Peggy made that happen."

"But I think Kendra and Krystal will be happier with a permanent home. Together."

"Me, too."

They reached the kitchen door and Kendra turned to Nancy. "Do you like ice cream sundaes?"

Nancy nodded. "Especially with caramel syrup."

Kendra gasped. "That's my favorite, too."

"Score one for Nancy." Jayden whispered.

"What's your favorite, Krystal?" Nancy touched the child's head.

"I'm happy with anything as long as I'm sharing it with friends." She shrugged her shoulders as she pointed to a vacant space at the table. The threesome found chairs and sat. "But chocolate holds a special place."

Krystal glanced at Nancy, continuing to answer the question asked of her before. "I'm more afraid of losing my sister. When she had surgery Friday night she was gone until Saturday. That was awful. We really want to stay together."

Nancy nodded. "Of that I am sure."

"So, Nancy. Can you keep us together or not?" Krystal's intense look made Nancy blink.

"The state of Oregon considers it a priority. I do, too."

"See? We've already got you trained." Kendra giggled. "I like that."

Jayden glanced at Baylie who sat listening to the exchange. "Sounds like the girls are going to sew this one up."

"Definitely." Baylie's eyes pooled. "I'm not sure who's more delighted—them or me."

Baylie finished her ice cream and as the noise of the children died down, she worked her way around the dining area, picking up sundae bowls, spoons, and soiled napkins. Lissa had taken the caseworker to her office to discuss the details of adopting Kendra and Krystal, leaving the girls looking bewildered, staring at the emptying dining room.

"What's wrong, girls?" Baylie drew near, pulling up a chair to sit. "You look overwhelmed."

Kendra puffed out her lower lip. "Just scared."

"Of what? The possibility of a new home?"

Krystal nodded. "We've liked living here at the ranch. If we leave, it will feel a lot like when our first case worker moved us after our Mom and Dad were killed."

"That was so hard." Kendra sniffed. "I don't want to do it again."

Baylie pulled the girls to her and wrapped an arm around each one. "You aren't going anywhere right away." She squeezed them. "Nancy has to meet with a committee to determine who might be the best fit for you. She also has to approach these families with the idea of taking twins. I think there are home visits after that. Don't be afraid to weigh in on how you feel. None of this is set in stone. At least not now."

"What if we don't like the people they choose or their place?" Krystal's worried face melted Baylie's heart. "Can we say no to an adoption?"

"I'm pretty sure you can object." Baylie paused. "Why don't you give this a chance before you think about not liking it?" Baylie kissed each girl on the head. "Nancy seemed pretty determined to make it right."

Kendra nodded. "I liked her a lot."

"Maybe you'll like the couple chosen just as well."

Jayden watched Baylie interact with the twins, ready smile and easy open heart making her adorable. He'd always considered her a good friend, a girl who rose above her circumstances and tackled the world with enthusiasm. Now he felt something more. The tug on his heart desired a deeper relationship.

She'd shared her story with him, a broken soul in need of repair, and she'd readily accepted his counsel as well as Parker's. Her healing amazed him, proof that the girl he'd always known still existed, her love for God and all that was His fueling her forward.

Jayden wanted to be her anchor in this time of soul searching, offering her a safe haven for her storm-tossed spirit and a shelter to share her heart. He wanted to capture her heart, if he admitted the truth, but he'd have to find direction for his life now that the military was behind him. School beckoned, and the cost would be offset by Uncle Sam, but it might mean separation for a time. Could their friendship survive another disconnect?

"Penny for your thoughts." Mom sat down beside him, beads of perspiration shining on her brow. She glanced from him to Baylie and back again. "You two seem to be getting rather cozy."

Jayden tapped the table. "We have always been good friends." He studied his mother. "This time around is a little different."

Mom smiled. "Both of you have matured and your needs have grown with time. She's a treasure, Jayden. Don't let her get away."

"Any advice?"

Mom stood and squeezed his shoulder. "I don't think it would take much to convince her of your intentions. Give her something concrete to hold on to."

"I have schooling ahead of me. Career choices."

"So?" Mom looked Baylie's way. "She's found a career here and the home she's always wanted. Be part of that."

"Working at the ranch isn't really a future for me." Jayden glanced around. "Kurt and Lissa have it well under control."

"This operation is always growing and changing." Mom winked. "Tell Kurt what you are thinking. You might be pleasantly surprised." She turned and walked away, untying her apron and hanging it on a post.

Jayden focused again on Baylie who still sat talking with the twins. She was definitely in her element, past history as a foster child, love of helping others, and a gift with words making her fit here at the ranch as if she'd been groomed for this job.

What about his past? What could his history offer others who might need a boost up? He'd not really succeeded with Cody, but in the end had earned enough of his trust that Cody let him know about George. He also believed Cody could yet benefit from an older brother figure in his life.

How many others like him were there that Jayden might help?

Baylie walked the twins back to their room after they'd met privately with Nancy to discuss their adoption and then said goodbye. The girls were quiet, subdued Baylie guessed, by the new future that might lay before them. She listened as they rambled, their secret worries tumbling out like nuggets of gold in a fast-moving stream.

"I might like having our own home again." Krystal kicked a rock in the gravel. "I like it here at the ranch, but being somebody's kid and part of a family would be nice."

Kendra glanced at Baylie. "They'd be our family, wouldn't they?

Baylie smiled. "That's what they want to be. A forever family."

"Nobody can promise that." Krystal frowned. "Not forever. Look at our mom and dad."

Baylie touched the girl's shoulder. "No one can see what life will bring. The new couple will do whatever they can, just like your parents did their best."

Kendra leaned against Baylie. "I want to give them a chance."

"Good." Baylie hugged her. "Why don't you go rest before dinner? You've had a busy day. And so soon after surgery." She pointed to the kitchen. "I need to help Melanie."

"Bye, Baylie."

She turned back toward the kitchen, thoughts on her forever home. What would that be like? Who would she share it with?

Jayden's image flashed before her eyes. Baylie hugged herself. What a forever that would be!

"Hey. Did you get the girls calmed down?"

Baylie jumped, breathing irregular, as the man in her thoughts appeared at her side. "I. . .I. . .I think so."

Jayden's brows rose. "Are you okay?" He touched her shoulder. "You seem a little panicked."

"I was just deep in thought." She tried to breathe. "You startled me, that's all."

Jayden's crooked smile lit his face. "You're cute when you're flustered."

"Who says I'm flustered?" Baylie tried to sound annoyed.

Jayden held up his hands. "No one said that." He lowered his chin, grinning at her. "But your face is red as a beet. And you're panting."

She swatted at him. "I'm not panting, just startled."

"Are you sure?" Jayden stepped beside her as she strode toward the kitchen, chin jutted out in defiance. "I'd kind of like it if being near me made you breathless."

Baylie stopped cold. "You would?"

Jayden chuckled. "I would." He took her hands. "I watched you today with the twins and I said that girl is one of a kind." He pulled her closer to him. "And if I thought being around me made you fight for breath, or turn red, or want to faint, I'd be the happiest man alive."

"You would?"

Jayden touched her cheek, pushing an errant curl back toward her ear. "I might even kiss you to make you gasp a little harder."

"Jayden." Baylie lowered her chin, her gaze on his shoes. She couldn't look in his eyes or she'd lose herself. "There are kids watching."

"Really?" He swept his arm to the right, then swung the other one to the left. "All I see are fields of green, children playing in the Frisbee field, and the sun's rays growing lower in the sky." He lifted her hand to his mouth and kissed it. "We're alone." He looked in her eyes. "What are you afraid of?"

Baylie trembled. Could he be serious? Could this guy she'd watched from afar really want to be more than a friend? He'd said that he did, but she was still having trouble taking it in.

He stood there, smiling, that endearing crooked smile on his face. The smile she'd known for years that made goose bumps pop up on her arms and warmed her insides. The smile was aimed at her. His hands caressed her knuckles. She could feel his breath on her face. Smell his after shave.

He lifted her hand to his chest, the beat of his heart beneath her palm. Not a slow steady beat, but a stronger one, a heart that felt like a runaway train. "Your heart is racing."

"Exactly. You're not the only one out of breath."

Baylie laughed. "Then kiss me already."

"I thought you'd never ask."

CHAPTER TWENTY-EIGHT

"Kurt?" Jayden caught sight of the man as he disappeared inside the barn entrance the next day and hurried to join him. The stable smelled like fresh hay in the warmth of the morning, the fragrant summer air wafting down from the loft above, bringing with it the sweet aroma of newly opened bales. Jayden could hear an intern above him tossing flakes of the alfalfa to the feeders, readying them for later in the day when the horses were brought in from the pasture. How many times had he done this same task growing up? Too many to count.

"What's up?" Kurt paused mid-aisle, a halter in his hand.

"I've been giving my future some thought and hoped to sit and talk with you about it."

"Your future here at the ranch?" Kurt jingled the lead chain. "Or your future in general?"

"Everything." Jayden wasn't sure what he wanted to do. Mom had said to run ideas by Kurt and so he was. Finding a career after spending four years as a soldier seemed daunting, but he had good skills that somebody could use. Surely.

"I've got some ideas you might consider." Kurt turned to walk, thumbing Jayden to follow. "Depending on what you see as your path."

"I've done mechanical work in the military. I've worked on my bike. I've grown up on the ranch which taught me a million things. I don't know how to compact it into a single job."

"Those all sound like solid skills." Kurt stopped at the end of the barn and opened the stall door. The horse, Whiskers, nickered. Kurt slipped the halter over the animal's head and snapped the buckle, then led Whiskers out of the stall.

"He's limping." Jayden pointed to the left front hoof which the horse favored as he followed Kurt. "Need a farrier?"

"Hmm." Kurt stopped and lifted the hoof. "He's got something wedged in the frog."

"I'll get the hoof pick." Jayden stepped down the aisle where the tools hung on the wall. He grabbed the pick and came back to where Kurt waited. "Does it look infected?"

"Smells foul." Kurt dug around the edge of the hoof, taking care not to dig into the tender part of the center. "He may need treatment."

"You want to clean it out now, or call the farrier?"

"Both. I'll clean it and call Dr. DeLorme to come have a look." Kurt worked around the sensitive tissue then lowered the hoof to the ground. "I removed the rock wedged there. But if he's bruised the frog, he may need professional help and a tetanus shot."

"Is Whiskers on the lineup for riding lessons today?"

"He was. That's why he was still stabled. I can have one of the kids catch a horse from the pasture and bring it up."

"I'll do it." Jayden reached for a spare halter hanging on the wall. "I haven't had to fetch a horse since I've been back."

"Remember how Lady used to follow you out of the pasture?"

"Yeah, after rolling in the mud and ruining my hard-earned grooming."

"I think she did that on purpose." Kurt pointed to the pasture below the barn, stopping to fill a small pan with grain. "Come on. We can talk while we play catch."

Jayden fell into step beside Kurt, his lame leg stretching to match the other man's stride. He'd be glad when the limp disappeared and his recovering knee found its ground.

"A rancher not far from here wants to sublet a portion of his property to someone who would establish a facility like ours." Kurt stopped at the fence and whistled. A roan mare lifted her head and studied him. After looking as if she was considering her options for a moment, she turned his way and ambled up the pasture. Kurt shook the little pan of grain he carried, and the mare sped up, nickering as she walked. "Come on, Ginger."

Jayden unlocked the gate and waited as the mare sought Kurt's treat. He stroked her neck as she gobbled, then slid the halter over her head and snapped the buckle. Kurt petted the animal, talking in soothing tones as he attached the lead rope and led her from the pasture.

"The rancher wants the place to be for boys who have lost their way." Kurt continued as if five minutes had not lapsed since he brought up the subject.

"Teens, I'm guessing?"

Kurt nodded. "He lost his son in a car accident. The kid who hit him had been drinking."

"That stinks."

"Yeah, his son was a good kid. Wanted to take over the ranch one day." Kurt looked out over the pasture and sighed. "The rancher hopes to honor his son's memory by helping kids like the one who killed his son."

"How much land are we talking about?"

"It's an alfalfa farm." Kurt stopped. "Lots of hard work. Plenty to keep guys involved most of the year round."

"House? Barns? Trucks?'

"All of the above. The foreman running the hay operation would work out of a separate set of buildings on the far side of the fields. The house and grounds of the family home would be yours to manage." Kurt led Ginger toward the round pen. "The operation would be funded by the sale of the hay."

"That sounds like a lot of work for one man."

"It would be, if not for the division of labor the rancher wants to maintain. The person running the hay operation will be a separate entity. Have his own crew. The boys' home administrator will oversee staff for the boys, a cook, and a housekeeper."

Kurt stopped at the gate and led Ginger into the pen. Bryn, today's riding instructor, came over and took the rope. "Ginger's in today?"

"Yes. Whiskers needs some tender loving care for a day or two."

"Thanks, Kurt."

Jayden continued their discussion as they walked. "Who is he considering for the position?"

"The thing is the rancher doesn't have anyone with the right set of skills." He pointed to the duplex. "Let's go talk in Lissa's office."

They entered the building, nodded at Baylie who sat at her computer, and traipsed on down the hall to the cubby Lissa claimed as hers. As per usual, Kurt grabbed chips from the stash on top of the refrigerator and tossed one to Jayden. He reached inside the unit and produced two cold drinks. "Talk better on a healthy snack." He winked.

Jayden chuckled. "I hope Lissa is that understanding about her missing inventory."

"Remember she keeps this here for me." Kurt grinned. "I'm special."

They munched in companionable silence for a few minutes, then Kurt tossed his bag in the trash and leaned forward. "The thing is, this ranch probably needs a partnership to run all sides of the operation."

"Sounds like it." Jayden tossed his bag. "Too much for one person, especially someone as inexperienced as I am."

"That's where you're wrong." Kurt rested back in the chair, hands clasped behind his head, focus on the ceiling. "You understand the foster care half. The boys who need a strong hand."

"But I know little about alfalfa."

"You don't need to know." Kurt leaned forward, elbows on knees. "The hay side of the ranch would be run by a foreman for the rancher. The house and its outbuildings would be part of the foster facility. The rancher will live off site."

"What kind of outbuildings?"

"That's the beauty of this. The house has a complete upstairs consisting of about six bedrooms with a full bath."

"Like your dormitory over the garage?" Jayden sat deeper in his chair. "So I would be on the floor with the guys?"

"No. Ground floor. Like a house father. There's an office, a full bath and a bedroom downstairs besides the kitchen and living area." Kurt picked up a piece of paper and sketched some squares on it. He turned the paper to Jayden. "This is the house. This is the barn. Tool shed. "He added some large spaces around the buildings. "Pasture for livestock."

"Looks a lot like what you have here."

"Yes. All circled by the hay fields." Kurt popped the pencil on its eraser. "The foreman for the alfalfa would supervise the kids he chooses to work on the hay. You would be responsible for their physical welfare, their counseling, and meeting the state's requirements if they come with baggage like felony convictions, terms of their parole, that kind of thing."

"Whoa." Jayden sat up straighter. "Sounds like a lot of responsibility."

"These kids need intervention before they are completely lost to society." Kurt studied him. "They've had abusive fathers. Neglectful mothers. Rough foster care situations. They need a fresh start."

"Sounds promising. The plan appeals to me somehow." Jayden fingered the crude map Kurt had drawn. "I'm a result of the guidance you and Peggy Blake gave me when I first entered foster care as well as the discipline the Marines taught me."

"You ought to go see Peggy. I have her cell phone number here." Kurt pulled out an address book. "You haven't been to see her since you returned, have you?"

"No. And I meant to."

"She could share the histories of the kids she and my buddy Foster mentored at their rescue ranch. Before I joined her operation."

"That's a good idea." Jayden stood. "You've given me a lot to think about. Thanks."

Kurt stood and offered his hand. "Don't forget to include Baylie in the mix. I sense she is part of your future, so she should know what you're thinking."

Jayden grinned. "This could make or break any future we might have together."

"No." Kurt shook his head. "She has a heart for hurting kids. She'd be perfect."

"But boys?"

"She kept you in line all through high school, didn't she?"

"Point taken."

All Baylie could think about was Jayden's kiss last night. He'd made it quick, light, but so tender she'd almost swooned. She could still feel his arms about her waist, smell his musky aftershave, remember the sweetness of his breath near her face. *God, if you don't mind answering another prayer, I'll be happy knowing Jayden has feelings for me. What a wonderful gift.*

She headed for her office, slowing her pace when Kurt and Jayden emerged through the front exit of the duplex. They appeared deep in conversation, stopping to shake hands as they parted. What deal had been struck? What agreement had they solidified? Her heart hammered out a staccato rhythm, imagining all the scenarios a discussion between Kurt and Jayden might produce. Could it be Jayden planned to stay on at the ranch? Wouldn't that be something?

Jayden turned her direction and seeing her, smiled and waved. "Good morning." He crossed the yard and stopped where she was.

"How's your day?" She swallowed her other thoughts, especially the one that whispered in her ear. *Kiss me again.* "Big plans?"

"Maybe." Jayden scuffed his boot in the gravel. "I'm heading over to see Peggy Blake."

"Isn't she the woman who first took you in as a foster child?"

"Good memory." Jayden pulled keys from a pocket. "She's retired now. Her ranch is managed by an overseer."

"I know how much you loved living there."

"I need to talk to her about her experiences as a foster mother." Jayden squinted at her. "Before I came along."

"Did she retire when she finished with you?" Baylie giggled. "That speaks volumes."

"Hey!" Jayden took a step toward her. "I was her favorite."

She raised a hand in defense. "Have a good visit." As he walked to his bike, she watched him go. *I'm sure you were her favorite. You are definitely mine.*

Jayden let the sun warm his back as he rode to Peggy's ranch. Not much had changed here since his days as a frightened child seeking to stay away from his stepfather George. Kurt had moved on. Peggy had retired. The barns and outbuildings, though, still stood as they had. Horses and other rescued animals meandered in the pens. Everything remained as he remembered.

He parked the Harley near the ranch house and walked up to the screened back door. No one, as far as he knew, had ever used the front door, so he raised a knuckle to the familiar casing, the cracked paint peeling a little more than he remembered.

Movement inside told him someone was coming, the scent of warm chocolate mixed with cinnamon tempting his nose. Finally, the door squeaked open, and a woman peered out at him, apron tied at her waist, nose tinged with a dusting of flour. He hid his surprise at the way the years had taken their toll, Peggy's face sporting wrinkles, frame more bent.

"So it's really you?" Peggy sounded out of breath, but the light in her eyes said she retained her spunk. "Kurt McKintrick called and warned me you were on the way."

"Yeah, it's me, Peggy." He raised his chin. "Jayden."

"Of course you are. No surprise there. You always knew when I was baking cookies. You and Kurt thieving my fresh baked goods." She chuckled, lifted the hook from its eye, and opened the screen door. "Come in and don't let the screen slam behind you. My kitchen timer is a dinging."

"Sounds like I'm right on time." Jayden slipped through the door, hooking the screen back into place. He turned and followed her down the familiar passage, the scent of hot cinnamon growing stronger with each step. He stepped into the tidy kitchen, Peggy's back to him as she bent over the oven, then she lifted out a baking sheet. He fought the urge to grab a hot cookie from the tray as he had done so many times before, always burning his thumb and tongue in his haste.

"What?" She straightened, setting the hot pan on the counter. "Not going to steal a cookie when I least expect it?"

Jayden chuckled. "I'm resisting the temptation, but I may be losing the battle."

"From the looks of you, other battles have been fought and lost before today."

Jayden nodded. "I was injured in an explosion in Afghanistan."

"An eye and it seems to me you've gained a limp." She took the cookie spatula, lifted four cookies from the pan, and slid them on a plate. "Stupid wars claim too many casualties." Handing him the plate, she pointed to a kitchen chair. "Why don't you sit a spell and tell me all about your adventures. It's been too long, Jayden."

He sat, enjoying a cookie as he recounted his war tales. An hour passed as they talked, Peggy nodding as she absorbed the nature of his war experiences. As the afternoon wound down, she reached over and touched his arm.

"I'm so grateful to God for bringing you home." Tears lined the edges of her eyes. "My Foster didn't get that privilege, you know. But I prayed you would be spared. Every day I prayed."

"You prayed for me?" Jayden laid his hand over her warm fingers. "I should have known your prayers were protecting me." Giving her a squeeze, he straightened. "You always knew how to lift me up. Thank you."

"I understand you are living at Kurt and Lissa's. Your mom, too."

"Temporarily. Which is why I'm here." He told her of Kurt's proposition. "He said you and Foster cared for some pretty rough kids."

"We did. But Foster knew young boys and I knew how to pray. We sent a lot of lost causes on their way from here to fruitful lives. One of our graduates, if you will, is currently mayor of Redmond."

"Wow." Jayden sat up, his respect for what she had accomplished growing. "That's quite a legacy."

"He thinks so, too." Peggy chuckled "Comes by to check on me about once a month. Though I have a foreman with a board of directors to oversee the Herrick Valley Rescue Center, I need advice on the changing tax laws and the goings on of Harney County. Wild horses still need oversight, though I don't foster boys anymore."

"That's the world's loss." Jayden ate the last cookie on the plate.

"But I think you could pick up the baton and carry on. Lots of hurting kids out there who need a man to guide them." Peggy winked. "You have your own experience from which to draw wisdom."

"Is that enough?"

Peggy folded her arms across her middle. "Your stint as a foster child and your time in the military more than qualifies you." She studied him. "I'd say you'd be great." She sat up. "Go for it."

CHAPTER TWENTY-NINE

THE ROAR OF THE MOTORCYCLE AS Jayden returned to the ranch later that afternoon made Baylie's heart skip a beat. They'd become good friends, their affection for each other bordering on the edge of a solid relationship, their future looming like a good romance novel. She resisted the urge to pinch herself in case she was dreaming. But if she was dreaming, she was doing so in living color in a real-life drama.

She logged off her computer, the story of Bossy almost finished. She'd had such fun writing the piece that the afternoon sped by. She glanced at the clock, noting that dinner preparations were only an hour away. Tonight Melanie was preparing a new recipe she thought the kids would like—pizza casserole. The dish sounded tempting—macaroni, hamburger and pizza sauce mixed together. What kid could say no to a pizza-like taste?

She looked to see where Jayden was headed. He carried his helmet to the apartment and disappeared. A minute later he emerged, limping gait filled with purpose as he strode to the barn. What was he up to?

She moseyed to the front of the office to spy. Jayden and Kurt appeared at the barn doors, deep in discussion. From the look on Jayden's face and the animated movement of his hands, the trip today had energized him. She'd never met Peggy Blake, but she'd heard a lot about her. After escaping the threatening environment of living with his stepfather, Jayden's memories of his time at Peggy's rescue ranch were always filled with laughter and happy thoughts. That's where he had met Kurt. Where he claimed to have shoved Lissa and Kurt together. Where he'd conspired with Peggy to get the McKintrick romance going. To hear him tell it Jayden had played the part of Cupid, complete with bow and arrow.

She chuckled under her breath. Jayden was a charmer. She'd known that in high school. Now he captured her full concentration. A handsome, matured ex-Marine with his sights set on her. She trembled. How happy she was to be the center of his attention.

She paused, glancing around to see where the two men had gone. She glimpsed them entering the ranch house, Gunner and Gage at their heels. A little disappointed, she locked her office and went to her apartment. Melanie didn't need her yet, so she'd take some personal time to check her appearance. Looking her best for Jayden seemed the sensible thing to do. At least it couldn't hurt.

The clock her grandmother had given her chimed three times as she reached for her hairbrush and mascara. Her mind wandered, thoughts on the conversation between Kurt and Jayden. She really did want to be a mouse in the corner. She couldn't wait to talk to him.

Her phone pinged. She glanced at the screen and gasped. The facility where her grandmother lived was calling. She closed her eyes and prayed before she pressed the answer button. Not Grandma. Not now.

"Hello?" Baylie held her breath.

"Baylie Summers?"

"Yes, speaking."

"This is Rhonda Davis at the assisted living facility where your grandmother, Laura Levine, lives. How are you?"

"I'm fine. How is Grandma Laura?"

"I'm sorry to report she took a fall and broke her hip. We transported her to the hospital where she is being prepped for surgery."

"Is she all right otherwise?"

"Pretty shaken, confused, calling for you."

"Yes, of course. Can I reach her at the hospital to talk?"

"Not right now." Rhonda paused. "She will be in recovery

tomorrow. Can you come and see her then?"

"I'll have to make arrangements with my employer. I can probably get away."

"That would be great." Rhonda's relief was palpable. "We'll look for you then."

Baylie clicked off the phone and sagged into a nearby chair. Grandma broke her hip? How would that affect her life? Baylie was all she had left. Would she need her? Baylie's spirits plummeted. The timing of this couldn't be worse but she would help her grandmother. Everything and everyone else would wait.

A knock on her door surprised her. She rose from the chair and went to the door.

"Hey, Bayles." Jayden's crooked smile spoke mischief. "How was your afternoon? "

"I wrote about Bossy." She stepped back from the door and gestured for him to come in, searching for the right words to tell him about Grandma. "How was your visit with Peggy?"

"Just like old times. She was baking cookies. I helped by eating a plateful."

Baylie laughed. "Why am I not surprised?"

"I'd like to talk with you about something, say, after dinner?"

"Sure. I have to make some arrangements with Lissa first, but after that I'm available."

Jayden frowned. "You seem pre-occupied. Everything okay?"

She blinked back the threat of tears. "The facility where Grandma lives just called. She has fallen and broken her hip."

Jayden reached for her hands. "Oh, Bayles. I'm sorry."

"Me, too." Baylie nodded. "She's on her way to surgery."

"That's fast."

"I know. I'm traveling to Bend tomorrow to find out the details. But I'm worried."

"Let's stop right now and pray for her." He held out his hands. Baylie grasped his fingers and bowed her head as Jayden prayed.

He looked up and caressed her cheek. "If you need company, I'm available. We can talk on the way."

"Only if we take my car."

"Deal."

Jayden volunteered to drive the next morning, but Baylie insisted the task would help keep her mind off the coming meeting with the hospital staff who awaited her arrival.

"If you drive, Jayden, I'm going to fidget all the way there, worrying about what the future holds for my grandmother." She touched his shoulder. "Is that a threat to your masculinity? I don't want to appear to be the dominant, take-charge Amazon woman who doesn't want doors opened for her. But I'm truly frightened."

"I understand." Jayden put his baseball cap on backwards. "I'll just slink into the seat and act like I'm a hitchhiker you picked up." He popped on his sunglasses. "Incognito enough for you?"

Baylie laughed. "You nut."

"Hey, it got you to laugh. Worth something."

The drive seemed to take forever, Baylie's mind fixed on the road ahead. Music played on the car radio sporadically, stations tuning in and out depending on what curve of the highway they were on.

Jayden tapped his knees and offered tourist-like appraisals of the scenery they passed—a herd of wild horses here, a fleeing antelope there, a piece of sagebrush in mid-air. Baylie grinned at the running dialogue, appreciating the way he kept her focused and relaxed. He couldn't be a nicer man if he tried. The fact that he was sitting in her car, concerned about her welfare, and totally comfortable with the situation gave her chills. Hunter would never have submitted to a road trip like this. She had forgiven herself for those days, but she still wondered how she could have been so blind.

The hospital loomed ahead, and she drove into the parking lot, finding a space close to the entrance. Turning off the key, she studied Jayden. "Not every day I can find a premium parking space."

"Thank you, dearie." Jayden spoke as if he were an old man, feigning a shaky voice. "Less distance for me to push my walker."

"Let me get it out of the trunk, you old codger."

Though the patients wouldn't appreciate their humor, they laughed together, the levity heightening her mood. "Let's go find Grandma."

After checking in at the front desk, Baylie led the way to the ward where Grandma was recovering, Jayden walking at her side. They paused at the reception area, then were ushered to a waiting room. A doctor appeared. "Baylie Summers?" At her nod, he extended his hand. "Dr. Hickman." He gestured for her to follow. "The front desk told me you were on your way." He led them into a small office and pointed to two chairs across from his desk. "Make yourselves comfortable."

"So how is my grandmother?" Baylie had wanted to see the woman first, but the attendant at the entrance had advised her to see the doctor instead.

"She's comfortable. She had an intracapsular fracture which is a break between the ball and the neck of the femur. We opted for immediate surgery. All seems well."

"How long is the recovery?"

"She'll be kept in the hospital for at least one week, possibly two. I will then send her to a rehabilitation facility. Could be six weeks or better."

Baylie glanced at Jayden. He quirked an eyebrow. She focused on Dr. Hickman. "Will she need someone to stay with her when she returns to her apartment?"

"That depends on her progress." The doctor hesitated. "But

someone her age can take six months to a year to recover from a fall like this."

"A year?"

"Yes. Even that timeline is generous." Dr. Hickman grew more solemn studying Baylie. "Broken hips in seniors are quite serious. It's important to keep their spirits up."

"What should I do?" Baylie leaned forward in her chair.

"I don't want to alarm you. Statistics in these cases are not favorable." He folded his arms, somber face stoic. "Your grandmother has a positive outlook, a great attitude. But her recent loss of Joseph could affect her thinking. A broken hip could bring on depression."

"How can I prevent that from happening?" Baylie bit her lip. "I live near Burns. Driving here every weekend could get expensive."

"She'll be well taken care of—both at the rehabilitation center and if and when she returns to the assisted living facility. I don't see her living independently in her apartment any time soon. A visit from you on occasion will keep her outlook positive." Dr. Hickman smiled. "Would you like to see her?"

"Yes." Baylie stood. "Very much."

"Great. She's in pain, but in good spirits. Having you here will do her a world of good."

Jayden walked beside Baylie as they followed the doctor down the hallway toward Grandma Levine's room. Baylie's mouth held no smile, lips pressed in a straight line. Though she held her head high, the battle to suppress tears didn't escape his notice. He reached for her hand. "I'm here."

Her eyes squinted closed for a second, mouth skewed as she held back what looked like the need to sob. She looked at him, tears pooled in her eyes. "Thank you." She spoke in a whisper. "What will I do if something happens?"

"Don't think like that." Jayden squeezed her hand. "We'll lend her all our support. She's important to me, too, remember."

"I know she is." Baylie slowed as Dr. Hickman stopped and opened a door. "Mrs. Levine? You have visitors."

Baylie stepped into the room and studied the face of her grandmother as she lay in bed. Grandma looked so fragile, tidy hair unkempt against the pillow, skin sallow. Baylie forced a smile she didn't feel. "Grandma! I've missed seeing you. Can I give you a hug?"

"Oh, Baylie, dear, you sweet, sweet girl." Grandma raised her arms and Baylie leaned in to give her a squeeze. "You didn't have to drive all that way to see me."

"Of course I did." Baylie straightened and gestured toward Jayden. "And I brought my favorite partner in crime with me."

"Not on that motorcycle again!" Grandma lifted a hand to Jayden. "How are you?"

"A bit shaky, I'm afraid." Jayden cast Baylie a crooked grin. "I rode shotgun this time with Baylie at the wheel. Not sure it's safer than my Harley."

Baylie gasped. "Hey!"

Grandma laughed out loud. "How fun. Thank you for making sure my Baylie gets to her destinations." She winked at Jayden. "I'm content knowing she's in capable hands."

"Yes, ma'am. I do my best, but this girl is a handful."

Baylie blew out air. "Don't believe a word he says, Grandma. I'm a very responsible driver."

Grandma clasped her hand. "I know you are. Thank you. I needed a laugh today."

Baylie sobered. "Are you in pain?"

"No. They've got great meds here." She yawned. "The hard part is staying awake."

"Rest is probably good for you." Jayden moved to the other side of the bed. "You don't want to complicate your injury. I had enough of that when I came back from Afghanistan."

"I'll follow your advice, then." Grandma arched her neck and lifted her shoulders. "My back gets tired laying here."

"You want me to call an aide to help you?"

"They'll be in to check on me soon and that will end our visit." Grandma sighed. "They are very attentive after surgeries. Visitation is limited."

Baylie stroked her grandmother's cheek. "I can always come back when they're finished." She swallowed. "Sounds like I might be here often."

Grandma shook her head. "That's not necessary." She pulled on the sheet. "I am being well taken care of. I welcome your company, but I don't want you trudging one-hundred miles down the highway every weekend to see me."

"But Grandma. . .'"

"No buts about it, girl." Grandma grew serious. "You have a wonderful job, a handsome fella for a friend, and a life to live outside of caring for me." She wagged a pointer finger at Baylie. "You go live your life and have fun. Then when you do visit, I can experience your adventures through your stories. You've always been a great storyteller. Now you can live some stories of your own."

Baylie glanced at him, face stricken. She looked back at her grandmother. "I'm available to be here for you. I'll even move to be closer to you."

"I appreciate what you are saying." Grandma Levine sounded more serious than Jayden had ever heard her. "This injury may take a long time to heal. It may leave me bedridden. I know the statistics. Don't make me sad by sacrificing your happiness to make me happy." She touched Baylie's hand then reached for his. "Jayden, promise me you won't let her do that."

"I'll try. She's determined, as am I, to make sure you are well cared for and comfortable." Jayden folded his arms and assumed a soldier stance. "You've always been important to both of us."

"You are so special, both of you." Grandma's voice wobbled. "I know you have the best intentions, but my contributions to your welfare, Baylie, and my support of you as your guardian over the years will be moot if I think you are compromising your life's ambitions to hover over me." Grandma clasped her hands together. "Let me see my efforts weren't wasted. Live your lives!"

A noise at the door caught Jayden's attention and he glanced up to see a nurse with a loaded cart waiting. She smiled, her hand on the medical supplies stacked on top.

"Are you here to check on Mrs. Levine?"

"I am." The nurse pushed the cart further into the room. "She needs to be kept off her injured hip, but also needs rotation to prevent bedsores."

"We need to leave?" At the nurse's nod Jayden gestured toward the exit, signaling Baylie to follow him. He leaned over Mrs. Levine and whispered. "I'll do my best to see that Baylie doesn't stray."

Grandma giggled. "I have every confidence she'll toe the line for you." She winked. "Now take her home where she can do what she needs to do and not fret over me. I expect great things."

Jayden straightened and met Baylie's gaze. "Ready?"

She gave him a gritty smile, letting him know she didn't like being led away, but she followed him out the door. Outside, she hissed. "I don't like leaving her."

Jayden shrugged. "You heard what she said. I'd say she has a full grasp of her circumstances. She's not one to beat about the bush."

"Still. . ."

Jayden took Baylie's elbow, turning her down the corridor. "I know how much she means to you, but you need to respect your grandmother's wishes. She's fragile, but she's in control." Jayden slid his hand to hers. "The best thing you can do is go home and live your life. That's what she wants you to do. That way you can bring her tales to brighten her day." He pulled Baylie to a stop. "I want to be part of those adventures."

Baylie's eyes moistened, smile wobbly. "I'm not sure which is better news, but I'll do my best to provide both."

They stopped at the front desk and left their phone numbers to be reached in an emergency. Baylie was insistent. "I want to be called whenever there is any change in her condition."

The nurse assured her they would do everything they could to apprise Baylie of any developments. She would not be left out of the loop. Satisfied, Baylie turned to him. "Does that make you happy?"

"I think what's more important is this will make your grandmother even happier."

CHAPTER THIRTY

THE RIDE HOME SEEMED AS ENDLESS as it had when she'd driven over. Baylie let Jayden take the wheel, her physical and emotional energy spent. She couldn't imagine Grandma left in a hospital facility indefinitely. Nor did she accept the doctor's prognosis that her grandmother might never return to her apartment. Baylie would do all within her power to see that neither of those scenarios came true.

"Penny for your thoughts." Jayden turned her way. "Or are they worth a dollar?"

"Ha, ha." Baylie slumped in the seat. "You probably wouldn't like what I'm thinking."

"Try me." Jayden tapped the steering wheel.

She didn't say anything right away, unsure she could voice her thoughts and not have him reinforce Grandma's edict. That's what it felt like, anyway. Almost as if Grandma was forcing Baylie out of her life. She knew that wasn't true, but the thought of not being allowed to care for the older woman at this point in her life when Grandma had always been there for her didn't sit well with Baylie.

"I don't know if I can just continue on when I feel such a responsibility to return all the favors Grandma has done for me. I want to care for her as she lives out her final years."

"You know what she said." Jayden slowed a little as he took a curve. "She wants you to bring her stories of your adventures."

"All I have are the experiences on the ranch." She looked at him. "How many Bossy the cow escapades can I retell?"

Jayden chuckled. "Bossy can probably provide you with plenty of material." He straightened in the seat. "Wouldn't you hate leaving the ranch? I had the impression that is where you felt you'd found a home."

"It is. If I left, though, the ranch would replace me. Life there would go on."

"Ouch." Jayden raised his shoulders. "I hoped you'd say I would be missed."

"I *will* miss you." She studied him. "I also know volunteering your time at the ranch is not your final destination. You'll be gone sooner or later."

Jayden didn't respond, turning his gaze out the window toward the desert land around them. He appeared deep in thought.

Baylie frowned. "You know something, don't you?"

"Yeah." He pursed his lips. "Kurt ran a proposal by me a day ago. I don't know if I'm up for the task, but the offer is tempting."

"What?" She twisted in her seat. "Can you tell me?"

"I can tell you some of it." Jayden glanced her way. "Part of it, though, could depend on you."

"How?" She touched his shoulder. "Jayden?"

For the next half hour, she listened to the plan Jayden had discussed with Kurt, amazed at the opportunity open to him, overwhelmed by the magnitude of it. Jayden had all the right credentials to take this project on, but to do it he would need support personnel.

When he finished he looked at her. "What do you think?"

She didn't know what to say. "Wow."

Jayden nodded. "That's what I thought."

"Where do I come in?"

"In the beginning you'd split your time between the newsletter you now write for the Mueller Ranch and a second newsletter, or some kind of correspondence, for the boys' home." He raised his eyebrows as if asking a question. "The boys' home will receive funding from the sale of the alfalfa, but I understand that won't be enough to keep it running when it is fully operational."

"So you'll need donors or sponsors from the community."

"Yes." Jayden drummed his fingers on the steering wheel. "My financial future would rest in your capable fingers."

"You certainly are trusting."

Jayden glanced her way. "If I can't trust you, who can I trust?"

Baylie grew silent. She couldn't be two places at once. If she left the ranch to care for Grandma Levine, she'd leave Jayden behind, dependent on someone else to share his future. But if she took on the extra newsletter, she'd have to remain here and not oversee her grandmother's care. The choice loomed like an insurmountable wall, and she'd never been good at climbing. How could she choose between them? *Lord, I know you are listening. Help!*

Jayden drove into the ranch and parked near the bunkhouse. After he'd told her about the proposal for the boys' ranch Baylie had been quiet the remainder of the journey. What did she think? He looked at her. "Want to do church with me in the morning?"

"I think that's a great idea. I could certainly use some teaching and encouragement, not to mention prayer time."

"You have a lot on your plate, Bayles." He touched her hand. "I'll join you in prayer lifting up your grandmother."

"Not to mention your job offer." Baylie's eyes grew round. "This is huge, Jayden. You know that?"

"Yes, I do. I'm going to run it by Mom tonight." He glanced at his watch. "She's probably too busy in the kitchen right now."

Baylie agreed. "I better go see if she needs any help."

"What's on the menu?"

"I think this is taco night." Baylie wrinkled her nose as if trying to remember. "I'm on lettuce duty."

"Maybe I can grate the cheese."

He followed Baylie into the kitchen, uncertain if she understood his dilemma. She hadn't acted excited, not for him, nor about her potential role in the operation of the boys' ranch. The dilemma she faced with her grandmother had taken precedence over everything else. Or maybe she didn't see herself in the middle of a bunch of boys. Her take on the proposed offer would affect his decision. He wanted her on board. Could she see herself in that situation?

Mom stood stirring the hamburger, the smell of cayenne and chili powder filling the room. She looked up from her pan and smiled. "Welcome back, you two. Are you here to help?"

"I'll grate the cheese." Jayden flexed his arm in a show of strength.

Mom shook her head. "I order the cheese already grated, but thanks anyway. How is your grandmother, Baylie?"

"She's in good spirits. The hospital is keeping her comfortable now that she's had surgery. She'll be bed bound for a while." Baylie sighed. "After that she may need permanent help."

"A broken hip is nothing to mess with. Her care could involve a long-term time commitment. She's fortunate to have someone like you to care so deeply." Mom ran a spoon through the meat. "Would either of you like to shred the lettuce?"

"I planned to do that." Baylie grabbed an apron. "Jayden wants to help, too."

"Great." Mom glanced his way. "Lay out the taco shells and find the sliced black olives."

"Got it. Sour cream, too?"

"Yes." Mom bit her lip. "I'm forgetting something. Oh, Baylie, when you finish the lettuce can you chop two tomatoes into chunks?"

The next half hour sped by as the time for dinner neared. Jayden wished he and Baylie could talk more, but the kids arrived, and the cacophony of sound grew louder as they waited for the signal to line up. Tomorrow after church would be a better time.

He had to find the courage to tell her what he was feeling. If she stopped him cold, that would determine his decision. Somehow, he didn't think that would happen, but she'd surprised him before. This was too big to not lay everything out on the table. He put plates and glasses in place as the two women finished the dinner. Later he'd talk to his mother. She would have the wisdom he lacked. She always did.

"See you tomorrow for church." Baylie untied her apron and hung it up on its hook. "You want to leave at the usual time?"

"Let's take your car so we can talk, okay?"

"What? No wild rides into the parking lot with the roar of the motorcycle announcing our entrance?"

Jayden grinned. "We can, as long as we find somewhere to talk after church."

"Sounds serious."

"You never know." Jayden removed his apron, holding it aloft. "I didn't really need this for the kitchen jobs I did." He added it to hers on the hook. "Can I walk you to your apartment?"

"Sure. I need a listening ear tonight."

They fell into step across the parking lot, the faint outline of the moon hanging like a slice in the sky. "The days are growing shorter." Jayden pointed to the stars peeking out. "Soon we'll be in full fall mode."

She glanced up at the darkening night, watching as the stars, one by one, made their appearance. "Hopefully by then I'll have answers regarding Grandma's progress."

"You heard what Dr. Hickman said. Your grandmother's recovery could take time."

"I know. I want to be part of that." She blinked away the tears threatening to spoil the discussion. "She's always been there for me."

"I understand. This is a tough problem to solve." Jayden stopped. "And I hope you'll want to be there for me, as well." Jayden stuck his hands in his pockets. "I'm trying to tell you I want us to have a future together." He glanced up, a spark of apprehension in his eyes. "I know Grandma Levine is important to you. I get that. But she made it clear how she felt about you hovering over her."

"Hovering over her? Is that how you feel?"

"What I'm trying to say is if you leave to care for your grandmother, however long it takes, we'll miss the narrow window we have to decide on this ranch thing."

"We decide?" Baylie frowned. "Jayden, what are you saying?"

He fidgeted, nervous energy making his heel bounce. "I know the timing is off here, but I didn't want to have you make plans about your grandmother's care without first hearing what I have to say." He glanced around the yard, mouth twisted, forehead furrowed. "I want us to have a future together. I'm falling in love with you and I don't want to lose you." Jayden's gaze grew intense. "I'm saying I want to marry you."

Baylie gasped. "Where did that come from?"

Jayden's smile sagged, face crestfallen. His voice became a whisper. "I'm in love with you, Baylie Summers. I want to discover if there's any chance you could love me, too?"

Baylie covered her mouth with her knuckles. She stared at the man before her. His eye was intent, its depths open and vulnerable. His lips pouted as if her response could destroy the quivering smile she saw promised on his mouth. Jayden was in love with her? Did she hold the key to his happiness if she said the words he longed to hear?

Her knees buckled as she trembled at his words. Every wish she could have dreamt now dwelt in the man before her, this wonderful friend declaring his love. She groped for something to say but no words came. All her concerns—worries about her future, about her grandmother's care, about finding a forever home—dissolved in those three words.

I love you.

"Aren't you going to say something?" Jayden reached for her hand and turned her to face him. "Or have I totally misread you all this time?"

"No." She stammered. "I mean I have given you—us—a lot of thought." She stamped her foot. "Oh, I'm making such a mess of this."

He pushed a tendril behind her ear, a smile breaking full force across his cheeks. "I love it when you're flustered."

"It happens a lot."

"No, it doesn't. Not to you." He pressed a kiss against her forehead. "But when it does, I feel as if I've found two misspelled words in your front-page story of the high school newspaper and you have to buy me a Dilly Bar."

"We were so silly then." Baylie cast him a shy smile. "I don't remember buying many."

"That's because you always found more typos in my sports column. I could never get ahead." He sighed. "I still remember the jog across the street to the Dairy Queen."

She touched his lips. "Poor baby." She ran her hand along his jaw. "I think you hit the jackpot tonight. I'll buy you a case of ice cream if you want."

He glanced at her, intensity in his eyes. "Ice cream is not what I want." He kissed her on the lips, loving how her eyes widened and her mouth hung open. "I want you."

"Let's go talk in the bunkhouse."

"Finally."

Stale air filled the bunkhouse, as if oxygen had been suppressed and a vacuum remained. Or maybe it was just his nerves cutting off his lungs. He prayed, knowing the discussion to come could reshape the landscape of his future. Baylie led him into her office, a more public place, but probably a wise choice if he considered what he was feeling.

"Want to sit at the desk?" Baylie pointed to the center of the room. "Or go grab chips in Lissa's office?"

"Let's sit at the desk." Jayden pulled out the familiar chair where he'd often sat across from Baylie as she worked. Where they'd talked. Where his fondness had grown for this girl he'd once known. A woman he now believed he loved.

Baylie sat in her swivel chair across the desk from him, vibrant green eyes wide, her face the picture of innocence. "You go first."

"I've been blind-sided by this whole ranch thing." He picked up a pencil and tapped it on its eraser end. That had been an honest answer. "But the ranching part is going to be handled outside of the boys' home operation."

"What part is yours?"

"The owner wants to leave the main house and surrounding barns to the boys' home. We'd have livestock, and boys, and counselors much like Kurt and Lissa have here."

"But the boys would be foster kids?"

"That's what I understand. Only older. Tweens and teens. Some may have had run-ins with the law."

"That's heavy."

"From what Kurt told me the rancher donating the operation wants to provide a safe haven in a productive environment. Those kids who are already on a path to destruction might be rescued. Maybe pointed in a different direction, complete with a healthy work ethic and hope for a better future."

"Sounds like a lofty goal." Baylie wiggled her chair side to side as if she was nervous, eyes staring at nothing while she listened.

"What role would I play?"

"You'd continue here as Kurt and Lissa's editor and you would create publicity for the boys' home. We'd need funding for the operation apart from the revenue the ranch produced."

"I'd live here, as I am now, and visit the boys' home for material?"

"That depends." Jayden paused before continuing. "If you and I moved forward with our relationship, you'd live there with me." Jayden gulped, nervous about the reaction he was sensing in Baylie. "That's what I hope will happen." Had she not heard him say he wanted to marry her? "You know. Like a wife."

Baylie grinned. "You *are* nervous. I heard you say that earlier, but I wanted to hear it again. Just to be ornery."

He shook his head. "I'm sincere, Bayles."

"I believe you." She leaned across the desk and kissed him. "I'm torn because of Grandma Laura. I can't abandon her. You understand, don't you?"

He swallowed to control his reaction. Not the answer he'd hoped to get. The sting of her response hurt. "I understand your loyalty to her. I had hoped your affection for me was just as great." He studied her. "What you need to realize is that this ranch opportunity will pass if I don't act upon it now, but I don't want to run it by myself. I want you there with me. If you leave to care for Grandma Laura, even for only a few short weeks, the window open to us will close. Is that what you want? That's what I'm hearing you say."

"It's not." Baylie wrung her hands. "The timing is off, that's all."

"When do you think the timing will be right? Even the doctor didn't guarantee a timeline."

"How can I consider moving forward with you, when the happiness of my grandmother stands in the way?"

"What about our happiness? Does it take a sideline?" Jayden

breathed deep. This wasn't going well.

"Jayden, that's not what I mean."

"Isn't it? Clearly your devotion to your grandmother takes precedent. What does that make me?" He huffed. "An *'also ran'*?"

Baylie bit her lower lip. "I want to pray over this."

"Alone? Or with me? Or in church tomorrow?"

Baylie folded her hands on the desk. "All of the above."

"I guess I expected more." He sighed. "You don't seem enthused." He pressed his hands together. "I will support whatever decision you make, Bayles, because I love you, but recognize some decisions can't be undone."

As Jayden gave her a peck on the cheek and said goodnight, Baylie's feelings of guilt needled her. He had grown quiet. She could tell she'd disappointed him, but he surprised her, and she'd said the first things that popped into her mind. Not good.

Had he really said he wanted marriage? To her? On a ranch? Going forward as husband and wife, as foster parents, their mutual experience in the foster care system giving them insights many people never learned?

Would this ranch become their forever home? Like Lissa and Kurt lived now? Baylie couldn't believe this was truly happening. Sounded too good to be true.

The only snag remained her grandmother. If Grandma Laura needed help, Baylie would have to postpone all of this to come to the woman's aid. The choice would be a bitter one, but she couldn't abandon her grandmother now after all the years she'd put Baylie first. Did Jayden understand?

Her heart ached, thinking of what might wait ahead. Losing Jayden would be a terrible price to pay. She'd longed for him in her life for what seemed an eternity. Now the door stood wide open—

all she needed to do was step through. But the door could easily slam shut in the wake of an unexpected complication, or a turn of events in her grandmother's health.

Tomorrow she and Jayden would attend church together. They planned to talk to the pastor about their plans and the obstacle threatening to tumble their dream house of cards. Pastor would have wisdom to share.

Baylie knew of a spot on the way home where they could stop and pray together—just the two of them. To think she might marry a man who wanted to kneel before God and ask His wisdom for them and their future together made her warm all over. She'd be a fool to let Jayden get away.

But Grandma had prayed over her life for years. The petitions on Baylie's behalf had been endless and no less important—always needed. Grandma made sure Baylie felt loved, not abandoned. Though she lost her parents at an early age, her grandparents' role in her life assured Baylie she had family on whom she could depend.

"God, this is so hard." Baylie's voice sounded hollow in the vastness of the empty office. "Please give the doctors wisdom concerning Grandma's hip. Please let her accept my help if it's needed." Baylie bit back the interference of tears. "If Jayden is lost because of this, please help me to accept your divine will." Baylie lowered her face into her hands, fingers growing damp as she let the tears flow. To lose Jayden would rip her heart from her chest. She'd never recover. "Oh, God. What am I to do?"

CHAPTER THIRTY-ONE

T HE RIDE TO CHURCH THE NEXT morning left Baylie's hands clammy, the clasping and unclasping of her fingers made palms already too warm sweat with more fervor. Jayden planned to ask the pastor for advice on their choices. Baylie considered that a good idea, but no matter what the pastor said, the bottom line rested with Grandma's future and Baylie's involvement in it.

"Hey, you two." The pastor stepped toward them, hand outstretched. "Nice to see you again." He glanced out at the parking lot. "Decided not to make a noisy entrance today?"

Jayden cast her a conspiratorial smile. "We didn't want to be the center of attention, so we came in Baylie's car."

The pastor chuckled. "However you came, you're welcome."

Jayden smiled. "We wondered if you would have time to speak with us after the service for just a few minutes."

"I can give you five or so. I have a deacon's meeting at 12:30. So if we meet before that, I can, but it will be brief."

"Great." Jayden shook the man's hand. "We're seeking advice."

"I'm always ready to help in whatever way I can." The pastor gestured toward the entrance. "But right now, we need to join the service."

Baylie glanced around the sanctuary today, thinking of how many people here she used to know. Thanks to Mary, her foster mother, Baylie had been an active part of the church's teen program. She saw a hand waving as she and Jayden worked their way forward to empty seats nearer the front. Not until she entered the pew and slid across to the center, did it register with her that Mary and Troy, her former foster parents, were here. Mary was the one signaling her. Guilt weighed on her. She should have come months ago, but she hadn't. Her history with Hunter and the remorse she'd felt had made her hide from those who might have helped her move on. Baylie could barely keep her mind on the message, eagerness to see her mentor burning in her head.

When the service ended and the benediction was sung, Baylie jumped up seeking Mary and Troy. She spotted them across the aisle and beelined her way there.

"Mary!" Baylie opened her arms and embraced the woman. "It's so good to see you again."

Mary hugged her about the neck. "I thought I was seeing ghosts when the two of you walked in." She held out an arm to hug Jayden. "You've certainly changed. What a man you've become."

Jayden's blush colored his cheeks and spread along his neck. He straightened, giving Mary the full benefit of his soldierly frame. "I'm recently returned from Afghanistan."

Troy held out his hand. "Welcome home, soldier. If we can help you in any way, don't hesitate to ask."

Jayden returned the handshake. "Thanks. It's nice you remember us."

Mary hooted. "How can we forget? You two power-housed the student newspaper. That April Fool's story you conjured up about year-round-classes made the school board members wet their pants."

Baylie lowered her chin, peeking up at Mary. "I still feel guilty about that story. I had no idea people were so gullible."

"You almost got us suspended." Jayden's smile said the memory still tickled him. "I could have missed the military because of an April Fool's prank."

"But I clearly stated in the masthead of that paper that this was a special edition in honor of April Fool's Day."

"That's all that saved you." Jayden's crooked smile let her know he was teasing.

"What are you up to these days?" Mary's question jerked

Baylie back to the present. "Am I to assume you two are more than friends?"

"We're working on that."

"Still writing?"

"Yes. I'm sorry I haven't kept in touch." Baylie inhaled a deep breath. "I write a newsletter for the Mueller rescue ranch, which takes in horses and offers a safe haven for neglected children. Jayden has a job offer we hoped to discuss with the pastor today. That may include me as well."

"Speaking of the pastor, he's glancing our way." Jayden touched her shoulder, then waved at the man.

"Can you excuse us?" Baylie stepped beside Jayden. "We won't be long."

"We have to gather up our brood." Mary tucked her hand in the crook of Troy's elbow. "We'll be outside in the parking lot for at least ten minutes."

"I'll look for you." Baylie turned the direction of the pastor.

Baylie sat with Jayden across from the pastor, the last few minutes an explanation of the dilemma they faced.

"I can understand your concern for your grandmother. She's fortunate to have someone like you to act as an advocate for her care. That you want to offer yourself to help with that speaks well of your character." The pastor tapped his desk. "Based on what you've told me, though, I doubt your grandmother would want to interfere with your future."

Baylie bristled at the comment. Her future meant making sure Grandma was well taken care of. Did he not see that? She could do no less.

"She's always. . ."

"Been there for you." The pastor nodded his head. "I get that.

That's what responsible adults do for their children and grandchildren." He leaned back in his chair. "They don't expect reciprocal actions from their offspring."

"It's the right thing to do!" Baylie sensed her anger climbing. "Isn't it?"

"It's wonderful that you care so deeply, but her recovery could be a long road ahead—months, years even. Have you thought of that?" The pastor studied her. "The bigger question is why would you make a decision that because of the time commitment might destroy the relationship you and Jayden share?"

Baylie kept her gaze on the desk, Jayden's glance her way burning a hole in her shoulder. She didn't want to lose Jayden. He was all she'd wanted for a long time. Yet Grandma was a priority. She raised her gaze to the pastor, then to Jayden. "I don't want that, either."

"Think how sad your grandmother would be to know she stood in the way of you and Jayden making plans for the future. Does she know what you are thinking? Doesn't she approve of Jayden?"

"Oh, yes."

"Then why would she be instrumental in tearing you two apart?"

Baylie's shoulders sagged. This was too hard. "Will you pray for us?"

"Rest assured I will." The pastor stood and held out his hands. Baylie took one and Jayden the other. The pastor bowed his head. "Lord, these two servants need your wisdom and direction. Grant them a clear understanding. Amen." He looked up and smiled. "I have a meeting waiting. Let's meet again soon."

Baylie followed Jayden out to the parking lot. She spotted Mary and Troy talking to another couple as five children circled them and the van.

"Baylie? Jayden?" Mary waved them over. "If you don't have lunch plans, why don't you follow us home and join our brood?"

She directed kids to the van while Troy helped buckle seat belts. "We have plenty to share." She turned. "We could get caught up. It's been too long."

"I wish we could, but I'm on lunch duty at the ranch today to give the cook a break. I skipped out yesterday to go see my grandmother."

"How is she?" Mary's face reflected surprise. "She was always such a pillar in your life."

"She broke her hip and had to have emergency surgery."

"Oh, no." Mary touched Baylie's arm. "Where is she? I'd like to go see her."

Baylie reached into her purse and wrote Grandma's address and phone on a pad of paper. "She isn't in her apartment right now. I put the address of the hospital where she's in recovery after her operation."

"She can have visitors?"

"Yes, but visits are kept brief. She can't move. I'm anxious to see how I can help her when she returns home. I may even move to be closer to her."

"But what about your job?" Mary's concern wrote lines across her forehead. "And Jayden?"

"I'll have to put them on hold for a while." Baylie swallowed her reservations. "Grandma may need me."

Mary frowned. "That would be quite a sacrifice and commitment of time, but I remember how much you depended on her. Knowing you, I'm certain you want to return her devotion." Mary glanced at Jayden, then back at her. "Not everything or everyone can always wait for later." She hugged Baylie. "Be sure your concern isn't misplaced. A wrong decision can alter a promising future permanently."

"Thanks. I will be careful." Baylie turned to see Jayden conversing with Troy. He caught her eye and nodded. She pasted on a smile she didn't feel. "Ready to head for the ranch?"

The picnic area beyond the kitchen buzzed with activity when Jayden drove into the ranch driveway. He and Baylie headed that direction. Lissa and Kurt were already on the scene, Lissa setting out paper plates and chips while Kurt fired up the barbecue.

"Need any help?" Jayden stood by the propane grill and held a hand toward the flame. "Plenty hot enough."

Kurt snickered. "This isn't charcoal where we have to wait for the coals to glow."

"Faster for sure, but how's the flavor?"

Kurt whispered. "The kids won't know the difference."

Jayden looked around. "Where are the meat patties?"

"Lissa should be bringing them out any minute." Kurt thumbed toward the kitchen. "Looks like she enlisted help."

Baylie walked toward them carrying a platter of raw meat patties and a long-handled spatula. "Kurt, do you have salt and pepper?"

"No." Kurt checked his work area. "I could use some barbecue sauce, as well."

Jayden turned. "I'll get it." He looked over his shoulder. "You want the buns, too?"

Baylie shook her head. "Lissa is preparing them inside. You know—mayo, pickles, lettuce."

"No ketchup?" Jayden picked up his pace. "I've got to save dinner!" The crunch of his feet on the gravel disappeared with him into the kitchen.

Baylie laughed. "What a character."

"He's always been a burger fan. Even when I first met him as a kid." Kurt lifted a meat patty with the spatula and slid it onto the hot grill. The mound of ground beef sizzled and popped as the heat of the grill turned it brown. "I'd say we can cook all of these rather quickly, wouldn't you?"

"Shouldn't take long." Baylie glanced toward movement from the kitchen. Lissa carried a tray of buns and Jayden followed with one bottle of ketchup and another of barbecue sauce. Gunner and Gage each carried a bowl. "Lissa's got the buns ready."

"Looks like the boys have the potato salad and the watermelon chunks."

"Great teamwork."

"When you work a ranch this size, you need everyone to pull their weight." Kurt studied her. "Has Jayden mentioned his new opportunity?"

Baylie nodded.

"He really wants you on his team."

"I know." Baylie felt the prick of tears in her eyes. "I'm giving it due consideration."

"Due consideration?" Kurt's mouth hung open, his eyes narrowed. "This is a chance for you two to find a forever together. Don't you love him?"

"Yes, I do." She bit her lip. "The timing is off. My grandmother may need help. I can't leave her in limbo."

Kurt stopped and studied her. "How much time do you think she will need? A week? A month? A year?" Kurt flipped the meat patties and moved them around the grill. "I understand broken hips mean a long road of recovery for the injured."

"I heard that, too." Baylie bit her lip. "I'm willing to give her whatever time she needs."

"Your grandmother's care may tie up several months, maybe years of your life. That's quite a commitment on your part."

"I hadn't thought about that." Baylie inhaled a deep breath. "I don't want to abandon her when she's so helpless."

"Your devotion is admirable." Kurt flipped a burger with a little too much force, the spatula banging on the grill. "That's a gold star in your favor," he looked at her and smiled, "but your future doesn't lie with your grandmother, Baylie." Kurt worked his way down the grill. "I'm willing to believe she'd tell you that herself if she knew what you're thinking."

Baylie remained silent, unwilling to share what Grandma had already told her. The thought of leaving her grandmother without a family member nearby didn't match her determination to assist. Grandma had never left her to struggle without a backup plan, how could Baylie not return the favor? Surely Grandma would see how much she needed Baylie at her side through this. Couldn't she?

"I'm praying about it." Baylie gave the expected contrite response, hoping Kurt would let the matter rest. "This is a lot to consider."

"Your heart will tell you what your mind can't." Kurt flipped the burgers again. "Jayden is a great guy. You won't find another like him any time soon." He looked at her. "I think I know what your grandmother would say."

Baylie bit her lip, the threat of tears burning in her eyes. Jayden circled the table helping Lissa set out the salads, plates, and plastic utensils for their picnic. He caught her glance, and nodded, his smile missing, mouth turned down. He turned away, heading toward the Frisbee field. She knew that look. She'd hurt him—something she never intended to do. Why could she never do the right thing the first time?

"These meat patties are ready for Lissa." Kurt handed her the tray.

Baylie carried the steaming meat to the food table and set it next to the buns. "Want me to fill the sandwiches?"

Lissa glanced up. "Sure." She grabbed a spoon. "I'll dish up the salad." She put a hand to the side of her mouth. "Jayden? Round up the troops."

Placing two fingers to his lips, he whistled. The children stopped what they were doing and gathered around him. He waved an arm and pointed to the picnic table. "Time to eat." He turned and the children followed as if he were the Pied Piper playing his flute.

Lissa laughed and glanced at Baylie. "He's such a natural leader." She spoke in a conspiratorial tone. "You are one blessed woman to hold the love of a man like that."

Baylie swallowed. Didn't these people know she was caught in a dilemma she couldn't resolve? She stepped up beside Lissa and assembled the burgers, her mind miles away.

After the children were seated and eating, she glanced around. "Where are the twins?"

"Spending the weekend with the family who plans to adopt them." Lissa's smile beamed, voice excited. "I think they may have found their forever home."

Baylie set the spatula down. "That's wonderful." She wanted to shout. "All Kendra and Krystal could talk about was going to a new home together."

"I know. And it's happening." Lissa did a happy dance, swinging the potato salad spoon.

Baylie sighed. A forever home. That's what all these kids longed for and deserved. She glanced Jayden's way. He wasn't paying her any attention. What if she had ruined her chances?

CHAPTER THIRTY-TWO

Monday Jayden hugged his mother, stashing the lunch she'd made for him in the saddle bags at the back of the motorcycle. Kurt had made arrangements for him to meet the rancher who wanted to create the boys' rescue home on his alfalfa ranch, a property fifty miles down the road. Today would be a scouting trip. Though Jayden knew in his heart the proposed home for boys was a venture beyond his skill set, he owed the rancher and Kurt an initial inspection. After that he could bow out with dignity, offering reasons that he must decline the offer. He planned to head back over the mountain to Pine Ridge where Parker lived, check out the programs at the university there and move forward with his life.

"I'm praying for you." Mom laid her hand on his shoulder. "This could be quite an undertaking."

"I'm only investigating the operation to be polite." Jayden stowed a bottle of water in the hideaway pouch. The early morning air promised heat later in the day so he packed an extra container for the journey, hoping to refill on the return trip. "I'm pretty certain it's more responsibility than I want to shoulder alone. Besides, being on this side of the mountain and knowing Baylie is nearby, but not available, would be torture."

"Have you talked to Parker?"

"He offered me a place to stay if I decide to move on from here." Jayden winked. "Before you two tie the knot."

Mom's eyes held moisture, mouth skewed as though she could break into tears at any moment. "I'm sorry, Jayden. I know Baylie is committed to her grandmother. I've encouraged her to stay close to the woman. I know, too, she is in love with you. Parker and I discussed it and he thought she was, too. Give Baylie time. I don't think she realizes the time commitment her loyalty may require of her. Grandma may need her help for years."

"Well, apparently I'm not a priority when it comes to her grandmother." He stopped himself. This wasn't him. He breathed deep. "I love Baylie and I want the best for her, even if it means losing her. But it hurts."

"I know it does."

He kissed his mother goodbye and climbed aboard the Harley. "Parker coming in today?"

"He's already here."

"Convenient."

Mom gave him one of her 'mother' looks, then raised a hand in farewell.

He turned the key and put the bike in gear. "I'll be late getting back." He gunned the motor and aimed the Harley up the driveway. Maybe he'd be gone a while longer. He had nothing holding him here. Not anymore.

Baylie sat at her computer Tuesday morning, trying to focus on the new feature story she needed to write for the next newsletter. She'd planned to put the spotlight on Melanie, but the interview she'd hoped to conduct had been postponed when Melanie returned late last night after a day off spent with Parker. She'd come in glowing, Parker's ring on her finger. The ranch staff exploded with excitement at the news. Baylie fought the lump in her throat. That enthusiasm could have been about her.

She hadn't seen Jayden since Sunday at the picnic. He'd taken off on his Harley after the burgers were cleaned up. Where he'd gone Baylie didn't know, but what she did know was Jayden had avoided her. She'd heard the bike return late that night and wondered what he thought of his mother's news. Monday when she went to work, he'd already left. She hurt for him. Two whammies in the same day—her reluctance to say yes to their future and his mother's eagerness to say yes to hers. A lot to take in.

The office phone rang. Lissa had come in earlier but hadn't approached Baylie. Not like her. No doubt Kurt discussed with Lissa the conversation he had with Baylie. Was everyone taking sides in this dilemma Baylie found herself in? Or was her imagination on overdrive? When the phone rang a third time, she looked to see if Lissa was still in her cubicle. A moment later Lissa came to her desk. "Phone call for you. You can take it in my office."

"Who is it?" Worried that the call might involve her grandmother, Baylie's heart raced. She hurried to the glassed-in cubicle. "Hello?"

"Baylie Summers?"

"Yes, this is she."

"This is the hospital nurse caring for your grandmother."

"What's happened?" Baylie sputtered in her distress. "Is Grandma all right?"

"Yes. She wanted me to get you on the line so she could talk to you." The nurse paused. "Here she is."

Muted voices occupied the background then Grandma's voice came on the line. "Baylie?"

"Hi, Grandma. Everything all right?"

"No. It's not!" Grandma sounded agitated.

"What's wrong?" Baylie held her breath, waiting for the bad news to slap her.

"Mary, your foster mother, was just here to see me."

"I'm glad she came, did you have. . ."

"She told me you were considering your options between caring for me after I leave the hospital and continuing in your relationship with Jayden. Is that true?"

"I merely said I might have to put him on hold for a while."

"Have you lost your senses, girl?"

"What do you mean?"

Grandma's sigh reverberated in the phone. "Baylie, dearest, I distinctly remember telling you not to plan your life around my surgery."

"I want to be there for you."

"I appreciate that. The staff at the assisted living facility will provide me with all the care I need when I can get back there, though it may be quite some time before that happens. But you taking a side road from your happiness to hover over me is not what I want. Absolutely not. Your grandfather and I haven't stayed by your side all these years to have you put aside your future in exchange for mine."

"I want you to be happy, well cared for, and surrounded by those who love you." Baylie didn't think she'd have to argue with her grandmother about this.

"I am happy, and I am well cared for. That's why Joseph and I moved into this facility in the first place. I have a housekeeper, a bath aide, and an onsite nurse. My needs have been met." Grandma paused. "I want to savor your happiness, too. When you come to visit, I want to hear you married your high school sweetheart. I want to know of your first child. I want to read your first book. That won't happen if you are hanging around my apartment in a facility for old people waiting their turn into heaven." Grandma harrumphed. "What a waste of a beautiful young talent like yours. You understand what I'm saying?"

Baylie was silent. Grandma had never told her off before.

"Baylie?"

"Yes, Grandma, I understand." She bit the pencil in her hand. "But my heart was in the right place."

"The only place your heart belongs is in Jayden's future. That boy is in love with you." Grandma sighed, the air whooshing into the receiver. "You aren't blind to that, are you?"

Grandma's words hit Baylie like a sucker punch to the gut. "No, but. . ."

"No buts about it." Grandma's words sizzled, her exasperation coloring every word. "Now if you haven't completely broken that boy's heart, you go find him and tell him how much you love him."

She suppressed a giggle at her grandmother's vehement declaration, but she had to be truthful. "I don't know if he will listen to me. I know I disappointed him."

"I'm heartbroken." Grandma cleared her throat. "Knowing I caused this to happen."

"I will try to fix things with Jayden. I promise."

"That's better." Grandma made a kissing sound in the phone. "I need to go take a nap."

"I love. . ." But before she could say 'you', the phone clicked. "'Bye." Baylie had her marching orders. She prayed she could still talk to Jayden. The wall of ice between them since Sunday might be difficult to thaw.

Jayden glanced out the window of his mother's apartment at the late morning sun, figuring in his head where Kurt might be at this hour. He'd gotten in late last night and risen equally late this morning. Shower and breakfast out of the way, he sat on his mattress thinking about what he'd learned yesterday. Kurt and he needed to have a discussion about the proposed boys' ranch. As he'd suspected, running a ranch like the one the rancher proposed to fund would mean a huge load of responsibility on Jayden's shoulders. Unless he found more help, he would have to turn the offer down.

A knock on the apartment door surprised him. Parker was in the kitchen with Mom putting lunch together. Aside from him and Parker, no one else ever graced Mom's front step. He rose and opened the door. Baylie stood on the other side, smile missing, eyes shuttered as if she feared looking at him. His jaw clenched.

No need to avoid me. The damage is done. I know where you stand.

He leaned against the casing. "Am I needed in the barn?"

"No. I, uh, don't think so." Baylie's eyebrows lifted, a furrow in the middle of her forehead, gaze clouded. "I hoped to talk with you, if you have the time."

"I need to find Kurt this morning, but I can give you a few minutes before that." He didn't like the sharp tone of his voice, but more conversation with Baylie seemed like a waste of time. Their lives were aimed in different directions. What was the point? "Let's go talk in the paddock. I need to feed Lady."

He headed for the outdoor corral, stopping in the barn first to grab a bucket of grain, then continued toward the space holding the horses. Private, but out in the open. No one could say he and Baylie were keeping secrets. Baylie stayed beside him, silent as they walked.

Lady nickered at their approach, the foal echoing the greeting as if he anticipated the coming grain as much as his mother. "Hey, girl. How's my favorite lady?"

The horse shoved her head over the top railing, nostrils wide as she sought the treat he brought. He didn't feel like laughing, but Lady prompted one anyway. He chuckled and opened the gate, stepping inside to pour the feed into the trough. Lady plunged her muzzle into the feed, a mix of oats and corn that smelled of molasses, the foal edging her out with his head as best he could. "Easy there, fella. There's plenty here for you, too." The sound of their chomping filled the quiet around him. Jayden stepped out of the corral and closed the gate. He leaned on the rail to watch the horses, speaking, without looking, to Baylie beside him. "What's on your mind?"

"I heard from my grandmother this morning."

"She anxious for you to move there?"

"No." Baylie's voice dropped to a whisper. "She gave me a lecture."

He looked her way this time, sizing up her statement. "That doesn't sound like your grandmother."

"Mary went to visit her." Baylie's voice wobbled. "Told Grandma what I said about putting you and me on hold until her surgery and rehabilitation is finished."

"On hold? Is that what you said?" Jayden fought his resolve not to get angry. "Like a telephone call you want to avoid?" He punched the fence post in front of him. "I told you I wanted to marry you." Even now the bitterness he'd felt when she dismissed his proposal threatened to color his words. "Didn't that sink in?"

"It did." Baylie was quiet. "I understood."

"Did you?" His voice rose, the pain of her rejection fueling his response. "You didn't even give me the courtesy of a maybe." He closed his fist and banged the top rail. "Baylie, I deserve better than that. I'm for real."

Baylie winced. "I never thought otherwise."

"That's not how you acted." Jayden tried to feel sorry for what he said, but he didn't. She'd made light of what he had proposed. Shoved it somewhere behind a dozen different things she needed to do for her grandmother. "Look. I know how important Grandma Laura is to you. I get your concern. I understand how much you love her, but I hoped to be that important, too." He knew where he stood with this woman. Somewhere at the bottom of her priorities. He sighed. "I love you, Bayles, and I want you to do what makes you happy. Even if that doesn't include me. Let's just part as friends, okay?"

Baylie inhaled, closed her eyes, and exhaled a slow breath. "I want to tell you how sorry I am."

"Don't." Jayden held up his hand. "You've made yourself

quite clear. We're not on the same path. I need to move on." He swallowed the agony those words inflicted. "At least I won't need to do a formal proposal if you weren't willing to discuss the possibility."

"I don't want you to move on." Baylie turned to face him, touching his elbow. "Marrying you is the one thing I've wanted since we were kids in high school." Sobs punctuated her words, tears running down her face. "I didn't mean to hurt you. I felt caught in the middle of what you wanted and what I thought my grandmother needed. I've really messed this up, Jayden, and I want to fix it." Her entire body trembled in her anguish. "Please forgive me."

He waited, letting her cry, the sound of her sobs mixed with the contented chewing of Lady and her foal. Sorrow and happiness blended in an outdoor kind of symphony.

He hated to see her in such pain—wanted to grab her and hold her in his arms, but she'd wounded him. Every ounce of courage he had went into asking her if she might consider marrying him. The brush-off in favor of her grandmother's needs cut deep. The gash still bled.

He found his voice. "I visited the ranch yesterday. You know, the one the rancher wants to turn into a boys' home?"

"Did you like it?" Baylie's eyes filled with a look of hope. "Were you impressed?"

"It will be a great facility when all the plans are complete." He looked at her. "But I'm not sure I'm the guy for the job."

"Why?"

"I'm heading over the mountain to the university. Parker's offered me a place to bunk while I pursue my studies." He turned and leaned against the railing. "I have no reason not to. The government is paying most of my bills. My future is wide open. All I need do is step into it."

"Without me."

The words were so soft he almost missed them, but she'd rejected the future he wanted with her. He would find a new one. "Yep. I'm following your lead. Now I have to find Kurt and tell him my decision, if you'll excuse me."

"I wish you the best, Jayden. I'm so, so sorry." She turned and walked away from him, steps hurried, cries breaking the silence of the morning.

He picked up the bucket and carried it to the barn. He heard Kurt whistling at the end of the aisle, the almost constant sweep of the broom in action. He stopped at the stall where Kurt worked and leaned on the gate.

Kurt looked up. "Well, good morning. How was the ranch tour?"

"It is an incredible opportunity. Going it alone would be beyond my skill set. "

"Alone?" Kurt leaned on his broom. "I had the impression you intended to include Baylie in your future."

Jayden turned his gaze toward the open barn door. "I did." He ground his teeth. "She's all caught up in her grandmother's injured hip. It's good to know she didn't mean to hurt me, but that doesn't change her plans."

Kurt frowned. "Are you sure that's what happened?" He leaned his broom against the side of the stall. "Or was she caught in the middle of two dilemmas, both of which she cared deeply about, and couldn't figure out the solutions to either fast enough?"

Jayden shrugged. "I thought if she loved me, she'd get excited, throw her arms around me, and squeal or something." He made air quotes with his fingers. "She said she'd have to pray about it. Like I was on one of her to-do lists." He kicked the straw away. "Slam dunk."

"Ouch." Kurt stepped toward him. "Lissa and I had our

troubles communicating when we were where you are." He laid a hand on Jayden's shoulder. "Let's go talk to her. She'll understand this better than I can."

Together they walked to the ranch house but found it empty. Duke yipped when they entered the yard. Gunner and Gage were giggling as they tossed a ball to Grayson. The toddler's little legs trotted to retrieve the toy. "You can do it, Grayson."

"Where's your mother?" Kurt snatched the ball as it rolled by his foot. "Here, Grayson, catch."

"She went to the office." Gunner caught the ball when Grayson missed it again.

Kurt gestured for Jayden to follow him to the bunkhouse. As they entered they heard voices, Lissa's calm and steady, and another that sounded broken.

Kurt walked on, but Jayden stopped. Kurt turned. "Sounds like you aren't the only one hurting here. She's in need of comfort and I'm guessing you can deliver it. Square your shoulders, soldier. It's time for truth."

Lissa's office door stood open, both women seated across from each other. Baylie's back was toward the door. As Kurt and Jayden approached, Lissa straightened. She nodded at Kurt, a signal Jayden interpreted as approval. He followed Kurt into the small office, the space confining as four adults crammed inside. Kurt pointed to a chair next to Lissa. "Sit there."

Baylie stopped sniffing and stared up at him, red-eyed and pale. Kurt slipped into the chair next to her, crossed a leg over his knee and leaned back. "Lissa, what do we do about these kids?"

Lissa grinned as if she were playing a script. "Help them realize they are hopelessly in love with each other but need a little help untangling the complex web they have woven around themselves."

"Sounds like us about ten years ago."

Lissa nodded. "Close. True love never runs smoothly, it seems."

"You two were like this once?" Baylie's mouth hung open. "You always seem so in sync."

Lissa chuckled. "Like when I took Kendra to the hospital and Kurt brought the kids without breakfast? "

Baylie chuckled. "I'd forgotten about that. I thought Kurt was in for a little trouble."

"He was." Lissa winked. "But all good men make technical errors from time to time, just like the women they love."

"That aimed at me, Lissa?" Jayden joined Kurt in crossing a leg over his knee. "I feel a lecture coming."

"No. No lecture." Lissa sent her husband a look that made Jayden blush. "Baylie has told me of the problem between you. You suggested Baylie marry you at the same time she learned of her grandmother's injury. She felt caught in the middle of two huge life crises she didn't know how to handle. She put you off. It isn't a bad thing for her to be faithful to her grandmother, but the way she did it was inconsiderate of your feelings. Your expectations weren't considerate of her feelings either. She is thrilled beyond happiness that you wanted to marry her."

"Strange way of showing it." Jayden folded his arms across his chest, resisting the spark of hope building inside him. Maybe he and Baylie could find a happy ending, after all.

"You ought to hear how Kurt and I acted toward each other when he and I were deployed, and communication broke down between us." Lissa's eyes snapped. "I was so mad at him. He seemed to fall off the planet."

"I witnessed some of that. You know—the skinny little obnoxious eleven-year-old who played matchmaker?" Jayden dropped his foot to the floor and leaned forward in the chair. "Peggy and I were on a mission. You two kept misfiring."

"I remember you. You were good."

Kurt laughed. "Look at us now."

"The point is you two need to sit down with each other." Lissa gazed at her husband, who nodded. "Kurt, Parker, Melanie and I had a powwow yesterday to find solutions. We agreed only the two of you can fix this. We're pretty certain you are in love. Tell each other how you feel. Apologize if you need to. Admit neither one of you will be able to live without the other one, and you won't. Grab hands, kiss passionately, and step into the future together." Lissa stood. "Now Kurt and I are going to leave, shut the door behind us, and give you time and space to find your way back to where you want to be."

Kurt wrapped an arm about his wife. "And I'm going to take my wife behind the barn and give her a great big smooch."

Jayden shook his head. "You two are hopeless."

"That's what love does, Jayden." Kurt led Lissa from the room, shutting the door behind them.

Jayden looked at Baylie. "I find it hard to believe you're really thrilled that I wanted to marry you. You didn't act like it."

Baylie blushed, a shy smile forming as she looked down at her lap. "Yes. I have thought of nothing else since you returned to the ranch."

Jayden's eyebrows rose. "I thought that's what I sensed coming from you. I took it slow, though, in case I was just an eager bag of hormones returned from the field. Marines get lonely when there's no female companionship around. We can get ahead of ourselves."

"I love you, Jayden." Baylie offered her outstretched hand across the table toward him. "I'm so sorry for hurting you." She squeezed his fingers in hers. "I lost sight of what was most important to me. Not because I got a lecture from my grandmother or counseling from Lissa. I love you because I can't imagine my life without you.”

"Up until five minutes ago that's not the impression you gave me, Bayles." Jayden held her hand in his, engulfing the small palm in his larger one. He covered her fingers with his. "I can't imagine living my life without you either."

"I really messed up. I was blindsided by Grandma's problems, but spending the rest of my life without you is not an option." She hiccoughed. "Please forgive me."

Jayden raised an eyebrow. "I've made my share of mistakes, too, Bayles. But as I told you in the barn that night when you heard Parker's counsel, how can I not forgive you when God has forgiven me of all I've done?"

"Thank you." Baylie smiled. "My life won't be fulfilled if you aren't in it."

"Nor mine without you." Jayden squeezed her hand and released it, hope swelling in his chest. "We've had a lot of experiences together. Similar life paths. We share a common desire to help those around us. We love the same Lord. Those are building blocks for a strong relationship." He narrowed his eye and felt lines furrowing his brow. "Now that I know where you stand, I'll ask you again." He held up his hand. "Be careful. This time I'm not scouting for clues like before. This is the real deal." He slipped from his chair and bent down on his good knee. "Will you marry me?"

Baylie's smile burst across her face. "Yes. A thousand times yes."

He reached in his jeans and removed a small velvet box. "This has been riding around in my pocket for a few days. I thought I was going to have to return it next trip to Burns."

He opened the box and took her hand, sliding the tiny solitaire on her finger. "I told you I was serious."

"It's beautiful."

He rose to his feet pulling her up with him. "Shall we go tell your grandmother?"

"No. Let's go tell Lissa and Kurt. And the pastor. And your mom. And contact that rancher about your new position."

"You think you'd like being a mom to troubled boys?"

"As long as I have a few boys of my own to guide through life."

"Then let's go tell the world our news." Jayden's fingers cupped Baylie under her chin. "First, though, this."

"Jayden?"

He wrapped his arms around her and drew her close, placing a kiss on her lips that left no doubt where he stood. When he came up for air, he heard clapping. Baylie laughed and pointed behind him. "Glass windows in the office."

He turned and saw Lissa, Kurt, Mom and Parker standing in the outer office hugging each other as if they had sealed a huge contract between them. "I think we've been played."

"Somehow I get the feeling they were plotting all along." Baylie smiled up at him, her eyes shining. "Is that a bad thing?"

"Not at all." He kissed her again. "Now we can find our forever."

"I can't wait." She wrapped her arms around his neck. "We'll write a really great love story."

"Maybe you'll win that Pulitzer you always wanted."

"Definitely a possibility."

Recipes from *In Search of Forever*

Muffin Tin Meatloaf

Ingredients
- 1 ½ pounds ground beef
- 1 large egg
- ¼ cup yellow mustard
- ½ cup ketchup
- 2 tablespoons Worcestershire sauce
- 1 cup panko bread crumbs
- 2 tablespoons minced onion
- ¼ teaspoon black pepper
- ¼ teaspoon sea salt
- ½ teaspoon onion powder
- ½ teaspoon garlic powder

Instructions

Preheat oven to 350°F.

1. Add meat, and every ingredient listed to a large mixing bowl and combine until mixed.
2. add meat to each muffin tin space. (an ice cream scoop works well)
3. Bake uncovered for 25 minutes.
4. Allow meat loaves to rest for 5 minutes before removing them from the pan.

Amber Kuehn: I think I got the idea of making mini meatloaves in a muffin tin years ago when I was doing a lot of freezer cooking. The recipe itself is a generic meatloaf recipe that I used as a guideline (but as far as my cooking is concerned, any recipe is one I got from somewhere years ago and don't follow it exactly (I consider recipes a guideline, not an exact science, so it changes depending on what I have on hand).

Provided from the kitchen of Amber L. Kuehn

Pizza Casserole

Ingredients

- 2 cups elbow macaroni
- 1 pound ground beef
- 1 (14 ounce) jar pizza sauce
- 1 (4 ounce) can tomato sauce
- 1 (4.5 ounce) can sliced mushrooms, drained
- 1 pound shredded mozzarella cheese

Instructions

Preheat oven to 350°F

1. Bring a large pot of lightly salted water to a boil. Cook elbow macaroni in the boiling water, stirring occasionally, until cooked through but firm to the bite, 8 minutes. Drain.

2. Cook and stir ground beef in a skillet over medium heat until meat is crumbly and browned, about 10 minutes; drain excess grease.

3. Mix cooked ground beef, macaroni, pizza sauce, tomato sauce, and mushrooms in a bowl. Layer half the macaroni mixture into a 9x12-inch baking dish; top with 1/2 the mozzarella cheese. Layer remaining macaroni mixture over the top; sprinkle remaining mozzarella cheese over macaroni mixture. Cover dish with aluminum foil.

4. Bake in the preheated oven until the cheese has melted and the casserole is bubbling, about 35 minutes. Let cool for 3 to 5 minutes before serving.

Provided from the kitchen of Lisa Sanetra

Author Note

No book comes together without the efforts of many individuals cheering from the sidelines, offering input into details within the storyline, and giving feedback on what is written. This novel is no exception.

I first want to acknowledge my critique group—Melanie Campbell, Dorcas Smucker, Becky Sue Harwood, and Amanda Bird—four women who have patiently read and reacted to each chapter, bringing with them wisdom from their personal experiences. I also thank Christina Suzann Nelson and Kathy Sheldon Davis who helped me sort out the complexities of the Children's Protective Services in Oregon. Any mistakes are mine.

I thank my publisher and editor Miralee Ferrell for offering me this opportunity to publish yet another book in the Mended Hearts series. This tale will bring closure to Jayden Clarke's story, a journey that began when Kurt McKintrick and Lissa Frye met at a Thanksgiving dinner in *Love's Autumn Harvest*. From there the sparks flew.

A special thank you to readers Lisa Sanetra and Amber Kuehn who entered my Easter giveaway by submitting recipes I could use to feed a lot of kids. Lisa sent a pizza casserole recipe and Amber submitted a muffin tin meatloaf creation—both of which merited a free book. Many thanks to these two women.

I thank my family for their willingness to give me the time to write the story, often stepping in to do chores that Mom used to handle on her own. To my husband, Loren, my son, Jon, and my daughter, Rachel, I love you. No wife or mother could be more grateful for the family with whom God has blessed me. Thank you.

Most of all, I give the glory and credit for this work to my savior, the Lord Jesus Christ. He has instilled within me a love of words, and a vision for scenes that make a work like this come together.

To you, my readers, I say thank you. Your reviews, your sweet heartfelt notes and your encouragement along the way have made the writing of this story possible. Enjoy this tale and let me know what you think.